THE SENTINEL

WHAT PEOPLE ARE SAYING
ABOUT **THE SENTINEL**...

"Wow... what a great book! Right from the prologue, I was drawn in and couldn't put it down. I finished reading it in only a few days! The plot is so intriguing and the suspense is intense. I highly recommend this book to anyone wishing to read a suspense thriller."

—By Caityb830

"I picked up this book with some extra time to spare and literally could not put it down! A really intelligent and suspenseful story! I would highly recommend to anyone looking for the next best seller!"

—By JBW3141

"Great suspense novel and definitely a page turner! Author shows insight in historical data and weaving a story line that brings the reader to a climactic ending."

—By Patty

"A page grabber from the beginning. This book shows the author's understanding of world events and very real possible scenarios. It kept me on the edge of my seat page after page. The link between the past and the present was masterfully presented."

—By NanaSzu

"This book is so awesome! I literally could not put it down and finished it within 2 days! I want more from Paul Bourdon!"

—By MollyL725

Paul Bourdon

THE SENTINEL

PROLOGUE

FAINT SHADOWS RHYTHMICALLY DANCED OVER ANCIENT stucco walls. A flickering candle fought to cast a warm glow amid unwelcome drafts of the evening's cold, damp air. Here and there, its flame shimmered as it bounced off the worn stone floor of the medieval Polish convent. Each slight depression in the floor appeared to shift back and forth like the gentle ripples of a mill pond that had received its last visitor in a mist-filled night.

The aura of the convent's tranquil beauty sat in stark contrast to the rolling pain that shot upward into the bony knees of its aged Abbess. As she entered her second hour of fervent prayer, her blood suddenly ran cold. Her breathing stopped as she caught a glimpse of the steady movement of Russian tanks and armored personnel carriers as they took up positions in the farmer's field across the road. She felt as if some evil presence had blocked her path. With a heavy heart, she turned her eyes away from the wavy glass window and focused on the crucifix in front of her.

"Please God, if it be your will, let this cup pass," she prayed. "It has been so long and this burden has taken its toll on me. I'm old and tired. Dear Lord, send me a new sentinel; someone to free me from the pain and misery of this lifelong bondage."

In her heart, Mother Anastasia knew the Russians had come for only one reason—to find the terror that lurked beneath the former German soil.

CHAPTER 1

DR. HANS BRANDT WAS LIVING HIS OWN HELL. EVIL WAS near, minutes away.

Situated on the corner of a once tree-lined avenue, his dental office was typical of the times. Like most clinics, it was fashioned out of the side of his modest home. When the momentum of the war turned for the worse, his list of clients dwindled to a few Nazi officials whose immediate dental pain was greater than their fear of moving through the horror that engulfed the city streets. His last patient of the day had left and his work was finished. It was the time of day he had grown to hate most. The sun would be setting soon and the blackout shades would be pulled down to prevent lamplight from becoming a beacon to nightly bombers.

He unbuttoned the collar of his white tunic, sat down and pulled a bottle of Schnapps from his desk drawer. His emotions had been frayed for over a year and he felt at wit's end. He had heard the rumors of the death camps and they sickened him. Many of his neighbors denied their existence, but he knew they were lying, trying to assuage their own consciences. The mere thought of having to work in some Nazi official's mouth made him feel dirty. He was tired and needed to relax.

Two shots later, the Schnapps had run through his veins, but his anger was born of shame and couldn't be smothered. How could we have allowed this to happen in our Germany? Hans thought. Are we not civilized? Maybe it was from living through the depression. People were starving, there was no order—no signs of hope. We could vote for the Nazis or the Communists, no one else. I never wanted Hitler, but the Austrian bastard made it clear that a vote for Communism was a vote for enslavement. Hell, he had that nation of peasants to the East to prove it. Our enemies from the last war had punished us beyond what was just.

Nazism lied, offering us a way out of misery. He made expansion of our borders appear to be our natural destiny. He said Germany had to stand up and tell the world: No more! I pray the Americans will take Berlin before the Russian horde rolls over us. If only I had political influence, I could still get Marta and my little Hanne out in time.

On instinct, he picked up the telephone, and then remembered there was no service in Berlin. He searched his desk for a note that had been delivered earlier. Hans wondered how his home and office had been spared from the incessant bombing. It seemed like an oasis in a sea of rubble and blasted-out buildings. He found the note and leaned back in his threadbare chair to read it. It was a reminder of his after-hours appointment. He looked around. Inch by inch, the walls of his office seemed to be closing in around him. The sulfuric smell of bombs hung in the stale air. Even his gritty eyelids seemed to be closing in on him. He felt as if he were mentally suffocating. The world beyond the ash-covered panes of his windows offered no hope of escape.

The sun was beginning to set. It lent a fiery glow to the smoky pall that hung over his city of birth. This harbinger of a looming hell cloaked Berlin's once proud monuments. Designed by Albert Speer, these sterile structures reflected the chip on Germany's shoulder. They stood in defiance of a world that denied her quest for a thousand-year Reich.

The pervasiveness of death and destruction was overwhelming. The horrifying sounds of the nightly bombing raids deprived him of the only respite life offered—blessed sleep. He looked again at the note:

GESTAPO WILL BE HERE AT 6PM SHARP. HAVE HILDA MEIER'S FILE READY.

Careful not to turn on the lights, his nurse entered the room, walked over and stared out the window. She observed the approaching darkness with apprehension. "Is there anything else I can do for you before I go home, Doctor?"

"No, thank you, fraulein, just draw the curtains. Don't lock the door. I have to wait for some Gestapo bastard to pick up one of our files."

"Doctor, I'm frightened. We must consider leaving Berlin if we're still able. It may be only a matter of days."

"I know. Come in tomorrow. We'll shut down the office and make arrangements to leave. We'll soon feel safe again... auf wiedersehen." Tilting himself upright, he spun his chair around, opened his file drawer and pulled out a worn, brown folder.

Hans sighed as he looked at the name that lay before him. His mind drifted. He seemed to do that often now, to a time and place that whispered serenity, to a time and place before the world went into terminal insanity. *I wonder why such a sweet young woman would volunteer to be Eva Braun's double. It couldn't be for money. I know her parents, and they live well. After all, they were given the confiscated house of the Schwartzberg's as a political favor. Could it be for position, patriotism? It doesn't make sense. What foolishness to get involved with those criminal thugs. Nothing good can—*

His worries were broken by a curt, double knock on the door.

"Come in. The door is unlocked," Hans beckoned.

"Dr. Brandt, Heil Hitler!" The stranger in black clicked his boot heels together, snapping his arm upward. Removing his fedora, he stopped and intensified his glare. He noticed the dentist did not return his salute.

With disgust simmering under his breath, Hans replied, "Yes, Heil Hitler. I've pulled Hilda Meier's file. What is it you want?"

Irritated that Hans remained seated and appeared not the least bit intimidated by his presence, the intruder swung his briefcase around, allowing it to slam on the desk. Hans jerked his head backward in surprise. The man in the leather coat slid his gloved hand into the soft-sided briefcase. Hans noticed the initials, JG, embossed in gold on the tab. The briefcase listed to one side but remained erect and open. The files of Eva Braun were removed and placed on the desk in front of him.

"Dr. Brandt, our Fuehrer is secure in his bunker and is making plans for the defense of Berlin. Eva Braun is there with him, but he wants to fly her to Berchtesgaden. For security reasons, you are instructed to exchange your files of this Meier woman with Eva's."

"I'll have my secretary make the changes in the morning. You can come by tomorrow and pick it up."

"No. You will make the changes *now*."

"But I'm here alone and this'll take time."

"I said *now*, Herr Doctor. I fail to see how a simple switching of records would require some grand effort by a secretary. I will wait."

Hans knew the argument was lost. "As I said, it'll take a little time to falsify the records. Have a seat if you wish."

"…A wise choice. Now, where is your water closet?"

"It's straight across the reception area, down the hall, first door on the left."

He watched the man walk past his receptionist's desk, and as Hans reached for his ink bottle, his elbow bumped into the already listing briefcase. Tipping over on its side, a second folder released from within. He looked to see if the goon was out of sight, and then opened the folder. One by one, he scanned the papers: Permits giving passage to Lisbon, tickets on a freighter to Buenos Aires, contacts in Switzerland and Marseilles.

What's this? A passport marked Hilda Maier, but with Eva's photograph? What are they planning to do to Hilda? He fought to regain his composure.

Hans heard the toilet flush. He shoved the papers back into the folder, returning it to the briefcase. The door squeaked open. He righted the leather case and reached for Eva's folder. Footsteps came across the reception floor. He slid several of Eva's dental impressions onto his lap. As Hans finished writing Eva's name on Hilda's records, the fiend entered the room and positioned himself behind his chair. Beads of sweat inched down Hans' temples. A shadow crept over the records.

"Are you finished, Herr Doctor?"

Hans shook his pen three times, feigning it was empty. He reached down and opened his desk drawer. "My pen's not working. I need to put a final note in the file." His right hand slid into the drawer while his left hand gripped a bronze bookend.

"That won't be necessary." With lighting speed, the man slammed the drawer shut, crushing Hans' fingers. Blinding pain raced through his trapped hand. He thrust the bookend up into the assailant's skull. The hulk staggered to one side, his knees buckled and he slumped to the floor.

It was all Hans could do to copy the information he found in the leather case. When done, he retrieved the fallen impressions of Eva from the floor and slid everything into a large envelope. With one hand, he tugged at his middle desk drawer, pulling it out of its track, and tightly stapled the envelope to its underside. He slid the drawer back in, stepped over the man and went to the adjacent room to dress his mangled fingers.

The pain in his hand began to numb over. He realized his only hope was to gather his wife and child and go westward to the Allied lines. But they will take us as prisoners, Hans thought. That's it—the records! I'll take the package to the Allies and use it as a bargaining chip.

Hans reentered his office; the leather-clad figure lay on the floor. He stepped over him. Terror exploded. A vise-like hand gripped his ankle, wrestling him to the floor. Fear turned to panic. He felt the barrel of a Luger press against his temple. The pistol discharged. Blackness came. Hans' body went limp.

Groggy, the stranger righted himself and pulled the dentist up into his chair, leaning him over his desk. As blood dripped from the side of his eye, the man placed the gun in Hans' right hand. He picked up the files and placed them into his briefcase. He straightened the lamp, wiping his blood off the bookend. He listened, opened the door and disappeared into the crisp night air.

CHAPTER 2

AS WINTER YIELDED ITS ICY LOCK ON NAZI GERMANY, THE Third Reich's winter of despair became a spring of horror. Everywhere, its once invincible army was in full retreat. The thawing earth that clung to the bodies of men trying to fight or sleep transformed into an unyielding quagmire. Under relentless cold rains, ground that had supported movement of troops now spewed forth an oozing morass of mud and slime. Clinging to the boots of the retreating men, it was as if the millions who had died in the war were reaching up from their shallow graves below. Cold, grey hands seemed to grasp at the heels of despondent, war-weary soldiers. Warfare's ebb and flow had lost all purpose. The Wehrmacht was losing more men in retreat than it had lost in its lightning push into Russia. To the worn-out soldiers, retreat felt like a futile passage to nowhere. They knew that death awaited them at the end of their journey. It would either come now or later, but later carried the shame of defeat.

Freezing rain tapped on the side window of the Mercedes sedan as it sped toward Berlin. Its slit headlights bounced a narrow beam of light into a darkness that mirrored the dying soul of its passenger, Albert Speer. Bombed-out debris lay strewn in the road. It popped into view as ghostly forms that rose and disappeared in cadence with the thumping of the sedan's wheels.

Am I traveling back to Berlin, or is this a continuation of my slow descent into Hell? The inner struggle with his shredded conscience gnawed at him night and day. We made our bargain with the devil, he thought. Ten years of diabolical depravity will have to be paid for.

A sudden drop followed by an upward thrust of the seat brought Speer's melancholy eyes back into focus. He looked into the darkness of the surrounding trees. Small farmhouses, with barely enough light

— 8 —

to make them visible, came in and out of sight. Like the Wermacht's defeated soldiers, endless pines, bent under the weight of the icy snow, broke into rhythmic view.

His mind drifted and flashed back three months, his last trip to the Eastern Front. He remembered every movement, every crying sound and every nauseous feeling of guilt.

***

He was driving alone in the frozen days of early January 1945. The leafless canopy of trees outside the town of Breslau allowed sunlight to flicker through their boughs and warm his tired face. He peered through the shimmering crystals that had formed on the windows of his camouflaged vehicle. The tranquility of the countryside was broken by the sounds of distant bombing. He shook his head to fight the drowsing effects of living without sleep.

They were coming—that god-awful Russian horde with their endless supply of Mongols to be used as human fodder—fodder that melted and twisted the German guns that never stopped firing into the mass of human flesh—fodder that paved roads for the Russian's ceaseless advance to the Fatherland. But that Fatherland was his and his father's and his father's father!

He was certain the war was lost, yet this "special" business required his attention. It was sadistic business and ripped at the tatters of what little moral fabric he had left. He hoped this business could salvage his dreams for Germany—not now, but later. This would be his gift to unborn generations. For him, National Socialism was not just a political movement; it was an expression of the psyche of German people. If he didn't believe this with every fiber of his being, he could never have lent his participation to such a chilling undertaking.

The snow-laden rooftops of "old town" Breslau exuded a surreal stillness that masked the insanity that had engulfed Europe. It spoke of a time line—a continuum that transcended new political ideas and human events. This old town juxtaposed against the sterile buildings he had designed for the Fuhrer in Berlin. Would those lifeless structures come to be viewed in the same light fifty years from now? Or would they be garish symbols of a period of national madness? Speer knew the answer and was ashamed.

When his car left the city, its buildings melded again into the rolling countryside. The strength of its forests tapped his genetic memory bank and spoke of his ancestral roots. He remembered Julius Caesar, who wrote of the strange people north of the Alps and their obsession to lay waste to the land around their territory by keeping it barren and uninhabited. It was considered a mark of honor and valor to have driven their neighbors from their land so no one dared to settle near them. In this peculiar behavior, they found their ultimate security.

Am I a prisoner of my heritage? Speer pondered. Have my actions been the manifestation of the blood that flows in my veins? The blood of my ancestors—that blood will fuel and drive all generations henceforth from which they too will draw their strength. He nodded his head in self-agreement. The purity of their bloodline—*that* is what will save them from the filthy vermin of the East. This, I promise.

Speer remained in his remembrance. He saw guard towers—towers securing the bleak compound that was the destination for his business. He had visited many concentration camps before, but they were different—pure death camps, efficient units of counter-production. This facility, however, had merit.

In his dream, he saw the high walls of barbed wire that surrounded the dismal rows of cheap, wooden housing. These buildings were not built for permanence. They were built for a short-term mission. As his vehicle turned left toward the facility, his senses became aware of a stark contrast. That contrast was between his camp and the stone walls surrounding the adjoining property. Those stone walls had housed the Convent of St. Mary Magdalene for five hundred years.

Five hundred years... Our Reich was to have lasted one thousand years. Odd... this convent filled with women, defended by nothing more than stone and a belief in God, has outlived a Reich that commanded the greatest army ever assembled by man. The irony sunk in. Humph. They are just women—an order of nuns. Is it true, the meek shall inherit the earth?

He remembered the fear that overwhelmed him in the middle of a blind curve. A large supply truck appeared. It bore down on him, halfway into his lane. He turned the steering wheel to the right. The car did not respond, its wheels sliding on an ice-covered patch. His torso braced for the crash. The truck grew to gargantuan size. He lost consciousness as the steering wheel collapsed under the weight of his chest.

Later, his eyelids struggled with a crust that had bonded them together. He winced, flickers of light reaching his pupils. The ceiling drifted out of a fog and into view. He leaned his head to the left and pain shot through his sternum, as if an elephant had stepped on his chest.

Disoriented, he cried out, "Where am I?" Cobwebs began clearing. The truck! Speer's body reacted to the image, shooting more pain into his chest. He was in a "hospital," but it was the one at the facility. Fear rose. Will I be safe? Have I been exposed to the biological experiments? Images flashed- -ghastly scenes bringing pain—sick people with gaping sores covering their faces and bodies. Speer closed his eyes. The images wouldn't go away. His hands shook, gripping the sheets. The devils that plagued his head refused to leave.

He saw zombielike people walking, aimlessly staring. They chopped wood, cooked meals and cleaned toilets. As if no one else existed, they obeyed orders and performed their tasks. Then more people, but this time they were normal people entering a building. Don't they know what we're going to do to them? Women, children—they too had fever-ridden bodies of oozing, puss-filled sores. No! No! This isn't happening! He remembered crying out as he saw the faces, the sores, the eyes—they're all looking at me. Don't kill them! You don't need to kill them! "I was an architect!" he blurted out. "Not a sadistic minister of pain!"

"Herr Oberst!" the nurse said. She reached over and gripped his shoulder.

Recognizing his surroundings, he inhaled. With every breath, his anxiety lessened. He looked away, out the window. The stone walls of the convent rose on the hill and came into view. It became clear what he must do. This facility will save our future generations. It will be their bloodline that will save them! This convent was here long before us and it will be here long after we're gone. I will give them this facility! They will take it and hide its hideous secret because I will tell them what we have made here and what horror it can produce. That knowledge will enslave them as surely as their God does.

But will those above me accept placing the fate of Germany and our grandchildren in the hands of insignificant women—religious women? They will, because they'll have no choice.

His vivid recollection continued. He was out of the hospital and had entered the convent. After cooling his heels for several minutes in the drafty foyer, he said, "Excuse me, Sister, but I was specific about meeting the Abbess."

"I can't help your expectations—Herr... Speer, is it?"

He nodded.

"I am the Abbess. My name is Sister, I mean, Mother Anastasia. Our previous Mother died last month. She came down with a horrid fever and became covered with sores. We couldn't save her, God rest her soul."

Speer shifted from one foot to the other. The Abbess noticed and her eyes turned cold. They told him she would yield ground to no one.

"Rumor has it that her fever was caught while ministering to the sick at your vile camp."

Speer was set back on his heels. As Armaments Minister, no one but the Fuehrer dared to question him. This diminutive, young nun had grown in stature. He paused, examining his new adversary.

Protruding from a habit that discouraged projection to the secular world was a beautiful face—soft and tender. Yet there was strength in her eyes—strength that came from within.

He was prejudiced by both her height and role as a nun. His first inclination was that she would never be up to this long, arduous task; let alone what he had in mind. But he was a good judge of character, and there was something about this woman that would prove formidable. This person could and would stand guard. Their reasons would be different, though. Fate had chosen this modest person, as it had chosen Joan of Arc for her role. She would be his unwilling keeper of the secret—his sentinel.

"You will have to excuse my unintended ignorance, Mother Abbess. I meant no disrespect. I assumed that an abbess would be somewhat 'older.'" He clicked his heels and cocked his head, reassuming his Teutonic posture.

"Perhaps 'taller' is what you meant?"

"In any case, Mother Abbess, I've come to make your religious order an unusual proposition."

She flashed Speer a piercing glare that went right through him.

This will not be easy, he thought. "I dare say this is an offer that even your God will not allow you to refuse."

"No, it is *you* who must excuse *me*. My God is also your God, Herr

Speer, and *He* doesn't suffer insolence. Is this offer somehow connected with your death camp?"

Speer's patience waned. He'd become agitated, strained. "Mother Abbess, I can assure you that our facility is not a death camp—quite the opposite. It is a hospital in which we conduct certain experiments for the sole purpose of extending life. I'm one of the few people within the Reich who believe we need a controlled workforce—a *living* workforce. When I'm finished, no one will die in any of our facilities. You see, we need a healthy workforce to serve a higher cause. I'm sure, Mother Anastasia, you can relate to a higher cause."

Speer paused, believing he had at least touched the humanitarian side of the woman. But would she take the bait?

With a heavy heart, she said, "Follow me." She turned and walked down the dark corridor to her office.

He closed his eyes and exhaled a breath of relief. This is for you, Margarete, and our children's children. He followed her down the stone-lined hallway and paused, touching the cold stone, his fingers tracing its grey veins.

When the sound of his jack boots stopped, the Abbess turned. "Herr Speer? ...This way."

Finding a chair opposite her desk, it became clear how and where he would attack. Everything hinged on the strength and finesse of his delivery.

"You may continue, Herr Minister, but bear in mind that God will be looking over my shoulder, and I dare say that *He* will be on *my* side."

He paused. He could make no mistake. He continued with slow and direct speech. He hoped this effect would create his web of entrapment.

"I have had a rather meteoric rise within the Reich," he said. "I have always been practical and blunt, and I shall be so with you." He leaned forward to increase his presence. "The facility on the adjoining property *has* been an experimental hospital, and we *have* done research in population control."

"I would remind the Minister that even here at the convent, we've heard the rumors of your population control methods. We are aware of your death camps!"

"This facility is *not* a death camp!" Speer blurted out. He realized he had lost control. "This facility has experimented in controlling people by administering, or shall I say, exposing them to various developed viruses."

"Viruses…? Did I hear you say viruses?" The nun was aghast. "Are you saying that you infect people here? You try to kill them with germs?" Her voice verged on hysteria.

"No! That is *not* what I said. We're not trying to kill them. We want to control them, alter their state of mind. We do this to make them productive workers within the Reich. As I said, we want controlled workers, and this course of action would allow us to shut down the other camps. We would be allowing them to live, not die." Speer shifted in his seat. "This is humane, no?"

"You will *allow* them to live? Do you Nazis believe you are God? How thoughtless of me, I should've realized how benevolent you people really are. And how many people will die in this... humane process of yours?"

"There may be those few that die, but I can assure you that most will live. I told you, Mother, I believe in keeping a living workforce, not a useless dead one."

"Herr Speer…" she started, fighting back the tears in her eyes as she thought of her deceased Mother Abbess, "I can't, no, I won't listen to you anymore. God has spoken to me, and *His* answer is an emphatic *no!*"

He smiled. "Excuse me, Fraulein Abbess, but I think it's *you* who doesn't understand." His voice rose with a forceful cadence. "You *will* do as you are told. You have no choice! The front is collapsing and the Russians will overrun our facility. It's a matter of months. We have discovered what we need to know and we *have* produced it. This virus cannot be destroyed. It must be hidden from the Russians. If you think Nazis are unscrupulous, think what the Soviet monsters will do if they find it. They will use it on *their* undesirable populations and on your own German people. They don't want workers. They want slaves for their gulags in Siberia. They want women to stock the brothels for their Mongol hordes. Is this the fate you want for your countrymen? We will evacuate this facility soon. No one else can hide this secret, and if you attempt to open the cylinders, you *will* spread its contents. Once this contagion is released, it won't stop until it reaches every person it is intended to infect.

"Hence, we intend to donate this property to your convent—under an assumed name. You *will* incorporate this property within your walls.

You *will* take this virus and hide it. Or… you can allow it to be unleashed on the world. The decision is yours. I will give you until morning to inform me of your choice. Heil Hitler!"

Speer rose from his seat, turned and slapped his gloves into the open palm of his hand. He put on his cap, ran his thumb and index finger across its brim and walked away in arrogance. He knew he had won. The secret would remain hidden. He had found his sentinel.

CHAPTER 3

PRESENT DAY

ASSOCIATED PRESS

MOSCOW - RUSSIAN PRESIDENT BORIS KERCHENKO WAS
admitted to a private sanitarium in Moscow. Unidentified sources in-
dicate that lifelong drinking habits have damaged his liver. Expectations
are that he will be interred for an extended period, after which, rest
and rehabilitation will take place at his countryside dacha. His duties
have been assumed by ultra-nationalist Alexander Konstantinov, who
will attempt to keep President Kerchenko's ruling majority intact. His
closest rivals, Vladimir Donskoy, head of the Motherland Party, and
General Gennady Zyuganov of the Communist Party have demanded
an immediate general election.

BERLIN, GERMANY

The day was fitting for a funeral at Holy Sepulcher Roman Catholic
Cemetery. Dark and melancholy, the sky set the mood with soft rain
falling. It was as if Heaven washed away the pain of those left behind.

Lisa Brandt stood by the grave of her grandmother with one arm
clasped around her mother, Hanne. The priest and a small cadre of
mourners left, leaving the two as the last to honor the passage of their
family's widowed matriarch. It wasn't until the last several years that
Lisa and her mother were able to know the lady held captive behind the
Berlin wall, unable to escape her communist homeland after the war.

"Life was cruel to your grandmother, Lisa. So many times I wished
she hadn't smuggled me out of Berlin. Life would have been hell under
the Russians, but at least we would've been together. I was such a
lonely child—"

"Things in life happen for a purpose, Mom. Only God knows
the plan."

"It's hard to fit those filthy Russians into any scheme connected with

God. If they hadn't overrun our city, Papa might be alive today."

"Mom, Grandfather committed suicide. It was the war—"

"No! No, it wasn't *the war*—that makes it too easy. I was smuggled out of Berlin and raised by my Aunt Gertie. You grew up in freedom and went to a good dental school in America. Don't you see? They suffered through the whole war. We never had to suffer—not like them. People that suffer are strong. They didn't take the easy way out. No, I will never accept that my Papa committed suicide—never!"

"I didn't mean to sound uncaring." Lisa squeezed her mother's shoulder while wiping her tears with her handkerchief.

"I know, dear," Hanne said. She grasped Lisa's hand and pressed it to her heart. "Let's drive over to your grandmother's house… we need to sell it now that she's gone."

"Mom, don't forget that it's in the old East sector. With economic problems haunting the European Union, you may not be able to sell it right away. Besides, I've heard there's a shortage of dentists in that area. Maybe there's an opportunity for someone wanting to set up a practice." Lisa's eyes twinkled as she opened a sly smile.

"You mean to use Papa's old office?" Hanne barely contained her joy. "…Why not?"

With another squeeze of her daughter's hand, Hanne smiled and said, "Come along then. Nothing would've made my Papa prouder, Lisa. I love you, lebchen."

***

Lisa stepped into the foyer of her grandparents' home. For the first time, she felt a bond with her past. Although the house was cold, light filtering through the partially drawn blinds gave its paneled walls a golden glow of warmth. Entering the reception area of her grandfather's office, however, her mood changed. She wasn't prepared for the scene that opened before her.

"Mom, this feels like some macabre museum. Why do you suppose grandmother never touched anything in this office? It's as if we've been thrown back in time. Nothing has changed. I mean, even his records are still on the reception desk… pens, appointment calendars, everything! It's like he's talking to us from the past."

CHAPTER 4

THE MOOD IN THE GILDED BOARDROOM WAS SOMBER AND reflective. A framed quotation hung between two antique tapestries. With a small light illuminating it, it stood out with prominence against the darker color of the walls. The quotation was more than just a reminder to those around the conference table—it was their mission statement. The quotation was attributed to the international banker, Rothschild, from 1938. It read:

> I care not what puppet is placed upon the throne of England to rule the empire on which the sun never sets. The man who controls Britain's money supply, controls the British Empire, and I control the British money supply.

Present were the hand-picked captains of Germany's largest industries, watched over by the real power brokers—the banks. They were an integral part of a global plutocracy that represented the financiers of Switzerland, London and Wall Street. These financiers had manipulated the Great Depression, initiated control by the Federal Reserve System over American banking, funded the Bolsheviks over the White Russians, and funded the rise to power of an Austrian paper hanger. This enigmatic cabal traced its roots back centuries. They influenced policy in both World Wars and reaped billions with no concern for the victor.

It mattered not that no one in this room had heard Adolph Hitler speak since January 30th, the date of his last radio broadcast. Rumor had it that Joseph Goebbels would soon announce that, "The Fuehrer is in Berlin and will die fighting with his troops defending the capital city." The end of the war that consumed the globe was drawing near. The Red Army had swept from the Oder River to the outskirts of the city. Plans needed to be set in motion for the future of the new postwar Germany and the subsequent billions that would be reaped in the rebuilding of Europe and the Far East.

Low, guttural whispers came to a halt as Albert Speer entered the room. He had been delayed, but the meeting couldn't move forward without his report. Gone were the customary clicking of heels and Nazi salutes. Instead, he set his briefcase and cap on the conference table, unbuttoned his soaking greatcoat and threw it over a leather chair.

"Was it an aimless trip?" one banker queried.

"No, it was not," Speer replied. He drew a breath and collected his thoughts. It had been years since he was Hitler's young lion of architecture. Those wistful days had been replaced by the drudgery and stress of providing a flow of materiel for a collapsing and encircled war machine. Facing a war-reduced population to staff his factories, Speer turned to the only source of available labor—the concentration camps. What he witnessed on the Eastern Front still repulsed him to his core. In just four years, he looked as if he had aged twenty. The war had taken its toll and he was weary beyond belief.

Speer wished he had been given time to rest prior to this meeting. For strength, he summoned an image of his wife and children, and began. "I've been working with Dr. Goebbels to convince our Fuehrer *not* to evacuate the bunker and move to Berchtesgaden. I can report that my attempts have been successful. He'll stay in Berlin and the bitter end will come sooner, not later. The sands of the hourglass have nearly run out. We can no longer bank on surrender, cutting our best deal with the Allies. We have—"

"A definite destination," interrupted the director of transportation.

"You are right, Herr Reuter, and that destination must be the United States. Like the mythical Phoenix, a New World Order *can* emerge from these ashes, but only if, through our group, Germany is able to infiltrate the victor. That victor will not be England or France—their glory days are behind them. Nor will it be Russia. Their peasant mentality will curse them for centuries. As you know from my previous report, America has beaten us in the race for the atomic bomb. Our intelligence informs us they will have the ability to deploy it by August—and deploy it they will. America will emerge as the real victor of this war and the spoils will go to them. We have made arrangements for them to capture the esteemed

Werner von Braun, and as a consequence, they'll have the technology to place their atomic bomb in our A-9 rocket. Within a few years, they will send it halfway around the world. The only thing lacking in the Americans is their will to conquer for territorial gain. Technology, *and* the will to use the power it yields, is the key to world domination. We have always understood this concept, but the Americans are a foolish, idealistic nation. That idealism has paralyzed them.

With this in mind, we have executed our plan to place someone on a course to come to prominence in America's postwar government, with, of course, the goal of ascending to its presidency. This person will be *ours*. He'll be positioned to protect the rebirth of Germany when we're ready to rearm. Hence, we will fulfill our destiny and ultimately the conquest of Russia. Russia must be conquered because of its overabundance of natural resources. We can only accomplish this with a rebuilt Germany shielded by the United States. The Nazis failed to do it alone and there is no reason to believe that Germany could do it alone in the future. Remember, Russia will strip us of everything they can get their hands on. On the other hand, the foolish Americans will want to rebuild our nation as an ally. Our people have proposed what they will call The Marshall Plan for postwar Europe."

"Your scheme becomes clear," chimed another banker. "But with all their military power, will we be able to manipulate and control the Americans?"

The third banker decided to give Speer a break. "I'm certain we will. It'll take forty years or more to rebuild Europe. The untold billions that we will reap from their Marshall Plan will be moved to Swiss banks and will be available upon need. Over time, we will clandestinely move the funds to Mr. Morgan's bank, and perhaps one or two others that are involved within their Federal Reserve. We'll buy a massive amount of U.S. security bonds and ultimately, we'll manipulate them from within." He turned his shoulders and pointed to the framed quotation on the wall. "When you own their *debt*, you own *them*. And all this will be at the expense of the American taxpayer. They are weary of war and will become preoccupied with their new affluence. But they will not see the crippling debt that will ensnare them. Odd, is it not? The American soldiers will have defeated us, but in the long run, *they* will unknowingly become *our* slaves."

"Herr Speer, what happens if the Russians also develop atomic bombs and A-9 rockets?" asked a banker. "What I mean is this: Will the Americans be willing to risk a future war with Russia?"

"They will protect Germany because they have no choice!" Speer snapped. He was in no mood to explain his position again. He looked over the men sitting at the table and thought, Am I the only person who understands that nation of economic whores? He clenched his teeth, took a breath to relay his impatience and tried to explain once more. "America is a melting pot of lowly immigrants without a national identity. They have no central purpose other than the acquisition of material goods. To them, money is almost a God, and I can tell you, if it came to a choice between money and God, the latter would die a quick death. With their abundant resources, they'll become the premier industrial giant of the world. But, here is the key: They will need Europe to buy the goods they produce. In order to achieve this, they will need a revitalized Germany to anchor and protect Europe against their new enemy, Russia. In summary, they *will* rebuild us and they *will* have to protect us."

He turned his head and looked at each member. "And everyone in our international group will make an enormous amount of money in the process. Frankly, we do expect Russia to become a world power. They'll do it because of the technology and reparations they will steal from us and the rest of Eastern Europe. But unlike America, it will be like an ape snatching a string of pearls. Their peasant mentality will doom them and they'll implode as a world power. Nonetheless, we are also making provisions to place one of our members into a family of high communist position in the Soviet Union as well. We have discovered a penchant for homosexuality in Victor Konstantinov, the Russian Ambassador to Sweden. It appears that he has a 'nephew,' Alexander, who has been 'away at school in Sweden.' I have chosen the 'nephew' myself."

Speer winced, for he believed his next statement was not what this group of power brokers wanted to hear. "It's unfortunate, but few of us will survive the length of time it'll take for this plan to come to fruition—it may take as long as fifty years."

A buzz of murmuring settled in over the gathering. Speer wondered if his message had fallen on deaf ears. The silence was broken by the head of Hueber Chemical.

"... And Herr Speer, can you tell us if our 'storage facility' is secure?"

"As far as we know, it's safe and camouflaged as best as is possible."

The head of Hueber Chemical again queried, "What do we know of our facility's contents? They are sealed and will last these fifty years?"

"They could last a hundred years."

"… Arrangements have been made for the transfer of the facility's property?"

"Completed," said Speer. He was weary and rose from his chair. He had delivered his dutiful message and wanted no more.

The chemical mogul raised his glass of water and toasted, "To the devil!"

"To the devil!" the others joined in.

Reaching for his briefcase and cap, Albert Speer let his water remain on the conference table. I'll toast our future, but not the devil, he thought.

Buttoning his greatcoat, he heard one of the bankers say, "… Good! Then let us proceed with our plans, Herr Speer. We'll await the coming of a new Reich! Heil Hitler!"

"Heil Hitler!" they all shouted.

In a tired voice, Speer responded, "Auf wiedersehen." Without the required salute, he turned and eased his way out the door.

A pall crept over the smoky boardroom as the receding sound of Speer's boots faded. The chemical mogul was the first to break the silence. "Pathetic, is it not? Herr Speer couldn't bring himself to toast the same entity that he sold his soul to."

"Even more pathetic," said the banker, "was how he told us 'we were going to make an enormous amount of money in the process.' He shows signs of understanding our core nature, but then falls short. We don't make or need money—we only need debt. Money has no value, other than what we say it is worth. We manipulate its value through wars, panics, recessions, depressions—whatever we deem necessary. No, it's debt that brings power. We gave the Bolsheviks enough credit to come to power and fight this war. The Americans have given England the credit necessary to rearm and fight. With our money, their banks will extend to Europe enough credit to rebuild. Therefore, Europe will be indebted to either the United States or to us. But it is *we* who have bought *their* debt. Therefore, everyone is indebted to *us*! And it is that indebtedness that gives us our ultimate power."

"That power has been in our hands since our ancestors, the great

Khazars, established their financial empire in the thirteenth century," said the second banker.

"To the Rothschild and the Warburg lineage!" toasted the chemical giant.

"…To all the great Khazars and their family trees!"

When the toasting had finished, the energy mogul asked, "Should we make a safe passage for Herr Speer out of the country?"

"No. There must be those who will pay for this Nazi mess."

CHAPTER 5

WEDNESDAY 15 APRIL 1945
THE BUNKER
BERLIN, GERMANY

WAITING OUTSIDE DR. THEODOR MORELL'S OFFICE, HILDA Maier paced back and forth. The lighting was dim and seemed to be absorbed by the dull, grey walls. She felt cornered, as if she were in a dark maze that offered no way out. She sat down in the straight-back chair and closed her eyes. When the tension in her body eased, she recalled her first public appearance at the Party Rally in Nuremberg, 1942.

***

Life was magical, mystical—the frenzied crowds, searchlights pointing upward into clouds seemingly lined with silver, the great circle of flags with their black swastikas emblazoned on crimson red, Roman-styled banners with eagles spreading majestic wings. It was all so exhilarating, so intoxicating...

Hilda's thoughts turned to herself as a girl growing up in Bavaria. She saw her mother's round face, calling her from their chalet. Papa, wearing his lederhosen, was laughing and tossing her up in the air, catching her at the last moment, and in one motion, sliding her under his legs. She could almost smell the sweet, green grass. Those were such happy and innocent times.

She saw grass turn to leaves and leaves blow away in favor of snow. Next, the ski trip to Berchtesgaden and the soft powdery snow that sprayed from the sides of her skis. A bump from the rear sent her body sprawling into the snow. She felt a hand reach under her arm and pull her up. A handsome young man fell over himself in apologies and introduced himself; it was love at first sight. Courtship followed—walks along the streets of Munich, conversations in the park while holding hands, loving words, loving touches. Soon, a proposal of marriage was joyfully accepted and the world lay open before them. Hilda remembered the young Wehrmacht soldier sliding a ring on her finger, the two of them walking down the aisle of the church and riding off to Innsbruck on honeymoon. Their deep, mutual love made her complete, and in her heart she believed it would last forever.

She remembered the pain that raced across her heart as a train whistle blew its final call. Rolf passed through billowing steam and boarded the troop carrier bound for the Eastern Front. Gone were their times together and gone was the young man that had captured her soul. All that remained were letters that arrived once or twice a month, then not at all. After a time, as the new life within her womb began to move, the dreaded notice came: Rolf had been killed. The crushing words struck like a dagger in her tender heart, she could scarcely breathe. Dazed, she stumbled down her front porch steps, crumpled paper still in hand, half running, half walking, blinded by her flowing tears. Where she was going didn't matter. She just had to flee—to anywhere. Hilda staggered into the street, trying to catch a trolley as it lumbered by. Her hand grasped the rear platform rail, but her feet missed the step. She was dragged till her arm could hold no longer, her body bouncing on the cobblestones like a discarded rag doll.

Hours later, as she gained consciousness, a second blow to her fragile spirit came. Their baby was dead. Severe depression followed the physical injury and her mind turned to suicide as the only way to be reunited with Rolf and her baby.

Days passed in recovery, and then by chance, Dr. Morell passed her room in the hospital. He stopped in his tracks when he caught glimpse of the woman who could've been Eva Braun's identical twin. Days later, he came to her house and recruited her to become Eva's double. Without a reason to continue life, she embraced his patriotic call and mindlessly plunged into the bizarre hell of the Nazi world.

A sharp pain from a repaired tooth returned her thoughts to the present. Hilda recalled the visit to her dentist two weeks earlier and the astonished look on Dr. Brandt's face when she confided her secret role to him. Astonishment turned to concern as her lifelong friend and dentist discussed the danger she could be facing. With his words fresh in her mind, Hilda closed her eyes and prayed for that danger to come. Only death would end the tortured pain of her miserable existence.

***

When Hilda heard her name summoned, she pursed her lips and entered Dr. Morell's office. She was startled to see a heavyset man in a black leather coat with a fedora pulled low, attempting to camouflage a gauze bandage that covered his eye. With his one good eye, he stared forward while clutching a black leather briefcase. Sitting at his desk was Dr. Morell, flanked by a slender woman Hilda recognized as the infamous Magda Goebbels.

"Good morning, Fraulein. May I present Frau Goebbels?" he asked.

Hilda's eyes met Magda's. The stiff woman nodded, forcing a condescending smile. The sinister hulk from Gestapo never moved.

"As you know, Fraulein, Berlin will soon fall," Magda began. "It's also not a secret that the Russians will overrun this bunker within perhaps forty-eight hours. If we are lucky, we will all be dead before then." She paused and fixed her intimidating glare on Hilda. "Have you been told of the treatment German women will receive from the Mongol horde?"

"Yes ..." Hilda was not sure where she was leading her.

"I must tell you, my dear Hilda," Magda continued, "that I know full well what this diseased vermin will do to me... to us... to my children. I will have no part of this. I won't let my body be desecrated by these filthy sub humans! Besides, for me there is no life without our beloved Adolph—I mean our beloved Germany *led* by our Fuehrer. No, Joseph and I have decided to die alongside our Fuehrer." She paused, her eyes misted over and she looked intently at Hilda. "And this includes my children. Do you *fully* understand what I am saying, my dear?"

"I think so," answered Hilda. The small room became hot. She felt faint.

"Now, the same pact has been agreed to between Adolph and Eva. He will mercifully give her a cyanide pill and kill himself. Their bodies will then be cremated, preventing mutilation of their remains. Do you still understand what I'm saying?"

"But how does this apply to me?" Hilda replied. She was in shock by the thought of Magda killing her children.

"Don't you see? Once Adolph and Eva are cremated, no remains will be found. The Russians will go on a manhunt looking for *them*, but if you are still alive, they will only find *you*. You are Eva's double, are you not? When captured, you will be identified as Eva Braun, and nothing you say will change their minds. These vultures will need someone's flesh to pick and you will be all that is left of Adolph's inner circle. You will be sexually and physically abused, mutilated and hung in triumph from the Chancellery flagpole, then—"

"Stop!" Hilda cried out. She covered her ears to make the sounds go away.

"Now, now, my dear, you can still spare yourself this torture. You see, Eva is carrying Adolph's child." Magda spoke with such intensity that Hilda was held spellbound. "We *must* save his offspring. Adolph's seed must live on to rule Germany and the world another day. Believe me when I say that there *will* be another time for the Fatherland, and it will be Adolph's child who will lead us then. It is Germany's destiny!"

With pain stabbing her heart once more, Hilda remembered the child she lost, the child that would never be. She broke down and wept. Magda Goebbels looked at the man from Gestapo, then at Dr. Morell. She shook her head, signaling them to do and say nothing. She knew Hilda needed to release her pain to move forward and obey.

When Hilda's sobbing reduced to sniffles, Magda continued, "Only you can save the baby of our Fuehrer, my dear, only you. We are asking you to step into the breach one more time for Eva. Let us remove her from Berlin to safety. You must take her place at Adolph's side at the final moment. You will save yourself from certain torture and you will save his baby. You must do this, Hilda—for yourself, for Adolph and above all for Germany."

Hilda closed her eyes and remembered her lost love and child. She thanked God for giving her this chance. Calmness infused her body and made her strong, once more looking at Dr. Morell.

"But why must we do this behind the Fuehrer's back … why not tell him what we are doing?"

Nervously, Dr. Morrell glanced at the Gestapo goon, then at Hilda. "You must understand, dear child, that the war has taken its toll on our leader. He screams incessantly. It's possible he may have had a nervous breakdown. No, it's better for us to help him in his hour of need."

"Do you think it will work?"

Dr. Morell nodded his head. "It can work. The Fuehrer has been complaining of his eyesight. I will give him a drug that will further affect his vision. He will again complain and I will administer eye drops that will make his already blurred vision worse. Coupled with the drugs he already takes, that should work. Will you do your country, your Fatherland, this one last honor?"

She saw this as an answer to her prayers. She could once again be with her beloved Rolf and their baby. "Yes ..." she whispered. "Yes, I will."

Knowing the time had come for solitude, Magda motioned for the two men to follow her out of the room. Hilda sobbed and then wiped her face with both hands.

"It won't be long, Rolf. I will be coming home to you and our baby."

CHAPTER 6

PRESENT DAY
ASSOCIATED PRESS

KANDAHAR, AFGHANISTAN: NATO PEACEKEEPING FORCES, U.S. COMMAND SECTOR – U.S. Forces marked the ten-year anniversary of their arrival in Afghanistan as part of a greater NATO Command trying to defeat the resurgent and combined al-Qaeda and Taliban forces. Although NATO started its mission with 60,000 troops from Europe, their number has dwindled to less than 20,000. Meanwhile, the number of American soldiers has swelled to over 100,000 with an additional 50,000 as support personnel. Despite total air superiority, U.S. forces have been bogged down in the Kandahar region with 5,832 killed in action since the surge began.

U.S. COMMAND CENTER
KANDAHAR, AFGHANISTAN

The job at hand seemed overwhelming, even for three career military leaders who had followed divergent paths to the pinnacles of power in their warrior profession. There was an enemy to fight. But finding that elusive enemy in the mountainous terrain of Kandahar had become a Herculean task that the combined minds of NATO could not solve. Inflamed by a hostile press corps that was neither understanding nor sympathetic, grousing and finger pointing had set in among the allies. Brigadier General James O'Donnell was a journeyman soldier who never viewed those in his command as pawns in a game of global chess. Staring at the latest casualty report on his desk, he ran his fingers through his military buzz. He was startled as his door opened allowing two of his superior officers to enter. O'Donnell jumped to his feet in rigid salute.

"Relax, Jim," said Major General William Sash, head of U.S. Forces.

"Where's that bottle of single malt hiding?" asked the Commander of NATO, U.S. Admiral Lawton K. Jones.

"Right where that little sweetheart always is—close at hand," answered Jim. He opened the lower file drawer of his desk and pinched three short glasses between his fingers. As O'Donnell poured the Scotch into the glasses, his superiors loosened their ties and dropped into the couch across from him.

"It's hard to believe that I was so full of hope when we completed that bridge over the Helmond River," mused O'Donnell, handing each man a glass of the amber liquid. "I still think of those sixteen hundred feet of pontoons in that brutal December water. If that damned rain hadn't flooded the Helmond, we wouldn't have needed that extra five hundred feet. Hmmm, ten years seems like a long time ago." He took a sip of his single malt. The liquid seemed to explode in his mouth and he felt its effects all the way down his throat. "Damn, I sure know good Scotch. That's Lagavulin for those of you who are part of the great unwashed."

"I love the nose—smoky, with lots of maritime aromas. That's peat, isn't it? No, Jim, I'm not one of the great unwashed. Anyway, I didn't believe you would ever finish that bridge with the shit-ton of problems that plagued the project. But when those first Abrams and Bradlees came rumbling across...well, let's just say that I was damned relieved," said Sash.

"Yeah, then one of our Humvees hit that friggin' IED mine right at Christmas. Remember how the pricks in the press were all over that hospital in Ghazni? You would've thought we lost the whole 709th, instead of one soldier losing his leg. Now, we're losing a thousand a month," O'Donnell said. He shook his head. "And there's no end in sight."

"Well, it looks like the French are going to see their end. They've announced they're pulling out," said Jones. "I talked to General Duperes this morning and it is official. That Couteau is an asshole."

"Can you blame them?" asked O'Donnell. "I mean, losing three thousand men to them is like losing thirty thousand to us."

"Let's not forget that this is our second go-around in this hellhole. We carried the brunt by ourselves for years. When is it our turn for a break? Shit, I knew when they were given Mazar-e Sharif there was no way they were gonna' hold that corridor. They were surrounded by the Taliban and al-Qaeda," said Sash.

"Well, maybe 'Frenchie' should have deployed more troops like we advised them in the first place," Jones interjected.

"Bullshit!" said Sash. "They had enough men. You just can't find al-Qaeda to fight them. On top of it, you have to deal with the tribal warlords."

"Well, I'm sick and tired of all their pompous pissin' and moanin,'" replied Jones. "It'll make my job a whole lot easier when they've packed their French asses the hell out of here."

"It won't when their body bags become ours," reminded Sash, his tone becoming irritable.

"What's this I hear about the Brits, Lawton?" O'Donnell asked. He noticed the need to calm Bill Sash down.

"Well, as you know Jim, the Labor Party won yesterday's election. Unofficially, they've stated that they will reduce, not increase their presence. Word's out that they were waiting for Frenchie to take the heat first. Now they can save face," Lawton said. Then, with a sarcastic British accent, "Very proper, don't you know."

"Hey, our political situation is not a whole lot different at home," said O'Donnell. "President Cook's been in nothing but a political heap of shit since his reelection last November."

"Yeah, remember his slogan, 'negotiate, don't obliterate?' Nothing but pure campaign bullshit," added Sash.

Jones defended his Commander in Chief, "Well, his options have basically been slim to none, other than to gradually add more troops."

"Tell me why he dropped a good man like Jenkins from his ticket three months before the stinking election? Hell, he was all right as V.P.; now we have that arrogant asshole Koernig to deal with," said O'Donnell. He took another long swig of scotch.

"I want to remind you that no matter what you think of him, he is *now* the vice president. And he's coming for a visit in ten days!"

"Let me guess, he's bringing along his handpicked Sec Def and maybe a few of his Ivy League toadies now that he's loaded those ass kissers onto the National Security Council."

"Jim, you've got to back off on Koernig," said Sash. "You can talk like that around me, but—"

"Screw him, Bill, I've never liked him and I don't like the way he's pushed himself and his cronies onto this country," interrupted Jones. His voice bellowed. "His 'accelerated gradualism' approach sucks. We have boys over here dying because of it!"

"Well, I'm not a political animal," said O'Donnell. "When we stood by and let Kandahar get overrun with the Taliban, we shot ourselves in the foot. When our troops are stuck in Taliban-held territory and right across the border the Pakistanis allow the a-Q to cross at will, what does anyone expect?"

"This shit, Jim...nothing but this kind of shit."

CHAPTER 7

VLADIMIR DONSKOY WAS A MAN WEANED ON THE DIRTIEST of political infighting. Adolph Hitler had been his hero, a hero on which he modeled his own political career. The Brownshirts, the beer-hall putsch, the time spent in jail, young Vladimir knew this was the grist of politics. Ally yourself with thugs, use them, and dig until you find enough dirt on them. When they're no longer of any use, you expose their skeletons in the closet and get rid of them. It's a blueprint for success; let them do the grunt work and carry you along to power. Then poof! You own them and you no longer need them. It worked then and it will work now. He knew there was nothing new under the sun and nothing changes.

The knocking on the door of his modest apartment was short and quick. The visitor looked left, then right, nervous to be exposed in the open hallway. He wanted to be sure that eyes weren't peering out of cracked doors or slightly pulled curtains. He raised his hand to knock again, but the door creaked open.

"You're late," Donskoy hissed. The smirk on his face telegraphed his disgust.

"I'm sorry comrade, but—"

"Don't *but* me, you idiot! Did they teach you to be late at FSB? The old KGB would have had your nuts on a platter for less than this."

"That was a long time ago, comrade."

"I know how long ago it was. Do I need to tell you the reasons for your dismissal again?" It's beautiful, he thought—you hold dirt on the man that gathers dirt for you. Look how I can make this pathetic excuse for a man squirm.

"No. What is it you need this time?"

"Information, you fool, always information!" Donskoy licked his thin lips. They broke into a twisted smile. His crooked yellow teeth were laden with plaque and leftovers from the previous night's meal. His eyes shone as the names rose in his mind, "I want to own Alexander Konstantinov and General Gennady Zyuganov. Do you understand? I want to *own them*!"

Donskoy saw fear rush through the ex-KGB's psyche. He knew he had raised the stakes. These weren't penny-ante party officials. The risks were higher and the fallout was deadlier if discovered.

With hesitation, the small man offered his proposal, "Well, comrade, you would agree that perhaps…certainly anything that I could find should be worth a little more? Yes?"

Donskoy turned red with rage. "Get out! Who do you think you are, you slimy little turd?" He raised his foot and kicked the prick's backside as he shoved him out the door. "Bring me the dirt I need by the end of this week or I'll have that picture of you and that naked twelve-year-old Chechen sent to your wife!"

CHAPTER 8

BRYAN HARMON SLICED A SMALL PORTION OF THE VEAL cutlet on his plate. He looked up and couldn't help but notice his German counterpart, Ernst Stihl, doing exactly the same. Same old restaurant, he thought—same white tablecloth and napkins. God, I'm bored with this life. It never changes—it's always the diplomatic way. Everything in its proper place, small talk laden upon small talk, meaningless reports stacked upon meaningless reports. All the real work is done in Washington. I'm just a glorified babysitter who shuffles paper. And I'm an assistant at that—an assistant who meets with other assistants and—

"Bryan?"

"Excuse me, Ernst, what was that?" asked Bryan. He hadn't heard a word of the diplomat's last query.

"What will be the official position of your government regarding Donskoy's claim to sovereignty over the Baltic Republics?"

"Ernst, President Cook certainly would never approve of this claim, and it's a moot point anyway since Donskoy hasn't been elected to anything yet."

"…Yet, may be the key word here, Bryan. After all, he's soaring in the polls and the people seem to want him."

"They don't want *him*; they want him to deliver half the garbage he's promising them. In any case, our official position is that he's a crude loud-mouth who won't be elected when push comes to shove." Bryan probed for information to pass to his ambassador. "By the way, has Chancellor Mueller reviewed the diplomatic statement in which we call for the buildup of German support forces in Afghanistan?"

"She has, but we've been forced to carry the bailout of the European Union's economic problems on our backs alone. We keep discovering more debt that these countries have promised their populaces. Bryan, I've seen these figures with my own eyes and it makes me sick. First we had to bail out Greece, then Portugal. Now that Spain is bankrupt, our coffers are down to nothing and Belgium and the Netherlands are begging at our door. How much longer can the French hold out? My God, the attitudes of these countries are so bad, they may not be salvageable. Fifty years of creeping socialism can ruin any society, even a German one." Looking around to make sure no one could hear, Ernst held up his thumb and index finger, indicating a small space. He whispered, "Believe me, we are this close to pulling the plug on the EU. Perhaps if President Cook would take a more sensible and realistic view of our need to return to our traditional borders east of the Oder-Niesse River, then—"

"Ernst, surely in light of Poland's entry into full NATO membership—"

"Still, you have a problem situation in Afghanistan, and I believe a quid pro quo would be in order. Wouldn't you agree?"

Accepting the fact that both sides had made their respective points, Bryan nodded. The two then settled in to the realization that they had received about all the tidbits of information they were going to get and were content to finish the midday meal in banal conversation.

Bryan Daniel Harmon was a young man who defined his whole being by one mistake, a mistake that left him unable to find his own forgiveness. He knew well the funk that he was in. It had occurred many times before, lately with more frequency. It was a void that blew across his soul like a hot sirocco carrying the parched pain of his youth to torment him again.

***

He had just turned sixteen; an age when all teenagers believe that life is eternal and requires no pain or penalty of action. Bryan did not revel in the status or privilege of being the first-born son and heir apparent to one of America's finest political families. His father, Blaine Harmon, was the American Ambassador to Switzerland…a plum appointment by any standard.

It was sunny and the air was crisp, the perfect day for his parents to drive from their home in Berne to Interlaken for a Saturday outing. Bryan and David were as close as two brothers could be. Being two years older was a blessing and a curse for Bryan. With the age difference came not only big brother worship, but also the begging from David to be included in Bryan's exploration of life's new-found pleasures. This day was no different. After several hours of boredom, David begged for Bryan to take them out for a joyride. Knowing the trouble he would be in if caught, Bryan resisted the steady drumbeat. But his resolve caved in when David called into question Bryan's budding and wobbly manhood.

"The roads are icy, so just a short drive," was the only resistance Bryan could muster. He had just received his driver's license and lacked the experience needed to negotiate the Swiss roads in winter. But it wasn't fear of the road that held him back. He and his brother were born late in life to his parents and there was a bond of love that only comes when a child is denied to wanting parents for many years. He knew he would be violating a sacred trust. It was a decision that would forever haunt his life.

Later, lying in a hospital bed, the horrid scene played in his mind. A truck—in front of me! Look out, Davey, look out! He opened his swollen eyes and saw his mother.

"Mom, where's Davey?" he whispered. His mother could only cry.

"Davey? Mom, where's Davey?" he shouted as the horror of the truth sank in.

She caressed his bandaged face. "Davey died. He was killed in the accident."

He turned his face from his mother in shame. The pain of his guilt was excruciating. The hospital seemed to crumble upon him. He searched the room, but his father was nowhere to be seen. Bryan knew that nothing would ever be the same. Darkness overcame him as he fell back asleep.

***

After a time, Blaine Harmon was appointed to the World Bank Board of Governors, precipitating a move back to Washington, D.C.—a change welcomed by the grief-stricken family. Trying to erase the pain of his brother's death, Bryan buried himself in his studies. Although he graduated third in his class at Yale and was voted "Most likely to kiss the maximum amount of ass," it was his father who planned his career and insisted on a master's degree in international law. Even his acceptance into the diplomatic corps was engineered by his father. Bryan wanted a military career, but his continuing guilt made him yield to his father's will.

CHAPTER 9

THE BRIGHTNESS OF THIS PARTICULAR DAY HAD FOOLED Lisa, and it wasn't until she stood in her grandfather's dental office that she realized how cold it was. It's freezing in here, she thought. I can't believe Momma had the gas turned off. If the temperature drops any lower, the pipes will freeze. A shiver ran down her back as she scanned the room. "I wish I had worn a heavier sweater," she whispered to herself. Thumbing through a few of her grandfather's dusty dental texts, Lisa was amazed to see how much dentistry had changed in the last seventy years. While her fingers turned the brittle pages, her mind wandered.

Grandfather had as much education as me, yet dentistry was so primitive, almost barbaric, she thought. In another seventy years I suppose my grandchildren will think of me as Granny Lisa, the barbarian tooth puller! Her lightheartedness turned to melancholy as she pondered how her grandfather had died. Suicide, hah! No one will ever think of me that way, she resolved. Sliding a book back on the shelf, she whispered, "Never!"

Never...She recalled her mother's words at the funeral two days earlier: "I will never accept that Papa committed suicide—never!" It's so hard to believe. Why did he do it? Even in a Russian occupied Germany, they'd still need qualified dentists. Her hand gently turned the pages of his yellowed appointment calendar. She focused on the first hour of his morning schedule, flipping forward and backward through several pages.

My God, I don't believe it. He attended morning mass every day! He must've been one devout Catholic. I may not be much of one, but I know that Catholics don't commit suicide. Odd, she thought. Her mind tried to reconcile the incongruity. Grandfather had several appointments scheduled for two days after his apparent suicide. That's not the action of a depressed person. There's even a notation to see if any cabaret was still open to take grandmother to celebrate her birthday the following evening!

Tuesday 13 April 1945...the day he died. His last appointment was in the evening: JG re: EB. I wonder what that meant. None of this has any logic. Momma said grandfather hated guns. Why would he have owned one if he hated them?

Turning around behind her, Lisa noted file drawers filled with dental records. Opening one, her eyes perused the tabs of the thickest files. He sure had an odd system for filing—alphabetical with each also assigned a number. Let's see, there's no file with the initials JG, yet he met someone with those initials. Maybe JG wasn't a patient. Huh, why is #8 in the B's missing?

Tugging hard, she pulled out the two files numbered 7 and 9. Opening #7, she examined the file, but found nothing unusual. As she picked up #9, a small handwritten note slid to the floor. Why isn't this in a file? It must have fallen in between:

EVA BRAUN - HOT & COLD PAIN - SCHEDULE FIRST OPENING

Lisa picked up file #7 and scanned the name: Bosch, Joachim #7. Looking down at the next file she read: Koln, Hannelore #9. My grandfather had Eva Braun as a patient? But where's her file? She would have been #8. Lisa turned and looked again at the appointment calendar. JG re: EB. EB had to be Eva Braun. But who's JG? He must've met JG to talk about Eva Braun before he died. Could she have been involved with his death? The picture of her grandfather was more confusing than ever. Suicide is a mortal sin in the Catholic Church. A man who went to daily mass wouldn't commit such a sin. Why would he act outside of his conscience, his church?

Lisa slid into the swivel chair and leaned back. She scanned the ceiling, the windows, the curtains, then rested on the large desk in front of her. They don't make them like this today. She slid her finger along its ogee edge.

"Hmm." She pulled on the brass handles of the center drawer; it didn't budge. Why won't this drawer open? "Ugh." I don't think it's locked, pull hard girl—must be swollen.

"Aagh!" she blurted out as her shoulders flew back against the chair, tipping it over, sending her and the drawer tumbling to the floor. Gathering her senses, she felt her face flush in embarrassment. Now, don't I look ridiculous! she thought. Looking up from her spilled position on the floor, she spotted an exposed manila envelope in the corner of the drawer recess. Reaching in, she removed the envelope wedged into the wooden slats.

There aren't any marks on the outside, she thought, turning the curious envelope in her hands. She opened the flap and pulled out its contents. What are these handwritten notes? They're passage papers out of Germany in the name of Hilda Maier. Who's she? And signed by Albert Speer! Ticket #09438 on the Juan Fuego to Lisbon, ticket #1643 on the Ponce de Leon to Buenos Aires, both marked for EB/HM...Eva Braun, Hilda Maier? Contact Kurt Koehler in Zurich, 1411 Rhone Strasse; Maurice Jadot in Marseilles, 368 Rue de Blanc; Heinrich Wetzel in Buenos Aires, Banc de Zurich, account #568-349-801, Frederick Stroessle.

Lisa's hands froze as she held the last paper. It was a note her grandfather had written. As she read, her emotions welled up:

EVA BRAUN'S DENTAL RECORDS CHANGED WITH HILDA MAIER'S.
JG—GESTAPO. MUST GET TO AMERICAN ARMY – INTELLIGENCE.
I LOVE YOU, LISL. LIVE FOR ME AND OUR BABY HANNE.
FOREVER,
HANS

Sitting on the floor, Lisa was overcome with her discovery. She leaned back against the wall and cried. "I love you, Grandpa..."

CHAPTER 10

ASSOCIATED PRESS

LONDON - LABOR PARTY LEADER CLARK GOODWIN HAS ANnounced the formation of a new ruling coalition after Centrist Liberal Democrats and defectors from the Conservative Party joined together to defeat Prime Minister Tony Blair. James Weaver, flanked by maverick Tory lawmaker Emma Nicholson, announced today on the BBC that his first act as Prime Minister will be to pull all British forces out of the quagmire in Afghanistan as soon as safety allows.

ASSOCIATED PRESS

PARIS - French President Jean Couteau, facing the largest mass protests of his presidency since the economic riots of December 1995, has ordered a sixth nuclear test in the Pacific Ocean. Amid the combined protests of Greens and NATO members, Couteau cited the escalating Russian tension in the Baltic Region as the reason France will continue its nuclear testing. Coupled with massive Muslim street riots fostered by discontent over its involvement in Afghanistan, France has become a political battleground.

MOSCOW

"Damn! What are you telling me?" Donskoy asked. His reaction telegraphed he hadn't grasped the gist of the information in his hand.

"What I'm saying, comrade, is that Alexander Konstantinov has no bloodline—at least not a Russian one. It's true that he has a birth certificate showing he was born in Stalingrad to the brother of Victor Konstantinov. And records do show the death of his father and mother during the German shelling of the city. But, there *was no* brother of Victor Konstantinov. He never lived in Stalingrad or anywhere else. This brother never existed. I have examined the minutest details of births, deaths, marriages, divorce, work papers—everything! And still, there is nothing!"

"But then, who is he? Where is he from?"

The ferret licked his dry lips and preened in front of the frowning Donskoy. He knew he had scored well and was now biding his time like an anxious sculptor, ready to pull the velvet shroud off his masterpiece.

He hissed the words out. "Nazis, comrade...filthy, little Nazis." His face tightened up, looking like a cunning weasel that had discovered a way into the hen house. "Apparently, young Alexander was delivered to Victor at our embassy in Stockholm. The log in the embassy archives shows he was delivered by Colonel Johann Kesserling." A slick smile cracked his face. "It seems old Victor Konstantinov used his position to keep young men from going to war. But only those of a 'certain sexual orientation,' shall we say."

Donskoy leaned back in his chair, his eyes focusing on the ceiling. The weasel stood across from him. "So," Donskoy mused, "we have ourselves a Nazi plant, do we?...Very interesting...a girly-man uncle who somehow wasn't his uncle. This is good. No, this is excellent!"

Donskoy returned a glare that sent chills up the spine of the informant. "Your sources are impeccable? This information will hold up under any scrutiny?"

"Comrade, please, twenty-five years KGB? I have markers to call in everywhere. Yes, this information is good and verifiable. Certainly, comrade, this information should be worth more than the usual amount, yes?"

"Get out! I said you'll get your money in the usual manner!"

As the door shut, Donskoy eased himself back into his chair. He clasped his hands behind his head and pondered the moment. He leaned forward and buzzed his secretary. "Call Konstantinov—tell him I want to meet tomorrow, ten o'clock sharp! Tell him that I will accept no excuse."

CHAPTER 11

PULLING OFF HIS SILK SCARF AND CASHMERE OVERCOAT, Bryan Harmon entered the door of the stately building and noticed the curvaceous figure of a young woman standing at the receptionist's desk. He decided the scenery in the old building had suddenly changed for the better. He shifted his direction to overhear part of the discussion.

"I'm sorry, Miss...?" The receptionist repeated. Her feigned lack of memory displayed her annoyance at being interrupted.

"Brandt, Lisa Brandt."

"Yes, well, Ambassador Barnes is in Washington for the week. Perhaps you'd like me to hold your packet of information and give it to him when he returns?"

"No!" Lisa said. She pulled the envelope back and clutched it in her breast. "I mean, I don't want to leave it unattended. I'd feel better if I gave it to the ambassador personally."

Perfect! Bryan thought. He sensed the timing was right to move in and feign a position of importance. "Excuse me," he said. He held out his hand in greeting. "I couldn't help but overhear your conversation with Mrs. Taylor. I'm Bryan Harmon, senior assistant to Ambassador Barnes. May I be of assistance?"

As their hands touched, Bryan felt a strange sensation. He was not only captivated by the beauty of her hazel eyes, but he felt as if he'd known her somewhere in his past—not casually, but somehow deeply connected.

"Possibly, my name is Lisa Brandt. May we speak in private?"

Bryan felt his face flush in embarrassment as he realized she was tugging to pull her hand away from his. He wondered how long he'd been staring and holding her hand? "I'm sorry, what was it you said?" Bryan replied. He was taken aback by his flight of mind.

"I asked if we may we speak in private?"

"Yes, of course. This way please. Mrs. Taylor, would you please hold my calls?"

"What a smarmy, little worm, you are." Mrs. Taylor whispered. Then she mumbled under her breath as she went out the door, "Yeah, use your hotshot title to impress her."

Closing the door behind them, Bryan motioned for Lisa to have a seat in the chair across from his desk. He hung his coat and scarf on the brass rack, never taking his eyes off her. He noticed her skirt rise, exposing her lower thighs as she sat down and crossed her beautifully shaped legs. His heartbeat quickened. Walking around his desk, Bryan paused and looked down at Lisa before sitting. The angle of her eyes, fully opened beneath the soft, light brown bangs of her hair, gave her an angelic look that Bryan found compelling.

What is it about her eyes? he thought. The strength, the sincerity in her face, he was hooked. Bryan eased himself into his chair, as dumbstruck as he had ever been.

The longer he stared, the more uncomfortable Lisa became. She shifted in her seat and tugged at her skirt to cover more of her exposed thighs. He's undressing me with his eyes! she thought. This isn't right. I don't need this crap and it's obvious he's not the one to help me. I'm going to leave and make an appointment with the *real* ambassador, not this paper fop.

"So, Miss Brandt, what can I do for you?

Lisa relaxed her grip on the package held against her breast and placed it on the desk in front of her, her hands still clutching its sides.

"This packet may contain nothing, but my grandfather wanted this information to get to the American Army in 1945. I think he may have been killed in his attempt."

Bryan reached forward to take the envelope, but Lisa pulled it back out of his reach. He smarted from the rebuff and leaned back in his chair. He scanned his fingernails and said, "Miss Brandt, I'm not sure that information from fifty years ago—"

"You don't understand. My grandfather thought it was important enough to—to die so that this information would get into American hands!" Lisa's anger rose to the forefront. Who does this arrogant, pretty boy think he is? How could he be so condescending?

Bryan was embarrassed by his failed diplomacy. He had made the mistake of tweaking a tiger's nose. He leaned forward in his chair and once again attempted to draw the packet from his guest.

"Miss Brandt, may I...?"

She looked down at his long, manicured fingers as he reached for the envelope. He looks more like a piano player than a diplomat, she thought. Her eyes looked up at his hair, then behind him to the coat rack. Razor cut, not one hair out of place, a thousand dollar cashmere coat, and a silk scarf! No, this silver-spooned boy's not the one to help me, she concluded.

"Miss Brandt?" Bryan again queried. This time he decided to use humor to soften the awkward moment. "What I meant was the war has been over for sixty years. If we had to sift through every piece of information that gets unearthed from the Nazi era, I'd be wearing green eye shades and have glasses an inch thick."

This was more than she was willing to take. Lisa shot up out of her chair, her eyes ablaze. "Damn it! My grandfather's death was listed as a suicide! Do you have any comprehension what it was like for his wife and daughter to live with that? My mother had to grow up with the realization that her father took the coward's way out. Suicide?...No way!"

Tears flooded her eyes momentarily. "I thought I might be able to change all that. To give back to my mother what was stolen from her— her respect, dignity, and memories of her father." Lisa took a steadying breath and exhaled, calming herself. "I thought somebody at this embassy just might give a shit!"

With resignation, she looked at the young diplomat, threw the large envelope down on his desk, and watched it slide to a halt in front of him. With all the disgust she could muster, she said, "Mr. Harmon, you can either act on this information or file it up your pampered ass."

***

Bryan stood at his desk in a state of total disbelief at what had just happened. He was stunned...and embarrassed! He had never encountered anyone like her in his life.

"Whew," he whispered. He sat down in his chair and attempted to write a report on his luncheon with Rolf Stihl, but words wouldn't come. He found himself staring at the closed door, remembering the image of her backside as she stormed out of his office.

God, she was beautiful...no, more than beautiful. I can't believe I didn't show more concern. That was stupid, Harmon—you owed the poor girl more than that.

His hand pressed the intercom button. "Mrs. Taylor, please have someone from archives come up to see me." He reached over and opened the packet.

CHAPTER 12

THE SILVER MERCEDES WAS PARKED WITH ITS ENGINE running in a modest, residential area of East Berlin. Steam rose from the car's exhaust pipe and faded into the air. Its occupant alternated between fidgeting with the temperature dial and checking her wristwatch. The Breitling hands never seemed to advance.

I swear! That girl has been tardy her whole life, Hannelore Brandt thought. If she can't get her little fanny here till eleven, why tell me to meet at ten o'clock? Then again, why did I believe she would be here on time? Let me guess, she'll arrive and have one more crazy reason why she's late for the thousandth time. Worse, she'll think I haven't heard it before. Maybe if I'd married a German instead of an American, she'd have been more punctual. I wish John had been alive to see her graduate. He would've been so proud. Where *is* she? I'm not waiting in this hot car anymore—I'll just go inside Momma's house. As she climbed the flight of brick steps to the front porch, Hanne thought, I'm so proud of her trying to do this. I just hope it's the right thing to do.

***

God, the traffic here is awful! There's nothing like this in the Western Sector, thought Lisa. She pounded the steering wheel with the palm of her hand. It's got to be the antiquated light system...not one of them is timed. Everything associated with the Communists is outdated and stupid. They need to spend money and computerize these things.

Checking her watch, Lisa again thumped the wheel in frustration. Damn! I'm an hour late. Finally! There's Mom's car. Uh oh, I'll bet she's mad! Deciding against honking the horn, Lisa slipped her Volkswagen Jetta in behind her mother's car. She watched as Hanne fumbled through her purse for the key. She steeled herself to face her mother's displeasure then opened the car door.

Hanne's key stuck three times before turning the corroded tumblers. The explosion was overwhelming. Doors and windows erupted into a million shattered pieces. Lisa was hurled backward into her car's seat by the impact. She saw her mother disappear into an orange and yellow fireball. Frantically pulling herself out of her car, she tried to run up the slope of the front yard. Her legs slipped out from under her. Her fingers clawed the frozen ground. She tried to go forward, but she was blown over on her side by another massive blast of heat. Her screams of horror were heard by no one as she sobbed through the singed hair covering her face. "Momma...Momma...Momma...!"

CHAPTER 13

ASSOCIATED PRESS

ISTANBUL, TURKEY - AFTER FAILING AGAIN IN HER ATTEMPT to forge a ruling coalition with the opposition parties, Prime Minister Adile Celik has turned over the government's reins to the Islamic Fundamentalist Party who called for a clerical government to be styled after that of Iran. NATO ministers have begun grappling with the problems raised by an Islamic state within its membership.

WASHINGTON, D.C.

The grandfather clock that adorned the foyer chimed its eighth bell as Ambassador Barnes drew the double doors to his den shut. He shut off the noise of running grandchildren and the endless prattle of the family get-together. Eight o'clock was the scheduled time. He knew the familiar ring code: Two rings, thirty seconds; one ring, fifteen seconds; then one ring again. After all these years, the calls still gave a fearful pause to his hand before he picked up the telephone to answer the third ring. The message was always the same: Proceed to the next level.

"Hello."

"Start Control Phase III." The voice on the other end of the phone was dry and raspy.

"Confrontation only?" asked Barnes.

"…No, total control."

The ambassador winced. "Is that to include giving him the envelope?"

"I said *total*. Have him show Cook the copies, then leave them in his pathetic hands."

"Are we a little soon? After all—"

"That is not your decision," interrupted the caller. "Koernig is to take control *now!*"

"What about the Iranian?"

"He's accepted our generous terms."

"When will he announce his call to Jihad?"

"No later than tomorrow."

"Make sure Mueller holds firm. She could be our weak link," said Barnes.

"She's not the problem." The caller cleared his gurgling throat. "It appears we have a problem...with the Russians."

"The Russians? Everything's in place there. How can they be a problem?"

"Alexander Konstantinov called. He's being forced to withdraw from running by Donskoy. Apparently, Donskoy traced him back to Stockholm...'45."

"This can't be. Has it been confirmed?"

"Yes. An ex-KGB operative pulled the connection and sent it to Donskoy. We picked him up and made him talk before he was eliminated. He had no information on the facility."

"But Konstantinov knows! What if Donskoy's thugs make him talk?"

"We're looking for him now. Don't worry—he'll be taken out."

Fear rose from the pit of Barnes' stomach. He too had information to be passed on. All information, even trivial, had to go up the chain. If he didn't tell him now, it'd be worse later on. He felt locked in a giant vise. His position, his family...everything could unravel. He felt as if the floor was turning to quicksand. His breathing labored as he tried to collect his thoughts.

"Certain..." He hesitated, the words not leaving his mouth. "Certain papers, uh...came into the embassy...three days ago. I, uh, was going to call then, but decided to check it out first."

"What papers? Why wasn't I told?" the voice thundered.

"They're old ones—dating back to '45. Apparently the office of Eva Braun's dentist was never fully sanitized."

"What's in these papers?"

"Everything that pertains to Eva...dental records, passage papers, names of contacts, bank account numbers."

The deafening silence on the other end added to the ambassador's rising angst. The room felt hot, the air thick. He jumped when the voice continued. "Any reference to our storage facility?"

"No."

"Where'd these papers come from? Are they original?"

"Copies, brought in by the granddaughter."

"I assume you've made all the arrangements? We have the originals?"

"The house was destroyed—the girl's mother with it."

The other voice shouted, "I asked you, do we have the originals in our hands—yes or no?"

The Ambassador's sternum tightened in pain. He slid his hand over his heart. Fear overtook him. Over the years, he had learned that every word must be guarded, every nuance cloaked. "No, but we're not sure that the granddaughter has them either. We…we don't know yet."

"Who handled this?"

"Bernhard did."

"I want those originals and I want the girl eliminated—now! Do you hear me?"

"Yes, yes of course."

"Who saw these papers at the embassy?"

"Three people—my assistant Harmon, his secretary Mrs. Taylor, and Conrad in archives."

"Eliminate the secretary and the archive man."

"But Mrs. Taylor is loyal to *us*."

"It doesn't matter. We're too close now! Eliminate her. Have you brought Harmon in yet? Is he one of us?"

"No. I didn't feel he was ready."

"Then eliminate him."

CHAPTER 14

THE MORNING CONFERENCE IN THE SITUATION ROOM promised to be exhausting. In attendance were President Peter Cook, Vice-President William Koernig, Chief of Staff Williams, Secretary of State James Holden, Secretary of Defense Charles Nelson, the NSC Chief, Chairman of the Joint Chiefs of Staff General Belden, and the heads of the four armed services. Uneasy when surrounded by uniforms, President Cook called the meeting to order and deferred to his SecDef. He opened up with the ever deepening quagmire in Afghanistan.

"Mr. President, as you are aware, the announced pullout of British forces leaves us in a tentative position. When the French officially announce their evacuation, it'll become a situation of crisis proportion. We'll need another NATO member to fill the gap or another massive buildup of our troops. However, I'm not sure *that* would be a good move as far as public sentiment is concerned. We just added troops over a lot of protest. This becomes a political decision that only you can make. General Belden, perhaps you could fill everyone in on our current situation?"

"Certainly. Sir, our forces are stretched beyond what any military analyst would consider prudent. You have a copy of our casualty report for this week. The numbers are disheartening. We could've picked up the slack of the British pullout, but with the French bailout, I don't see it—especially the Mazar-e Sharif corridor. In light of the political situation in Turkey, coupled with the Islamic call to Jihad, I would advise that we consider our own withdrawal as an option."

"Well, I appreciate your candidness, General, and maybe—"

"Excuse me one moment," interrupted Koernig, "but, we seem to be jumping ahead without considering the ramifications of German troop inclusion. Perhaps you've forgotten their offer to participate?"

Cook retorted in kind. "I haven't forgotten their so-called 'offer.' Maybe I don't want to be blackmailed into sanctioning their old borders at the Oder-Neisse River in return."

"When one considers the French nuclear tests and the Russian threats against the Baltic countries and Poland, certainly one could forgive German anxiety if…" Koernig paused for emphasis, "…if one takes enough time to examine and put together the pieces."

"May I remind everyone that Poland is now a NATO member?" interjected Secretary of State Holden.

"That's exactly it!" declared Cook, his blood boiling. "How in the hell are we going to give Germany part of a NATO member's sovereign territory? They ask too much!"

"Hasn't quid pro quo always been a sound basis for international relations?" Koernig shot back. "As I see it, we need Germany as much as they need us."

Cook pounded his fist on the table. "As long as I'm President of this country, there'll be no changes in the European map—period!"

"Mr. President, I'm afraid you're naive in such matters and—"

"*President* is the key word here, Mr. *Vice* President. I'm still the damned President!" Cook bellowed. "Gentlemen, this meeting is over. The Vice President will remain!"

As the last of the participants filed out of the room, Cook rose and shut the door behind them. Koernig remained in his seat. He tapped his pen on the conference table with an air of indifference that cut to the President's frayed nerves.

"Bill, I won't tolerate this insubordination. I know you and I haven't exactly—"

Koernig was ready for his long-awaited grab for power. "May I remind the President that *you* are not in a position to argue with *me*? You may still be 'the damned President of this country,' but you forfeited your leadership when you couldn't control your demented sexual appetite."

Confident that the time was right to wrest power from Cook, he raised his briefcase from the floor and placed it on the table. He pulled out a large manila envelope. Like a predator inflicting pain upon his prey, he pulled out the contents, one obscene photo at a time. He flipped each one so it landed face up in front of his target.

"How well do you think these pictures will play in Peoria?" Koernig hissed. The President's hand shook as he held the photo of himself naked from the waist down. A voluptuous young woman was performing a lewd act on him.

"Uh, how about looking at these shots of your White House bedroom while Mrs. Cook was in California—or perhaps this one, or this one?" Koernig would not relent.

Cook erupted into a verbal tirade. "Where did you get these, you stinking, Nazi-loving bastard? I'll—"

"You'll do what?" Koernig shouted back with equal voracity. "You'll do exactly what you're told to do. Now sit down and shut up."

As Cook picked up the last of the sleazy photographs, a look of resignation crept over his face. He eased himself back into his chair, covering his eyes with his hands.

"I might consider supplying the congressional committee that is investigating your 'investments' certain copies of which I have here. I not only have copies of the missing trading records, but also the records that allegedly burned in that bank fire. Maybe, as the icing on the cake, we could play a tape recording of you soliciting illegal contributions right here in the White House. No, Mr. 'still the damned President,' you'll just finish out your term and do precisely what we tell you to do."

Koernig tossed another envelope to Cook on his way to the door. "Those were a warm-up. Here's some more late night reading for you. Don't worry—I'm sure I have more copies if you need them. Please, do try and play the game, old sport."

CHAPTER 15

THE FLOW OF AUTOMOBILE TRAFFIC WAS MODERATE FOR A Tuesday, considering the normal noonday crunch of commuters out for lunch. Slouching in her VW, Lisa Brandt peered over the newspaper she had been using to cover her face. Her anxiety rose with each pedestrian or car that passed her parking space near the embassy's main entrance. The explosion at her grandmother's house had left Lisa in a state of shock. Her paranoia was fueled by the indifference of the police to her mother's "accident." Bent on wrapping up this case in the quickest and simplest manner, the investigators paid scant attention to the fact that the gas had been turned off. Lisa was convinced that the explosion was not only meant for her, but was connected to the information her grandfather had left behind.

Where is he? She looked over her newspaper and glanced at her watch. Lisa's mental stability was in tatters. Damn it, doesn't he ever eat? Who's that man over there? She raised the newspaper and covered her face again. Where are you, Harmon? Can I even trust you? She lowered the newspaper. Where'd that man go? Is he behind me? Oh God, he's gone! He's disappeared! Stop it—maybe he was just a tourist. Shit! I'm so afraid. I know it was a bomb that killed Momma. They wanted me. The gas was off! Why won't those bastards believe me? I'm to blame—it's that Eva Braun stuff. Harmon's the one who took it from me. Oh, Momma, I'm so sorry. Please forgive me. Tears welled up as more confusion gripped her mind. There he is! Oh, God, I can't trust him, but who can I turn to? Why is that car slowing down? They're looking at me!

Bryan Harmon descended the steps of the embassy, turned onto the sidewalk and tucked his newspaper under his arm. The honk of a car horn broke his stride. He looked to his left and saw a VW pulling up alongside him, its window rolling down.

"Please! Get in—I need help!" Lisa shouted. Without hesitation, Bryan jumped into the car. He hadn't pulled his right leg into the car when Lisa stepped on the gas pedal. Bryan's head hurled backward as the door crashed onto his leg.

"What the hell's going on?" Bryan blurted out. He struggled to pull in his aching leg and shut the door. Lisa's eyes darted back and forth between the rearview mirror and the front windshield. She said nothing. Slamming on the brakes, she made a quick left, followed by another screeching turn down a narrow street to the right. She stared again at the rearview mirror. She was confident that they weren't being followed.

"...Miss Brandt?"

"Please. Don't talk—not yet." She slammed on the brakes and veered her car into a parking space. "We can talk in this konditorei. Let's go."

As Bryan eased out of the car, he saw Lisa's tension as she slammed her door behind her. She took the lead to the pastry shop and opened the door herself.

"Zwei cafe, bitte," she said. She stood at the counter, her eyes scanning to see if anyone had followed them. Trailing behind her to the table, Bryan felt ridiculous, like a wayward child in tow. This is crazy. What is it about her that I can't seem to—?

Lisa raised her eyes and met his.

"Please. I'm so frightened and I don't know where to start. I don't even know if I can trust you." She ran both sets of fingers through her long hair, tossing it straight back.

"What are you talking about?"

"Look, there are questions that I need straight answers for." She gained strength and courage with each sip of coffee. "Did you check any of the papers I handed you on Friday?"

Bryan looked perplexed, somewhat defensive. "Well, not personally, but I told my secretary, Mary Taylor, to pull up our archives on Eva Braun. They arrived yesterday morning. I also had her check the archives database to see if your grandfather's name came up in any old newspaper clippings, birth records, medical records, obituaries, the whole nine yards. Those haven't come back yet." Bryan wondered if he had overstepped his bounds.

She struggled to continue. "Do you know my mother was killed?"

"What, when?"

"Sunday morning."

"…How? I mean, I'm sorry, Miss Brandt. How did it happen?"

"She was killed when my grandfather's house blew up." She paused, dropping her face into her hands.

"Are you talking about the house on Lindenstrasse? That woman was *your* mother?"

"Yes."

"I saw it on the news, but nobody reported that someone was killed."

"They acknowledged it today in the papers. Did you read the article?"

Bryan felt guilty. "No, I only read the international news. Why?"

"They reported it as a suicide, a woman who was distraught over her mother's recent death. It was ruled an accidental explosion while she was trying to asphyxiate herself."

"Maybe—"

"Don't you understand?" she snapped. "It happened when she walked in the front door. I saw it with my own eyes!" She could scarcely talk, her voice quivering along with her chin. Bryan offered his handkerchief and squeezed her wrist. She shook her head no and wiped her face with her fingers. "She was to meet me there. I was supposed to be there first. It was meant for me! Oh, God, I was an hour late—the traffic was horrid. I pulled up as she was putting the key in the door. She opened it and walked in…Oh my God…" Lisa's pain was overwhelming. "Don't you see?"

"But maybe the gas—"

"No!" Lisa half shouted. "My mother was afraid of gas, so she had it turned off the day after the funeral. Only the electric was left on. I tried to tell her the water pipes could freeze, but she wouldn't listen."

"But who would do this? And why?"

Losing her patience, she snapped back, "Are you that blind? It's those notes I gave you!"

"But they're over sixty years old!"

"Someone in your embassy wanted me dead," Lisa said. "Will you help me? Please?" With that, Lisa covered her face with a napkin and began sobbing again.

Bryan reached across the table and put his hands around her wrists, gently pulling them from her face. As her eyes rose to meet his, his brother David's face flashed in his mind. At that instant, something compelling came over Bryan, striking him deep. He knew his life would never be the same.

He answered, "Of course. Now, we need to make sure you're safe while I do some investigating. Do you have a place to stay tonight?"

"Yes, my mother's house."

"No. That's the first place someone would look. Anywhere else?"

"I could stay with my friend, Anna. She's my old college roommate."

"Okay, but be careful. Call me—no! Get in touch with me tomorrow—same way, same time."

"Mr. Harmon, this could be dangerous for you too."

"I know."

CHAPTER 16

ASSOCIATED PRESS

PARIS - PRIME MINISTER JEAN COUTEAU FORMALLY AN-nounced the withdrawal of all French troops under NATO command from Afghanistan. The pullout will commence immediately and will be completed within three months. At the same time, France has expressed grave concerns over the American request that Germany supply enough troops to make up for the losses of the French and English withdrawals.

ASSOCIATED PRESS

MOSCOW - Newly elected Russian President Vladimir Donskoy has sent troops across the border of Estonia to protect the Russian minor-ity. Estonia has sent a formal protest to the United Nations and has requested its assistance in this crisis. Sources claim this movement is in direct response to Germany's desire to extend its borders east of the Oder-Niesse line.

HARRISBURG, PENNSYLVANIA

Looking down the tree-lined road, Franz Kreuger sensed the strong undercurrent of positional power emanating from the sprawling manors that defined this suburban countryside. Below the magnificence of the massive century oaks and running like a continuous ribbon on either side of the road were vine-covered, brick walls spaced with intermittent, lighted columns that defined the estates of their ultra-wealthy owners. As the black Mercedes glided along the asphalt road, he knew this was not just a moneyed neighborhood; this was an "old money" neighbor-hood. These were families of prominence and power, the kind of power that discreetly passes from one generation to the next.

    Kreuger knew perception was the key. If one had enough money and displayed the credentials of a proper bloodline, questions were seldom asked. Basking in the warmth of reflected glory was a sport that had been raised to the highest pinnacles of social dignity. Society's snobs were also the easiest to dupe.

Within a moment of arriving at the bronze gates, the forged letter K in the center split and opened back to itself, as if a giant hand was sweeping out an invitation to proceed. Franz was taken aback by the long drive that drew his vision upward to the majestic turn-of-the-century, English-styled mansion. He snickered when he thought of who had been inserted into this highest level of society almost fifty years ago. Glancing over at Otto Kunsler, Franz nodded his quiet approval. He knew that their leader could have placed even the likes of himself there. Not that he was jealous, for Franz loved his work and took great pride in knowing that, although killing was his trade, he was a highly skilled professional.

A manservant answered the door, acknowledged the two visitors with a curt nod of his head and directed them to the drawing room.

After several minutes of perusing artwork, Franz looked at his watch and flashed a frown of irritation toward Otto. Looking back up, he saw Ingrid enter the room, her ageless demeanor as fresh as her flowing pastel gown. Still the grand lady, he begrudged, shaking his head in disbelief. I remember when she was but a fifteen-year-old gutter-snipe begging for food in bombed-out Berlin. She was as easy to recruit as I was. All it took was a little bread and a roof over your head. But she got the cushy assignment. Otto elbowed Franz and the two stood in unison to greet their charming hostess.

Franz grimaced as he caught sight of another servant entering the living room carrying a silver tea service. The hair bristled on the back of his neck. It was her—that bitch slut from the devil! He could tell by the large double mole under her left eye. When tea had been served, the servant stood waiting to draw the large doors shut. Ingrid Koernig never acknowledged the servant's presence or even passed a glance her way.

"That will be all, Ilsa," said their hostess after testing her first sip of tea. "She is such a fine servant. I want to thank you, Otto, for recommending her. I don't know what I would have done without her after my husband's death. She was so helpful to him when he got sick. It was a total shock. I mean, he had been so healthy—never a day in the hospital."

"We are both very sorry to hear of Wilhelm's death," said Otto, feigning sympathy.

"Thank you. He had no pain of course. He died in his sleep, thank God. He never stopped believing, you know?"

"Yes," said Franz. "There will never be another corps like the SS—such bravery, such—"

"Such focus! Such unity of purpose," interjected Otto, raising his index finger into the air.

Sitting upright and proper on the couch, Ingrid stared at the cup of tea in her hands. "Well, Wilhelm and I have always been loyal to the mission. Just like you were nine years ago, Otto."

"Yes, getting that much money transferred without notice was quite a trick."

"This is such a strange and expensive country! I wouldn't have believed that it would cost sixty million dollars to purchase a senate seat," added Franz.

Ingrid raised her head in pride. "Yes. But without that money, our dreams wouldn't have come true and our mission would not have succeeded. Now my son, William, is vice president."

"Yes, but getting the money was easier than getting him elected to the Senate," said Otto. "Individual people are no problem to control—a whole population we cannot. But with that weakling Cook in the White House, all avenues are open to us."

"Sex and greed, that is all it takes," added Ingrid. "It's a good thing a man is there. They are easier targets to blackmail than a strong and principled woman."

Changing the subject, Otto asked, "How's your health these days, Ingrid?"

"Just fine, thank you my dear Otto. I'm seventy-six now and have never spent one day in a hospital. God willing, I should live another twenty years, or at least long enough to see my William fulfill his destiny."

Franz looked over to Otto and nodded his head. He rose politely, indicating their short visit was over. With a courteous bow and click of his heels, he took the hand of his hostess and said, "Wonderful! And I can assure you, his destiny *will* be fulfilled. Ingrid, it has been a pleasure seeing you again, but we must be on our way. We will be in touch with you and William—Auf wiedersehen."

The two men walked down the flagstone steps and climbed into the Mercedes. Looking at each other, their eyes mirrored approval.

"I trust everything is in place?" asked Franz, turning on the ignition.

"Yes, her servant, Ilsa, is the best you know—and loyal. You had an assignment with her in Berlin, did you not?"

Franz ground his teeth and stifled his revulsion. "That was a long time ago. Some things are best forgotten. How long will it take that bitch this time?"

"Twenty-four hours. No more."

CHAPTER 17

ALEXANDER KONSTANTINOV KNEW FROM THE MOMENT HE returned the phone to its cradle he was a hunted man. He also knew a hunted man was a dead man. The information that entrapped him was in his head and there was no way to remove it. The pact he had made with the devil would have its price, and that price would be his life.

His thoughts drifted as he stood on the ever-tightening subway platform. People, crammed together, all waiting, all pushing for that last inch that might be the difference of getting on the next train or not. It seemed as if the train would never come. His memory wandered back to when he was a boy of thirteen, the glory of the Hitler Youth flashing through his mind. Even as a child he was a fervent believer. Then the bombing started and never ceased; his mother was all he had left. Then she too was killed. That incessant bombing…those explosions! Bloodied and broken, his mother's arm was the only part visible beneath the charred wood and brick rubble that were the remnants of their apartment building. His fingers tore at the crumpled heap that covered her. He pulled it away piece by piece, until he finally saw her face. Momma, why you? You can't leave me! Why had I rebelled against her? She was a kind soul. Her only crime was that she taught Russian at the university. I hated the constant taunting: "Erich the Red." On and on it went—your mother is a Russian whore…commie pig lovers! Yes, I could speak Russian, but that was my only crime. Then, he remembered the arm of Albert Speer as it gently came to rest on his shoulder. He remembered his comforting words: "Everything will be all right. Come, my young man, we will take you away from all this."

The shrieking of the subway whistle broke his trance. He looked around. Am I alone? Am I safe? I could go to Sweden. I could hide there for a few years. For a man of my position, false papers are easy to come by.

As the doors to the train opened, Konstantinov felt the crunch of tightly packed bodies surge forward. A man suddenly fell against him. My God! There's a knife in his back! It was meant for me! Panic struck. He clawed his way to his left, forcing his body through the swelling mass of humanity. His briefcase was ripped from his fingers, swallowed up by the crowd. Don't stop, let it go! There—the stairs! No matter how hard he tried, his body seemed to move in slow motion. It was as if he were hovering above, watching himself. Halfway up, he broke clear of the crowd. The steps were open. He took them two at a time, his arms flailing as streaks of sunlight broke through. As he reached the top, a wide shadow blocked the light. Two men in trench coats grabbed him by the arms.

CHAPTER 18

ANNA'S APARTMENT BUILDING WAS TYPICAL OF THE THOU-sands that had been built in the city after its division by the communists in 1961. It was a cream colored brick building of no discernible style, with two stories raised over an open parking garage. More so than most cities of its size, space was Berlin's dearest commodity and because money and time were also a premium in post-war Germany, style suffered to cost and efficiency.

Driving up to the building, Lisa wondered why she remembered it as being more welcoming in appearance. With its Linden trees having yielded their summer leaves to the winter season, even the street was dreary.

Turning into the narrow drive, she saw Anna's white Volvo parked in her designated spot. Lisa was grateful. Seeing the rusting automobile in its familiar space gave her a feeling of comfort and warmth, a subliminal lifeline to her past—that carefree time before her mother's death. As she pulled into an open space, Lisa grabbed her purse and overnight bag. She opened the car door and climbed the exterior staircase to the first level. Its overhead lights were out, making each step upward a descent into fear. By the time she reached Anna's door, doubt was in control; every minute sounded a warning. She knocked. Across the street and out of sight, a small flash of light emanated from a van parked in the street. Its occupant lit another cigarette. He was watching, waiting.

Why doesn't she answer? Lisa thought. Her car is here—she must be in the shower. She fumbled through her purse, found her old key at the bottom, and unlocked the door. She held her breath as she eased it open, her hand feeling for the switch. The light revealed a disheveled apartment that shocked her senses. Anna is such a neat freak, she thought. She forced herself to take one slow step after another. The coffee table, the chairs…their feet are not even in the crush marks on the carpet. No, that's not my Anna.

"Anna? Anna?" The silence was deafening. She walked toward the kitchenette, dropping her bag on the couch. She looked at the sink—dishes were still in it. Anna never left for work without doing the dishes. She opened the refrigerator door. Plenty of food—she must've just gone to the market. She closed the door and noticed a half cup of coffee and a bowl of hardened oatmeal. Coffee was spilled on the table. Why is some on the floor? Anna would never leave a—what's that? Was that noise in the bedroom? The muffled squeak sounded like a creaking floor.

"Anna?...Anna?" She entered the bedroom and noticed the unmade bed. What's going on? She scanned the small room—a photograph of herself and Anna on the nightstand. She picked it up and sat down on the side of the bed. Hugging the picture, memories came flooding back. Lisa thought of growing up together...double dating, going to the dismantling of the Berlin wall, candles held high in the night. We were thousands...tears of joy streaming down. If we could go back in time... She must still be at work. Where's her phone book?

She found the book, picked up the phone, and held it to her ear. She listened for the dial tone. Was that a double click? No. It can't be! Lisa hung up the phone and gingerly picked it back up while holding the tone button down. She unscrewed the mouth piece. It's bugged! She froze. Oh, Anna...no.

Out of the corner of her eye, she saw Anna's pepper spray on the nightstand. She picked it up, turning it in her hands. Anna never went anywhere without her spray for protection. Gathering her wits, Lisa walked to the bathroom and turned on its light. There on the counter was the make-up bag that she carried in her purse. Oh God, Anna. Have they hurt you too? They couldn't have! How could they know? Who are these people? Her thoughts ran crazy. She panicked. I've got to get out of here—now!

She crept back to the living room, her right hand grasping the heavy overnight bag. The floor creaked behind her. She spun. A face! It lurched at her from behind. She raised the pepper spray and discharged its contents. With all her strength, Lisa swung her bag against the assailant. The blow hurled him over the couch, onto the floor. She raced to the door, fumbling with the chain. It finally gave. She ripped the door open, her hips bounding into the handrails, her feet negotiating the descending flight of steps. She struggled to unlock her car door—it finally opened. She hopped in and pulled the door shut. She slammed the gearshift into reverse, then into drive. Out of nowhere, her attacker exploded in front of her, his face ablaze from the headlights. Her charging vehicle threw him aside with a thud. She pulled out onto the street, tires screaming. She looked back and saw hot exhaust rising from the back of the parked van. Its lights flashed on and the van lurched forward.

"Oh God, help me!" she screamed. She looked into the rearview mirror—the van was gaining on her. She looked ahead and saw the railroad crossing lights flash red. The guard rail started to lower down.

"Oh God...Hurry...Hurry!" Her speedometer read eighty kilometers per hour. The crossing gate was halfway down. The light from the approaching train was almost upon her.

"Oh...please!" Her Volkswagen jolted from side to side as the gate dropped to its lowest position, slamming onto her trunk seconds before the train roared by. The blaring of its thunderous horn broke the stillness of the night.

The driver of the van slammed his foot on the brakes. They couldn't respond fast enough. He raised his arms to cover his face. The van swerved, flipped over, and hurtled itself into the deafening diesel engine.

As Lisa sped away, she saw the massive fireball reflected in the mirror. Anna's face flashed before her, then her mother's. Her chin quivered and tears rolled down her cheeks, "Oh, Anna, not you too?"

CHAPTER 19

ASSOCIATED PRESS

HARRISBURG, PENNSYLVANIA - INGRID KOERNIG, MOTHER of Vice President William Koernig, died in her sleep last night at 11:00 p.m. A spokesperson for the family said her health had long been failing and her death was not unexpected. The vice president was immediately notified and returned from Washington to make the necessary arrangements.

BERLIN

The vehicle with the crushed trunk lid circled the block of the U.S. Embassy. Its occupant, sleep deprived and running on adrenaline, became more frustrated with each pass of the entrance. With her head turning from side to side, her anxiety level was in high gear. Lisa Brandt had completed her sixth such drive-by. Where is he? she wondered. The skin of her fingers ached from clutching the steering wheel. Looking left, she noticed two men sitting in a grey Mercedes fifty meters from the embassy's entrance. Where'd they come from? They weren't here on the last pass. Wait, I've seen them before! No, maybe not. Why would two men be sitting in a car, waiting? Am I going crazy? I don't know. I've never been so afraid and alone.

"Where *are* you, Harmon?" she screamed out. Her fist pounded the wheel.

Lisa made a sharp U-turn past the end of the embassy complex. This time at least I'll see your faces as I pass by. There he is! He turned the corner down there—I know it's him! Slamming her foot on the accelerator, she lurched past the Mercedes without even glancing at its occupants—her focus was on the man she must trust with her life.

As she passed, she saw the man in the passenger seat lean forward enough to see Bryan Harmon turn the corner on foot. His quick slap on the shoulder of the driver signaled him to start the engine and begin pursuit. To avoid the attention of the embassy's Marine sentries, the Mercedes eased out and made the turn at the end of the compound. Thirty meters from Bryan, Lisa honked her horn and swerved the car over into the opposite lane, her tires rubbing against the curb in front of him. Without hesitation, he bolted to the side of her screeching car and jumped into its passenger seat.

"What's going—?"

"Never mind!" Lisa snapped. She hit the gas pedal. "Are we being followed?"

He looked around. "I don't know. Well, maybe...I'm not sure."

"Damn it! Be sure! They're after me!"

He looked again. "Well, I think there's—yeah, a grey sedan, two men."

"That's them, hang on!" Lisa made one quick left, then another.

Bryan's hands grabbed the dashboard as she passed a slow moving bus, weaving between two oncoming cars. Her car careened down a narrow alleyway scraping the side of Bryan's door against the side of a building. The Volkswagen sped out of the alley and onto a cobblestone street. She made a sharp right and came to a screeching stop.

She swung her car door open. "Come on! Grab your briefcase." Within seconds, she was chasing down an electric trolley. When the bus slowed to a crawl, they jumped on. Lisa dropped in the tokens and they moved to the rear. Bryan, breathing heavy from trying to keep up with his athletic counterpart, stared at the floor. Without notice, Lisa bolted upright and headed out the rear side door.

"Hurry!" she hollered. She ran across the Schlosspark to the edge of the River Spree and jumped onto a waiting water taxi. Bryan was the last to jump on and the taxi shoved off before he was able to take his seat. He lost his balance, falling onto an adjoining passenger.

"Miss Brandt—"

"Don't say anything, please." She looked around, holding back the urge to cry. Finally, her eyes met his. His gaze caressed her soul with a tenderness she had never felt before. As his hand slid over hers, Lisa knew that she was, for the moment, safe. She told him of the apartment, Anna, and the chase.

"Mr. Harmon, I'm so frightened—first Momma, now Anna. I know they've hurt her, probably killed her. I'm so alone, I—"

"You're not alone, Lisa—not anymore." His hand lifted her face to meet his. In her eyes he saw his Rubicon and knew this was the moment to make his crossing. Alea iacta est, he thought, the die is cast. "I'll take care of you. I promise."

"You can't help me. You can't see them—they're everywhere! People I love are being killed and I don't know how to stop it. I don't even know why." Her voice trailed off. "Just leave…"

With both arms, he drew her in close and in a tender voice he whispered, "I can't leave. Not now."

"I'm so tired," she said. Placing her head on his shoulder, she closed her eyes.

***

In a small café on Salzburg Strasse, a young waiter threw a white towel over his shoulder and pulled an order pad out of his apron. He approached the booth that was situated in an isolated, rear corner.

"Zwei café und strudel, bitte," Bryan ordered.

When the waiter departed, Lisa displayed the positive effects of her short nap on the water taxi. "Did you find anything in those papers I gave you?" One part of her wanted answers, but the other was afraid of what she might hear.

"I've found plenty. There was a ship named Juan Fuego and it did embark for Lisbon in May of '45," Bryan said. He scanned his sheaf of papers like a lawyer preparing for an opening statement. "Let's see, Maurice Jadot died in Marseilles in the first week of May '45, no cause of death given—you know, Vichy Government and all. Much of this I found in our embassy archives, but the rest came from an old friend from law school, Jose Merido. After graduation, he went back to Argentina and set up practice in Buenos Aires. His practice is in real estate law, so it was easy for me to get the remainder of the information. Apparently, Heinrich Wetzel died in 1950—an apparent suicide. His wife and children died in an automobile accident one month earlier—"

"Shhh!" Lisa whispered as she noticed the waiter approaching with his tray.

"Zwei café, strudel, und strudel," the waiter announced. He placed the dishes in front of his customers.

When the waiter went back to the kitchen, Bryan continued. "So anyway, Heinrich Wetzel ended his life and willed his house and property to, whom else? Hilda Maier! But catch this, the records that Jose was able to pull up show a signature on the will that is not even close to that of earlier documents that Herr Wetzel had signed. Hilda's still alive. She's frail and elderly, but still kicking. And guess what? She still owns the property. A live-in nurse attends her."

Bryan stopped to sip his coffee and took a bite of the strudel. "Now," he paused again and took another sip, "the records show that a son was born to Hilda in 1945 at the Hospital de Las Cruces. However, he died at age five. Jose said there is a death certificate, but he couldn't find the cause of the child's death—no hospital records, no coroner's report—nothing."

Bryan paused, but only enough to note the puzzled look on Lisa's face. "Can I finish eating now?" he asked. A twinkle appeared in his eyes.

"Depends…anything else?"

"Oh, yes, there is one more thing…Kurt Koehler, Banc Zurich? Nine years ago he was accused of mishandling funds at the bank. Sixty million dollars was transferred to the United States. There were no records of its source or its final destination. Only that it was the last transaction that Koehler handled. Next day, they found him in his home with a gun in his mouth."

***

The backstreets of what was old East Berlin were not familiar to either Lisa or Bryan, but they both knew that gutter snipes and urban decay would offer the temporary haven they needed. His instincts preferred the protection of the embassy, but she insisted that whoever was trying to kill her had deep connections within the embassy walls. He wanted to argue, but her case was overwhelming. Something ominous was going on at the embassy and he knew she was right. Constantly looking behind to see if they were being followed, they circled many streets, even to the point of pulling into dark alleys with lights off, watching to see what or who might pass. When they were convinced that they were not being followed, they parked the car she had rented and walked several blocks to the Altes Plate Hotel. As they climbed the worn limestone steps, Lisa turned for one more look before passing through the paint-starved doorway.

The night clerk observed the well-dressed, young couple approach his front desk. He pulled the cigarette from his lips, kicked his legs off the desk and stood up with an all-knowing, sarcastic smile on his face. I'll give them one hour to work off their young fever, he mused, as he undressed Lisa with his yellow eyes. They look nervous—bet they're screwing around behind their spouses' backs. That should add an extra five Euros to the room rate. And I'll bet I get it.

"Do you have a room for one night?" Bryan asked.

The clerk responded with a sneer, "Yes, one night, sixty Euros."

As Bryan pulled out his Visa card, Lisa reached out and pushed his hand down. "No! I mean, let's pay cash." Fumbling to open her wallet, she said, "Here, I have it in my purse."

Counting the cash in his hand, the clerk lowered his brow, smiled and said, "Room 202…that would be right above me, the stairs are over there. Have a nice sleep." His voice trailed off in sarcasm as they came to the first step. The clerk sat back down, kicked his feet up again and waited for the base, passionate sounds of sexual fury that would resonate through the floor boards to his eagerly awaiting ears. He opened the evening newspaper and draped it across his lap.

Bryan unlocked the hotel door, and as he pushed it inward, a sense of awkwardness overcame him. He looked down to the floor, stepped back and allowed Lisa to enter first. After suffering the humiliation with the sleazy clerk, they awkwardly entered the room. Bryan locked the door behind him and Lisa felt exhaustion as she picked up a chair and placed its backrest under the doorknob. Neither the sounds of the bed springs squeaking under her weight nor the creaking of the armoire doors mattered to Lisa. As her head came to a rest on the wafer thin pillow, the stale smell of cigarette smoke made her nauseous.

"Look, I don't want you to feel uncomfortable about this," Bryan said. "I don't see any other way to watch out for you. I'll sleep in the chair and you can have the bed. It's old fashioned, I know, but it'll work." His voice trailed off as he turned clutching a blanket, only to see Lisa on the bed, trembling in a fetal position.

"I'm so cold. I don't think I'll ever get warm again."

Bryan shook the blanket open and placed it over Lisa's quivering body. Kneeling down at the side of the bed, he brushed her hair from the side of her tear-streaked face. He watched as she fell asleep.

***

Morning found Bryan staring out the window at a sunrise that even the window's soot could not hide. Lisa stirred. One eye opened, then two. She raised herself up on one elbow. She saw Bryan standing at the window. A strong, not-too-muscular body, she noted. Thank you, God, she thought. Thank you for the gift of this man. What is it about him? He seems taller today, stronger too. "Good morning," she said.

Bryan's head turned, a smile opening on his face. "Sleep well?"

"Actually, I did—very well. Have you been up long?"

Letting go of the curtains, Bryan walked to the bed and sat down opposite her. "I got up about an hour ago. I've been trying to figure out where we go from here."

"Mr. Harmon—"

"Bryan. Please call me Bryan."

She smiled at the use of his first name. "Bryan, I think we both know that our answer is in Buenos Aires. And please, call me Lisa."

"Do you have a passport, Lisa?"

"Of course."

"Well, then, let's get going."

CHAPTER 20

ASSOCIATED PRESS

MOSCOW - A GOVERNMENT SPOKESPERSON ANNOUNCED the rebellion in Georgia was crushed. After Russian troops secured the city of Tbilisi, rebel leaders surrendered rather than face annihilation. Russian President Donskoy also warned the "gangsters in Ukraine" not to make the mistake of disobedience as the Georgians did, or face immediate reprisals. He repeated Moscow's claim that the government of Ukraine must stop the wholesale dismantling of its nuclear missiles, which he asserts, are still the sovereign property of Russia.

BUENOS AIRES, ARGENTINA

As the metal baggage carousel meandered through its fixed track, the cargo load dwindled as the last remnants of luggage came out of the tunnel and were pulled off by eager owners. Lisa looked at her watch, then at Bryan and back to the carousel that had run its empty course and come to a halt.

"Well, isn't this lovely," said Lisa. "If I wanted our bags to go to Rio, I would've picked an airline other than Lufthansa."

"Relax, maybe there's a simple explanation. Either they didn't get unloaded or they're on another incoming plane."

"Well, let's go. If our luggage was left on board, we'd better get up to the ticketing counter before this plane takes off again."

"I'm terribly sorry, Herr Harmon, Fraulein Brandt," said the crisply dressed, Lufthansa supervisor. "I've had the ground crews check all arriving and departing planes, including all the luggage vehicles—all to no avail. I'm afraid your luggage is not in Buenos Aires. It is not in Berlin either. Lufthansa regrets the inconvenience we have caused and would be pleased to extend hotel accommodations for you while we trace your belongings. Please be so kind as to fill out these forms. We hope to expedite the swift return of your belongings. We want to ensure that you have an enjoyable vacation in our lovely capital."

When he completed the last line of the last form, Bryan's patience had worn thin and was about to break. He slid the forms across the desk, gritted his teeth and gave Lisa a frustrated but assuring nod.

Placing his hand on his telephone, the supervisor asked, "Now please, may I make hotel accommodations for you?"

"No, that won't be necessary. We'll find our own, thank you," answered Lisa.

"May I encourage you to use my phone to find one? That way I'll know where to contact you the moment your luggage is located," he persisted.

"No, thank you," replied Bryan.

"Perhaps I could arrange for a taxi?"

"Please!" Bryan blurted out. "We'll handle this situation ourselves, and when we do, we'll call you. Now, would you point me in the direction of the exit?"

As they walked out the door, the supervisor dialed his telephone. His eyes never left Bryan and Lisa.

"They are leaving."

"Where will they be staying?"

"I don't know the name of the hotel…they wouldn't take one of ours."

"The bags?"

"They're in the closet behind me."

CHAPTER 21

"MERIDO LAW OFFICE, MAY I HELP YOU?" THE SECRETARY queried. The harsh singular click of the incoming call struck a sore nerve. I hate it when people don't have the common courtesy to admit to a wrong number, she thought. Reaching over, she pushed the third button on the intercom panel and heard the familiar buzz in the rear office.

"Yes, Maria?"

"Jose, I'm leaving to deliver the document package to Señor Rodriguez. With good traffic, I'll be back for lunch. Don't forget, Bryan Harmon should be here soon. Why don't the two of you go ahead and start reminiscing? We'll eat when I get back. Oh yes, Francesca will cover the phones—bye, Love."

As Maria Merido stood to leave, she scooped up the stack of documents on her desk and slid them into a manila envelope. Closing the door behind her, she walked down the hall and stepped into the ladies room to refresh her lipstick and hair. Pleased that every hair was in its proper place, Maria closed her purse, tucked the envelope under her arm and opened the door. Startled, she gasped and stopped in her tracks as she almost bumped into a tall, Aryan-looking man walking past the door. More surprising was the reaction of the well-dressed man. The door had barely opened when the man's body went rigid, his left arm rising up to defend his head while his right clenched a fist in a karate pose. The suddenness of his movement caused Maria to step back and blurt out a frightened yelp. With the same quickness, the man recovered his tight composure. He stood erect, nodded an apology to Maria and continued down the hall. With her hand pressed against her heart, Maria walked to the elevator and proceeded downward to the ground floor.

**

The steeled Aryan stopped outside the door with the glass panel painted: Jose Merido, Attorney. He looked left and right before turning the door knob. He opened the door and entered the elegantly appointed law office.

"Francesca," the voice in the intercom resonated, "would you please bring me the Diaz file?"

"Si, Señor Merido, right away," she answered.

Like a robotic machine programmed to respond to sound, the intruder's head snapped around in the direction of the voices. His hand eased into his suit and pulled out a pistol with a silencer attached. Approaching Francesca's office, he saw her standing and sorting through the files of an upright cabinet. Finding what she was looking for, she turned to return to her desk. The long silencer extended from the gun, loomed as large as a cavern, inches from her eyes.

"Wha–"

SPIT! SPIT!

Francesca's body stood rigid for a few seconds, then wobbled, teetering to the right. The Aryan's powerful arm shot out and caught her fall with little effort. Without a sound he eased her crumpled body to the floor. His menacing eyes again scanned the office. He crept toward the sounds of Jose at his desk, his large muscular body filling the doorway. As Jose picked up several papers, he sensed a body in the door opening.

"Thank you, Francesca, br—"

SPIT! SPIT! The bullets entered his right eye. His head fell backward, caught by the back of his chair, one lifeless eye still open. Blood spewed from the other.

***

Having paid cash and registering under the name of Mr. and Mrs. John Trent, Bryan and Lisa carried their bags of newly purchased clothing and personal articles to the room of the moderate, yet chic hotel.

"I'll call Jose and let him know we've arrived," said Bryan. "You're going to like him. His will be a pleasant face after what you've been through."

"Good. I'll only need a few minutes to freshen up. I slept most of the flight, as you know…sorry."

The unanswered phone at Jose's office left Bryan perplexed. Redialing the number, he received the same results, and after several rings, canceled the call.

"What did he say?" Lisa asked.

"Nothing. There was no answer. I dialed four times."

"No answer? That's odd. Didn't you say he had a secretary?"

"Yes, two—one of them is his wife, Maria."

"Maybe they went to lunch?"

"It's only 11:30 here."

"Well, let's go over there anyway. I'm sure they will be back by the time we arrive. Do you know how to get us there?"

"No, but I'll find out at the front desk." He picked up the phone again. "I'm going to call the Embassy in Berlin. I told Mrs. Taylor that I wouldn't be in for a couple days, but I want to explain my absence to Ambassador Barnes directly."

"Bryan, is that wise? What if someone else listens in on the conversation?"

"I'm not convinced that there's a problem within the Embassy, but I'll use a secure line."

***

Sitting in the back seat of a well-used taxi, Bryan felt a joy of anticipation. The thought of seeing Jose opened a flood of memories that had him smiling and staring out the window. Lisa's hand moved to cover his as it rested on the seat.

"Getting anxious?"

"Huh? Oh, I was just thinking of the first time I met Jose...what a character. But don't worry, I haven't forgotten the real reason we're here," Bryan said. The smile on his face disappeared. "Jose has an extensive packet for us to pick up; background papers on Hilda's residence, her estate, her nurse and, oh yeah, he also said he found something else that could prove to be very interesting."

"What's that?"

"I don't know. He was on the line with a client when we spoke, so he could only fit in a few words, and I didn't want to push him."

"I suppose it doesn't matter. We'll know soon enough."

He turned his head and stared out the window again. "Funny about Jose..."

"What's that?"

"He was such a ladies man—and I do mean the quintessential 'ladies man!' He graduated second in our class and had offers from big firms coming at him left and right. I'm talking starting at over one hundred G's right out of law school. It was everything he ever wanted; live in the U.S., make big bucks and bring his family over. You know, the American dream as seen by most poor foreigners. Then this girl comes out of nowhere. He told me she was the one he had been waiting for all his life, and after just one date—one date! I mean, he could've had any woman he wanted. She tells him that she wants to move back to Buenos Aires and raise a family. So what does he do? He says yes in a heartbeat and moves with her back to Argentina. Go figure!" Bryan shook his head in mock disbelief.

"Go figure what? Why do you find that strange?" Lisa asked.

"I guess I don't...anymore. Now I can't wait to tell him just that."

"Tell him what?"

"That I finally understand." He squeezed her hand and cracked an impish smile.

The taxi swerved to the curb and came to an abrupt stop. Lisa felt her body roll against Bryan. A warm flush came over her and she blushed, this time with pleasure.

"This must be it." He looked up at the tall glass office building. "Whoa...didn't I tell you this guy was first rate?"

When they got out of the taxi, Bryan stood motionless, staring at the building. Lisa stepped forward and said, "Are you going to stand here pie-eyed all day, or are we going up?"

"Huh? Oh yeah, I'm just impressed. Jose's got to have it made."

"It's only impressions, my dear. Let's go see the real Jose...the one you've been telling me about."

Bryan felt his anticipation rise as his body leaned toward the opening elevator doors. Before Lisa stepped out of the elevator, he was off and down the hall to the door of Jose's office. As he reached for the knob, he was embarrassed when he noticed Lisa lagging ten feet behind him.

"Sorry," he said. "I'm just anxious to see him after all this time."

Opening the door inward, Bryan's single step forward came to an abrupt halt at the sight before him. His mind couldn't comprehend what his eyes saw.

"What the hell?"

The large reception room with its richly appointed furnishings was in shambles. Desk drawers lay helter-skelter about the room with their contents strewn in every direction. Leaning over the arm of a sofa, a large lamp lay broken with its shade crushed amid cushions pulled up and disheveled. Bryan felt terror. The meaning of what he saw sank in.

"Bryan?…Oh my God," Lisa cried out. Her hands rose to cover her mouth.

"Wait here," Bryan commanded. "Let me go in first."

Inching his way forward, Bryan's heart pounded, his palms moistened. Each step propelled him deeper into what he feared was a ghoulish nightmare. What will I find? Is danger still here? Is an assailant waiting to attack? His imagination raced. Beads of sweat broke out on his forehead. His eyes and ears set to fever pitch as life itself hung on the slightest movement of his body. Bryan feared the noise from the crumpled papers beneath his feet would betray his arrival. It was impossible to avoid the obstacles. He found himself in the first small office. The scene made him wretch. A young woman was sprawled on the floor in a pool of blood. He turned toward Jose's office. He swallowed hard, fighting for air. He knew the worst was yet to come.

Reaching Jose's door, Bryan forced himself to overcome his fear and look in. He saw mounds of overturned furniture and files. "Oh no…Oh shit! Shit!…Shit!" Jose's blood-soaked face had come into view. Bryan's stomach muscles wretched again. This time, they lost control. He fell to his knees, bent over and vomited.

A hand touched his shoulder. He jerked around and set his body into a quick, defensive posture. His arm swung wildly, almost catching Lisa's face with the back of his hand. The terrified look on her face touched him with a depth of emotion that he hadn't felt since his brother's death— emotion he thought he was incapable of ever feeling again.

"Lisa, it's my fault! I should never have called him. Why? Why Jose… why the woman? No!…Oh my God, is it Maria?" Like a man possessed, Bryan scrambled to his feet. He stumbled his way to the first office. Afraid of the truth, he stopped at the office door, forcing himself to walk in. He knelt down and rolled the woman's body over. "Thank God, it's not her!" he blurted out. "But where is Maria? She's his secretary…she should be here!

Breathing hard and confused, he looked about. Fear gripped him again. "Lisa?" he shouted. "Where are you?"

"I'm here, Bryan, I'm here." She ran to him, wrapped her arms around his head and drew his face to her bosom. He mourned deep from within his soul and was lost in her safe embrace.

"This can't be true," he sobbed.

"Bryan, stop! We've got to think. They must have been killed for the information Jose had. Maybe they didn't get it. Quick, start looking. You check that room. I'll check Jose's."

CHAPTER 22

MARIA MERIDO STOOD IN FRONT OF THE DESK OF SEÑOR Raul Rodriguez. Tall, slender and blessed with Castilian beauty, she radiated a subtle air of authority. She was Jose Merido's strongest business asset. Understanding the law was one matter; securing clients was another. To this end, Maria was a natural.

"I am sure, Señor Rodriguez, you will find the papers in order. If you find everything agreeable, this deal should close the day after tomorrow." She handed the large envelope to the wealthy industrialist. She also gave her trademark smile. It was subtle, but most men withered.

When he opened the package and slid out the contracts, Rodriguez noticed a smaller envelope fall to his desktop. He picked it up and read the Anglo name handwritten on the envelope: Bryan Harmon. Turning the envelope over in his hands, he asked, "Is this meant to come to me?"

"Excuse me, Señor Rodriguez. That was put into your package by mistake. I was in a hurry to leave the office. Here, I'll take it." She apologized and reached for the envelope.

Within moments, her client perused his papers in a general manner and proceeded to square them on his desk. "As always, that husband of yours is a deal maker, not a deal breaker. Everything seems to be in order, Maria. Please inform Jose I will study them in detail tonight and call him in the morning. If all is correct, I'll sign and execute on Monday—it will take until then to have funds in place."

He extended his hand with the anticipated joy of having even the smallest contact with the Castilian beauty.

"Thank you Señor and good day. Please give my regards to Señora Rodriguez."

***

Maria exited the elevator on the third floor of her building, grateful the ladies room was close at hand. Pushing on the door of the restroom, she looked down the hall and noticed the door to her office ajar. Forgetting her momentary urge, she walked to the door, hesitating before entering. She heard the rustling of papers and the murmurs of strange voices within. As she entered, her knees weakened.

Maria cried out in terror. "What is going on? Who are you? Jose…?"

Bryan jumped to his feet. Half startled, half in panic, he bolted from Jose's office. He ran to prevent Maria from entering further. The shock on her face said it all. Bryan talked on the run, "Maria, thank God you're alive. It's me, Bryan—Bryan Harmon."

"Bryan?…Yes, but Jose, where's my Jose? What's going on?" Terror gripped her. She looked left then right, trying to see around Bryan into Jose's office. She broke. "Where's Jose?" she screamed.

"Maria…" Bryan paused. He reached to draw her into his arms.

"No!" she screamed. "No…Jose!" She tried to dart past him. Bryan spun Maria around and locked his arms around her. She pounded on his chest to free herself.

"Maria, please…please listen to me. Maria, please stop! Jose is dead. He, he's been killed." He pulled her head to his shoulder. Her body went limp, collapsing in his arms. He beckoned to Lisa with his eyes.

"Let her cry, Bryan. It needs to come out."

When Maria's crying subsided, he nudged her body away from her husband's office.

"Why…why my Jose?" she whispered. "He is such a gentle man. He loves his children."

"I think the answer is in a package of information Jose had gathered for us, Maria. We looked but couldn't find it anywhere."

"I have that envelope. It's in my briefcase. I picked it up by mistake."

"We must leave—and now," Lisa said. She realized how harsh she sounded. "It pains me, Maria. But you have to get to your children—you can't help Jose now. You must leave—you're in danger! Whoever did this will think you have the information elsewhere. They'll stop at nothing!"

Lisa led the way out while Bryan steadied Maria with his arm and followed close behind. Maria Merido stopped at the door, looked up and ran her fingers over Jose's name one last time.

CHAPTER 23

ASSOCIATED PRESS

KABUL, AFGHANISTAN - NATO PEACEKEEPING FORCES, U.S. COMMAND SECTOR - Admiral Leighton Smith announced the deployment of another twenty thousand U.S. troops to the peacekeeping role in Afghanistan. Admiral Smith said the men are in response to both French and English pullouts and the newest wave of terrorist bombings by the Islamic Jihad.

ASSOCIATED PRESS

WASHINGTON, D.C. - A State Department spokesman acknowledged that Germany petitioned the U.S. to support its request for a return to prewar borders at the Oder and Niesse rivers. President Cook is said to be studying the request with a cautious, but open mind.

EXECUTIVE OFFICES
PARLIAMENT BUILDING
MOSCOW

Vladimir Donskoy's boorish style was reminiscent of days gone by when the Soviet Union was ruled by totalitarian edicts enforced by brute militarism. He was a man who longed for those days and demanded their return. His national security meetings were run in the old, threatening manner. Gone were the times when Boris Yeltsin sat in the middle of the conference table as if he were chairing a meeting of equals. He removed the old, smaller conference table and installed a longer one in its place. The difference was that he was now positioned at the end of the table, and meetings would never again be a gathering of equals. All eyes were required to focus on him. Raw intimidation was the key operative, and the hierarchy of the Red Army paid homage to the man whose maniacal glare weakened the knees of all who surrounded him.

Donskoy opened the meeting as he had the last—the subject was Alexander Konstantinov. The man had become his newest obsession. True, Donskoy had found dirt on his rival and ruined him politically, but that wasn't enough. Deep in the pit of his stomach, Donskoy knew that there must be more. It was bigger. It had to be. He knew it. Why would the Nazis have set him up in the first place? he thought. Why or who would keep this man in a position of power, always on the outside of the bubble, waiting? There had to be a purpose. What was Konstantinov's mission?

"So, Comrade Gorgin, what do we know of our little Nazi traitor? Has the purpose of his mission been defined?"

The Director of Central Intelligence Service (CSR) cleared his throat and shifted in his seat. He knew the question would be asked, but that gave him no solace, as he also knew he didn't have the answer the chairman was looking for.

"I am sorry to report, Comrade President, but Konstantinov has resisted all our efforts to make him talk. He denies our allegations, and I can assure you that no amount of coercion has been—"

Donskoy's face twisted into a mocking sneer as he interrupted. "What the shit is this 'no amount of coercion?' I want answers! Damn it to hell...I want that wretched son of a bitch singing like a canary! Do whatever it takes." Donskoy's voice quieted to a menacing growl. "You make that scum talk within forty-eight hours or I'll have your resignation on my desk and your nuts hanging from my key chain! Am I understood?"

"Yes, Comrade President, but these are not the old days of the KGB," Gorgin pleaded. "We have laws now—and the press—"

"Forty-eight hours, you gutless wonder—not one hour more!" Donskoy caught himself, realized the tirade he had just let loose and proceeded to clear his throat. "Now, let us get to the business of regaining our former Soviet Union."

As Donskoy's endless words droned on, General Strelnik raised his eyes to meet those of General Asimorov. Conversation or facial grimaces were not needed, for their eyes spoke volumes.

"I don't care *what* the world thinks!" Donskoy's rant was relentless. "Yeltsin cared, and look what it got that miserable asshole: He screwed up in Chechnya and I had to clean up his shit-mess. He screwed up Georgia, then Armenia, then Azerbaijan, and *again* it was me who had to clean up his garbage. Well, I'm *not* going to screw up in Ukraine, and I'm sure as hell *not* screwing up in Belarus! This is *Soviet* land, bought and paid for with Russian blood. Any moves on this land will be paid for with someone else's blood! I stand on the Helsinki Accords of 1975, including that shit-hole of a country, Poland. The borders will not move!"

The room hung in dead silence. Foreign Minister Zhukov sat fidgeting with his pen, waiting for a pause in the Russian President's long harangue. When he was comfortable that there was a pause, he carefully structured his response, hoping that he would not become the target of another outburst. He couched his words and said, "Yes, Comrade President, the Helsinki Conference on Security and Cooperation in Europe did accept the new borders as inviolate, with the exception of, 'revision by peaceful agreement.'"

The explosion was as loud as it was instantaneous.

"*Peaceful*? Do you call those bloodsucking gangsters peaceful?" Donskoy screamed. Spittle formed in the corners of his mouth. "They are nothing but blight on Mother Russia. I want to cleanse her sacred body of those filthy maggots!"

"But it appears the Americans are going to sanction the German request for restoration of Germany's former borders," the Minister dared to say. "Poland has agreed, but requires *their* prewar borders to be honored from Wilno to—"

"Vilnius! Vilnius, you fool! I don't care if those idiot Poles want to give up their land. That's their problem, not mine. As for those sniveling Americans, those bastards are as depraved as their leader Cook. All they care about is money and which hole their dicks are going into next."

General Strelnik's patience was worn. "Comrades, please!" he said. "Must I remind everyone here of the American nuclear arsenal...their missiles—their technology? Does the name 'Desert Storm' mean anything to you? 'Operation Ir'—when shock and awe overwhelmed Iraq? I don't think—"

"You don't think?" interrupted Donskoy. "You don't think shit, General Strelnik. You screwed up in Chechnya and you let that vermin rabble run you around like a confused peasant chasing a chicken for supper. No, General, I will not hear you. Let me tell every single one of you in this room, that not one millimeter of Soviet Union territory will ever be permanently surrendered. Not ever! I can back down those American eunuchs with one submarine parked off Washington! You hear that—one fucking submarine!"

CHAPTER 24

WALKING DOWN THE WELL-WORN, YET ODDLY CHARMING cobbled street in the old residential district, one could point out, with a reasonable degree of accuracy, the portion of the population that carried a German bloodline. Scattered amidst the Spanish-styled homes, complete with terra-cotta colored roofs and stucco facades, were the transition houses of the Germans. They were still clad with a stucco face, but usually limited to the first floor level. The second floor carried dark, vertical wood siding that rose upward to a cedar shake roof.

The residence at 622 Avenue de Los Arboles Rojos was one such house. Overall, its outside was neat, but the shrubbery was overgrown and its paint was in need of attention. The interior of the home was a reflection of its exterior. Within, most of its old, yellowed shades were drawn, providing an antique hue that bathed its beamed ceilings and wood-paneled walls. Dust balls clung to deer antlers, which had been fashioned into a dining room chandelier. An ornate cuckoo clock chimed the relentless passage of time.

In the bedroom, an elderly woman lay in her bed, staring at the dingy ceiling that matched the grey of her hair. Her daydream had turned to pain and her whispering was audible.

"My darling baby, don't cry…momma loves you. No, lebchen…no, you cannot stay with momma…you must go. You—Stop! Don't pull his arm!" Her head rocked back and forth and her body squirmed. "He's just a baby boy…go on Albert; it will be all right. I said don't hurt his arm!" A tear formed in the corner of her eye. "Oh, please baby; don't cry…momma will always love you." The sheets were damp with sweat. "I can't stand the pain! Oh, take him quickly!" She heard his crying voice calling to her; first loud and painful, then soft and faint, and finally fading to nothing. Momma! Momma! Momma…momma…momma…

Her body bolted upright into a sitting position, causing the newspaper to slide off her lap to the floor. "Albert!" she shrieked. "Albert!…My baby boy!"

Hearing screams from the bedroom, the nurse jumped from her chair, spilling part of her burning coffee on her fingers. She grabbed her small medical kit and within seconds entered the room. She pulled a hypodermic needle out of her kit and squirted the needle upward to check its contents. As she inserted it into Hilda's IV tube, a hand grabbed her wrist and a startled voice cried out, "Who are you? I don't know you!"

"I'm Nurse Froehling. I'll be attending to you today. Nurse Menendez is ill, so the agency called me. It's all right, my dear Eva. It's time for your medication. Don't worry—everything will be fine."

Hearing the nurse call her by her real name, the name from her distant past, Eva Braun let her upper torso lay back down. She took a deep breath, knowing her long life in hiding would soon end. She closed her eyes and smiled, remembering the handsome man that strode into the Eagle's Nest at Berchtesgaden…

"The Fuerher's plane's been delayed. Sit down and tell me the news from Berlin." She patted the cushion on the sofa next to her.

"I just came from Breslau, where we have a…facility. And what I've seen, I cannot talk about. It wrenches my stomach."

She placed her hand over his and the softness of her touch sent needed warmth through his body. He had always desired Eva, and she his young, firm body. Passion exploded from the emptiness within and they made love in a desperate frenzy. Albert Speer needed the comfort of human touch to block out the nightmarish images he had just witnessed, and Eva's long abstinence with Adolph made her desperate for more than affection.

Eva's memory drifted in and out like a raft at sea, but she saw flags waving everywhere. Red flags, flags with swastikas emblazoned on them, and lights...haze...smoke. Then cheering, screaming crowds, lights swirling upward as if coming from Hell itself. Arms raised and stretched straight outward amidst the chants: "Sieg Heil! Sieg Heil! Sieg Heil! Sieg Heil! Sieg..." Her dream faded to blackness.

In the kitchen, the nurse picked up the telephone and dialed the familiar number. She heard the man's raspy voice answer, "Yes?"

"It's done," she said.

"How long?"

"The usual—twenty-four hours."

CHAPTER 25

BRYAN SAT AT A SMALL DESK IN THEIR HOTEL ROOM. HE opened Jose's envelope and thought of his lost friend. Why did such a gentle soul have to be brutally murdered...and for what? How did they even know about him? The answers he needed wouldn't come. What do they want? And who the hell are they? Lisa hung up the phone and broke his pensive stare.

"Maria's safe. She gathered her children and is in seclusion at her cousin's country home. She called the police from there and they've provided protection," Lisa said. She eyed the partially opened envelope. "Are you all right with opening it now?"

"Yeah, I think so. Sorry, I just can't get that horrid image of Jose out of my mind." Bryan pulled the contents out of the envelope. The typing became blurry as his eyes filled with tears and his chin quivered. He took a long breath, wiped his eyes and refocused on the information. "Let's see, this is a copy of Wetzel's will, giving the title of his house to Hilda Maier. And, uh, a copy of a birth certificate for her son, Albert Wilhelm Maier, and a couple of newspaper clippings. The first one talks about the death of Heinrich Wetzel. Let's see...he committed suicide after his wife and children were burned to death in an auto accident."

"Does that mean anything to you?"

"No, but this second one's got a picture with it." He handed it to her. "It's an article on the death of her son, Albert. The picture shows a scene at his funeral. Jose said there was something else—but what? And where?" He turned the clippings in his hands, looking at both sides.

Lisa took the articles from him and examined them. "Is there anything else in the envelope?"

"No." He shook it upside down and peered in.

"Hmmm? There *must* be something here. Could there be anything at all in the picture? I don't know...maybe something in the background?"

Tilting the lampshade upward for more light, Bryan held up the newspaper photograph closer to his eyes. "I don't know. My eyes aren't good enough. Maybe there's someone in the crowd. This picture is grainy and old…I'll need a magnifying glass. I'll call the front desk and find out if there's a pharmacy nearby." He dialed the telephone on the nightstand.

"Yes, this is room 306. Where I can find the nearest pharmacy?"

Lisa continued to peruse the papers. In particular, she noticed the deed. "Well, at least we have Hilda's address."

The hotel concierge answered, "Certainly Señor Harmon. It's at 135 Toledo Boulevard. Take the first street left of the hotel entrance, then down one block. You shouldn't miss it. Is there anything else I can help you with?"

"No, thank you." Bryan placed the receiver down and stared. His mind clawed through his memory for details, no matter how small.

"We can go to Hilda's tomorrow, Bry—" her voice stopped as she turned and caught his puzzled look.

With a sudden twist of his head, his attention zeroed in on Lisa. "Wait! We paid cash for this room, didn't we?"

"Of course we did. What's the matter?"

"What name did we use?" He snapped his fingers.

"Uh, it was Trent. Yes, Mr. and Mrs. Robert Trent. What's going on?"

"The concierge called me Mr. Harmon, Lisa—*Mr. Harmon!*"

"What?" Her apologetic posture turned to serious concern.

"Mr. Harmon. How the hell did he know my name was Harmon?" Fear gripped him. He scrambled to make sense of it all.

Lisa's mind snapped into focus. "Come on—there's no time! We've got to go! Grab your briefcase and the papers. Leave everything else!" Her body moved on instinct. She grabbed her purse off the bed. Reaching the door, Lisa slowed her movements, twisted the doorknob and eased the door open…just enough to peek down the hall. Confident all was clear, she nodded Bryan to follow.

As they ran down the hall to the elevator, Lisa pulled up her hand, blocking Bryan's path. She saw the old, clock-like arm of the rising elevator. "The stairs—go for the stairs!" Her hand shoved Bryan backward and to the left.

They reached the staircase door. His body came to a sudden halt. He slammed into the door—it wouldn't open. He grabbed the knob with both hands and twisted it violently. It still wouldn't budge. He looked back at the elevator. The arrow passed the second floor and made its way toward three. He squeezed again and slammed his shoulder into the door—nothing. He slammed into it again. This time it broke free. They descended two steps at a bound.

With a universal ding, the elevator announced the third floor. Its doors opened, its two occupants surging forward. Outside door 306, guns were drawn and silencers screwed on. The first man leaned back and kicked open the door. The second hurled himself forward, hitting the floor rolling. In one smooth motion he was up on one knee. His weapon searched the room for its prey. There was no one. He jerked his weapon upward and to the left. The first man responded and searched the bathroom while the other provided silent cover. Rising to his feet, he walked bow-legged to the balcony door, his gun never leaving its two-handed extension. No one was found. Without a word spoken, the weapons were returned to their holsters. They looked at each other, frustration showing on their faces.

CHAPTER 26

THE FUNERAL OF INGRID KOERNIG WAS IN ITS SECOND hour and the Lutheran minister showed no sign of easing up on his eulogy. He enjoyed hearing himself proselytize to the great unwashed, and a gathering of Washington dignitaries, socialites and press corps offered an opportunity he couldn't resist.

Vice President Koernig sat in the center chair opposite the flag-draped coffin and no longer fought to keep up an image of paying attention to the long-winded zealot. With his arms folded and his eyes staring at the ground before him, his mind wandered back to the painful images of his youth.

He saw a boy of five being pulled away from his mother as he stretched, crying and screaming, for one last touch of the woman with the loving face. That image was replaced by a boy riding in a black Mercedes up a tree-lined drive to a mansion in the Pennsylvania countryside. The boy sat small and alone in the backseat. The image of the driver, with his right ear missing, haunted his dreams still.

Next, he pictured his new parents, Wilhelm and Ingrid, sitting stern-faced on a sofa in an immense drawing room. After a long pause, Ingrid was the first to break the awkwardness of the moment. "What a beautiful boy, so strong and handsome!"

"Are his papers in order?" asked Wilhelm. He commanded center stage by slapping his newspaper against his leg.

"Yes," responded the driver. He scratched the scarred flesh that was once his ear. "I have every detail of his birth—certificate, immunizations, hospital records—everything!"

Wilhelm signaled the butler by snapping his fingers and nodding toward the boy. The manservant walked over to the child, raised him by the arm and escorted him up the stairs to his new bedroom.

Sitting on a large bed in an oversized room, the bewildered boy started to cry, furious at being abandoned by his mother. With hatred mixed with tears, he erased his mother's face from memory. How could she have abandoned me? I will never forgive you!

Then he saw himself as a slightly older boy sitting on Ingrid's lap, listening to her read one of his favorite stories. When Wilhelm entered the house, Ingrid motioned him to get down and run to the opposite chair. She hid the book behind a cushion. Wilhelm entered the room, flashed a stern look at the boy, and asked if his studies were finished. The boy whined an answer in the negative. It was matched by a swift backhand to his face. The servant was summoned and the child was hauled off to his "thinking" room.

"Please, Wilhelm, he's just a child," she said, fearing his predictable response.

"Shut up. You're half the problem!"

The door opened to a small, windowless closet. Koernig saw the boy enter. The door was closed on him and locked. Blackness shook the frightened boy.

The vice president inadvertently shivered, causing his head to rise. His attention returned to the present and ever-droning minister. Seconds later his breathing slowed once again and the images returned. He saw a teenager playing with a Golden Retriever puppy. The memory was warm until Wilhelm's face appeared. His stern face nodded a directive to the servant, who then looked at the boy's dog.

The hard face faded to doors of the drawing room bursting open to a waiting Wilhelm. "Where's Schotzie?" the lad screamed. "What've you done with my dog?"

Wilhelm's cold eyes never left his newspaper. "You were too close to that dog. I told your mother not to buy it in the first place. It was not good for you." Then, with an air of indifference and finality, he said, "The animal has been disposed of." The teen turned his rage to Ingrid, whose face turned from him in shame.

A feeling of happiness took over when he remembered a beautiful blonde girl at his college graduation party. As their eyes met, she blushed and looked downward. The strong hand of Wilhelm came to rest upon the shoulder of the young man.

"Her name is Barnes, Nancy Alicia Barnes. Her father is Peter Barnes of the diplomatic corps. You will learn to love her in due time. Beyond that, you have nothing to do. Everything has been arranged."

Nancy's blushing face faded into a scene of Wilhelm's dark, mahogany casket being lowered into the ground. William saw himself sitting between Ingrid and his wife Nancy. His steeled face turned to Ingrid, and their dry, emotionless eyes met. Their heads nodded ever so slightly as they squeezed each other's hand. Ingrid rose, followed by Nancy, William and the children. She picked up a clump of dirt and cast it on the coffin. Nancy and the children did likewise. William Koernig simply passed by, his youth fading away.

The picture in his mind changed to a man, a vice president. He was alone again in the library of his own house. The telephone rang and he heard a voice as real as if it were being spoken in front of him.

"She has become a serious liability. They could make contact with her, and in her medical condition, we don't know what she might say. We're not looking for your permission to terminate—only your acceptance."

The loving face of his mother, Eva, crying as he was pulled from her at age five, came back into view. But with the cold detachment of a heart that had ceased to feel emotion, he did not hesitate. He whispered, "Of course. Do it."

Straightening his body in his seat, William Koernig's attention returned to the present. As the minister concluded his eulogy, Koernig looked over and his icy eyes met those of Ambassador Barnes—all was in order.

CHAPTER 27

OUTSIDE HILDA'S HOUSE, THE DARKNESS OF EVENING BEGAN to tiptoe in. The warm glow of the streetlights began to flicker and various lights inside the residence went on. Two figures sat huddled together in the shadows, watching—waiting.

Inside the bedroom, Nurse Froehling checked for a pulse, and when she found none, she placed her fingers on Hilda's carotid artery. Convinced that her work had been completed, she turned and set the timing device. As her foot kicked against the fallen newspaper on the floor, she looked down and noticed a piece torn from the front page. Puzzled, she picked up the paper, glancing at the floor. Pulling back the blanket on the body, her eyes caught the time on the nightstand clock. Realizing time was running out, she gave up the search, pulled off her latex gloves and stuffed them into her pocket.

Taking out a handkerchief, she walked to the front door and wiped the doorknob to erase any fingerprints. Her years of paying attention to every minute detail had left a hollow feeling inside her. She paused, the missing piece of newsprint bothering her. She grimaced and locked the house behind her. As she walked down the sidewalk to the street, she slipped the handkerchief and key into her purse and passed within inches of the pair huddled in the bushes. The street lamp lit the hard Teutonic face, exposing the double raised moles under her left eye.

Lisa looked at Bryan. He jumped to his feet and ran crouching to the side of the house. He motioned for Lisa to follow. Running and staying low, she reached him within seconds. She saw his hands cupped together and inserted her right foot. Her body was hoisted up to the window. Scanning the living room and dining room, she saw no one. She tapped Bryan's head to drop her down.

"What'd you see?"

"Nothing. That window over there must be the bedroom." She

pointed to the rear corner of the house. They moved to that window and he again hoisted her up. This time Lisa saw a figure asleep in bed. She strained her head, checked to see that no one was with the woman and jumped down.

"This has to be Hilda's room...the house looks empty."

"Well?"

"Bryan, we *have* to get in and look around."

His eyes scanned the neighboring yards and houses. A swift kick from his shoe sent the glass shattering to the basement floor. Dogs barked in the distance.

They reached Hilda's bedroom. Bryan put his index finger over his lips and motioned to Lisa as he eased the door open. He made his way to the dresser and looked back, his sleeve catching a perfume bottle. It fell over onto its tray with a clank. His body froze. His breathing stopped. His head swung in the direction of Hilda, but her body didn't move. He eased over to her bed, looking to Lisa for guidance. She shrugged her shoulders. He wet his index and middle fingers with his tongue. He slid them under her nose...nothing. He reluctantly placed them on her neck...still nothing.

He whispered, "I think she's dead."

Lisa crept over and picked up Hilda's wrist and checked for a pulse. Holding Hilda's hand, she felt a small, crumpled paper wadded in her grip.

"What's this?" Spreading Hilda's fingers, she removed the newspaper clipping. She turned on a lamp and read it aloud:

ASSOCIATED PRESS

HARRISBURG – Vice President William Koernig attended the funeral of his mother, Ingrid Koernig. At his side were his wife and three children. The ceremony was attended by many dignitaries, including Peter Barnes, Ambassador to Germany and Blaine Harmon, former Swiss Ambassador and current World Bank Executive Director. Conspicuously absent was President Cook or any representative of his administration.

"Shhh! What is that?" Bryan blurted out. He heard a low, rapid beeping.

The explosion was deafening and everything went black. Bryan and

Lisa were hurtled sideways to the floor. Flames engulfed the living and dining rooms. Bryan regained his consciousness. He fumbled around in the smoke and darkness, desperately trying to find Lisa.

"Bryan!" she screamed.

"Here, right here." He pulled her shocked body closer to him.

"I'm okay," she whimpered. "Let's get out of here."

He grabbed a small chair, smashed it through the window and helped her to the ground. A soft rain began to fall as they ran supporting each other down the driveway. A second explosion blew its fury out the windows and doors. They were thrown forward onto the wet grass, tumbling under its impact. Running down the road, they looked back to see the house engulfed in a ball of flames.

CHAPTER 28

FOR WHAT SEEMED TO BE HOURS ON END, BRYAN AND LISA aimlessly walked the back streets and alleys of old Buenos Aires. Each car that passed and each person they encountered loomed as a potential enemy, a threat to their lives. They were lost and their nerves were stretched to the breaking point. The hotel they found was the only thing that appeared "safe" to them. Apart from its location in one of the sleaziest areas of the city, its shabby exterior was matched only by the dank, moldy smell of its interior. Lisa sat on the side of the bed, shivering and soaking wet. She glanced over and saw Bryan looking down at the street between a slit in the drawn curtains. She was physically exhausted, emotionally drained and tired of the chase, fear and death that surrounded her.

Watching him stand guard, a comforting sense of security came over her. Is this the same person I found at the embassy? Somehow he's different, older...stronger. Is it because I need him, or have I fallen in love? No, I can't fall in love—not now—my life is a living hell. She looked at him again. Warmth came over her and she felt the love as if it were about to carry her away, away to some safe haven where nothing would hurt her again.

He looked back at her, but she neither turned away nor blushed. Her eyes told him what he dared not ask. He walked over, picked up a comforter and gently wrapped it around her shoulders. Nothing needed to be said as she felt warmth flow throughout her body. Her pulse quickened and her cheeks turned red, flush with a rising passion. She felt an ache in her heart. She wanted him to take her away—nothing else mattered. They looked at each other again, only this time, their eyes locked. With every fiber of his body pulsating, he took her hands and pulled her to himself. Their lips touched—soft, yet tentative. They kissed again, then again and again, until their heads swirled and the world disappeared as they lovingly surrendered to each other.

CHAPTER 29

ASSOCIATED PRESS

BERLIN - A SPOKESPERSON FOR CHANCELLOR ANNEKE Mueller announced the deployment of 20,000 German troops to Mazar-e Sharif, Afghanistan. The troops will be under the NATO peacekeeping flag, although it is widely known that they will operate under American direction. Russian President Donskoy has sent a formal protest to both the United Nations and Washington.

NOVA KAZALINSK, KAZAKHSTAN

The government of "independent" Kazakhstan had always maintained proper relations with its acknowledged benefactor, Russia. It stayed within the sphere of the Russian Federation and never questioned the true ownership of the missile sites its borders housed.

In the underground control center near Nova Kazalinsk, the mammoth computers and control screens on the concrete walls continued to hum and blink in perpetual harmony. With no perceived enemy threats to fear, life in the post-Cold War era was monotonous in the cavernous missile facility. The only "enemies" the Kazak technicians feared were the arrogant Russian supervisors regularly sent in to monitor their efficiency.

Colonel Viktor Polgrad had always taken sadistic pleasure in making his presence felt when he stood face to face with the weak Kazak director. He knew he was going to take that pleasure to a higher level today, for he would be issuing new orders, orders he knew would guarantee and secure his authority for a long period of time.

As a large steel door struggled to open to its maximum with a loud metal thud, Colonel Polgrad tilted his head backward and inhaled through his nose. Straightening his posture, he proceeded into the control room as if he were leading a long parade of imagined dignitaries. He came to an abrupt halt at the center desk and slammed his metal briefcase down, announcing to all his arrival. As always, the director scurried from his office like a sycophant lapdog to greet the impatient Russian.

"Comrade Director, you do have your key, I presume?" the Colonel asked. He stared down his nose, his head tilted backward.

"But of course," the Kazak said. He nervously fumbled through his pocket.

After inserting their mutual keys in sequence, the Russian opened his briefcase and pulled out a small envelope, its seal intact and witnessed by both men.

"These are your new coordinates, comrade. You are ordered to commence retargeting immediately."

The Kazak opened the envelope, and with great care, pulled out the discs and down-loaded them into the computer's mainframe. Reacting slowly, the coordinates showed themselves on the screen. He was dumbfounded. An ashen color came over his face.

"With all due respect, Colonel, these coordinates are not allowed under any of the Salt Agreements! Some of these are civilian targets!" he whispered.

"That, my dear Comrade Director, is not your concern."

"But this cannot be!"

"Nonetheless, they are your orders, Comrade. They come from the highest levels," the Russian replied. His anger grew with each deliberate sentence. "You know the procedures as well as I. Perhaps you would like me to call General Vasilov and tell him of your reluctance?" Pausing, he said, "Or should I call President Donskoy himself?"

The Kazak's eyes fell in resignation to the floor. He leaned back in his chair and pulled out a handkerchief to wipe his upper lip. He had no stomach to defy the rabid dog in Moscow.

"No, Comrade Colonel. The programming will commence immediately."

***

WHITE HOUSE

EXECUTIVE OFFICES CONFERENCE ROOM

WASHINGTON, D.C.

Vice President Koernig was in his element. He knew full well that this morning's meeting would be chaired by the President, but orchestrated by none other than himself. "Why I have to suffer this fool, I'll never know," he whispered under his breath. He knew the Chiefs of the Armed Services would back him, as would the Secretary of Defense and National Security Adviser James Peters. The CIA was iffy and Chief of Staff Waring was definitely not his, but overall, this meeting would belong to him and him alone.

As the President entered and sat down, the folders that were placed on the table at each chair were picked up and opened in unison.

"John, would you bring everyone up to speed on the latest information?" Cook asked his CIA director.

"Yes, Mr. President. Gentlemen, last night, Langley picked up information from Moscow. Apparently, Donskoy has ordered the retargeting of its missile sites in Kazakhstan. Their retargeting includes our missile sites and those of England and France. It is also rumored, though not confirmed, that civilian targets are included. The retargeting has already been put in place. In addition, Russian technicians have been installed to take over manual control at most sites in the Ukraine."

"John, any word on the missile sites within Russia?" asked NSA Director Peters.

"No. I'm sorry to say we have no confirmation one way or another. However, it is our opinion that Russia is using Kazakhstan as a trial balloon before retargeting its own. Within the next twenty-four to forty-eight hours we'll know. Believe me, we are working on it."

"Well, John, what does all this mean?" asked Cook.

The Vice President knew it was time to make his move. "Mr. President, it means that they have violated our agreements and the United States is in jeopardy. Once again, it is under your watch!"

"I know that!" said Cook. "But why? Why are they doing this? I've bent over backward to appease them."

"It's obvious, Mr. President, your policy has backfired. We have to look at an immediate quid pro quo to back them down, or if that doesn't work, something more drastic. Depending on the retargeting of the rest of their missiles, it could require the threat of a preemptive strike."

The President's face blanched in disbelief. His jaw dropped. "What did you say? You can't be serious!"

"Sir, it's an option that certainly must, at the very least, be looked at," said the Secretary of Defense. "James?"

The NSA Director paused before giving his measured response. He turned his palms upward in a gesture of resignation. "Well, Mr. President, we must, of course, consider all of our options. There certainly is no reason to leave any option off the table. In the short run, all options should be open for discussion."

CHAPTER 30

AS THE SUN POKED ITS HEAD ABOVE THE HORIZON, ITS FIRST beaming rays pierced the side windows of a jet bound for Atlanta. With a flight pillow tucked between her head and the window, Lisa's right eye cracked open enough to see the sunrise. She tucked her flight blanket up over her left shoulder. That was as much of the early morning that she wanted to enjoy.

Waking hours had always been difficult for Lisa. Her biological clock was set to that of an evening person, and in her mind, the only thing she wanted to see at six o'clock in the morning was the back of her eyelids. The wee hours didn't particularly bother her, as long they were experienced by someone else.

Bryan awoke with a start. He shook Lisa's arm and pulled the blanket off her shoulder. "Lisa…Lisa!" he whispered.

"Huh? What?"

"That newspaper clipping—the one that was in Jose's packet. Where is it?"

"What newspaper?" She shifted and stretched her body. "Oh yeah, it's in my purse—just a second." Groaning with exhaustion, she reached down, yanked open her purse and handed it to him with a long sigh. "Here, can I go back to sleep?"

"No. It's him! I know it is! It's my old law professor, Frederick Werner."

"Who are you talking about?"

"Freddie the Wiener! Well, that's what we used to call him behind his back at Yale." He turned the news clipping in his hands.

"How can you tell?" Lisa mumbled through a yawn.

"Pull out the magnifying glass and I'll show you."

Adjusting the glass in and out for enlargement, he pointed with his index finger. "See how he's kind of looking sideways?" With his finger tapping the old photo, he said, "Well, look at that ear."

"What ear? I don't see an ear."

"See the patch of hair missing over and behind it? It looks light a crescent moon. I'm telling you, it's him! That's Freddie's trademark. He called it a birth defect, but we all believed it was a war wound and that he was some old Nazi in hiding."

"Are you sure it's him?"

"Positive. I stared at that gross trademark for many boring lectures. See how there's still a sideburn? Oh yeah, it's him alright. That's why Jose said there was something else to show us. He was in all my classes with Freddie. In fact, it was Jose who gave him his crazy nickname."

"Why's he in that picture? Why do you think it was important to Jose?"

"I don't know, but that would be about his age in the early fifties."

"Bryan, I don't know what this means, but we need to get to Washington."

"Why?"

"Think about it," she responded. The cobwebs had cleared and her mind was focused. "Eva Braun changes identity and becomes Hilda Maier. Then she slips out of Germany, ends up in Argentina, has a child and the child dies. Jose looks into her background and gets killed. You call your embassy and hotel employees who shouldn't know us suddenly do. We get to Eva's place and she's dead with a news report buried in her hand. Someone then tries to blow us up inside the house. And what's the article that she clutched in her hand about? The Vice President of the United States burying his mother!"

"And the connection is?" he asked.

"I'm not sure, but I think we need to find this 'Freddie the Weiner.'"

"You must be right. I don't know why Werner is in that old photo, but if Jose died because of it, we'd damned well better find out. When we land, we can rent a car and drive to D.C. We'll notice if someone's tailing us. We can stay at my parents' home and no one will know we're there."

"Aren't they home?"

"That depends on where you call home. They maintain a home in Geneva, but they also have a Brownstone in Georgetown. They use it when Dad's there in an official capacity as the U.S. Governor of the World Bank. Right now, they're scheduled to vacation in Geneva. Dad must have flown back for the funeral of the Vice President's mother. I noticed his name in that press release—but they wouldn't have stayed over."

CHAPTER 31

THE WATER-STAINED CEILING FLOATED IN AND OUT OF Alexander Konstantinov's semi-lucid state of consciousness. There were times when the stains appeared just as they were. Other times they became great vortexes that sucked him forward, swallowing him up, denying him his very breath. It was at these moments when his greatest fears were met head on, for he shared this turbulent gorge with all forms of despised creatures: snakes with jaws agape, hissing and snapping their fangs at his face. He tried raising his hands to parry them away but they wouldn't move. His arms were belted to the bed. Rats were chewing and gnawing on the sides of his hands. Get off! Get off! Stop this, please!

"What?…Where am I?" he whispered.

"You are in Russia, Herr Weber—at a hospital for the criminally insane. Do you want to talk about your mission?"

"No! I'm Russian—Russian I tell you! Konstantinov—Alexander Konstantinov! I was born in St. Petersburg." The stains on the ceiling again came into view. He didn't want to go back to that maelstrom. He felt his wrists burning in pain as the restraints burrowed into his raw flesh.

"Herr Weber?…It is Herr Weber, you know," said the man in hospital whites. "We know all about you and what your little mission is, Jurgen. Do you want to talk about it? After all, they say confession is good for one's soul."

"No, damn you! I've told you my name is Alexander Konstantinov. I am a Russian diplomat. I was born in—"

"You may relax, Herr Weber. You're not going anywhere and you will talk soon enough. We'll take a short break for you to collect your thoughts. I shall return in ten minutes. If you don't talk about your mission, we will have to visit your 'little friends' again. Do you like your 'little friends,' Herr Weber? Perhaps with a stronger dosage, we could add a few more."

Konstantinov watched the door shut behind the man with the white coat. As his head turned the other way, his eyes fixed on the intravenous stand next to his bed. The devastating effects of the continuous flow of drugs into his body had taken its toll. He felt weak and knew he couldn't hold the truth back any longer. Of his own imminent death he was certain. He hoped that the welcomed end would come first.

The white coat of the departed attendant caused his mind to drift. He remembered the rows of beds with patients sitting upright against iron headboards. Covered with open running sores, their faces stared blankly forward. The men in white coats jotted onto their clipboards. This scene had crept into his mind a thousand times over the years.

He turned his head and faced the window. Rain was falling, tapping the black grimy window and running to the ground below. From there it flowed away, pulling his mind with it. Barely visible beyond the dark window was the convergence of the Oka and Volga rivers, their icy waters rushing together to form an even stronger current. The teeming eddies of water soon took on the look of another maelstrom. "No, please not again. Don't let them bite me. Make them go away," he whispered to no one. A line of tears crept down his cheek and disappeared into his pillow.

CHAPTER 32

THE RAIN HAD FINISHED FALLING, ALLOWING THE STREET lamps to give a picturesque sheen to the posh residential section of Georgetown. That was where the elite of America resided, and anyone who wanted power knew that was where they had to live. Deals were made there, as nowhere else. However, acceptance into this clique was sparse and always with a sponsor.

As his rental car came within half of a block of his parent's house, Bryan killed the lights and parked the car in an open spot two doors away. Before getting out, he scanned the neighborhood, paying close attention to the parked cars that dotted the street. Feeling sure that the cars were empty and no one was watching, he motioned to Lisa.

The walk to the front door was short, but Bryan felt as if they were in an illuminated fishbowl. Every drop of rain that splashed onto a fallen leaf pulled his attention. As his thumb pressed the door latch down, he looked around once more and prayed his parents had not changed the security code. Holding his breath, Bryan waited for the system to disarm. Seeing the green light come on, he exhaled and gave a relieved look to Lisa. He ushered her in and locked the door behind them. Worn out from the flight, he let his travel bag drop to the floor and headed for the library to find the nearest couch.

Still wary, Lisa walked around, checking for anything that might seem amiss.

"Do you think anyone is around—a maid, a housekeeper? Don't you think we should check it out?"

He jumped up and moved toward Lisa with a guilty look. "Sorry. I guess I felt like a kid again—home, safe and sound. No, they don't have any live-in help, but let's look around anyway."

A careful search produced nothing. They relaxed and after Bryan had his fill of snacks, they went to bed, made love and fell asleep in each other's arms—exhausted.

Bryan's sleep was deep, but Lisa tossed and turned—the events of the last two weeks preyed upon her mind. The scene of her mother entering that fiery door exploded in her nightmare. She awoke with a start.

She looked over at Bryan sleeping and then slipped out of the tall, four-poster bed. Wrapping an oversized terry robe around her, she descended to the main level. The aged mahogany staircase creaked under her steps and she paused as she heard Bryan stir. Comfortable that she hadn't disturbed him, she crept into the kitchen, poured a glass of juice and took two cookies into the library.

With casual curiosity, she perused the voluminous bookshelves and noticed a framed picture of Bryan's father with J.P. Morgan, Jr. and Joseph Kennedy. Next to it was one with President John Kennedy and Vice President Johnson, followed by one with Nixon, then Ford and last, Carter.

The man certainly has friends in high places, she thought. I guess party politics was only a minor nuisance. Moving to the next set of shelves, she noticed the familiar face of Willy Brandt, then Helmut Kohl. True to form, Bryan's father stood next to each man, looking as relaxed as if he were a roving big brother at a fraternity party.

That's the key, she thought. The world runs on decisions made by a few...a handful of elitists. Lisa felt the story that the cozy walls were telling her. This man is the U.S. Governor of the Board of the World Bank—how convenient. Yes, these people transcend nations. I wonder how many phone calls were made right here in this study that set global actions on a predetermined course. How many billions of dollars traded hands each time interest rates were tweaked? Where does the world's money go when stock markets suffer their "Black Tuesdays?" The money goes in and multinational corporations receive and spend it, but then it disappears when all the markets take a dive. One day the money is there, the next day it's not. It's like a global shell game, but a game nonetheless, and its players are few in number.

Her eyes continued to scan the room and she couldn't help but feel was that something out of place. The whole room was a rogue's gallery, a veritable "who's who" in big time geo-politics. This is a man's room, but the man doesn't seem to value his family, she thought. It's all about power and connections—that's what drives this person. Why aren't there any pictures of his wife on display, or Bryan or his brother? There's no happiness or joy in this room, no pictures of happy times that normal families cherish and put on display.

Her thoughts turned to Bryan. Who is this person I've fallen in love with? Good God, will he turn out like his father? No, I can't believe that…he's warm and has depth in his heart. I wonder what he was like as a boy. I'd love to see some of his baby pictures. There must be a family album.

She looked down and opened a door in the cabinets—nothing but clutter and periodicals. Opening another door, she saw several photo albums standing in a row, their dates on the cover in chronological order. Pulling one out, she saw what she recognized as more current photos. Oh look, she thought, pictures of Bryan's graduation from Yale! He looks so young…Christmas shots…this looks like his mother's birth-day…this must be a vacation, perhaps in Switzerland. Yes, definitely in Switzerland. What a cute picture of Bryan and his mother standing on a verandah with mountains in the background. Oh, there's his father bent over talking with two men at a table…My God! It can't be! One of the men is missing an ear—there's a bald spot around it—he's Frederick Werner! Why is he there? Why would Bryan's college professor be *there* with his father? That can't be a coincidence…

Lisa skipped to the third album in from the left, the time period shifting to his parents' early marriage years. She flipped through the wedding photos; his father in uniform, then his mother smiling and pregnant. They looked like happy times…two people starting out their lives with high hopes and expectations.

Turning the pages back to earlier years, her mood shifted. She became somber as she saw the photos of Bryan's father sitting in uniform at his desk, then shots of him walking through bombed-out streets. Buildings were left half standing amid mounds of crumpled concrete, brick and steel. In the background, scavengers picked through debris for anything to sustain their meager lives. Was this Berlin? she thought…Hard to say. His father is in uniform, talking with…she strained to look at the grainy photos…looks like German bureaucrats. I remember that matters concerning Berlin were decided by an inter-Allied council called…Oh what was it? Kommandatura! Yes, this must be one of those meetings.

The next photo showed the same people. This time something caught Lisa's eye. Under a civilian fedora was a man with a missing ear—it's him! So, Werner again, she thought. The man certainly gets around. What's the date? Pulling the photo out of its black corner holders, she flipped it over and read the small caption on its backside: Berlin, 1946.

Bryan was in the middle of a fairly pleasant dream when the lights flipped on. He looked up and saw Lisa standing in the doorway with several books under her arms.

"Bryan, it's time for you to wake up."

CHAPTER 33

BERLIN - AN ESTIMATED 10,000 SKINHEADS RAMPAGED through the city during the night. Rioting, looting and destruction were the worst in this country since the infamous "Kristallnacht" of the 1930s. Unable to control the outpouring of violence with local police, Chancellor Anneke Mueller has called in the army reserves to restore order. A spokesperson for Mueller said the skinheads are demanding the deportation of all Polish migrant workers and a return to pre-World War II borders. Hans Baecker, leader of the skinheads in Berlin, has called upon German nationals everywhere to begin protests.

ASSOCIATED PRESS

WASHINGTON, D.C. - Press Secretary Morton Price announced that the Russian retargeting of its Kazakhstan missiles has left the U.S. with "no alternative" other than to retarget its missiles back to the coordinates that existed prior to the conclusion of the Salt Agreements. He also announced that the administration does not know if this move by the Russian government signals an actual return to the Cold War, but the U.S. is prepared to match the Russians step by step.

NEW HAVEN, CONNECTICUT

Lisa had a feeling of déjà vu as she watched the flowing mass of students walking the sidewalks of Yale University. Although it had been a little over one year since her graduation from the University of Florida, the events of the last month made it feel like an eternity. She looked at their carefree faces and felt a distance of age that belied the timeline difference.

"Nice campus, Harmon. It must've been a tough three years for you—you know, talking with that silver spoon in your mouth."

Bryan smiled. "An absolute ordeal, that's for sure. Oh, there's the Law

Building, third down on the left. It's a venerable old place, huh? You can park out front and I'll run in and make an appointment with Freddie."

Climbing the steps of the ivy-covered building, he felt as if he were still in school. He paused as he reached for the door of the secretary's office. An image of Jose jumped in front of him and caused him to stop in the middle of his step. A coed leaving the office almost bumped into him and Bryan apologized before entering the room.

"Hello, my name is Bryan Harmon. I'm a former student of Dr. Werner and I would like to schedule an appointment with him, please."

The student secretary looked surprised. "I'm sorry, but Dr. Werner has taken an extended leave of absence."

"When will he return?"

"I'm afraid we don't know. Dr. Werner had a stroke three weeks ago and he's been in critical care at University Hospital ever since. We have no idea when he'll return because of his medical condition. I haven't known him all that long, but he seems to be the nicest—"

"Pardon me," Bryan interrupted. "I know he's wonderful, but could you tell me his hospital room number? It's important that I talk to him."

"Well, certainly, but they won't let you visit—intensive care and all that, you know? Anyway, he's in room 210 in the critical care ward. Apparently he's rarely conscious, and when he is, he only babbles incoherently." She turned red as she realized Bryan might be a family member. "Oh gosh, I'm sorry—I assumed everyone knew about that. Professor Deland has taken over as interim department head. Maybe I could make an appointment for you with him?"

"No, but thanks anyway." Bryan looked over his shoulder and down the hall. The first door on the left opened and a student walked out with folders under his arm.

"Is that one of Dr. Werner's family members?"

"No. He's a student that Professor Deland sent over for some notes on a class. I guess he must've had a hard time locating them. He's been in there for a long time."

As the young man passed, Bryan excused himself, turned and followed him out the door. Running down the steps, Bryan raced to Lisa and jumped in.

"Quick. Follow that student in the blue jacket, but stay back."

She held the car back and they sat in silence as they followed the young man for several blocks to a student parking lot.

"That's strange," Bryan said. "He was supposed to be getting class notes from Werner's office to take to the lecture hall. Instead, he's getting into his car and leaving. Look! Some 'student' car—a brand new BMW!"

"What's going on?" Lisa asked.

"Let him go and turn left over there. I'll explain on the way to University Hospital."

***

Walking down the hospital corridor, Bryan tugged Lisa's arm to change direction as he spotted a blue and white hospital sign labeled: Critical Care. He looked over the duty nurse's shoulder and saw his old professor lying in a glass CCU cubicle.

"Excuse me. My name is Bryan Harmon. I'd like to see Frederick Werner, if I may."

"Are you a member of the immediate family?"

"Yes, a grandson from out of state, and she is my fiancée."

"Okay. Follow me, but you can't stay longer than five minutes. He's a very sick man and seldom regains consciousness. I'll bring you in another chair so you can sit by his bed."

"Has he asked for anyone or anything?" Lisa asked.

"No. He just mutters something about the HRS, but this behavior is not uncommon for stroke victims."

"HRS?"

"Yes. More like, um, he 'heard the HRS,' or something close to that."

"He 'heard the HRS?'" Lisa asked again.

"Yeah, I must have heard him say that dozens of times—always with a sense of anxiety. I guess he's desperate to talk about the HRS."

"Bryan?"

He thought hard for a few seconds, then frowned and shook his head. "I don't have the slightest idea."

The nurse checked Werner's tubes and monitors and brushed the hair off his forehead. "If you need me, press this button. I'll be close by." The nurse left the room and closed the door. Lisa's eyes trailed behind her. Through the glass, she saw another nurse staring with a frown as she picked up the telephone and dialed a number.

Lisa's attention returned to the lifeless body on the bed. "He looks pathetic."

"Professor?…Can you hear me? It's Harmon, Bryan Harmon. Do you remember me?"

Like a pair of dusty tomb doors, his grayish-blue eyelids cracked open.

"Harmon…Blaine? It's…to see…"

"No, Professor. I'm Bryan. You know, Blaine Harmon's son. How are you, sir?"

Frederick Werner's hand shot up and clutched his visitor's shirt, as a man drowning in water would grab at a life preserver. His filmy eyes pleaded Bryan as if this was his last chance.

"Blaine…" He coughed and his lungs wheezed. "I was always loyal… always…"

With each cough, Bryan felt his old mentor's fingernails dig deeper into his skin.

"Hurd…vee…HRS…" He coughed again—deep, guttural. A large gob of phlegm came up into his mouth. His shaking hand tried to reach for his spit trough, but couldn't reach it. Lisa grabbed it and held it under his mouth, allowing Werner to spit it out. "Hurd…HRS." His grip slackened and his hand slid to the bed. His eyelids closed once more.

"Professor? Professor…?" Bryan knew there wouldn't be an answer—at least not now.

***

As cars passed by, Bryan stared straight ahead, his mind racing, his driving on mental autopilot. Concerned, Lisa turned to look at him. He seemed lost in thought. She turned her head forward again. Her whole body jumped as Bryan's palm slammed onto the dashboard.

"That's it!" he shouted. "Freddie hadn't *heard* anything about the HRS. He was saying HURD versus HRS! H.U.R.D.!" He grinned in triumph as he spelled it out. "Listen. It was a Supreme Court case—HURD versus the HRS. Werner used it as a prime study case back when I was in law school. There was this child, Thomas Hurd, who was adopted by this couple. When he reached adulthood, he went to the HRS to get information on his biological mother who had given him up at age five. HRS wouldn't release the information under privacy laws, so he sued them and lost. He appealed and the lower court ruling was overturned.

HRS then appealed to the Supreme Court and they *lost*. Werner always thought this was a landmark case in privacy law."

Lisa was bewildered. "What does that have to do with us?"

"I'm not sure, but he thought I was my father. For some reason, Werner wanted to tell him about this particular case."

"But he was drugged and delirious," Lisa argued.

"No. Not really. He was in and out, yes, but when he was conscious, he *needed* to talk about this case. I'm telling you, I felt him grip my arm. His nails dug into my skin—hard. He looked straight into my eyes as if the fate of the whole world depended on me getting this information. He needed my father to *know* this."

"Why are you turning around?" she asked. "Where are we going?"

"Back to Yale. We've got to get into his office...before someone else does."

CHAPTER 34

AN OVERSIZED LEATHER CHAIR STRAINED UNDER THE weight of the obese man who leaned back with a phone tucked between his ear and shoulder. His fingers rolled a silver dollar back and forth across their tops in a motion that tried to calm his frayed nerves. The dollar dropped to the floor as the call rang in.

"Where are they now?" His voice sounded hoarse, almost desperate.

"They're at the father's house in Georgetown. Do you want them eliminated?"

"No. Not in Washington! Did you tap the phone?"

"We're recording as we speak."

"Good. He'll call his father, and when he does, they'll go to him in Geneva. Otto will visit them after he calls. He will take them out there—all of them."

"You can't mean Blaine Harmon?…His wife? Surely you can't—"

"I said *all* of them!" he growled, then lit another cigarette. "It will appear to be a terrorist act. Feed the media an anonymous call. Contact me when it's done—not before."

***

U.S. COMMAND CENTER
KANDAHAR, AFGHANISTAN

Staring at the map on the wall in front of him, Brigadier General James O'Donnell stood with his hands clasped behind his back. His long military career had taken its mental toll on him. He shook his head in disgust, let go of his hands and walked back to his desk in a sour mood.

As he approached his chair, a framed photo of his wife and two children caught his attention. For a moment, his feelings of frustration and inadequacy left him and he clung to the warm sensation that overtook him. God, I miss them, he thought. Tim and Julie are two years older than this picture. Warmth turned to sadness again as he realized he had seen them only three times in the last two years, and even those visits were short. Shit, I couldn't even make Tim's graduation. You call that a father? Hell, I prayed for this chance; anything was better than directing the "meals on wheels" campaigns in Haiti and Somalia, but this is worse—acting as a backyard fence between people whose hatred goes back centuries. I can't seem to win this war, and can't stop the bloodshed either. Hell, I can't even—

A buzzing from the intercom interrupted Jim O'Donnell's rambling thoughts. For a brief second, he didn't remember his surroundings. "Yes?"

"Sir, Major General Sash is on line one," announced his aide.

"Thank you."

Looking down at the flashing button, Jim hesitated to pick up, for he already knew the topic of conversation. With a sigh he said, "Good afternoon, Bill."

"Jim, I just got off with Chief Belden and he's in agreement that we need to pull back."

"I'll set up a line along the Eastern sector," he replied with a heavy heart.

"Jim, this is no reflection on you. I want you to know that no one else could've done better. This one just wasn't in the cards, but we do want you to pull back to Ghazni and await further orders for a pullback to Kabul."

"Kabul? Bill—"

"This is not open for discussion, Jim," Sash interrupted. His voice changed to firm and short. "We can't take any more losses from the Taliban. The air strikes haven't had the effect we were hoping for. In fact, they've actually hurt us on the diplomatic front. Sorry, Jim, I'm afraid it's Ghazni."

"I'll begin withdrawal preparations immediately," O'Donnell replied. He tried not to show the disgust he felt.

"There's a bigger picture here, Jim, you know that. We've got to secure our position—however precarious it is. By the way, did you hear that the asshole Ruskies announced today that they've sent security troops flooding across the Ukraine border?"

"What?"

"Yeah, Donskoy says their sole mission is to protect Russian-owned missile sites from destruction. We think they're going to retarget them on Europe. Looks like these troops may only be a precursor to their total takeover."

"Damn those stinking bastards! What the hell are they trying to do, start fucking World War Three? Ike and Monty should have listened to Patton." He shook his head in disgust. "Anyway, Bill, thanks for the kind words and consider it done."

CHAPTER 35

LISA LOOKED DOWN HER NOSE AND DREW A DEEP BREATH. She raised her eyes to the ceiling and exhaled loudly for emphasis. The student secretary of the Law Department was reasonably seasoned, but wasn't prepared for the rapid fire onslaught being leveled at her.

"I don't think you understand. Professor Deland is in the middle of his lecture and he needs Dr. Werner's reference book—now!" Lisa shouted. She bent over the reception desk and placed her nose several inches from the intimidated girl. "Do you know what the word *now* means?"

"But you don't have any identification."

"I told you, I left my ID in the lecture hall. Would you like me to run all the way back and get it so some pencil-pushing witch like you can prove that I am, in fact, myself? Never mind! Give me your name so I can tell Deland who screwed up his lecture."

"Oh, all right! Go on in. Next time make sure you bring your ID."

Lisa walked past the receptionist's desk and down the hall. She breathed a sigh of relief after she entered Werner's office, closed the door and leaned back against it. Now, find that damned book and get the hell out of here, she thought. Okay, black book set...these are maroon...these are beige...Supreme Court decisions...19...79. I haven't seen this many books outside of a library!

Okay! Here it is...Supreme Court Decisions, 1979! Ugh! It's wedged in tight. Now, getting it out is the next trick. As she continued to tug at the book, it broke free, tumbled through her hands and hit the floor with a loud thud. She picked it up and spotted some papers sticking out between the pages. She opened the book and examined its contents. What's this?...An old copy of a birth certificate...in Spanish? It reads: Albert Maier, February 27, 1946, Church of San Carlos, Buenos Aires, Argentina. Let's see...this one is a death certificate: Albert Maier, June

22, 1951. Hmm...This one's a—

Her body froze as the door opened behind her. She turned to launch another tirade against the nosey receptionist. This time she was accompanied by a man—she assumed another professor.

"Did you find what you needed?" He looked at the book in Lisa's hands.

"Oh, uh, yes! Yes, of course," Lisa stammered. "Right here, thank you. I'll tell Professor Deland you were most helpful—good day." She tucked the large text to her chest, looked down at the floor and walked past the pair into the hall.

It wasn't until she saw Bryan pulling up the car that her heart stopped its intense pounding. Then she heard him speak. "Did you have any problems?" he asked.

In a flash, her emotions poured out and she spun around and screamed, "I hate this! I hate all of this shit. Don't ever make me go through this again. I can't...I just can't..." Lisa covered her face with her hands. Her body went limp. The cumulative effect of the murders, the bombings, the stalking and the relentless pursuit was finally breaking her. At the same time, she felt the shame of having dumped on the person she loved.

Bryan saw a small parking lot and eased the car into a space. He looked to see if they had been followed. It was safe. His looked back to Lisa. He knew her pain, her fear. He also knew that this woman had been sent to him...but why? He didn't know, but that feeling was there—that same haunting feeling he had when he first met her. Or was that the first time? Somewhere in his past—he couldn't put his finger on it, but it was real. She was real, as if they had been soul mates for eternity—not just in his head, it was deep and it cut to the very core of his spirit. Look at her pain, he thought. It tears my heart apart to see her in this pain. She is my heart and her pain is mine. "I love you, Lisa." He pulled her into his arms.

"I'm sorry. I was afraid that I'd get caught. So much has gone on for so long and I took it out on you—the person I love." Her grip intensified as if he might disappear like her mother.

"I know, I know."

She pulled her head back. All was right—no words were needed. They embraced again, and for the moment, time disappeared.

After a while she pulled away and ran her fingers through her long, shimmering hair, pulling it back. "I'm okay. Let me show you what I found."

Without thinking, he asked, "Did you get the right year?"

Her face turned to granite. With eyes that made him feel two inches tall, she cracked a sarcastic smile, continuing the icy glare.

"Sorry," was all he could muster. Even that was barely audible.

"Not only did I get the right book, but maybe you'd like to see a death certificate for Albert Maier, or this, a copy of a birth certificate for William Koernig."

Puzzled, he held the papers in his hands. Bryan tried to make the connection. His eyes darted back and forth. Lisa opened a thin grey booklet and said, "Try this."

Shaking his head in confusion, his jaw dropped open, leaving his mouth agape. "A passport?...For William Koernig? That's the Vice President! This picture is of a boy, what, five or six? The address is in Harrisburg, Pennsylvania—that's where the Vice President was raised. What's this all about?...Why would Freddie have these documents hidden in his office?"

Lisa flipped the next paper over and read it aloud. "This is a letter of transit. It allowed one Fredrick Werner to leave Berlin on an American military plane, acting as a diplomatic courier. It allowed transit to Zurich, Marseilles, Tangiers, Buenos Aires, then to Washington. Look at the signature."

He took the document, scanned the front and turned it over. His hands quivered. "Blaine Harmon?" The color drained from his face.

Lisa handed over the next paper with a solemn face. "Look at this one. It's an approved letter of withdrawal for Werner. It allowed him to withdraw one million U.S. dollars from an account at the Banc of Zurich. It's also signed by your father."

Bryan Harmon, always quick with words and glib of tongue, said nothing. He handed the documents back to Lisa, put the car in gear and drove off. For miles his head never moved and his eyes stared straight ahead. Silence held...fifteen, twenty minutes—it seemed like an eternity.

When she could bear it no longer, she asked, "Where are we going?" There was no response. "Bryan, please!" she begged. "At least you have your father and mother alive. Don't shut me out. I don't have anyone but you."

"We're going back to the Brownstone to pick up our things. I also want to pick up some memorabilia. It's time to visit my illustrious father."

"In Geneva?" she asked. "Are you going to call him first?"

"Oh yes. You can be damn sure of that."

CHAPTER 36

ASSOCIATED PRESS

BERLIN - THOUSANDS OF GERMAN ULTRA-NATIONALISTS and brown-shirted skinheads crossed the Oder and Neisse Rivers and began rioting in Polish cities as far eastward as Wroclaw (formerly Breslau). Polish police, dressed in riot gear, were dispatched to the cities, but have yet to restore order. The Polish government appealed to NATO and will send a formal protest to the United Nations tomorrow, arguing that Germany has given benign approval to the riots. In response, Germany stated it cannot stop the riots, short of sending its own troops across the border into Poland.

ASSOCIATED PRESS

WASHINGTON, D.C. - White House Press Secretary Morton Price stated at a news conference today that Vice President William Koernig will be flying to Germany to review the situation in Poland. He will meet with the Chancellor on Friday morning.

ZURICH, SWITZERLAND

As the gilded grandfather clock reported the first of its scheduled nine chimes, the phone rang. The heavyset man entered the den and closed the door behind him. "Yes?"

"They're on their way."

"Geneva?"

"Yes," said the caller, wanting to venture nothing more than needed.

"When do they arrive?"

"Tomorrow, two p.m., Swiss time. What about Otto?"

"He'll be there."

"Will he need help?"

"No—fewer complications that way."

"Anything else?"

"Remove the tap on the phone and sanitize the Brownstone. The Harmons won't have need for it anymore."

CHAPTER 37

PRESIDENT COOK SAT AT THE CENTER OF THE LONG CONFERence table. His irritation shifted to embarrassment as he fidgeted with the pen in his hands. The full security staff sitting around him was complete with the exception of the Vice President. Cook stood up, turned and began pacing. Chairman of the Joint Chiefs of Staff Belden looked across the table to SecDef Collins and telegraphed the feeling that something was about to hit the proverbial fan.

"Where the hell's Koernig?" Cook blurted out. "He knew damn well this meeting started at nine sharp!"

"Mr. President," said Security Advisor Peters, "I believe the Vice President is on a call with the German ambassador as we speak."

"So I guess we all just *wait*, but for what?"

"Sir, the German situation *is* half of this meeting," said John Martin of CIA, "and I'm sure whatever information the Vice President can provide will be—"

"I know! It just pisses me off that I—" Cook's voice came to an abrupt halt as the opening of the door announced Koernig's entrance. He strutted in with the air of a peacock.

"Mr. President," he said, giving Cook a curt nod of his head. "Sorry gentlemen, but I had Ambassador Siedler on the phone. Shall we begin?"

The last question rubbed a raw nerve with Cook. He ground his teeth. His blood boiled. He was about to unload on the Vice President when a lewd picture of himself with an eighteen-year-old woman flashed in his mind. He felt the heat of embarrassment, as if everyone in the room had seen the image in his head. Instead, trying to maintain what little dignity was left, he dropped his eyes and stared at the table. "All right, let's hear from CIA on those missiles in the Ukraine...John?"

"Excuse me, Mr. President," interrupted Koernig. "I think we should address the Polish situation first."

Lowering his eyes again to the table, the Commander in Chief replied, "That's fine...I guess."

Koernig smiled. "Now, as I was saying, I talked with Ambassador Siedler. It appears, gentlemen, that the German-Polish Border Treaty is about to be buried, and may it rest in peace. The German people have—"

Cook squeezed his pen, nearly breaking it in half. "But this is an agreement that both countries signed in 1990, Mr. Vice President, and it's sanctioned by NATO—of which *both* countries are now members."

"Yes, Mr. President," replied Koernig, "I know the history. It started with Gerald Ford and his ridiculous Helsinki Accords, and it is true that Helmut Kohl brokered this silly border treaty, but did it ever occur to you that no one bothered to ask the German people themselves whether or not *they* accepted it? Or did anyone consult with the Polish people? In the aftermath of the war, thirteen million Germans and five million Poles and Balts were relocated under international law. Whoever spoke for *them*? The boundaries of this whole area are a result of the United States, England and Russia deciding unilaterally on what they thought might be in their own interest. The further fact is that it affected untold millions of people, left a thousand years of history in a state of flux and is only now returning to its natural boundaries."

"But, Mr. Vice President, the reality was that the Soviet Union had more to say about this than the Allied Powers, and still does," SecState Holden interjected.

"Soviet Union?" bellowed Koernig. "What Soviet Union? We are talking about Russia. *Russia*, gentlemen, and right now they are nothing but an economic basket case. Apparently the Secretary of State has forgotten that the Soviet Union as we knew it is dead and in shambles. Donskoy rattles sabers and moves his troops around, but the bottom line is that he doesn't have the financial resources to extend power beyond his own borders. It took them years just to put down the Chechen rabble, and not even Donskoy is certain that they have succeeded. No, Mr. Secretary, I think not."

JCOS Belden was the next to offer his opinion. "With all due respect, Mr. Vice President, we still have the matter of Russia's rattling of her sabers that you wisely acknowledge. There's only one problem—those sabers are ICBM missiles—and they are being retargeted as we speak."

Koernig yielded no ground. He looked at Cook and said, "Of course, the ultimate decision rests in the hands of you, Mr. President, but I strongly recommend supporting Germany's desire to recertify its prewar borders beyond the Oder-Niesse line. Moreover, it would be foolish not to support our only remaining ally in Afghanistan. Without the English and French, German troops will be our only ally, and without them, our mission will turn out to be another ten-year Afghanistan quagmire. Let me be clear, gentlemen, Germany *will* ultimately reclaim its land. It will happen sooner or later...and it *is* the natural order."

With the demeanor of a man beaten, Cook stared down at the conference table. His voice, sullen and barely audible, mumbled the words, "I understand the Poles have petitioned NATO and will make a formal protest to the Security Council tomorrow."

"That is correct, Mr. President," said Bert Holden.

"Then have the proper, well-couched response on my desk by this afternoon for my approval. Something to the effect that although the U.S. still supports the German-Polish Border Treaty in principle, it must acknowledge that the accord does allow for peaceful modification of boundaries according to the will of the people. Then follow up with a call for a peaceful solution. This will placate the Germans, and maybe the Polish government can gain control of the situation. Now, what about those missiles in the Ukraine, John?"

"Sir, the information I have is current as of this morning," replied John Martin of the CIA. "We have confirmation that the Russians are in control of all missile sites in Ukraine. The retargeting of these sites isn't known as of this time. However, the rumor is that they'll be targeted at Germany and possibly at our positions in Afghanistan."

"Damn! John, I want that information to me as soon as it comes through."

"Immediately, Mr. President."

Koernig leaned forward, placed his elbows on the conference table and clasped his hands. His eyes met every person's in the room, drawing all of their attention to him as if he were the command center. "Mr. President, I believe we're in the midst of an emergency that's already equal to the Cuban Missile Crisis." He shook his head in feigned disbelief. "Apparently your quid pro quo policy hasn't been successful. Our actions haven't caused any alteration of Russian behavior. They've simply not worked. Therefore, I recommend that we consider a far stronger response."

"Do we know of any additional troop movements, John?" asked JCOS Belden. He focused on John Martin, then on SecDef Collins.

"No confirmation as of yet, but there are reports of a series of mobilizations forming," replied Martin.

"Any probable destinations indicated?" asked Belden.

"These are old Warsaw Pact divisions and their probable course could only be westward. And that course would be Poland," said Martin.

"Alright then," said Cook, "let's talk about Afghanistan."

"Situation deteriorating, Mr. President," said Collins, "and in rapid order."

CHAPTER 38

DRIVING UP THE LONG GRAVEL APPROACH, OTTO REMEM-
bered the last time he had visited Blaine Harmon in the cream-colored,
stucco chalet. It was nine springs ago and the tulips had just opened
their buds, yielding their splash of color that foretold the change of the
season. Otto had just returned from the Banc of Zurich with a suitcase
of money to be couriered to the United States. He then thought of Kurt
Koehler, his contact from the bank. It was unfortunate; I'd known him
since 1955...Nice man. He was always good to me. I shouldn't have had
to kill him, but then, orders are orders.

The sound of the doorbell brought him out of his pensive state. Same
door chime, he thought. I always liked that tune. As the door opened,
Otto saw that Blaine Harmon was stunned by his presence. "Otto? Otto
Kunsler...Is that you?"

"Yes, it's me...Good to see you again, Herr Harmon."

Blaine extended his hand in greeting, but tried to block him from
coming into the house. "Otto, what, uh...what brings you here? It's been
what...ten years?"

"Nine to be exact, Herr Harmon." His voice was low and guttural,
showing not the least emotion. "May I? It's been a long journey getting
here." He forced a step forward.

"Oh, yes, please come in." With his arm extended, Blaine motioned
him toward the living room.

Otto led the way, enjoying the view of the snow-covered mountains
that lay beyond the tall walls of glass. He turned in front of a semicircu-
lar sofa and sat down, his back rigid and straight. "Herr Harmon, I wish
I could tell you that my visit is not business, but I cannot. How is your
lovely wife Mary?" He scanned the room, his ears open for the smallest
of telltale sounds.

"Mary? Uh, she is well thank you. She is in town, picking up something from the market."

Otto knew exactly what had to be done. He was sure he could take all of them out at any second. Mary? No problem. He would wait for her to return and let her discover the gruesome scene before he disposed of her. Otto liked that scenario. It was the sadistic pleasure of watching his intended victims squirm in fear and mental anguish that excited him. Besides, he had a fierce dislike for Blaine Harmon—that nose-in-the-air asshole who acted like he was above all this. Worse, he couldn't tolerate Blaine's son becoming one of them. Why should this panty-waist have the plum job? Why should he have the son and family I sacrificed?

"And your son, Bryan?"

"Bryan, is coming for a short visit. He's bringing a young lady with him—I believe that means he's settling down."

"Yes, Herr Harmon, I *do* think he is getting serious...perhaps too serious."

Blaine caught the inflection in Otto's voice. "Whatever do you mean?"

"Your son, Herr Harmon, has come across certain information—information that could possibly jeopardize our entire mission."

"What?" Blaine's jaw dropped. "What information are you talking about?"

"He knows about Hilda, Eva, Wetzel, Koehler and Werner..." Otto paused, intensifying his glare and lowering his brow, "and also Eva's son."

"How do you know this? How can you be certain?"

"Because of the girl your son is bringing to meet you. Her name is Lisa Brandt. Does her surname ring any bells, Herr Harmon?"

Blaine's face wrinkled, showing the strain of recollection. He queried further, "Brandt...where've I heard that name before?"

"You may recall, Herr Harmon, Eva Braun's dentist was a Dr. Hans Brandt—Lisa Brandt's grandfather. He's the one who switched her dental records. This girl, Lisa, got your son involved after she stumbled onto notes her grandfather had made about the identity change with Hilda Maier."

"Of course, I remember; the switch was essential to get Eva out of Germany with Adolph's child, but didn't the dentist commit suicide?"

"Ah yes, Herr Harmon, I almost forgot...you have always been naive. No, he didn't commit suicide. He was...shall we say, disposed of—but in an untidy manner. Somehow, Dr. Brandt made notes of Eva's passage to

Argentina, which included Koehler and Wetzel. He also left a message to get the information of the switched dental records to the American army. We're not sure how, but this grandchild must have discovered them in her grandfather's office."

"How could this have been allowed to happen? That house should have been thoroughly sanitized or destroyed."

"Need I remind you that it was 1945? There wasn't any time left. The Russian army was ready to overrun the city. In any case, Herr Harmon, that is all ancient history, is it not? We must deal with the facts as they are now. And those are that Lisa Brandt took the information to the U.S. Embassy in Berlin, and to Bryan, I'm afraid. Of course, our contacts in the embassy notified us immediately." Otto sensed that Blaine's patience had grown thin.

"Why wasn't this handled at that time?" Blaine blurted out. "Why wasn't my son shielded?"

"Several attempts were made, Herr Harmon, but either this young woman is very lucky indeed or there is more about her than we know. In any case, she *did* get him involved and he seems to be a willing accomplice. Be assured, we have followed their moves—everywhere."

"Everywhere? Just where in the hell is everywhere?"

"We tried to control her in Berlin several times. Each attempt was thwarted—some with the help of your son. Her mother and roommate were killed, but she got away."

"*Killed*? What do you mean killed?" Beads of sweat appeared on his forehead and upper lip. He pulled out a handkerchief and wiped his face.

"Would the word eliminated soothe your tender feelings? As I said, Herr Harmon, you have always been naïve. Money and power were what you wanted, but you were always happy not to know the mechanics that are necessary to achieve our mission. The mother, the friend...let's just say that they were expendable. The target was the girl. What she knew had to be controlled, contained. She eluded us, thanks in part, to help from your son."

Blaine shifted in his seat. "But he's being groomed to be one of us!"

"Well, apparently no longer, I am sorry to say," said Otto. "Unfortunately, he is now part of the control problem. Lisa and your son went to Buenos Aires, where he had an attorney friend living down there—a man named Jose Merido. We controlled him, but—"

"What?" Blaine interrupted, "Jose is dead?"

"Yes. A most unfortunate turn of events," Otto replied, his words as cold and icy as if he were discussing the weather outside. "As I was saying, Herr Harmon, we controlled him. Unfortunately he had already provided your son with information—information which led him to Eva. They were in her house the night she was killed. We don't believe they had time to find anything, but they were able to follow Merido's leads to our common friend Werner—and hence, our mission."

"Stop! This is ludicrous! What information could've been available?"

"Information on Wetzel…birth certificate, death certificate…" His voice trailed off.

"You mean Wilhelm Maier…William Koernig?"

"Yes. Do you see our concern *now*, Herr Harmon?"

"Yes. Yes of course, but what about Frederick Werner? He has always been loyal. Surely he said nothing."

"We don't know. Werner had a stroke before we could control him. After his stroke, he became a babbling idiot. Your son visited him in the hospital, then went to his office and removed a book. We don't know what was in it, but we fear your son found something. We believe that is why he wants to see you now."

"What could Werner have that would jeopardize our plans?"

"Herr Harmon, we all have information that is vital for the completion of the greater mission."

Wiping his forehead again, Blaine thought, why does he keep calling me Herr Harmon? It's as if I'm someone he's never known?

Blaine Harmon, man of power, wealth, diplomatic skill, felt naked and impotent. In a matter of minutes, everything he had—money, influence, title—had been obliterated. He felt fear—raw fear. He feared for Bryan, his wife, Mary…and even himself.

"Are you sure of this, Otto? Couldn't there be some mistake? I mean, I'm sure that—"

As Blaine pleaded, he saw a small, menacing grin crack on Otto's face. "We both know that answer, Herr Harmon, and we both know what must be done."

Blaine could sit no longer, his legs ached and his body felt as if it had been slammed against a wall. He rose to stretch his legs and relieve his tension. In a lightning move, Otto reacted by thrusting his hand into his jacket. Blaine saw the swift movement, the bulge in Otto's suit. He sat back down and Otto's hand eased its way back out in unison. He knew he was trapped. He was a fly caught in a web and the spider was moving in for the strike.

"Danke, Herr Harmon. Please, make no sudden movements again. Now, what time did you say your son and his friend would arrive?"

"Twelve o'clock or thereabouts, that's about..." Blaine made a quick move with his left hand to expose his watch. Out of the corner of his eye, he again caught the flash movement of Otto's hand. He froze. Blaine knew he had made another mistake. "Sorry. Maybe ten minutes, maybe sooner."

"As I said earlier, Herr Harmon, I am here to control an unfortunate situation...not necessarily to kill. When your son arrives, perhaps a little discussion might aid us in our judgment of his actions. Perhaps we should give the young man the benefit of a proper explanation. Yes?"

Blaine's voice quivered. "Yes, yes."

"And your wife, Mary, she is to return when?"

"She said she would return before they arrived. I don't know what's taking her so long."

"Relax, Herr Harmon. For some reason you seem anxious."

Blaine's hypertense body jumped as he heard the sound of one car door shut, then another. He thought to himself, God, help me, what have I done? His anxiety was overwhelming. He was not sure he would ever breathe again. Sixty seconds. Then ninety seconds. Time seemed to stand still as if he were suspended in a cloudy void.

The doorbell chimed. He focused his attention on Otto, who motioned him to answer the door. He hesitated for a moment, then walked to the door, opened it and extended a stiff handshake. "Bryan. Good to see you again. How is Berlin? I trust you are advancing at the embassy." Blaine tried to telegraph a message for Bryan to look over his shoulder.

After raising his arms for an embrace, Blaine dropped them instead for a stilted handshake. Bryan's eyes met his father's and read the message. He looked over his father's shoulder. Blaine followed the trajectory of his eyes and knew that he saw Otto and sensed the danger. "I'm doing fine, Father. Let me introduce you to Lisa Brandt. I, uh, brought her here to meet you and Mother. We're engaged. Father, this is Lisa. Lisa, this is my father, Blaine Harmon."

Lisa stood dumbfounded by the statement. Blaine rushed forward to rescue the moment, hoping she would be quick on the uptake and catch his drift.

"I'm pleased to meet you, young lady. Please, come in. I have an unexpected guest today—an old wartime friend, Otto Kunstler. We haven't seen each other in years. Come, I'll introduce you both."

While the banalities of introduction took place, Blaine's mind formed a plan of action. He took special care to seat Bryan and Lisa opposite Otto and himself.

Following discussions of political events at the Embassy, Otto was ready to be prosecutor, judge and executioner. His burning eyes were set on Bryan. With a clearing of his throat, Otto began his interrogation. "So, young man, it's my understanding that life in the diplomatic corps can sometimes be exciting and dangerous."

"Not really," Bryan answered. "Mostly, it's mundane conversation over endless meals."

"But sometimes, is it not possible for skeletons from the past to emerge...especially in Berlin, with its Nazi past?" Otto pressed.

"Anything in life is possible."

"Is it not possible that one could come across old records that were never meant to see the light of day?"

"Anything is always possible, Herr Kunsler," answered Bryan.

"I imagine that someone could find something regarding, say, Adolph Hitler, or possibly his mistress, Eva Braun. Is this not true?" His glare pierced Bryan, his voice dripping with anger.

"I'm sure that any information on a woman who passed away fifty years ago would be of no interest to anyone outside of an historian." Bryan glanced at Lisa. He telegraphed for help.

Lisa took the cue saying, "So, Herr Kunsler, how are you finding the weather here in Geneva this time of year?"

Annoyed by the petty attempt to change the subject, Otto raised the tempo in his voice. "I have no knowledge of the weather here in Geneva, Fraulein Brandt, anymore than I know about the weather in Buenos Aires or Washington, D.C." He stared down Lisa. He looked like a hunter about to strike. He leaned forward and hissed, "Perhaps, *you* could tell *me* what the weather is like this time of year in Buenos Aires, Fraulein Brandt?"

Lisa returned his glare with equal intensity. "I wouldn't know, Herr Kunstler."

Blaine Harmon shifted nervously on the sofa. He had been watching Otto's every move. It was up to him to save his son's life. "Well, Otto, I'm sure that life in Berlin for two young lovers must be different than what you or I might suspect it would—"

The sound of gravel crunching in the driveway caused Blaine's head to turn, breaking off his sentence. He switched topics. "I think I heard a car drive up; it must be Mary." His head pounded as his heart burst into a throbbing beat. The moment had come—every second counted.

"Hellooo," Mary sang out as she walked through the door. Blaine's focus shot to Otto. He saw a weapon emerge from Otto's coat. Terror swept over him. No time for fear, no time to plan. He lunged at the would-be assassin, his hand coming down on the weapon. He screamed to Bryan, "Look out!"

His move was too late. Two bullets ripped into Bryan's shirt. He bowled over his chair, hitting his head on the corner of a table. Mary dropped her groceries, screaming at the sight of her son. The glass top of the coffee table smashed under the weight of Otto and Blaine. They hit the floor—ensnared in a death wrestle. The gun careened away. Otto reached out and grabbed a long shard of glass. With an upward thrust, he plunged it into Blaine's abdomen. Blaine's body went rigid as he felt the shard rip, tear his organs apart. Blood pouring from his mouth told the story. He freed himself from Otto, rose and staggered to Bryan, collapsing at his side.

Shocked by the sudden explosion of violence, Lisa saw the gun careen toward her as Blaine's body hit the floor. She lunged, grabbed the gun and pulled off three shots—two entered Otto's chest. He was on his knees as the bullets entered. His bloodied hands grabbed his chest. He looked up in disbelief and fell sideways.

Lisa cried out, shaking the gun from her hand as if it were burning hot. Sobbing, she half rose, grabbed a chair for support and stumbled her way to Bryan. She cradled his bleeding head in her lap and prayed for God's help.

Blaine struggled to regain consciousness. He gripped Lisa's arm and fought to drag his body forward and get his head onto her knee, next to Bryan's ear. He raised his hand, placed it on Bryan's face and whispered through his tears, "Bryan, I'm so sorry...I've always loved you..." His hand dropped and clutched Bryan's shirt. He groaned, dragged himself closer to

Bryan's ear and whispered, "...Key." He summoned the last of his strength. "...In the clock...mantle...Banc of Geneva...Jim...Marston..."

Bryan's eyelids cracked opened, searching for focus. As his father's head fell on his shoulder, he heard his last words.

"Forgive me..." Blaine's spirit closed to final darkness.

"Help me!" Lisa screamed to Mary. "Now! Quickly! Check Blaine." Mary, frozen in shock at the enormity of the carnage, heard Lisa's plea and moved to her husband. She saw his lifeless body and assumed the worst. She knelt over Blaine, petrified to touch him, as if her touch would send him to his death. With all the strength she could muster, she reached out her hand and touched his neck, then his chest—nothing. As the tragic moment ripped her heart, Mary screamed in agony, clutching his body in her arms. She pleaded, "No...no! Please, Blaine, come back." Letting go of his shirt, she sat back on her legs. Looking toward heaven, she wailed even louder, "No God, no. Don't let this happen..."

The sound of Lisa's crying reached Mary's ears. She wiped her cheeks with the palm of her hands and looked down at Bryan. With hesitation, she looked up at Lisa and asked, "Is he...? No, no, please not Bryan too. Oh, don't let this be."

Opening his eyes at the sound of his mother's grief, Bryan whispered, "Mom, I'm still here, it's just my shoulder. Let me see—aagh," he grunted as he pulled his shirt back. "I think only one went in...the other one grazed me."

Lisa turned to Mary, "Do you have any gauze, bandages, water—any towels? We need to stop his bleeding."

Lisa helped Bryan get up on the couch. She remembered Blaine's last words, looked around the room and spied the clock on the mantel. She sprang to her feet and hurried to the fireplace. She examined the clock, saw a brass latch on the back and carefully opened its door. Only one key, she thought, but it's the winding key. Putting it back on its hook, she closed the rear door of the clock. As she turned to walk away, Lisa pondered Blaine's words, "key...clock." She reopened the back door and slid her slender fingers upward. Her fingertips felt another key hanging above. Perusing the key in her hands, she noticed the initials, BDG, engraved above the number 622.

Bryan grimaced and turned to Lisa. "What's that?"

"Your father said to get the key from the mantel clock. Here..."

Her arms laden with towels and bandages, Mary came back into the room and saw Blaine again. She broke into tears. Feeling the pain of losing her own mother, Lisa walked to Mary, put her arms around her and drew her in.

"That man was after Bryan and me—to stop us. Your husband was involved. I don't know how or why, but he died trying to save us. Mrs. Harmon, please help us—we don't know what to do. They'll kill us unless we can expose what they want kept secret. You've got to handle this horrible mess here so I can get Bryan to a doctor." Thinking aloud, Lisa continued, "But not a hospital—too many questions. Call the police, but don't tell them about us—not yet. Do you have a family doctor that will respect your diplomatic immunity?"

Mary softly answered, "Yes, I think so…let me get his address. I'll call him and tell him you're on the way."

His body numbing to the pain, Bryan focused on Otto's body. "Lisa, search him. There could be something on him. Mom, wipe the gun and put it in Dad's right hand." Mary obediently placed the gun in Blaine's hand and looked back at her son.

"Mom, did Dad ever talk about this key?" He turned it in front of her. "It's to a safety deposit box."

"Yes," she said, squinting at the key for identification. "Your father told me that if he ever died unexpectedly, to take the contents of the box to Jim Marston—he'd know what to do with it."

"Jim Marston, the ambassador to Poland?"

"Yes. They've been friends since they worked together in the occupation after the war."

"Mrs. Harmon," interrupted Lisa, "do you know what's in the box?"

"No. Blaine made me promise never to ask or look. He said it was sensitive government information that I shouldn't see."

"Bryan, we must leave," Lisa said. "Mrs. Harmon, we need the contents of that safety deposit box—today—*now*! These people are powerful. They'll block you from getting to the box if we delay. You must go there now and call the police when you return. I'll take Bryan to the doctor and—"

"No!" interrupted Bryan. "I can wait a bit longer. We'll follow Mom to the bank and you can go inside and help her, Lisa. I'll wait in the car. Mom, I know this is difficult for you, but our lives depend on it. It's asking a lot, but please, don't call the police until you return home. And Mom, change your jacket, Dad's blood is on it."

Still in a daze, Mary asked, "What's this all about?"

"I'm not sure, Mom, but I think we'll find out after we get that box—time to go."

CHAPTER 39

ASSOCIATED PRESS

VILNIUS, LITHUANIA - RUSSIAN ARMORED TANK DIVISIONS rolled across the borders of Latvia, Lithuania, Estonia, Belarus and Ukraine in a surprising sweep to secure their borders with Poland. NATO intelligence was caught off guard by the lightning speed of the advance. A spokesperson for Russian President Donskoy stated that the mobilization is meant only to defend the borders of the former Soviet Union against harassment by Germany or Poland. He also stated that under no circumstances will any Polish land be annexed by Germany.

ASSOCIATED PRESS

BRUSSELS - NATO commanders scheduled an emergency meeting for tomorrow to review "the Polish Crisis." Admiral Smith, Commander of NATO, stated that any Russian movements into Poland will be met with the gravest response. All forces have been put on highest alert.

EXECUTIVE OFFICES, WHITE HOUSE
WASHINGTON, D.C.

Closing his manila folder and rapping it with his knuckles for theatrics, Vice President Koernig stood rigid at the conference table and stated, "Mr. President, I've finished discussions with Chancellor Mueller and NATO. In light of a confirmed Russian plan for their repartition of Poland, the consensus is that all NATO countries should go to DefCon status."

Looking around the table for support, Cook asked, "Do we know for certain that their troops will cross into Poland, or is it just a show of force? John, what about CIA?"

"I'm sorry, sir. Our information says they *will* cross the border within days."

***

ZURICH, SWITZERLAND

"What the hell do you mean the police have been called?"

"Harmon's wife just called the Geneva police and said her husband has been murdered and the man who killed him is dead in her living room."

"Did you remove the tap?"

"Not yet. Remember, Otto was to sanitize the place?"

"Can the tap be found?"

"No. I don't make mistakes."

"Neither did Otto! Pull out and return to the house tomorrow if it's safe."

Hanging up the phone, the large man pulled off his glasses and in one furious motion, threw them on his burl-topped desk. Leaning back in his chair, his nicotine-stained fingers massaged the bridge of his nose. He sat upright again and dialed the phone. The voice on the other end answered, "Yes?"

"Apparently it seems Otto *did* need help after all."

"What? Is he—?"

"He's dead. Get to Zurich on the next flight out and drive to Lucerne. Call me when you arrive."

"What about our problem couple, Herr Oberst?"

"They're alive, damn it! Why else would I be calling you?"

"Where do we meet?"

"The usual restaurant in Lucerne, I'll let you know the time."

***

GENEVA, SWITZERLAND

The walls were papered with the type of design one usually associates with doctors' offices—bland, nondescript and of a trendy style ten years past its time. Looking around, Bryan wondered if there was some sort of international course required in medical school for this kind of deco-rating. "Where the hell is he?" Bryan asked aloud, hoping the nurse would hear him. "How long do I have to sit on this table and...aagh!" He grimaced as another pain shot upward from his shoulder.

Sitting in an uncomfortable chair next to Bryan, Lisa stood, set the envelopes on a chair and hugged him in an emotional embrace.

"I love you, Bryan. I can't stand to see you hurting like this. Maybe we should stop."

"A month ago I could've stopped, but not now. There's—"

The doctor entered the room, stopped and chuckled, "Well, I can see I have a lot to learn about bedside manner. Perhaps I should write this on the prescription—take three times daily."

As Lisa pulled away, Bryan smiled but grimaced again with pain. "Sew me up, doc...I need more of the medication you just prescribed."

The doctor laid his hands under Bryan's shoulders and eased him backward to the examining table. "Lie back down so we can get a look at you. You say this was an accident?"

"Uh, yes...a hunting accident...on my parents' estate. I fell and the gun went off. I guess I didn't have the safety on."

Lifting his head up, the doctor stared at Lisa. "You know that I have to report this to the authorities."

Bryan looked over to Lisa, then back to the doctor. "You've known my parents for over twenty years. Fix me up and please, just wait until tomorrow to report it. I'm serious. If you don't wait, it could mean our lives."

"The wound I can fix, any other problems, I can't. Nurse, bring disinfectant and sutures," he said, yielding to his Hippocratic Oath. "Miss, would you step out into the lobby please?"

Relieved at not having to watch, Lisa picked up the rolled envelopes that had been found in Blaine's safety deposit box. She walked into the lobby and sat down amid the year-old periodicals. After sitting and staring at the envelopes, she forced herself to pull out the yellowed dental records contained within. The name she saw written on the cards screamed at her.

EVA BRAUN

With trained, yet apprehensive eyes, Lisa studied the nuances of Eva's dental care. She was pained when she saw the name of her grandfather, Dr. Hans Brandt, D.D.S. She closed her eyes and saw her mother walk up the steps of her grandfather's house, then the explosion. Her fingers crushed the edges of the records as she whispered in anger, "I won't run anymore, you bastards!"

With new resolve, she opened the second envelope and pulled out its sordid contents. A puzzled look reshaped her face as she examined the sepia-colored photographs. The first photo showed a long line of war prisoners in full-length trench coats passing through a large iron gate. Armed guards stood watch and the eerie scene was surrounded by barbed wire and lit by tower spotlights. Lisa tried to put the pieces together. These men look like Russian soldiers entering a concentration camp, she thought. That's odd…there are no barracks, just a singular concrete building. What is this place? Turning the photograph over in her hands, she saw the writing on the back:

05 DECEMBER 1944, BRESLAU FACILITY, CONTROL GROUP 30A

The next photograph showed a line of guarded prisoners entering the building. Moving to the next picture, Lisa saw a horde of naked men entering a room with the German word for "Showers" stenciled above a steel door with a small viewing window. Oh my God, she thought. What's coming next?

Hesitant to look at the next photo, she was surprised to see the same men coming out another door with "Exit" painted above. To the right was a staircase with an arrow pointing down and the word "Hospital" stenciled on a concrete wall. I thought this was a gas chamber. These men appear healthy. Why are they going down to a hospital? Wait! Why are the guards wearing gas masks and dressed in white body suits?

She flipped back to the previous photo with naked men entering the showers. The guards were wearing uniforms with SS lapel insignia, but no gas masks. Examining it further, she noticed concrete walls, a ceiling and a floor, but no windows or openings. Lisa returned to the first photo and confirmed that only one building appeared and it contained a single, heavy-looking entrance door—again, no windows. Why such a small building over what appears to be a massive underground basement? Why underground? And why would a hospital not have any windows? Moreover, what are the gas masks for?

In the next picture, Lisa saw long rows of hospital beds, all with patients lying face upward. Within the room, attendants were wearing gas masks and protective clothing. Over the next several photos, she saw close-ups of patients who appeared to be writhing in sweat-drenched seizures, their bodies covered with oozing fever blisters. Her stomach turned nauseous. Turning one over, she saw the familiar inscription:

07 DECEMBER 1944, BRESLAU FACILITY, STRAIN #24, C.G. 30A

Nausea turned to shock as she pulled up photos that showed facial close-ups. Covering their faces were festering, pus-filled blisters, eyelids crusted shut and tongues bulging out of split, swollen lips. She fought the urge to gag, but was surprised to see the next picture show the opposite side of the room with patients sitting upright, no apparent sickness at all. Even though the patients appeared normal, the attendants and guards were wearing the same protective gear she had seen earlier. Turning this photo over, she saw a different notation below the customary date:

NORDIC DESCENT, CLEAN BLOODLINE

Returning to the close-ups of the infected men, she reached a slow, startling conclusion. Wait a minute. These men are of Mongol extraction—dark hair, mustaches and almond-shaped eyes. Flipping the last three photos over, she read the notes on the back of each:

MONGOL BLOODLINE

ALAN BLOODLINE

SIBERIAN MIX

Lisa stopped while trying to ponder what heinous crimes had been committed so long ago, and to what purpose. Her face turned ashen— the gas masks, the suits—she wanted to scream. Those men had been infected with some insidious germ. These are photos of germ warfare experiments—on real people. It had to be!

Lisa grabbed the remaining black and whites. As fast as she could, she flipped through the next several batches. Oddly, the close-ups of the infected men showed their conditions improving. What are the dates? Turning them over, she read:

13 DECEMBER 1944

Frowning, Lisa recognized the same men sitting upright in their beds, but their blisters had disappeared. However, something appeared amiss—they didn't seem to fit the mold. Then it hit her. She noticed all the men were in the same position—a pillow behind their backs, arms resting at their sides, palms down on neatly tucked bedding.

"That's it!" she whispered aloud. The look on their faces—it's the same on every one of them: expressionless, zombie-like, staring ahead as if they were drugged...but I don't see any IVs, nor any sign of an attendant injecting them. The date read:

15 DECEMBER 1944

The last two photographs showed the men being led out of the building, but this time the guards were in regular German uniforms and not wearing any gas masks. Lisa spied a small #24 written in the upper, right-hand corner of all the pictures.

Lisa looked around to make sure no one was watching. Comfortable that she was alone, she pulled the remaining papers out of the envelope. Opening them, she read the caption:

TOP SECRET
Results: Control Group 30A, Strain #24
10 January 1945, Breslau Facility

Having the customary Nazi identification emblems, the documents appeared to be authentic. They were divided into four main bloodline categories: Mongol, Alan, Siberian Mix and Varangian Rus. Listed below each category were the names of thirty-five men. Linear, across the page were columns for age, weight, height and blood type and a larger space for notes marked "Other."

Lisa saw that only four men died out of a total of one hundred and forty. Two were in the Mongol group and two were in the Siberian Mix group. Page six contained the results of the experiment. Again, it was divided into the four bloodline categories:

Mongol Group

Results: Strain #24
Same results on C.G. 30A, C.G. 24A - 29A
All reacted, 3% fatality rate.
Incubation: 24 HRS.

Symptoms: Violent, flu-like. Duration: 5 days.
Recovery: 3 days.
Motor Skills Loss: None. Memory Loss: Total.
Communicative Skills Loss: Near total.
Reproductive Ability: Total sterility.
Other: No aggressive tendencies exhibited.

Alan Group

Results: Strain #24
Same results on C.G. 30A, C.G. 24A - 29A
All reacted, 0% fatality rate.
Incubation: 24 HRS.
Symptoms: Violent, flu-like. Duration: 5 days.
Recovery: 4 days.
Motor Skills Loss: None. Memory Loss: Total.
Communicative Skills Loss: Moderate.
Reproductive Ability: Total sterility.
Other: Minor aggressive behavior exhibited
only after excessive physical abuse.

Siberian Mix Group

Results: Strain #24
Same results on C.G. 30A, C.G. 24A - 29A
All but one reacted, 4% fatality rate.
Incubation: 12 HRS.
Symptoms: Violent, flu-like. Duration: 3 days.
Recovery: 2 days.
Motor Skills Loss: None. Memory Loss: Total.
Communicative Skills Loss: Near total.
Reproductive Ability: 80% sterility.
Other: Aggressive behavior returns after minimal
physical abuse.

Varangian Rus Group

Results: Strain #24
Same results on C.G. 30A, C.G. 24A - 29A
None reacted.

CONCLUSION

Strain #24 appears to infect only those descendants of the Mongolian/Steppe/Caucasus regions. Peoples of Pure Scandinavian descent are not affected. Strain #24 does not affect Germanic peoples of pure Aryan descent. Parallel tests were conducted on dissident German prisoners and defectors in Control Groups 24B through 30B. Only nine reacted, but it was determined that their bloodline had been contaminated by inferior species. The loss of life in all cases is minimal and cannot be definitively concluded to have its origins in Strain #24. Equal results have been observed in both male and female subjects. The lasting side effects of memory loss, diminished communicative skills and reduced aggressive behavior are all viewed from the positive side. The continued motor skills levels can make for an excellent workforce that can be both productive and controlled. The sterility factor is considered excellent, both in the short- and long-term analyses. Strain #24 is highly contagious and can be stored for an indefinite period of time in vacuum-sealed containers at moderate to cool temperatures. Reproduction is quick and cost effective.

Lisa's face reflected the horror—she had heard all this before. She had visited Dachau as a teen and had seen the gruesome photographs, but now, to have *this* in her hands…to hold the proof! It was as if it were happening now, but to her. She wanted to scream. Is this what they don't want us to know about? Who the hell are *they*?

Voices began stirring opposite the door to the receptionist. She grabbed the papers and refolded them. As she shoved them back into one of the envelopes, she noticed there were two more papers inside. Opening the first, she read a letter addressed to Oscar Blitzer, ordering him to begin the production and storage of Strain #24. All further experiments were to cease. It was signed by Albert Speer and dated 19 January 1945. The final paper Lisa scanned, as it was a German document that had the blanks filled in Polish. It appeared to be a deed for transfer of property.

As the voices came closer, Lisa returned everything to the envelopes, put them under her arm and stood as the door to the lobby opened. Bryan led the way with his arm in a sling. The doctor followed behind and motioned for Lisa to come forward. When she had given Bryan a careful hug, the doctor directed his instructions to her.

"The bullet passed through clean, without touching any bones.

Change the dressing once a day and make sure he gives it plenty of rest. Here are his antibiotics; he must take three a day. If he does as told, the wound should heal fast."

The smile on the doctor's face disappeared and he looked behind himself to see if anyone was listening as he eased the lobby door shut. "Because of my respect for his parents, I won't report this for twenty-four hours—that's the best I can do. I don't know what kind of trouble you're in, and I'm sure it's for the best that I don't. Be careful."

Walking to the car, Bryan noticed Lisa's ashen face, her arms clutching the envelope. "Are you all right?"

"The contents of this envelope are the key to everything. Its implications are heinous. What's in my hand is bigger than the both of us."

CHAPTER 40

A WHITE COVERING OF SNOW WAS BROKEN ONLY BY A narrow wisp of smoke rising from the chimney of a dacha. The sense of purity was contrasted with the evil atmosphere that pervaded the inside of this country house. With its cream-colored stucco and stone walls and wood-slatted roof supported by stout brown timbers, the dacha was the extended womb of Boris Donskoy. It was here that he found his deep sense of connection with Rodina, his Mother Russia. It was here that his ancestors' blood stirred the passions of his soul. His every fiber craved one goal: A Russia restored to its peak of world power. Not a foolish communist state, but a vast empire. Not only reaching its former borders, but this time, a Russia with *purpose*—with oneness of mind, and that purpose was to be total domination. Not the weak leadership of Kruschev or Brezhnev, not the self-flagellation displayed by Gorbachev, or worse yet, the comic opera of that fool, Yeltsin. No, *his* Russia would be about control. The gutless vermin in Ukraine and Belarus would soon know the heel of his boot, and the arrogant Germanic types of the Baltic States would feel his iron fist, but it was the "yellow skins" and the "darkies" to the south and east that made his blood boil. Soon enough that rabble in Chechnya, Georgia, Dagestan and the rest of that cesspool of humanity would come to know his plans...his ultimate *solutions*.

"Well, don't just stand there! What have you got?" Donskoy snarled.

He knew his Chief of Internal Security felt confident. Gorgin took two tentative steps forward and slid into the wood chair across the table from Donskoy. "I have the information you have been waiting for—and on time, Comrade President."

Donskoy stared straight at him, sat up and rested his arm on the table. Without relinquishing the pressure of his glare, he slid a bottle of vodka and shot glass slowly across to Gorgin. "This material that you have for me, for your sake, it better be good."

Gorgin took his shot of vodka for strength and opened his brief-case. "It appears, after all, comrade President, that Konstantinov *was* a Nazi plant. He was recruited during the war and has been methodically working his way inward and upward into the Soviet, now Russian bureaucracy." He looked down again at the vodka bottle. Donskoy blinked approval. Gorgin took another shot, slid the papers across the table and said, "On page three, you will see that Konstantinov talked about a secret, stored virus. This virus was developed by the Nazis and has the capacity to neutralize and ultimately eliminate all of our undesirable races." Gorgin smiled as he saw his leader's attention snap into focus. "Apparently only clean Russian stock would be saved; all corrupted races would be affected." Gorgin eyed the vodka bottle again.

In the flash of a second, Donskoy's forearm swept the bottle from the table, sending it crashing to the floor. "No more vodka! Tell me what this means!" he bellowed.

Gorgin shifted in his seat. "Yes, comrade President. Once the undesirables have been infected, they become docile robots—a free and controllable workforce." A sinister smile opened up on his face, exposing his half-rotted teeth. "And best of all, this workforce will become sterile and unable to reproduce. What I am saying is that if this virus falls into the wrong hands, your dream of another Soviet Union is gone, unless we create it by military force. If we control this virus, Holy Mother Russia can weed out the entire rabble from our society bit by bit. Then we can turn it against Afghanistan, even China and Turkey—wherever we wish."

Donskoy's thoughts intensified. "Yes," he hissed, "a Russia that even Stalin would have coveted." He leaned back and tilted his head to the ceiling; his stare went blank. After a minute, he bolted from his chair, causing a startled Gorgin to almost fall backward in surprise.

"Konstantinov—he is the key! He can lead us to this virus, correct?"

Gorgin's pulse quickened as he mapped out his words before he spoke "Well, comrade President, that is, I mean no...he can't. You see, Konstantinov is dead. He died." The two shots of vodka now had a reverse effect. Donskoy saw Gorgin could no longer couch his words; awkwardness had set in.

"What do you mean he is dead?" Donskoy shouted. "I gave no orders for him to be killed. Who is responsible for this? I want that bastard arrested."

"He's dead, but no one is to blame. You see, he killed himself. He tugged at his IV stand and tipped it over onto himself. He increased his dosage and—"

"Shut up, you incompetent fool! I want to read this report in silence."

Moments later, Donskoy sat upright in his chair and said, "This report says the virus is stored in Poland. Is this information true? Has it been verified?"

"We have not verified it as yet, comrade President. Our ability to spy is not what it used to be under the old KGB."

"And why not? What the hell does it take to get information out of that shit-hole Poland—a country I could crush with the mere snap of my fingers?"

"The best we got from Konstantinov is that the experiments were carried out by the Nazis somewhere in the Breslau area."

"The Breslau *area*? Do you know how large an area we are talking about, you idiot? I want our agents combing that city! You tell those incompetent fools to check every stinking record—no stone unturned."

"As you have said, comrade President, it *is* a country we no longer control. Polish troops are everywhere trying to suppress the German skinheads."

With a look of contempt, Donskoy growled, "Then with that much confusion, it should be *easier* to gain access to their old archives."

"I see, but—"

"No buts!" he thundered. "If this Strain #24 exists, I *must* have it, and I want it *yesterday!*"

CHAPTER 41

STARING OUT THE WINDOW INTO NOTHINGNESS, WILLIAM Koernig leaned back in his comfortable chair, propped his feet on his desk and locked his arms behind his head. He was lost in a dream-like trance. In his vision, he saw streets filled with throngs of cheering people, their emotions running wild as endless lines of missiles, tanks and goose-stepping troops paraded by. Spotlights lit up the evening sky in swirling patterns choreographed to the intoxicating sounds of "Deutschland Uber Alles" blaring from thousands of loudspeakers surrounding the red-stoned Kremlin of Moscow. With every note sung, hundreds of thousands of candle flames danced in the hands of people with arms locked together. They rhythmically swayed with joyous tears, flowing in harmony. All hearts were moved as the spotlights continually crisscrossed the black, red and gold banner of the German flag raised high above the Kremlin tower. Thousands more hung from street lamps. There to witness it all was him, the American President, William Koernig. His arms were raised above his head, waving triumphantly as he stood next to the German Chancellor on the viewing platform above Lenin's Tomb in the ancient Kremlin Castle. The mass of humanity reacted with tumultuous cheers as he told them, "The process of confronting and overcoming the past is now buried as deep as Lenin's Tomb! You have accomplished what our ancestors have dreamed of for over three hundred years! Long live your new Reich! Long live Germany!"

His intercom buzzed. In an instant, the dream disappeared and his feet dropped to the floor. "Yes?"

"Mr. Vice President, Ambassador Barnes is here for his appointment."

"Send him right in, Mrs. Corbin. Thank you."

He stood and composed himself as the ambassador entered the room. "Good afternoon, Peter, please, sit down." He gestured to a chair across from his desk, said, "Would you care for a drink, perhaps coffee?"

"No thanks, Bill. How are Nancy and the children?"

"They're fine, but I'm sure you're not here to ask me about family matters."

"You're right. We do have a problem. It appears that Blaine Harmon's son has received some fairly sensitive information."

"Such as?"

Peter Barnes drew in a deep breath and said, "Your birth certificate from Argentina..."

As the words hung in midair, Koernig's face paled. He struggled to speak. "What did you say? That's not possible."

"It's worse—he also received all the papers tracing Eva to Argentina and you to the United States."

"How the hell—"

"Through Fredrick Werner and Blaine Harmon," the Ambassador interrupted. "Werner talked to us before he died and Harmon was killed in Geneva."

"Shit! Who else knows about this?"

"The whole group. I was called this morning."

"What do they want?" He rubbed his forehead with his palms.

"First of all, Bill, they want the heat turned up on Cook. They'll provide the Senate Subcommittee with a few more incriminating tidbits and leak it to the press. We think the beginning of impeachment proceedings could be close—looks strong for obstruction of justice. You've got to be ready to fill the breach. Secondly, we also have word that Donskoy has found out about the virus."

"That too? How much does he actually know?"

"He knows *what* it is and that it *does* exist, but fortunately, only that it's somewhere in the Breslau area," Barnes said.

"Are they close?"

"We really don't know. However, the group wants to push the skinheads and nationalists into Phase II. The Russians are going to go nuts, so we have to be ready to react."

"What about Harmon's kid? Who's going to get rid of him?"

"Jack Dillon is handling that."

"God, Peter, it's like everything's beginning to unravel. I'm...I mean, *we* are so close now." Urgency made his voice quiver, "Make damned sure that kid is stopped—too much rides on this."

CHAPTER 42

"CAN YOU MAKE OUT THIS LAST DOCUMENT?" BRYAN asked. He handed Lisa the faded photocopy.

"Let me see." She turned her body to put more light on the paper. "It's definitely some kind of deed...a transfer of property. Yes, here it is...it's a deed of conveyance, a description of the land and any appurtenances that are being conveyed to the...looks like the Sisters of...the Order of Saint Mary Magdalene, in Krakow."

"Who's the conveying the deed?"

"Looks like a German company. I think...Hueber Chemical, A.G.," she replied.

"Where's the property located?"

"Uh, it's in or looks like it says Breslau. That's Wroclaw now, isn't it?"

Bryan nodded his head in agreement as his mind churned. "Why would a German chemical company donate a piece of property that was located in Germany to a group of nuns in Poland?"

"I'm not sure, but I know that this document relates to the germ experimentation that was going on in those photos. We were never meant to see this, and a lot of people have died because we have. I have a feeling our answer is at this convent." Reaching upward, she placed her palm on his cheek and caressed it. "Our lives will never be the same. Maybe that's why God put us together at this particular moment in time." She sighed and continued, "I love you, Bryan Harmon. No matter what happens to us, don't ever forget that."

"I love you, Lisa—forever." His upper and lower lip tugged slightly on her lower lip, his tongue touching her upper lip. She responded with a shiver. The embrace turned into frantic undressing and then tender lovemaking. Finally, a sweet moment of surrender carried them away.

Lying in her tender embrace, Bryan was awakened by Lisa's soft words, "Sweetheart, we must leave for Poland, but you should call your mother first. She's probably out of her mind with worry and grief. She's going through hell and needs comforting. She could also be in grave danger, so we need to get her somewhere safe." Arising, she handed him the phone. Her eyes watered as she thought of her own mother. "I know the pain you're both feeling."

Dialing the number, Bryan thought of the documents, the pictures and then his father. How the hell did you get involved with these people, Dad, and for God's sake why? The break in the ringing interrupted his rising anger. "Hi, Mom, are you okay?"

"Oh, Bryan, thank God you called! Are you all right? Did Dr. Boucher take care of you? Is your shoulder—?"

"Mom, slow down," he gently interrupted. "I'm okay, really. My shoulder is better and Dr. Boucher went out of his way to help us—more than you'll ever know, but how are you? Have you made arrangements for Dad?"

Mary attempted to ease Bryan's anxiety. "I called the embassy right before I called the police. They've been most helpful. Jim Marston called and had an army of people here to make the arrangements, including handling the police. I just wish some of the people he sent were as nice as he's been. I mean, Jim's the one who's Ambassador to Poland, so why would they be asking *me* questions about that country?"

"Mom...what questions?"

"Oh, just a barrage of inane questions," Mary replied, trying to put it all out of her mind.

"Mom, please—think—it's vitally important. What inane questions?"

"Well, for instance, did your father and I ever visit a convent in Wroclaw? Or did your father ever correspond with the Sisters of St. Mary Magdalene in Krakow? In the first place, why on earth would we visit a convent? They know perfectly well we're not Catholic. In the second place, your father and I have never even been to Poland. I must have been asked that question a dozen times, in a dozen different ways. It was almost like they were trying to trick me."

The silence on the other end of the line was deafening. Mary was concerned they had been cut off. "Bryan?" she asked.

"I'm here, Mom. Did they ask anything else?"

"They seemed unduly interested in your dad's stock portfolio. They asked if he had any papers or stock in the Hueber Chemical Company in

Germany. I showed them all his important papers and there wasn't any-thing regarding a chemical company, but they kept on asking anyway." Her voice broke with emotion. "That's what seemed important to them, not that my husband had been murdered."

"Mom, the people that weren't very nice…were they from the State Department?"

"Yes. They said they were."

"Did they show you identification?"

"Well, no. They arrived right after the nice people left and I assumed they were sent by the State Department like the others. They told me that Jim had sent them over to keep all your father's governmental papers in order and secure, but they were so pushy with all their questions. Don't these people talk to each other? They were the same questions I answered earlier."

Bryan hesitated, not wanting to ask the next question for fear of the answer. "Did they ask about the safety deposit box?"

"Yes, but I told them I didn't know if he had one or not. I don't think they believed me. Oh, they also questioned me about you and your young lady friend."

"What did you say, Mom?"

"I didn't say anything because I don't really have any information to give. Bryan, what's going on? I'm so confused and exhausted. When are you coming home? I need you here."

Her last comment devastated him. "I wish I could tell you, but I don't know. Mom, I'm in a lot of danger, and so is Lisa." He hesitated, knowing the pain his next words would inflict on her. "I can't be there for Dad's funeral…I can't even be there for you. I'm so sorry, Mom, but it's not safe for us—not right now."

Sobbing, Mary forced herself to speak, "Sweetheart, I can handle this, I really can—as long as you're safe. Please be careful, and promise me I won't be put through this again…"

"I'll be careful…I promise you. Mom, listen carefully. This is vitally important. As soon as the funeral is over, I want you to go and stay at Aunt Sara's house. Don't tell anyone—not Jim Marston—no one! Don't take any clothes. No luggage. I'll call you as soon as I can."

ZURICH, SWITZERLAND

"Did you trace the call?"

"Yes—Hotel St. Jacques—Geneva—low rent district. There *was* a safety deposit box; it's been cleaned out."

"What else?"

"The mother knows nothing; she's been kept in the dark. Young Harmon and the girl are going to Poland. Do we monitor the old lady?"

"Till she leaves, then follow her every move."

"It would be easier to get rid of her—she knows nothing."

"Do as you're ordered!" The large man growled and slammed the phone into its cradle.

He rubbed his chin and decided to make another call. This one he dreaded. He was no longer in charge. Now *he* was the underling doing the bidding.

"Hello?"

"They're on their way to Poland," he said between deep breaths. His obese body struggled to take in air.

"Do we know where?"

"Breslau, we assume."

"What about their itinerary—arrangements made?"

"Two things are certain. They *will* go the convent and they *will* be taken out there."

"Need I remind you that you've told me this before?"

He gritted his teeth, bristling at the sarcasm. "No," he whispered.

"We won't tolerate two screwups. You know that."

"Understood…"

"What about backup?"

"The best."

"Try second best. You said Otto was the best. Now he's dead."

"They *will* be controlled…" His voice trailed off as he heard the phone disconnect.

CHAPTER 43

EXITING THE TAXI, ILSA BACHMANN INHALED DEEPLY, looked up at the dark, wooden restaurant and felt a homey welcome. Her pride swelled as she straightened up in the lightly falling snow, recognizing this feeling as one would an old friend. It had come to her many times over the fifty years that she'd been in service to The Cause. It was her inner strength of knowing that what she did mattered for the greater good. It had kept her going all these years. It had been drawn upon time after time when nights became sleepless and the faces of her victims danced in her head like some macabre ballet. She suppressed her feelings of guilt because those victims were the enemy and she was, after all, a soldier. A soldier in a nameless shadow army, but a soldier nonetheless, and she always followed her orders to the letter. Her eyes misted over as the thought of again being summoned to duty raised her chin high with pride. She took off her wire-rimmed spectacles and wiped her eyes, taking care not to irritate the protruding double mole beneath her right eye.

As she entered the restaurant, the maitre d' approached her, only to be waved away with a curt motion of her hand. She stood erect with her head cocked back. Looking down her nose, she scanned the booth section and at last found the object of her search. Walking with the upright air of a bureaucrat who should be recognized for some minor accomplishment, she came to an abrupt stop at the rear booth. The man looked up and acknowledged her. She clicked her heels, slapped her gloves into her opposite palm and sat down with a rifle-straight posture, chin held high.

"Good God, woman! Must you be so damned conspicuous with your pompous crap?"

"Excuse me, Herr Oberst. I was extending to you the same respect that I would want as a loyal soldier to the Fatherland," she said, maintaining her Teutonic dignity.

"I don't want your respect, you imbecile," the man retorted. "You're an assassin with a job to do, nothing more. You are paid very well for your service—no different than a prostitute. Let's cut the shit and get down to business, shall we?"

Watching the folder as he slid it across the table, Ilsa Bachmann felt the rigidness in her body diminish to a slouch as the echo of the man's words deflated her ego. Something was wrong. It was as if her soul had been stabbed and her strength was bleeding out. She felt weakened, out of place.

"The first photo is one Bryan Harmon, a young American diplomat stationed in Germany. The second is Lisa Brandt, a German dental graduate."

"She is German? No one told me she was German."

"I wasn't aware that I was required to tell you anything. Your job is simple. You're to eliminate her. Inside the folder is a plane ticket to Krakow. A car will be waiting in the first stall of short-term parking. The keys will be inside under the mat. In the trunk will be the habit of a nun of the Order of St. Mary Magdalene—along with your tools. Drive to Breslau and go to the Hotel Odra on the western side of the city. There you will find Franz Kreuger. His cover is a priest named Wetzel."

"Kreuger?"

"I'm sure you remember him from your Leipzig mission."

She responded with any icy glare. "I know him, Herr Oberst, but I work alone."

"How nice of you to remind me what an insufferable bitch you are—not this time."

"And who will be in charge?" she growled.

"Kreuger," he snapped, asserting his authority. "You report to him."

"But—"

"Frau Bachmann," he interrupted, "you work for me, not I for you. Your orders are in the folder and *don't* screw them up. Your flight leaves in two hours." A sarcastic smile appeared on his face as he dismissed her. "Now, leave me alone, I'd like to enjoy my meal."

Walking down the steps of the restaurant, Ilsa fantasized about the miserable, fat swine soon having to go to a hospital, where she could be a *very* attentive nurse. As the taxi pulled along the curb, she vowed that this would be her last mission for these bastards.

CHAPTER 44

POLAND HAS ALWAYS BEEN THAT BEAUTIFUL PLAINS country which its neighbors have coveted and stolen, yet cannot keep. It is a country with a rich tapestry of history that has wound itself through the millennia...beautiful brocade, but nonetheless, a tapestry that close examination reveals the continuous errors of its weavers. Born the bastard son of a Swedish Viking rape, Poland rose to become a land of princes, castles and wealth unmatched by its neighbors whom it dominated in power and trade. Its boundaries stretched beyond the Amber Road in the east and included most of Ukraine, Belarus, the Baltic States and Slovakia. Jewels such as Kiev, Smolensk, Riga and Vilnius were in the crowns of its princes, but it was those jewels that were coveted by enemies in all directions of the compass. From the north it was the Swedes, from the south it was the Hungarians or the Turkish hordes of Sultan Muhammad. From the west it was the Germans, and from the east, it was the Mongols and Tatars who swept the plains and forests in 1241. Throughout Polish history, its magnificent cavalry of Hussars with their long lances and lightning speed held off its enemies without having sufficient numbers to turn the tide to a final, perpetual victory.

Valor was never the error of the weavers of Poland. It was its political fabric that left it the stepchild of Europe, for it has always been a question of who could rule Poland best. Its great magnates owned overwhelming tracts of land which survived constant erosion in the great river of Polish political torrents. In the absence of a central power to reign in their allegiances, these magnates elected the king of their choice and often granted this title to someone outside their borders. The stage was thus set for other countries to see this rich land as a pawn to be brokered, or at worst, as a wanton whore who would serve their monetary needs.

WROCLAW, POLAND

"Yes, Father Wetzel, your room is ready and all arrangements have been taken care of. Your room is the fourth door left of the elevator as you get off on the second floor. I took the liberty of putting you in that wing, as it is unoccupied and you will have privacy and quiet for your meditations."

With a hardened face, Franz Kreuger took the key and entered the elevator. As the doors closed, he looked back at the clerk and forced a smile. Priest! I'll meditate all right...I'll meditate on getting out of this bullshit disguise.

Once inside his room, he threw his suitcase on the dresser, took off his black coat and removed his holstered Glock. Yanking off the Roman collar, he sat down on the bed and dreaded working with the old swine bitch from Berlin. I've never been able to stomach her, he mused. He lit his cigarette and took a long, hard drag. "A priest and a nun," he said thinking aloud. "Can you believe this shit?" Well, that ugly hag should have been a nun, he thought, taking another drag on his cigarette. Who the hell thought up this fucking cover anyway? Why not take them out in their sleep or their car? I don't need this bitch and her stinking needles.

He took one more puff, laid his head back on the pillow and with a sweep of his arm, extended his hand to the ashtray and only half put out the cigarette, allowing the stench of the smoldering nicotine to permeate the room.

Blankly staring at the ceiling, Franz surrendered the swirling plaster pattern to a sea of nothingness. It was Berlin all over again; the sanction was his. Why had they sent her in? I told them I would handle it! It was a perfect setup...a fourteen-year-old prostitute found strangled by a belt in his hotel room. It would have worked—no politician could ever recover from that kind of scandal. He would have told me what we needed to know. Then all I had to do was put a gun barrel in his mouth and poof, another suicide! It could've been so simple, so clean.

But no, that bitch stuck her nose in where it didn't belong. Save the poor German child. What the hell did her being German have to do with it? She sneaks into his room, gives him a drug to make him talk, and the son of a bitch dies of a heart attack. I know they blamed me...that fat prick Dillon said I waited too long. I only waited to find a child prostitute, you asshole. It had to be a child…nothing else would have worked!

As Franz's hands squeezed the blanket on the bed, he fantasized his hands were wrapped around her throat. He rubbed his eyes and tried to put it out of his mind. Sleep came slowly.

CHAPTER 45

A FREEZING MIST HAD APPEARED FROM NOWHERE. AS IT transformed into biting sleet, the road became a hazardous obstacle. Bryan noticed icicles hanging from the red and white candy-striped gate that blocked the road entering Poland. Rolling down the window of the grey rental, he felt the stinging sleet on his face as he handed the border guard their passports. The young soldier took off his glove and breathed on his hand for warmth. He flashed a light inside the car and caught their faces with the beam. Bryan was weary from the dangerous drive, but refrained himself as he watched the guard walk back into his hut with a puzzled look. After a moment, the gatekeeper returned with an apologetic, but firm demeanor.

"I am terribly sorry, Fraulein Brandt, but you are a German national and the border is closed to *all* Germans. In light of the problems we are experiencing, you can understand our refusal to admit you."

"No. We don't understand!" Bryan barked out. The veins in his neck bulged as he tried to control his frustration. "Did you not notice my diplomatic status? Miss Brandt is my assistant and as a member of the American Embassy in Berlin, I am here to gather firsthand information on this crisis for my government. Without American assistance, this situation could explode with dire consequences for Poland."

Bryan's bellicose attitude set the guard back on his heels. He became nervous as he weighed the waking of his superior officer against allowing the couple to pass. "Then please to understand, Mr. Harmon, you accept full responsibility for the actions and whereabouts of Fraulein Brandt at all times. And this will be in my log."

"I understand."

"Proceed." The guard pushed down on the counterweight of the gate, allowing them passage.

As the power window sealed off the outside chill, Lisa looked over at a very confident and self-assured Bryan. "Wow, you're good!"

"Maybe I should be in the diplomatic corps."

***

U.S. EMBASSY

WARSAW, POLAND

Although his office was spacious, Ambassador James Marston felt small and was as despondent as he'd been in a long time. The death of his old friend Blaine Harmon had come as a shock, but it was more than that—it had shaken his core. Was this the sum total of all he and Blaine had worked for over the years? He had attended church every Sunday with his wife Sally, but it had been for show; a requisite for any diplomat in the religious country of Poland. Religion meant nothing, for Jim was a closet agnostic. It wasn't that he disliked the concept of God—he had no use for it. Nor was science his God, as those matters had even less value to him. He didn't care because he saw no monetary value in God.

But now, thoughts of the existence of evil had crept in and clouded his thinking. Had he unwittingly made a pact with some evil entity? Was there such a force as a netherworld? And was that force a mire of quicksand, allowing no escape? He had no place to turn, no one with whom to share his fear. These questions dominated his thoughts. Sleep no longer came quickly, as he would toss and turn for hours. Would he end up like Blaine Harmon, his stomach spewing forth, lowering the curtain on his life? He closed his eyes and gnashed his teeth. If he had a soul, was it lost to eternal damnation? The buzz of his intercom brought sweet relief. "Yes, Millie?"

"Ambassador Marston, there is a personal call for you on line three. It's Blaine Harmon's son, Bryan. Do you want to take it now or would you prefer to call him back?"

"I'll talk to him now, thank you." He paused before punching the blinking button. "Hello, Bryan? Let me say how sorry I am for you and your mother. Your father was a wonderful man and a great friend. He will be missed."

"Thank you, Ambassador, I—"

"No, please," he interrupted, "call me Jim. Is everything going all right with your mother? I hope you don't mind, but I took the liberty of sending some embassy people over to help her with the funeral arrangements."

"Not at all, thank you, Jim. Mom is holding up under the circumstances. She wanted me to personally thank you for your help. Believe me, it was appreciated," Bryan lied.

"Am I correct in understanding that the funeral will take place in Georgetown on Thursday?" Jim asked. "I'd consider it an honor to be a pallbearer—if that's acceptable to you?"

"Yes. It'd be fine, and thanks for offering."

"If there's anything else I can do, please let me know. Your father and I went back a long way and if you have any questions about anything, I—"

"Ambassador, that is Jim," Bryan cut in, "there are some things I need answers to. Would you meet me before you go back to Washington?"

"Certainly. I can redirect my flight to Geneva before—"

"I'm not in Switzerland...I'm in Poland."

"What? Poland?...But what about your mother?"

"Please, one question at a time. I need to talk about the work you did with my father after the war. Did you also know Fredrick Werner?"

Marston's solicitous demeanor vanished. He froze at the name.

"Dad told my mother that if he ever died unexpectedly, she was to deliver something to you." Bryan let the words hang. He sensed the diplomat was stunned. "He told her that you would know what to do with it."

Still, he could not answer. For sixty years, Marston had hoped this day would never come.

"Jim, that task has passed from my mother to me. Was my father correct?" Bryan wasn't sure if the person on the other end was still listening.

In fear, Jim whispered, "What was it he wanted you to give me?"

"The contents of his safety deposit box."

Marston fought to keep his composure. "Where in Poland are you?"

"I'm in Wroclaw."

"Okay. There's a restaurant on the western bank, in the Inner Town, called the Polanie. It's situated two blocks from the Cathedral of St. John the Baptist. I can be there in about four hours and meet you there. Bryan, your father and I...we...never mind, we'll discuss this later. Be careful of the rioting."

CHAPTER 46

JAMES HARRINGTON MARSTON WAS THE QUINTESSENTIAL career diplomat. To anyone who knew him, Jim was a likeable man who was always in the right spot at the right moment. Such was the situation in the chaos that followed World War II. He was never a fighter. The thought of going to Europe and dying so that some Frog or Pole could be free was of the question. After all, he was a Yale graduate, class of '41, with a double major in pre-law and German. Realizing that graduation cancelled his deferment, he applied for and was accepted in the master's program for political science at Harvard. It was there that he had his epiphany—diplomacy would be the great savior of this skewed planet. Marston graduated in 1944 believing that the war would grind down in about a year. Markers were called on his behalf and the Army rushed him through Officers Candidate School.

Upon receiving a call from his local congressman, the Army was coerced into recognizing the little jewel that they had. They assigned Lt. Marston to General George Patton's Army where he was assigned as Assistant to Colonel William Sutherland in the Pacification and Administrative Corps.

It was in Berlin 1946 that Major Marston met Colonel Blaine Harmon. In the aftermath of the Third Reich's traumatic meltdown, Germany was a country that lay prostrate, waiting to be divided by its victors. The Great War machine was in chains and had become a sniveling, begging dog. Half of its near-death body was in the skillful hands of the western surgeon, George Marshall. The other half was under the heel of the eastern Hun, Josef Stalin. Its devastation was complete and its children had to pay for the sins of their fathers. Every aspect of civilized life came to a grinding halt. In the midst of overwhelming confusion, misery and suffering came millions of war-ravaged refugees, forced into exile as the victors played a gigantic chess game with postwar Eastern Europe. People became meaningless pawns as traditional borders shifted like straw in the wind. To accommodate the insatiable appetite of the Soviet Bear, four and a half million Poles were forced to relocate westward into old German territory. In order to balance the Soviet Union's devouring of one third of its land, Poland was given half of it back by shrinking Germany's borders to the Oder and Neisse rivers, displacing nine million German nationals.

Compounding this intolerable situation, the scales of Lady Justice heaped more misery upon misery. Every function of government, national or local, came to a complete standstill as a poisoned society was put under the microscopic eye of its victors and systematically leeched of its Nazi blood. In Berlin, Germany's greatest treasure, the calamity read like a chapter from Dante's *Inferno*. Its buildings lay in bombed-out heaps surrounded by people picking through the rubble like vultures cleaning day-old roadkill. Widowed women and fatherless girls sold their once chaste bodies for soldiers' rations. Even able-bodied men became beggars and were willing to do anything—short of admitting complicity in the Third Reich. Women and children cried in the streets for any scrap of information on husbands and fathers that would never return from the savagery of the East.

Into this quagmire came the likes of Blaine Harmon and Jim Marston. They were the "Kommandatura," that group of men given the task of sorting through the broken pieces of government like a person working a jigsaw puzzle without the benefit of the picture on the box cover. The pile had to be sifted to find all the pieces with a straight edge in order to put together a wobbly border. Subsequently, the power they exercised over peoples' lives stroked their collective egos. The corrupting influences they encountered were intoxicating. Opportunities for the accumulation of riches and power were placed at their feet daily, begging to be picked up. Only those of the strongest moral fiber and courage could resist its corrupting call. The weaker would succumb. Blaine Harmon and Jim Marston were strong at first, but in the end, the strength of their character proved not to be deeply rooted.

In the beginning, petty bribes were justified as the perks of the job. After all, they were the ones who sacrificed by remaining and not going home. Marston would approach Harmon and ask if a peculiar situation was all right or if that opportunity would be okay. Blaine Harmon would wince and feign minor discomfort of conscience, but his reply was always the same: "Yeah, sure, why not? Hell, everyone else got to go home to their families. Let's not make a habit of it, but be certain something is in there for me."

Over a period of time, Marston's timid need for approval evaporated and the two men came to feel neither pain nor shame. Perks blossomed into deals and deals turned to graft. When enough money had passed their hands, it came time for others, whose power transcends governments, countries and war itself, to call in their markers. Photographs were discreetly revealed to the pair and their money left a paper trail that was indisputable. Blaine Harmon and James Marston would never resist again. The outsiders had become the insiders.

CHAPTER 47

U.S. EMBASSY

WARSAW, POLAND

WITH COLD AND CLAMMY HANDS, MARSTON CAUTIOUSLY dialed the number he hated most. Covering the receiver with the palm of his other hand, he nervously peered at his door, hoping no one would enter or hear his conversation.

"Hello."

"Harmon's son just contacted me and wants to meet."

"Where are they?"

"Poland...Wroclaw."

"Where are they staying?"

"I don't know yet, but I'll find out." He knew it was information that he should have already secured.

"When do you meet?"

"Tomorrow at noon!"

"You don't seem sure."

"Of course I am. I said tomorrow at noon."

"Where?"

"Polanie Restaurant...Inner Town," Marston replied. He waited for a quick response, but it didn't follow. His heart throbbed. Does he suspect that I'm lying? Sheepishly, he asked, "What do you want me to do?"

"Just be there."

"I make—"

The phone clicked off.

Jim didn't like lying to his superiors. Why do I feel the need to hedge my bet regarding Harmon? he thought. If only I could turn back the hands of time. Blaine's dead—that's my warning—the shot across the bow. I could be next. No, we can work around this...Dillon always does.

He tried to write a memo, but the pen went limp in his shaking hand. The words were unreadable. He grabbed the paper, crumpled it in his hands and threw it toward the basket. "Shit!…Damn you Blaine!" His fist hit the desktop. "I told you I wanted to retire ten years ago…I told you it had been too long."

CHAPTER 48

PICKING UP THE RINGING PHONE, THE DESK CLERK SAID, "Hotel Odra. How can I help you?"

"Father Wetzel's room," the gravelly voice demanded.

"Ah yes, let's see…Father Wetzel. We put him in room 204, so it will be nice and quiet, he could—"

Dillon interrupted, "Just connect me through, you idiot!"

The ring of the phone startled the assassin. Franz Kreuger cautiously picked up the receiver and responded, "Yes?"

"Has Bachmann arrived yet?"

"No."

"Harmon is in Wroclaw as we speak."

"Do you know where?"

"No. Start checking the hotels. He'll be meeting Marston at the Polanie Restaurant tomorrow at noon—be there. Take Bachmann with you so there's no screwup."

The hair on Kreuger's neck bristled at the cutting remark. It was all he could do to grit his teeth and keep his cool. "What about Marston, do I take him out with the other two?"

"No! Only if you have no choice, then make it appear that rioting was the cause. Am I clear? We still need him."

"Yes," Kreuger hissed, bristled at the caustic comment.

Franz Kreuger was a professional assassin who seldom disobeyed orders. Over many years, he had stayed alive by following his keen instincts for survival. These core instincts had always served him well. Even though the cobwebs had not cleared from his sleep, he reached for an unfiltered cigarette. With a low, hardened hack for impetus, he felt the lump of nicotine-filled phlegm rise from his throat and enter his mouth. He looked for something to spit into, then decided to send it hurtling to the carpet below him.

The first drag of a cigarette in the morning was always the most pleasing. His raw nerve endings would mellow out as the smoke reached his blackened lungs. He was a hard man who eschewed life's pleasures and was content in knowing that he was a man well trained in his killing craft. Once a contract was sanctioned, he completed it—never leaving a trace back to his benefactors.

This morning seemed different. His honor had been questioned and he felt betrayed. It was that pig bitch with her sickening needles, he thought. He couldn't get the putrescent vision of working with her out of his mind.

That's it! It's the goddamn needles, he thought. That was the only fear he had ever known, and this weakness preyed upon him. Now I've got to be wet-nursed by that old bitch and her needles, 'just in case I screw up!' "Bullshit!" Franz hollered out and put the half-drawn cigarette into an empty beer bottle next to the bed. All these years, I've never botched a sanctioned contract. Who the hell is he to send in that bitch? It was Otto who screwed up in Geneva and I'm not taking the heat for someone else's screwup.

Running his fingers through his hair, his left hand grabbed the side of his head while his right firmly gripped his jaw. With a quick snap, he cracked his neck and decided that he would ace his benefactor's half-ass plan by taking out the American couple before the old hag got involved. What if they're supposed to meet at the Polanie Restaurant today, instead of tomorrow? What if that louse Marston was lying? There it went again—that feeling deep in his gut that told Franz it was going to happen early.

He knew it. His instincts were never wrong. They rose to the top and took control. He reached over and grabbed his Glock pistol. As his fingers caressed the black weapon, Franz pictured the young couple in his mind…he felt the raw heat of anger. With blinding speed, both hands clasped the gun and spun around. Drawing an imaginary bead, he saw their foreheads explode, the impact of the bullets snapping their necks backward. Pop, pop! No problem. No traces, very clean. "I still have what it takes," he whispered to himself.

After his shower, Franz walked back into the dressing area, drying his gray, flattop with a towel. He spotted the black suit with the Roman collar hanging in the closet. A sneer of disgust formed on his face. I hate this kind of shit, he thought. Why can't they let me take them out like I always do? I've made up my mind right here and now…there is no way I'm going to defile this body with that stinking disguise! Hell, even priests are allowed to go out in street clothes today, he rationalized. He smiled as his plan coagulated in his head. Oh, yeah—this works.

He slung his shoulder holster over his head and inserted his trusted weapon. Over all of this went his tailored jacket. As he preened in front of the mirror, he made sure his weapon did not show. He couldn't help but wonder if the disgusting, old pig-bitch had a special holster for her stinking needles. "Fuck her," he said aloud to no one. I haven't been this pissed off since Berlin. That sanction was mine. I had it all set up. Then *she* comes in ahead of me and screws it up. Well, that won't happen this time, Fraulein, you miserable bitch!

CHAPTER 49

THE POLANIE RESTAURANT WAS AN EATERY TYPICAL TO A thousand cities around the world. To describe it as unpretentious would be paying it a liar's compliment. Its exterior stucco was yellowing and it had blackish-green shutters, which were slightly askew to the windows and barely hanging with rusted screws. Peeling window jambs held wavy glass where several sun-bleached portraits of the beloved Polish Pope and the Black Madonna, Our Lady of Czestochowa, were taped and curling on the inside.

Because the building was narrow and deep, the seating inside was comprised of two long rows of booths with high backs that afforded reasonable privacy. Years of scrubbing gave the wooden table tops a faded, mellow sheen. Dim lighting gave the Polanie an overall ethnic charm that made up for its middle-class menu.

Studying each patron that entered his humble establishment, Karol Tciuszko prided himself on knowing his patrons' business.

"Ah, I see you be Americans," Karol said, his beaming smile preceding his words. With a slight bow and welcome sweep of his arm, he seated his two guests in one of the rear booths. He liked having his patrons close at hand.

"Very observant," Bryan replied in good humor, "although I'm not quite sure how to take that. Is being an American a compliment?"

Lisa allowed Karol's observation of ethnicity to stand uncorrected.

"Oh yes, ha ha! Please, do not take as insult. I should wish that our poor city could attract more tourists...American tourists, that is. Right now, we are awash with these bastard Germans to visit us, but then," he paused, lowered his voice while looking around cautiously, "maybe we get the filthy, Ruskie pigs back, too." Karol made a quick sign of the cross, then looked at his guests and said, "Please to forgive. You want that I should bring two lovely people something to drink?"

"Start us off with two coffees, please," Bryan said. "We're waiting for someone else."

"Is this man, woman?" Karol asked.

"An elderly gentleman."

"Good. I will bring two coffees and send friend back as soon as he comes."

He grabbed two mugs and began pouring the dark brew into them. Karol Tciuszko's mind drifted to a scene of his grandfather and grandmother pushing a two-wheeled cart that used to be pulled by an old, worn-out nag. The cart was heaped high with a threadbare blanket tied over the top. They passed a bombed-out train station with the city name, Lwow, stenciled on a sign that hung on an angle by one hinge. It creaked as it swung in the slight breeze, mirroring the movement of the broken refugees. His grandmother was wiping her tears with the edge of her long, brown babushka. Her rounded back strained under the weight of a large bundle of clothing like a sapling in a wind storm.

All along the westward route were Soviet soldiers armed with carbines, some mounted on horses, the rest standing. All were barking their harsh orders with looks of contempt on their surly faces. As the Russian troops stormed through his village, they killed any who resisted the shifting borders of Poland. In the background was the family farmhouse that had been carved out of the forests by his ancestors a hundred years earlier. He saw the face of his great uncle dying on the porch step, his resistance over. Karol's hatred of the Russians ran long and deep.

As it overflowed the second mug, the hot coffee burned his thumb. The scene in his memory disappeared as fast as it had come. Rounding the corner of the kitchen with the hot drinks, Karol noticed a distinguished looking, silver-haired gentleman enter the restaurant.

"Ah, Mr. American, your friends are back here. Please to come and sit with them," Karol said. Carefully setting the full cups down and pulling the towel from his shoulder, he wiped the seat and motioned for Jim Marston to sit.

Bryan slid out of his booth and stood, hand extended, to greet the elder diplomat and his wooden smile.

"Jim, thank you for meeting us," Bryan said.

"Bryan, let me say how sorry I am over the passing of your father."

"Thank you. Oh, excuse me…Jim Marston, this is my friend, Lisa

Brandt. Lisa, this is Jim Marston, an old family friend."

"I'm pleased to meet you. " She was polite, but began sizing up the visitor.

"Enchanted my dear, I've heard much about you, Miss Brandt."

Bryan's brow furrowed, trying to remember when he'd had any discussion with him regarding Lisa.

"Please to excuse, but I brought you some coffee also," Karol interrupted.

"That sounds like something I could sorely use," replied Marston.

"You like to see menu?" asked Karol.

"Yes, but I would prefer to wait a bit, thank you."

As Karol walked away, Bryan nodded to Lisa and she produced one of the manila envelopes and handed it to him. Opening the top flap, Bryan took a long breath for dramatic purpose while turning the folder in his hands. "I believe this is why my father was killed. He said you'd know what to do with it."

The diplomat became nervous, finding himself at a loss for words. "Bryan…your father and I made some mistakes a long time ago. The times were different. I wish that…well, you have to understand, there was confusion everywhere. All those people were desperate and had so many needs…we couldn't help everyone. The pressure was intense…so much money, that—"

Bryan interrupted the stumbling diplomat. "Please, I know now there are things that my father did that are going to sicken me. That's why he's dead—he paid the ultimate penalty. He had information of such consequence. We have that information and that's why there are people who would kill me…and Lisa." Sliding the envelope across the table, his eyes locked on the diplomat. "And, I believe, it's why they'll also kill you."

Marston fumbled as he pulled several copies out of the envelope. He froze at the name on the birth certificates.

"It's your Vice President, isn't it, Ambassador?" asked Lisa. "He's Eva Braun's son."

CHAPTER 50

MARSTON'S HEART BEGAN TO POUND AT THE SOUND OF her name. The game was over. Resignation engulfed the tired diplomat. "Yes, it's Koernig." He paused and dropped his head into his open palms. Seconds passed, but time seemed an eternity as he gathered his composure. Staring only at the table's surface, the Ambassador began his overdue confession.

"Koernig was handpicked to lead a new confederation—an economic union of the United States and an expanded Germany—a new world order if you will. Not just a political entity, but an economic powerhouse…a global government that'll not only control people, but resources and industry as well. All within a peaceful framework—a framework that will allow capitalists to grow, individuals to prosper, poverty to be eliminated, the overpopulating of the earth to be reined in—controlled." Marston, the apologist, switched gears to become Marston, the salesman. His pace quickened and his face returned to its normal color. In a convoluted way, he suddenly felt righteous.

"Yes. Of course, your father and I knew of this and were damned well instrumental in it, but no one wanted us dead because of it. Bryan, you were being groomed to take my place, to become a part of all of this. You still can, don't you see? Listen my boy, let me take the packet and give it to my superiors. We'll tell them you were already coming to me… to make damned sure that you were really in on it, or—"

"Ambassador Marston, please!…Stop all this!" Lisa looked at Bryan and moved the second envelope sideways to him. "Show him the rest."

"Jim," Bryan said, "this isn't about Koernig, or economic power, or your so-called global government. Is this how you plan to control the world's population?" He tossed the envelope across the table.

Marston looked confused as he opened the envelope and began pulling out its sordid contents. Confusion turned to concern, then to astonishment. The gaping of his mouth revealed everything. After several minutes, he put the papers down, arranged them in a neat bundle and slid them into the envelope. He stared downward to the tabletop, allowing the data to sink in and expand its hideous message. Little by little his eyes rose to meet Lisa's, then Bryan's. "Listen. I mean...your father and I didn't know...we—"

"Yes. He *did* know, damn it!" Bryan slammed his palm onto the table. "He *did* know! That's why he put this in his safety deposit box. He knew!" Bryan's voice trailed off as he turned his head to see if his outburst had been heard. "But he chose to do nothing about it...not until the very end. Jim, he said you'd know what to do with this. I think, down deep, he believed that there was still good in you. That you'd do what he couldn't—do what's right, fix what he didn't have the strength to do." Lisa reached across the table and firmly placed her hand on Marston's trembling wrist.

"I don't know. How do we know that they even want this virus?" Marston asked. "How do we know if it even exists, or after all these years that it's any good, or alive? I mean, it's a virus—how long could it last?"

"Ambassador," Lisa began, "I'm a doctor of dentistry and I've taken numerous courses in bacteria and viruses. Of all the enemies of the body, the virus is the least complex. Simply put, it's a protein-coated bundle of genes carrying DNA, which are its blueprint for reproduction. You see, it hasn't any reproducing mechanism, so technically, it's not alive—until it enters one of our body cells. Then our cells become the factories to produce new, *living* viruses. Each virus can produce thousands of copies of itself, each killing its host cell, but, and here's the catch, *only* if its DNA instructions tell it to. Don't you see, Mr. Ambassador? If kept in a vacuum-sealed canister at a proper temperature, this virus could be available forever. It's not alive, at least not until it is targeted...at *specific* peoples' DNA!"

Marston no longer looked at Lisa. Staring at the table, he spoke in a whispered voice. "This storage facility, it's now a part of the convent property, isn't it?"

"We believe it is," Bryan said.

"So the Germans deeded the property over to a remote convent so the virus could be kept hidden, protected by unsuspecting nuns. Rather brilliant, in a twisted sort of way," Jim added with sarcasm.

"But why haven't they retrieved it before now?" asked Lisa.

"That would have caused too much attention," replied Marston. "Poland and East Germany were two of the most closely guarded countries under the grip of the old Soviet Union—KGB controls and agents were everywhere. Without a doubt, the safest place to hide something would be in a cloistered convent. As long as it was there, the virus would be in safe storage."

Marston paused, the grand scheme coming to view. "It all fits into a neatly timed package. I thought the plan was only for Germany to recover its former borders—to be stronger both economically and politically. With a refurbished army, they would stand alongside the United States and create a new world balance. Russia would no longer be the second military power—Germany would be. This union would be a counter balance to a nuclear China and an emerging nuclear India."

As Marston shook his head, his voice and demeanor rose. "Germany doesn't need this land in Poland to assert their military or economic power. Where in the hell have I been? They want the border moved so they can control Wroclaw, move their people and relocate the convent. They'll do it with legitimacy and later work their insidious plan with this virus."

His mind continued to race as he paused for a long slug of coffee. "Sure," he said, "they are looking eastward, but their goal is to take all of Poland, then Russia itself. Then they will have a ready-made workforce of mindless minions. Two thirds of the old Soviet Union will die off after a generation or two, then half the Chinese. With Koernig as president, this union would have virtual global control. And this cabal of financial elitists would control the money supply of both the United States and Germany. Control the money supply of that economic union, and you control more than half the world."

Marston's anger flashed like a beacon. "This is what these bastards have waited for—the timing is perfect! Donskoy has rolled his armies through its Federated Nations and put them under his control. The world sees him as the aggressor. His troops are massed along the Polish border and are ready to carve up it up like they did in nineteen thirty-nine. He could even be blamed for causing the viral outbreak. He'd be painted as practicing biological warfare against his conquered populations...who will be falling ill by the millions. No one from the West would come to the aid of another Hitler in the making."

The Ambassador paused and then clutched at Bryan's forearm. "No, this time, the Western nations with Koernig in power would welcome and support a German countermove against the Soviets, especially if they are a nation that is too sick to defend itself!"

CHAPTER 51

STANDING AT HIS COFFEE STATION, KAROL TCIUSZKO heard the bell jingle as the door to his restaurant opened. Grateful for another customer, he turned the corner to the dining area and stopped in his tracks. His jaw dropped as he took in the image before him. His breath came in short gasps. Who…where? I've seen this man before… where? He stepped back behind the square column, his back pressed against the wall, his mouth dry. He felt something dark and ugly stir from within. These were deep, burning feelings of hatred that had been suppressed; only now they exploded from the recesses of his mind. What was it was about this chisel-jawed man who stood in the entry slapping his glove, impatiently waiting to be seated? Karol poked his head around the corner, squinting for a better look. His head snapped back. Is it him? His family jolted into his consciousness.

He recalled his sister as she carried soup to the table, placing it in front of his smiling father. "Karol, where are you hiding? Come, it's time to eat." The face of his loving mother came into focus. She turned from the black stove, wiping her hands on her embroidered apron. "Karol? Where is that imp?" she said. "He always plays his hiding game at the dinner hour. Sweet Mother of Jesus, I'm going to box his ears if he doesn't come this minute!"

His father finally shouted in exasperation, "Karol! Come now."

The door! It burst open, showing a hulk standing and holding a weapon. His mother shrieked. His father rose in panic. The long, black gun swung its deadly aim. The blast! Oh my God—it's Papa. He shot Papa! The man moved smooth and swift, like a killing machine. The gun pointed to his mother, spit once. She fell against the stove, then slid lifeless to the floor. His sister, gripped in terror, couldn't move. Two more shots spit out. Her body bolted backward into the open fireplace, soup splashing everywhere.

The man-machine looked around. He searched every room, every corner. Karol laid his head on the floor of the loft. Sweet Saint Joseph, please protect me. Don't let him see me. He felt hot urine release into his pants. Please! Please. Jesus...

The killer placed his gloved hand on the latch of the door. He stopped. The first drip of urine passed through the floorboard, hitting the stone floor below. He turned, looked upward in the direction of Karol, his weapon followed, sweeping for a new target. His glare pierced every timber, every slat, looking for a shadow. The cruel face of the killer was now exposed, burned into the memory of Karol. He would never forget it. The door creaked as the wind opened it again. Then noise, voices... his neighbors were stirring. The killer looked in the door's direction. A second drip released itself. Looking again at the loft, he drew aim in Karol's direction, fired three shots and left.

Is it him? Could it be him? Karol wiped the sweat on his forehead with his towel. It could be...he's older, grayer. Confusion crept in. Karol looked again and thought, It can't be. Maybe he's just another Kraut from the mob that had come into Poland. Wait! This one's different—cold, menacing. He scans with the eye of a hawk. It's him—the killing machine! Has Satan returned?

Karol summoned every ounce of courage as anger trumped his fear. He pushed off the wall in the direction of the impatient intruder. He approached the malevolent stranger, forced a smile and cautiously asked, "Would you like that I should get you table? I have one right here," he said, pointing to the first table in.

Kreuger looked over Karol's shoulder and cracked a satisfied grin as he honed in on the three Americans in the rear booth. "Nein, I want that one right there, bitte."

Karol felt an icy chill run up his back. It's him. I know it! The man walked past him to the center booth and sat down, his piercing glare never leaving the three visitors.

CHAPTER 52

MY INSTINCTS WERE RIGHT, KREUGER THOUGHT. HE PIC-tured the three people slouched in the booth with blood gushing from bullet holes in their foreheads. He felt good. Closure was at hand without the bitch and her needles.

"May I start fine gentleman with coffee?" Karol asked.

"Coffee is fine," Kreuger said, still honed in on his targets. Karol smelled the danger. He doesn't want me—he wants *them*! He snapped the damp towel off his shoulder and swabbed the table in broad, rapid swipes. His forearm brushed against the intruder's jacket. The assassin's hand lashed out and pushed Karol's wrist aside.

Karol maintained his decorum and thought, I was right; he's wearing a gun. You have to get up plenty early to fool Karol Tciuszko, but what does he want with these Americans? I must to help them. I'll never again lie still in fear. Never!

"I shall start you with my delicious coffee and bring you menu in moment, please." He tried to appear nonchalant, but his thoughts wouldn't stop. He is nothing but a killer—a cold-blooded killer. When he is finished with the Americans, he will harm me and then my Katerzina. He will leave no witnesses. A plan formulated in his mind. With shaking hands, he pulled out his billing pad and scratched out a bill for the three in the rear booth. On its backside he wrote his warning.

"Jim, will you help us?" asked Bryan, with a heart that was unsure of the response.

"Bryan, I don't know what to say, other than yes. Let me take the packets. I'll need them if I can get in to see the President himself—alone."

Lisa's hand immediately pushed on Bryan's leg. He looked over and saw concern written on her face, but she nodded approval. Bryan squeezed her hand and said, "My father told my mother you would know what to do with this, and I guess we have no choice but to put our trust in you—and that includes our lives."

"Ambassador," Lisa added, "do you think going to the President is—"

Karol interrupted, his index finger patting the back of the small paper for emphasis. "Here is your bill, fine people, please to pay when ready."

Bryan looked up. He saw Karol with a deep frown, his eyes darting toward Kreuger. He then moved to pour more coffee, buying time.

"What's this?" Bryan whispered, turning the bill around to read the handwritten note.

"What does it say?" asked Marston.

Bryan whispered, reading the note aloud. "Do not turn around—man in other booth—gun under jacket."

"What?" Lisa said, louder than Bryan's comfort level.

"Shh! Don't turn around," he whispered forcefully.

"Anything else I may bring fine people?" Karol asked in a loud voice as he returned to their table, his back to Kreuger. "Is very hard to be good Western capitalist if nobody eats." He then lowered his voice to a whisper. "There is back door in kitchen, across from toilet, not see hallway from booth. Man and woman go toilet, then get out." Reaching across the table, Karol grabbed a menu, opened it on the table and raised his voice again. "Nobody wants food anymore; how can I feed my poor family?" He closed the menu and reached to place it in its holder. "Please to make run out of here," Karol whispered to Bryan. "As I pass his table, push me into him; maybe I give you ten seconds, no more."

As Karol turned away, he feigned hearing something from Lisa, stopped and replied loud enough for the stranger to hear. "What? Oh, please to forgive, toilet down hall on right," he said, pointing to the rear. Passing Kreuger, he muttered to himself loud enough to be overheard, "Sure, flush as many times as you want, I make so much money on coffee."

With a slight nod of his head to Lisa, Bryan slid out of the booth and stepped aside allowing Lisa to get out. Casually, she walked down the hall toward the lavatory as Bryan sat back down. Kreuger let go of his pistol and slid his hand out of his jacket. Bryan counted to thirty and gave a nod to Marston, who followed Lisa's lead. Raising the bill close to his face, Bryan pretended to study it and looked at his watch. The seconds ticked off, unmercifully slow. His heart pounded, the blood rushing to his neck as he prepared to make his move.

Terror choked the very air out of Bryan. His hands became clammy as he nervously faked looking at the bill, the pain from his shoulder wound intensifying with each heartbeat. He looked again at his watch, just one more minute to go. *God, why doesn't my heart slow down? I can't stand this!* He cautiously glanced at his watch again—thirty seconds.

Karol grabbed the coffee pot and began walking up the aisle. He passed Bryan, giving him a nod with his eyes. Summoning all his courage, Bryan slid his right leg over the edge of the bench and ever so slowly slid his left hand till it gripped the edge of the table. As Karol came to within a few feet of Kreuger, he hollered out, "You want I should pour more coffee?"

Now! Bryan bolted from his seat and lunged forward up the aisle. Kreuger saw him move. With the instincts of a trained assassin, his hand raced into his open jacket and withdrew the semiautomatic pistol. Bryan's age had the advantage as he quickly reached Karol and pushed him, coffee and all onto Kreuger. With the hot brew scalding his chest, Franz screamed out in pain, and with a mighty sweep of his hand and arm, smashed the gun into the side of Karol's head. Karol's body slumped to the table and then to the floor. Franz kicked him with a thrust of his foot.

The few seconds were enough as Bryan raced through the door before Kreuger was able to draw a bead on him. Fighting his way up from the booth, he saw Bryan leap into an open back door of a grey Mercedes as it sped away.

"Fuck!" he blurted out. He then kicked Karol's limp body again and again in the groin. He looked down, anger welling up as he bent over and placed the gun barrel next to Karol's temple. "Polish dog!"

"Karol?" A frantic voice resonated from the kitchen.

Kreuger's attention snapped from the crumpled mass to the kitchen. He pulled up the Glock, slipped it into his holster and spit on Karol. Within seconds, he vanished.

CHAPTER 53

"AMBASSADOR MARSTON, WE'RE GOING TO NEED SOME help, our clothes are still at the hotel and now we haven't a car."

"You don't need a car, Lisa," he replied, "at least not yet. You two are going back to the embassy in Warsaw with me. One thing is for certain, they will be watching your car at the restaurant and they may have even discovered where you are staying. Do you have your traveling papers?"

"Yes, but—"

"No buts! Tell her, Bryan, you know I'm right about this."

Bryan sat staring out the window. His mind seemed a thousand miles away, yet he heard the conversation. It was not just the shock of the restaurant, everything seemed a blur. Nagging details about their encounter with Marston had not added up and needed to be squared in his head before he could go any further. At last, his silence was broken. "Jim, you told Lisa back in the restaurant you had heard a lot about her. When the hell did you 'hear a lot about her?'"

"Well, I guess you must have told me on the phone when you called," he stammered.

"No! No, I didn't. And how do you suppose that assassin knew we were going to meet at the Polanie?" Bryan demanded.

"I don't know, I—"

"I think you *do* know!" Whatever the truth was, Bryan had to know it, or maybe he already did.

Jim shot back, "All right, God damn it!" Anger engulfed the normally smooth diplomat. "I was called by one of our members—he knew you would be contacting me. I told him the two of you were in Wroclaw, but I swear, I told him we were to meet tomorrow at noon, not today! I've stuck my neck out Bryan, and there's no going back with these people."

"You want us to trust you, when you damned near got us killed? How do we know that you're not setting us up now, or that you're even going to President Cook with this?" Bryan turned his head and again stared out the window. He felt a twisting in the pit of his stomach.

Marston fell silent. "I guess you don't." Then, in an apologetic tone, he continued, "I can't roll back the clock to convince you, nor can I change what your father and I did—God knows I wish I could. While I don't have the power to alter the past or change the present, I can tell both of you that, unlike your father, I do have the opportunity to rewrite the future—but only if you let me."

Bryan looked over to Lisa and saw her tentative nod of approval. "I just don't see that we have any choice but to believe him," she said, assuring him with the strength of her stare.

***

Looking in the rearview mirror for what seemed to be the hundredth time, it slowly became clear to Marston that they had, in fact, made their escape. His relief allowed his thoughts to focus on other matters. Noticing his cell phone mounted on the console, he saw that four calls had been logged in from his embassy, all with the urgent code prefixed. "I need to call the embassy," he said, wondering how much more pressure he could tolerate as he dialed directly to his secretary. "Millie! It's Jim."

"Ambassador, oh thank God you called. We've been frantic around here worrying about you. You said you wouldn't be back until late, but no one knew where you had gone, and with the riots and all...then you didn't answer your cell phone. Anyway, there's been no confirmation as of this moment, but apparently the Russians have moved troops across the Polish border. The Secretary of State wants you in Washington ASAP for a briefing. I've got a military plane waiting on standby for immediate departure as soon as you arrive. I've also called Mrs. Marston and she's packing now."

"Millie, you are a gem! Please call Sally back and tell her to pack for both of us. And tell her to expect a slightly longer stay in Washington this time. I should be back in two hours." He slowly replaced the phone and checked his rearview mirror one more time.

"We'll go with you as far as Warsaw, Jim, because we need you to secure a car and find some clothing, but then we're going back to Wroclaw—to the convent of the Sisters of St. Mary Magdalene."

CHAPTER 54

OVAL OFFICE
WASHINGTON, D.C.

"GOOD MORNING, MR. PRESIDENT."

Cook looked up and greeted Chief of Staff Waring, "Morning John."

"Do you want to review today's schedule now or have another cup of coffee first?"

"I think I could use one more, need to clear out the cobwebs."

"No problem, sir. I could use another myself."

"You know, all my life I wanted this job," the President said, tilting his chair backward. "Every damned move I ever made—I had the Oval Office in mind. Now I detest it. Sometimes, I swear I'd like nothing more than to chuck it all and resign. God, it was so much easier when I was governor of Tennessee—a woman waiting any night that I needed some ass. Just get in the car with the security troopers, official business of course, and they had the babes waiting for me in some apartment— always good-looking chicks, too. Nobody really gave a damn back then. Hell, I ran that state slicker than a dog's dick and if anybody dared to step on my toes—boom! They were out on their asses. Ahh, that's good coffee."

"I'm sure those were the good old days, Mr. President, but—"

"Damn! Then that lousy trailer trash had to slap me with that lawsuit—what a crock," he said, shaking his head in disbelief. "Hell, she wanted me to slip it to her. Then she pulls that 'I'm insulted' crap. I mean, what did she think I was doing—inviting her up there for a little conversation? Besides, she looked like a whore, big hair and all, but never were there pictures...till I got to Washington."

Waring tried to control his sarcasm and said, "Well, I'm sure having the ladies right here in the White House would be a little risky, sir. You had to know there'd be fallout if you got caught."

"Bullshit. Let me give you a little lesson in politics. I've set myself up as being too damned likable, too sincere. Hey, you pick the right moment in front of press, then you bite your lip, quiver your chin and let your eyes water up…bingo! Women totally eat it up and want to comfort you. You see, I'm like someone's wayward son. In the first place, if the kid does something wrong, you don't believe it. In the second place, if you do end up believing it, you hate like hell to punish him because you love him so much and know he's basically a good kid. The only ones that get punished in politics are the ones that you don't like in the first place. You know, like that surly Nixon with the sweat ball on his nose. Hell, even his most ardent supporters disliked him. Nobody minds kicking a brooding asshole, you know what I mean?"

"Uh, that I do, Mr. President, but please keep in mind, the Senate is zeroing in on the other problems, and not just the women."

"Shit, come on John, those were just some well-timed investments. Everybody in government comes to power and fattens up their wallets. Besides, that was when I was governor and—"

"Mr. President," Waring interrupted. He was nervous about crossing the line, but said, "I'm talking about the obstruction charges. You're basically right about everything else, but it's not the public who will judge those charges. We now have to deal with the Senate. You have enemies in that august body, and if an impeachment vote were to come, we're not even close enough to use Koernig's vote in a tie."

"Bullshit!" shot back Cook, slamming his fist on the desk. "All of these problems have their roots in Koernig. That rotten, Nazi bastard has been nothing but a damned millstone around my neck. I should've never agreed with Jack Dillon to pick him."

"Dillon's still your biggest supporter, and without his millions in the beginning—"

"That's crap! He's hedging his stinking bet! That's why he pushed me to drop Akers in the first place and switch to Koernig. Don't you see what's happening? Koernig's hammering me and he's Dillon's hand-picked golden boy now—like I once was. And on top of all this, you're telling me I've got to make a heavy decision on Poland today." Cook sighed then mumbled, "God, I need a good screw right now."

Waring winced. "Well, I'm sure a good screw is what you need, sir, but we'd better review today's schedule—time's getting spare."

"Yeah, I know. What've we got first, those pimp lawyers or the

Polish crap?"

"The crisis in Poland is at the top of the agenda, Mr. President. We conference at 8:30 with State and that'll run to about 9:30. Then National Security at 10:00 sharp. That will run through lunch until 1:00, then the impeachment defense team from 2:00 to 4:00. That gives our PR people plenty of time to spin both crises before the evening news comes on."

"Okay, maybe I'll go knock some off with Rosemary on my break," Cook said.

"Sorry, Mr. President, but the First Lady has a Women's Conference luncheon today."

"Sarcasm, John, just sarcasm. I said I could use a good screw, not a screw with her icy highness. I wouldn't screw her with…well, never mind."

Waring raised his eyebrows, wondering if his president was beginning to lose it. He shook his head once in disbelief, checked his watch and said, "If you're ready sir, it's time for State." Waring stood, adjusted his tie and was grateful the conversation was over.

The president pushed his chair back from his desk, stared down at the carpet and thought, God, it really was better back in Tennessee. He rose to face yet another meeting.

CHAPTER 55

"GOOD MORNING, GENTLEMEN, PLEASE BE SEATED," COOK said as he entered the room. Pulling his pen out of his pocket, the President nodded to SecState Bertram Holden. "Bert, why don't you start us off with an overview?"

"Certainly, Mr. President. As you can see, I brought in Peter Barnes from Germany, Jim Marston from Poland and Ernest Niles from Russia. Each will be available for their assessments as needed. Now, we have confirmation from Langley that the Russians have, in fact, crossed the border into Poland. We don't have a final appraisal of the total strength of their troops, but their destination appears to be the Oder and Niesse Rivers. Their official excuse is, 'to protect Polish sovereignty from the ravenous appetite of NATO.' Donskoy has invoked the old Warsaw Pact treaties and doctrines, which he claims are still in effect unilaterally, because Russia never gave its approval for Poland to join NATO. Bottom line, he claims Russian troops will not leave Poland until all German nationals have been expelled. The official Polish response has..."

As Holden rambled on, Jim Marston felt the effects of jet lag on his well-worn body. After all these years, it was something he'd learned to compensate for, but never really mastered. Stifling his yawn, Jim stared long and hard at President Cook, noticing how particularly aged and haggard he'd become since he last saw him. He wondered how the President would react to the information he was about to unload on him. Would it change his thinking? Would he be able, or even willing, to do anything with it? Marston still wasn't sure how to approach him concerning the information. Should I go through the Chief of Staff? he thought. How do I keep Peter Barnes from finding out? I don't think Holden is part of the group, but I really can't be sure.

Suddenly, the solution came to him like the switch of a light in a dark closet and he quickly jotted a note on the top of his report.

Looking down to the floor at his right side, he saw his half-opened briefcase. He reached down and pulled out another copy of his report.

"...and so, Mr. President," continued the Secretary in the same monotone he began with, "my recommendation would be that a joint statement be issued through NATO condemning the invasion, but leaving the door open for quick negotiations to diffuse the situation. Bill Thomas has talked to the Russian ambassador who has assured him that this action is only a supportive police action to bolster the Polish government. Now I know that this seems to fly in the face of what Donskoy has stated, but the ambassador has assured us that this is temporary in nature and that there will be room for discussion as long as this is kept on the international forum."

Realizing that the long monologue was finally finished, President Cook quickly shook his head once to clear his delirium. "Thank you, Bert. Do we have an official response from the Polish government?" Cook asked, running the risk of another long response.

"We do, Mr. President," chipped in Bert Holden. "Of course, it's one of condemnation and concern, followed by a demand for both Germany and Russia to extract their people from Polish borders. They have also sent an appeal to the Vatican, for whatever good that will do."

"And do we have an unofficial response?" begged Cook.

"Neither we, nor any of our allies, have had any requests for military support. Jim Marston discussed the situation with the Polish ambassador and may be able to shed a little light there. Jim...?"

Seizing the moment, Marston stood, scooped up his sheaf of papers with both hands and nervously walked over to the President's side. "Sir, the Polish ambassador would welcome any help the United States may give, short of direct military intervention. He reminded me of how long his country had been under the shackles of Soviet domination and believes the situation would be best resolved politically rather than by military confrontation. He has a sequential outline of steps that he feels could dissolve the problem and I have put them together in this report. His thoughts are succinct and clearly worth noting." Jim slid the packet under the President's eyes with his index finger gently tapping the faint handwritten note.

"Excuse me, Jim," Holden said with a disturbed tone in his voice, "but don't you have a copy of that report for me?" The clearing of his throat only highlighted his glare.

Feigning awkwardness, Marston quickly handed the other copy to the angry Secretary. "Of course, excuse me, Mr. Secretary, as you know I only arrived this morning on a red-eye, so this is hot off my laptop, and my jet lag may be responsible for any lapse of etiquette."

As the President looked down at his report, he missed the penciled note in the upper right corner:

Urgent to discuss events in Poland—must be *private*!

Cook opened the folder and feigned interest by turning a couple of pages upward. He then swiftly closed the manila folder and said, "Gentlemen, thank you. I think we'll close at this point. I have National Security next on the agenda. Thank you for your time, and be prepared for another briefing. Bert, I'd like you at the 10:00 a.m. meeting." Picking up the packet of papers, Cook retreated to his office. Marston's heart sank.

***

CONFERENCE ROOM

WHITE HOUSE

10:05 A.M.

Chief of Staff Waring knew he would be bombarded with barbs as he entered the conference room and saw anxious faces turn to disappointment. He would have to get control immediately. "Gentlemen, Mr. Vice President, I'm sorry but President Cook will be just a few minutes more, then we'll quickly get started."

"Well, I wonder who he's hitting on now?" the Vice President opined, his sarcasm loud enough for everyone to hear. "Besides himself," he quickly added.

As the controlled chuckles subsided, John Waring cleared his throat for order, then asked of the CIA Director, "Do we have the recon slides from Langley set up?"

"Set up and ready to go with full reports at each seat," John Martin replied.

After several minutes, the grousing again peaked. Tapping his fingers on the long mahogany table, Koernig took the lead. "You did say ten o'clock sharp, did you not, John? If we're having a meeting, maybe someone should knock on his honor's bedroom door and tell him not to catch anything in his fly when he zips up."

The room again filled with low, guttural laughter. "Perhaps he should just bring the bimbo in with—"

The turning of the door knob sent the room to dead silence.

"You were saying, Mr. Vice President...?" the wily Chief of Staff asked dryly.

"Nothing," Koernig snorted. "Mr. President, are we finally ready to go?"

"Gentlemen," Cook said, nodding to the assembled men. "As usual, I'm quite sure our European affairs expert, the Vice President, would like to start the meeting by enlightening us on the unquestioned, territorial rights of the German people."

His sarcasm was biting to everyone except its intended target. Koernig scanned those present as if nothing had been said and began his diatribe against Russia. "Mr. President, I...excuse me, *we* have been patient for too long, supporting the failed policy as advanced by a Department of State that is in desperate need of a spine donor. This policy of appeasement with Donskoy has brought us right to the very crisis we are about to discuss. As you know, I've long argued in favor of allowing the German people to reclaim their prewar borders. I repeat again, the current borders go against the natural order of history and a correction has been long overdue. Now we have exactly the worst possible situation with Russian troops reoccupying Poland. Had we allowed the Germans to reestablish their borders before Donskoy came to power, we wouldn't be having this conference.

"There are always golden moments in history. One of these moments was when the Iron Curtain fell and the Baltic States were freed. The Soviet Union ceased to exist and its offspring, Russia, was left as an economic basket case. We had our chance to fully right Europe, but we allowed that chance to come and go. The primary question is: What will we do about it now? How will history judge us for our actions at *this* moment?"

SecState Holden had been biting his tongue and could tolerate no more. In total exasperation and with firmness he rarely displayed, said, "Our policy, Mr. Vice President, has never, at any time, been a policy of appeasement. I would remind everyone here that we have one hundred and fifty thousand military personnel bogged down in Afghanistan... and there still appears to be no hope of resolving that conflict. In the report lying in front of everyone, you will see that even as late as last night, the Polish ambassador himself is *not* recommending direct military intervention."

"Excuse me, Mr. Secretary, but I don't see where the Polish government has much of a voice in this matter. Part of what is now Poland is still legitimate German land. Germany is still our only ally left in Afghanistan. Do you possibly think that you have the *German* position clearly spelled out in this report?" Koernig hissed.

Cook intervened in a calming manner. "Gentlemen, please! I think it wise to first review the intelligence we have from Langley. Then I'd like to hear from the Joint Chiefs to see what our military options may or may not be."

"Director Martin has some slides to review first, Mr. President, if you are ready..."

***

Pacing his office like a caged animal, Jim Marston was having a difficult time waiting and knew only too well what was going on in the National Security meeting.

He second guessed himself and thought, Why I didn't put the contents of the envelopes in with my report when I gave it to the President, I'll never know. He could be using that information now. He could be making it clear to everyone what's really going on.

Coming full circle back to his desk, Jim saw a picture of Sally and his children. Suddenly, they came alive inside the frame. They'd soon know his dirty secret and they would have to share in his shame.

Maybe I should've trusted the Secretary with the information, he thought, his eyes still staring blankly at the picture. Why didn't I at least feel him out? He began pacing again. Has the President been mortally wounded with this impeachment crap? Shit! When does he get out of that meeting? The unanswered questions tortured his mind. What about young Harmon and the girl? I wish they weren't going to Wroclaw. His hands began clenching and unclenching in frustration. Damn! The President has to call me, he just *has* to!

The picture in the gilded frame jumped out at him one more time. He slumped into his desk chair. The moment of truth had finally arrived and he cringed at its consequences. What, on God's earth, will I ever say to Sally?

CHAPTER 56

LISA'S HEAD TURNED AGAIN TO HER MAP. "THE ROAD FORKS up ahead, stay to the left. See, the sign for Wroclaw? We're only about an hour out."

"I see it," Bryan acknowledged. "I'm just not sure what good we can do. It'll be in the hands of the President, maybe even as we speak."

"The President? It said in the paper this morning, your senate released another bombshell yesterday—someone testified that the President ordered him to shred documents that had been subpoenaed. This could lead to his impeachment, Bryan. If he's impeached or resigns, that leaves Koernig in charge. You know who this man is, and you know he's part of this global spider web. If he allows those people to get hold of this virus, millions and millions of human beings are going to become mindless robots and eventually die. Don't you see? There won't be any stopping them. You know this, Bryan! There won't be a life for us or our children—or for half the world. Wherever this virus is, it has to be destroyed before it's too late."

Bryan looked straight ahead at the road and glanced to the left. The trees passed by, creating a green and black hypnotic scene that drew his every thought. His sense of resignation felt complete. "The Russians will probably beat us," he finally ventured, turning back again to Lisa. "They've already crossed the border and are heading this way."

"That's all the more reason for us to get there first."

"Look, I'm a diplomat. What do I know about destroying some stored virus, a virus that I don't know the location of or even whether it exists?"

"What about the owner of that restaurant...the Polanie?"

"Karol? What about him?"

"Maybe he could help us, or at least tell us who could."

"Hell, we don't even know if he's still alive, and if he is, why would he want to risk his life again?"

"He will, because he did it before—when he knew nothing. This time we'll tell him everything."

Bryan knew it was fear that was now driving his thoughts. For the first time in his life he really wanted something, and that something was a life with this woman. And yet he was afraid of losing it. "We can't go back there Lisa, they'll be looking for us and it's far too dangerous."

"I don't see that we have much of a choice, I just don't," she said, squeezing his hand with hers.

Bryan looked over and when he saw the courage in her eyes, his own strength returned.

***

Kreuger combed through all the hotels of Wroclaw. Money, the international influence of choice, opened all the registers and forgetful minds of sundry desk clerks. He knew he'd eventually find the hotel they had stayed in, that wasn't the question. He also knew there was no probability that they would stay at that hotel two nights in a row.

Kreuger was still groused over being told how to perform his tasks. Just give me the assignment and it'll get done…my way. It always has. Then this asshole Dillon comes along. This arrogant piece of shit who thinks he can micromanage everything. I'll give him the name of the hotel, and he can stick it up his ass for all I care.

He entered his room and closed the door behind him. Standing in front of the steam-fogged mirror, Kreuger grabbed a towel and wiped away an area in front of him. As his body came into focus, the reality of the moment haunted his glare. Rage welled up inside him like a pot that hums as it begins to boil. The red scald mark on his chest revealed the naked, cutting truth—they had gotten away, and he had failed. For the first time in his life, Franz felt his age and wondered if it wasn't time to get out. He didn't need the money; he had enough stashed away in a Swiss account to ride out the rest of his life in comfort, but he couldn't walk away from this one, not now. No, they'll die all right, but it won't be by some damned needle shoved into them by that miserable pig bitch. She's not going to one up me.

Kreuger's head snapped around at the startling sound of the telephone. He grit his teeth in disgust and threw the towel on the floor. He knew only too well who it was.

"Yes?"

"What happened at the restaurant…are they dead?" asked the gravelly voice.

For the first time in his life, Kreuger felt the shame of his own failure and it stung. His ego was bruised and he fumbled his words to cover his error in judgment. "No. They didn't show."

"What do you mean they didn't show? Marston himself told me he was meeting them there at noon today."

"I said they didn't show!" His voice rose in tension from his deliberate lie.

"Were you at the right restaurant, the Polanie? He said the Polanie."

"How many restaurants do you think are named the Polanie in this shit-hole city?"

"What about the hotels, I assume you found where they were staying?"

"Of course."

"Well, were they there?" asked Dillon.

Kreuger was tired of the conversation. Who does he think he's talking to…some rank amateur? "If they *were*, they would be dead, now wouldn't they?"

"Bachmann's in room 203 next to you. Get in disguise and go with her to the Convent of St. Mary Magdalene—that's where they'll go. Your papers are from the Seat of the Archbishop of Krakow. They'll give you permission to stay there for three nights, but you won't need that long. *One* of you had damned well better be successful!"

CHAPTER 57

WHEN THE POWER POINT SLIDE SHOW HAD FINISHED ON the large screen monitor, Vice President Koernig was the first to let his voice resonate. His petty glare scanned the members seated around the long table and he raised his arm straight out, palm up, at the projection screen to accentuate his words. "I hope that these pictures leave no question in anyone's mind that a Russian invasion of Poland is fully underway. No doubt the State Department would like to begin negotiating with Donskoy to get back *half* of the land they've already taken."

"Mr. President...can we please stop the sniping?" appealed the exasperated Secretary of State.

"Bill, we're all aware of your total dislike for State, so I would ask you to keep the level of sarcasm down. All right, I would agree with the Vice President that a Russian invasion of Poland is fully in effect. Chuck, what has been the unofficial reaction from NATO?"

"Well, sir," the SecDef responded, "as always, the wheels of NATO move slowly, even when one of its own members is invaded. I'm afraid our English and French allies do not appear to have the stomach or the will for a direct confrontation at this moment over Poland. They have issued the perfunctory condemnations, but you must remember that they just completed an agonizing and embarrassing retreat from Afghanistan. The consensus is that NATO may have been premature in admitting Poland into the organization. Frankly, they feel they have been caught a little off balance."

"How does Germany feel?" Cook asked.

"Outrage, of course, but it *is* their citizens who have initiated this crisis. They're going to stay low on this one—until the U.S. reacts, anyway. Even then, you must remember, they *have* made a major commitment to the effort in Afghanistan. We can't count on them for both fronts."

Cook requested to hear from the Chairman of the Joint Chiefs of Staff Belden. "Howard, I'd like the short straight facts. What are our military options?"

"Sir," the General addressed his Commander-in-Chief, "from strictly a conventional military standpoint, I'm afraid our options are minimal to nothing. By talking in terms of a conventional military response, I'm limiting myself to ground combat, air supported, of course. Containment of the enemy, militarily, is not possible under any scenario without putting whatever troops we may send at considerable risk. We do have our rapid deployment forces available for immediate insertion, but without any ability to back them up quickly, I'm afraid their impact would be minimal at best, and a continued retreat westward would have to be envisioned. In order to support the RDF quickly enough, we would be required to siphon off troops and materiel from Afghanistan, and that's an option that would be ill advised. Our abilities to effect coercion of the enemy by sea are nil, and to be effective by air would in all probability require the employment of tactical nuclear weapons."

With a long pause for emphasis, Belden scanned the room looking for affirmation of his judgment. His eyes returned to Cook and he leaned back in his chair, uncomfortable with the role of talking like a "Dutch Uncle" to the President of the United States. The mere thought of what he must say sent a chill down his back. "Mr. President, the only option we see from the military side is either the use, or the threatened use, of our full nuclear arsenal—and that becomes an extremely difficult, political decision."

The Secretary of State's face lost its color, his gaping mouth a witness to the incredulity of what he had just heard. "Mr. President, certainly under the concept of mutually assured destruction, we don't believe we can win some sort of a nuclear exchange."

"Perhaps not," interjected Koernig, "but do I need to remind anyone here of the Cuban missile crisis? When the Soviets not only believed in our nuclear ability, but our *resolve* to use them as well, they ultimately backed down and removed their missiles."

Ever the diplomat, Secretary Holden tilted his head and peered over his reading glasses. "May I politely remind the Vice President that the missiles we had clandestinely installed in Turkey were also removed in a rather silent, quid pro quo? What do we possibly have to offer the

Russians this time in return?"

Koernig dropped his head to his chest theatrically. Looking left, then right, he shook his head and sat back down. He then fixed his glare on the Secretary of State. "Where, may I ask, is it written in stone that we always *have* to offer something in return?" His voice now rose in a crescendo. "This is *their* invasion, not ours. It is an invasion with troops and tanks—not mere citizens!" His icy glare froze Holden. "We have," his voice receded, "no choice but to give our ultimatum for them to retreat—*and* to back it up by going to DefCon status."

"Mr. President, may I speak?" Security Advisor Doering asked in a barely audible voice.

"Certainly, Norm, all opinions are needed."

"Sir, this decision is ultimately yours to make, and I do want to be very clear that I agree with the Vice President on this matter, but in light of its potentially grave consequences, I strongly advise that our allies be informed of our decision, while at the same time be convinced that this decision is in our mutual interest, but is nonetheless, nonnegotiable. The raw truth is that NATO marches to the drumbeat of the United States. Of course, time is of the essence, because obviously by these intelligence photos, the Russian advance is moving rapidly and unabated. Therefore, Mr. President, should you decide to issue this ultimatum to the Russians, our allies need to be briefed immediately. I might also add that the window for issuance of this threat to the Russians is quickly closing. We either act immediately, or we stand down and do nothing."

Deep in thought, seconds slipped by as all eyes centered on the President. Finally, Cook opened his eyes and raised his head back up. A pained look of resignation came over his face.

"Chuck, your opinion?" he asked the SecDef.

"Mr. President, I agree with the Vice President and Norman. The only advice I would add would be to inform the leaders of Congress at the same time we inform our allies."

With a nod of his head, the President agreed. He looked at Koernig. He saw the power and the resolve this man had to destroy him. This intruder was picked by others more powerful than himself, not only to succeed him, but to control him like a puppet. It was similar to a recurring nightmare where everything is level, smooth and serene, and then the tranquility is disrupted by some violent agitation. Cook felt powerless to exert his will, as if he were being sucked into the center of an abyss.

Looking down at the table again, the President weighed his decision at length. Finally, with a rising of his head, the decision was made. "Gentlemen, the ultimatum will be issued tomorrow," he said, his teeth now locked as he scanned the table. He noticed Koernig breathe a sigh of relief. "I want a copy of the announcement to our allies on my desk by 3:00 p.m. today, Bert. Chuck, prepare us for DefCon status tomorrow. John, you set a meeting with the Senate and House majority and minority leaders for 7:30 a.m. tomorrow. I want all here present. Bert, schedule the Russian Ambassador for 1:00 p.m. Norman, you draft the ultimatum for my review at 3:00 p.m. today, and give a copy to Chuck for his review before it hits my desk."

"Excuse me, Mr. President," said Waring, "the press, you know they're all over this."

"Right, John, Bill Koernig will handle that with the press secretary. That will be all for now. Wait, one more thing—if one word of this leaks—"

CHAPTER 58

GAZING INTO THE MIRROR, ILSA BACHMANN COULDN'T shake the odd sensation she was experiencing as she adjusted the large rosary belt around her habit. I look almost angelic, she thought to herself. I've devoted and sacrificed my entire life to a cause, just like these nuns do...no husband, no children...but at least they have a God that loves them in return. Me? I only have a cause...a cause that doesn't even respect me for what I have given. Ilsa put her hands together in a prayerful pose. Looking at herself one more time in the mirror, her mind drifted as she pondered a make-believe life as a nun. There would be no killing, no weeklong bouts with chronic depression...just nights free of those recurrent, horrid nightmares.

A curt knock on the door jolted Ilsa from her fantasy. Her hand instinctively slipped under her habit, unzipped the leather pouch and gripped one of several hypodermic needles contained within. As she opened the door, she was poised to pounce on her prey. Seeing Franz in his priestly garb relaxed her fingers, but not her tension.

"Oh, it's you…enter," she said.

"Danke, Frau Bachmann. Or should I call you, the most holy Sister Ilsa?" The words rolled from his tongue, dripping with disgust.

"Let's keep our petty, little jibes to ourselves, shall we, Herr Kreuger? I'm sure this mission can be completed successfully if you just follow my advice."

"Frau Bachmann, must I remind you that I'm in charge and you will do as *I* say in this operation. Am I perfectly clear?"

Ilsa's jaw stiffened as her teeth ground together, the words bristled through her ears. Her hand again slid to the pouch concealed under the layers of her habit. With her hand clutching the needle, she willed herself to release the syringe and regain control.

She vowed to maintain the professional dignity that had been so important in her life, all the while fighting the feeling that it was being stripped away. "On the desk is a layout of the convent, our papers and photographs of our targets. Additionally, Herr Kreuger, there is a sealed envelope addressed to you. Feel free to review these and I will dutifully await your plan."

Kreuger licked his nicotine-stained index finger, wasting no time sorting through the packet of information. "I'll need fifteen minutes to finish my review. Then we'll check out the convent and its grounds." He reached into his inner coat pocket and without looking, he tossed a flask of schnapps to Ilsa who reacted instantly and caught the flying object.

Leaving her no dignity, he continued with a sneer, "Make yourself useful and pour some of this over ice for me."

Ilsa pursed her lips, turned and closed her eyes. In her mind, she saw a long needle enter the lower part of Kreuger's spine—his whole body going rigid from the shock, his eyes bulging from their sockets. Ilsa smiled. The scene gave her pleasure.

CHAPTER 59

AT FIRST, A SOFT RAIN HAD CREPT IN, BUT IT CHANGED and pounded the windshield of their car with such ferocity that Bryan could barely see the road, let alone the street signs of Inner Town, Wroclaw.

"Damn it, is it this street or the next?" Bryan snapped.

"Next left, then down about two blocks on the right. Be grateful, I think the rain will at least give us some kind of cover. Let's park in the back, maybe Karol left the back door open,"

"It'll help our cover only if we can read the damned—"

"There it is!" Lisa cried out. "Be careful."

Bryan sharply turned the steering wheel and pulled the dark Mercedes into the rear alley. Its surface was barely covered with gravel and had deep ruts filled with rain. As soon as Bryan had negotiated the potholes, he turned off the car lights and scanned the surroundings. Lisa sat motionless, staring at the rear kitchen door illuminated only by a rusted lamp swinging in the wind suspended only by its wires. They sat in silence until she looked over at Bryan and asked, "Ready?"

"No, but let's go anyway."

As she turned to open the car door, Bryan's hand grabbed her arm. "I love you."

"And I you," she replied, putting her hand over his with a firm squeeze.

Within seconds both car doors opened and they bolted out into the pouring rain toward the protection of a small, corrugated overhang above the door. As Bryan's hand turned the doorknob, there was a sudden screech and a loud thud near the trash bin next to Lisa. She stifled a scream and fell against the door, causing it to slam shut just as Bryan had begun to pull it open. A black cat jumped and ran away. Bryan, stunned by the noise, still had his hand on the doorknob.

Suddenly, the knob turned in his hand. He froze, then felt the door begin to open. His heart jumped into his throat and he reached to protect Lisa with his other hand.

"Who's out there?" Karol shouted. His head peered around the door, followed by the gun in his hand.

"Karol, don't shoot! It's us, the two Americans," Bryan blurted out.

Looking up at the bandages on his head, Lisa felt shame for causing his pain. "Are you all right, Karol? Are you alone?"

Karol looked past and around his uninvited guests and said, "Yes. Please to come in."

He grabbed Bryan by his coat, pulling and directing the two inside. When he was comfortable that no one had seen their arrival, he put down his revolver and quietly locked the door.

Once inside the empty restaurant, Karol led the young couple through the kitchen and into the dining area. Motioning with a quick snap of his wrist, he indicated a rear booth to sit in, then walked to the front door, locked it and turned over a faded sign that read CLOSED. Nervously, he peered over the sign and through the wavy glass pane, searching methodically left and right for any suspicious bodies or lurking shadows. Finally convinced no one was watching, Karol returned and slid onto the bench next to Lisa.

"Please to forgive, but it does not give my bruised body pleasure to see you again," he said, pointing to his bandaged head. "But why is it you come back?"

Lisa placed her soft hand on his arm. "Karol, we owe you so much and I don't know what to say or where to begin, but we're not here to just thank you—we need your help again!"

"Again? I don't know if much more my poor body can take. I am thinking that you people much in trouble." He looked straight into Lisa's eyes and said, "Besides, please to forgive this old fool, but I think that you not American citizen—I think you are German."

Looking down, Lisa nodded in shame. When her eyes returned to Bryan, a soft whisper was all she could muster. "We need to tell him the truth...only this time, we tell him everything."

The minutes rolled by and soon became an hour. Patiently, Karol listened to the long tale of corruption, murder and deception. All his life, Karol Tciuszko had been a person who wore his soul on his face, so

Bryan easily read his shock, surprise and even disbelief. Karol winced and frowned as the memories of his own family's haunting past flashed in and out. Scarcely a day of his life had passed that the dreaded visions didn't torture him. He carried the shame of not having stopped the killer, as if a boy of seven could ever have made a difference. In his pained mind, he had convinced himself he was a coward—a coward who had only wet his pants in a crisis.

Even the loving Abbess of the convent who had taken him in could neither soothe his grief nor ease his shame. Karol had become docile and passive over the years—someone the Russian soldiers could take advantage of whenever a free meal was expected or a favor demanded. Why always him? They would walk into his eatery and sit down without even a by-your-leave. He was expected to know each and every soldier's face and what their "usual" was, so they wouldn't be inconvenienced by having to order. When Karol would make an occasional mistake and place a wrong plate in front of one of them, it was quickly cast upward into his face. Karol would then ask forgiveness as he groveled on the floor, cleaning the mess. The kicks and laughter only added to his shame. And never was a meal paid for. His wife begged him to protest, but he was a man defeated. God, how he loathed the Russians...and how he hated himself.

When Lisa finished her story, Karol slowly shook his head, all the while unconsciously wiping the table with his cloth in a rhythmic manner. The clouds in his head cleared. At long last he understood the reason for his family's tragic murder.

"The curse!" he blurted out. "One by one, all stone masons who work on walls of convent died or were killed...all within six months of finish. Our town people called it the Curse of St. Mary Magdalene. All these people...killed to hide some sickness? My Papa, Momma and baby sister...they were killed for *this*?"

As if he had been exorcised from an internal demon, Karol Tciusz-ko felt both the freedom and responsibility of rebirth. Tears filled his eyes as he said, "So this is why I was spared. God spared me for this moment, this I know!"

Moments passed in silence. Finally, Karol wiped his eyes and spoke again. "Please, I must to help. I have friends...let us say people I know, who can help. You see, when filthy Russian pigs leave Poland, they in big hurry. Much military things return to Russia, but young soldiers just want go home, not to clean up. Much things left behind, and of course, we proud Polish want that we should help them to go home fast. So we help them to load—this box for them, that box for them...oops, this box for us...that box for them. Some boxes have guns, some hand grenades, some explosives...Karol has friends and Karol will help."

Feeling the strength of Karol's conviction, Bryan knew it was time for his own redemption...in a way, to make up for his brother's death... to make his own future. It was time for him to take control. He quickly formulated a plan in his mind. "Listen, I think I know what we must do. Karol, you need to go to your friends and get enough explosives to blow up an underground storage area, plus several hand grenades, just in case. Then—"

"Please to tell me," interrupted Karol, "how big is place? I need to know how much place we try to explode."

"I don't know, Karol, but bring enough to blow up, say two or three of your restaurants." Karol let out a whistle as he crossed himself. "While you're doing that, Lisa and I will go to the convent tomorrow morning and see what information we can gather."

Lisa frowned, "And just how will we get in? I can't tell them I'm a nun or that I'm looking for my long lost aunt."

"You won't have to," replied Bryan. "Jim Marston gave me these blank embassy documents to fill out if the need arose. We'll tell them that we're from the American Embassy in Warsaw and we're gathering information on the Russian invasion to take to the Vatican. You know, so the Pope can possibly be used as a broker in this crisis." He knocked on the wooden table top and crossed his fingers, saying, "Who knows? It just might work."

"When we make this explode?" asked Karol.

"Tomorrow night," Bryan replied.

"You ask much in short time, but Karol will do this."

"Karol, can you find us a place to stay? I'm afraid to stay at a hotel," asked Lisa.

"Of course. You may stay with my beautiful wife, Katerzina, and me. We do not live much like bureaucrats, but our humble home is clean. And we have extra bed, but..." Karol lowered his head and voice as if someone were watching. "You must not tell Katerzina anything about this, or what I will do. And," Karol suddenly got a sheepish look on his face and shrugged his shoulders, "please to tell my beloved wife you are married."

CHAPTER 60

THE HAIR ON THE NECK OF THE PRESIDENT BRISTLED AS Harwood Naisbitt rose to courteously shake his hand. "Senator," was all Bob Cook could utter through gritted teeth. *This is the same son of a bitch who stands in front of the TV cameras day after agonizing day and berates me as a whore monger and a thief. Now he's smiling as if he were some cock-o'-the-walk that I should suck up to. God, I hate this political shit!*

"Mr. Speaker," Cook said as he turned to acknowledge the distinguished congressman from Texas. As they shook hands, Cook thought, *Another asshole. Who the hell's idea was this anyway?*

President Cook quickly shifted mental gears and said, "Gentlemen, please be seated and we'll get right into it. I've brought you in this morning to brief you on the crisis in Poland, and hopefully our government will put on a unified face...at least to the rest of the world. As you are aware, having secured the cities of Bialystok, Lublin and Krakow, the Russian Army is advancing across Poland at an alarming rate. They've stopped short of Warsaw, apparently for political reasons, but their armies are moving north and south of the city and will probably have it encircled by the end of the day."

Yielding no time for them to respond, the President continued with a rapid fire of facts. "On the wall monitor is a map prepared by the Defense Department. You can see that the shaded area is that portion already controlled by Russia. Resistance is nonexistent, and CIA tells us the old communist bureaucrats are pouring out of the woodwork in support of Mother Russia. It is our belief that Poland will be completely overrun within two days. Couple this with a Russian sweep through Belarus, Ukraine and the Baltic States, and you almost have a return of the old Soviet Union, complete with that lunatic Donskoy as its puppet master."

As the President finished, he tapped his fingers against each other and looked from left to right down the long conference table for emphasis. Scanning the assembled group of men, his demeanor soured at the sight of the Vice President leaning back in his chair, arms folded and a Cheshire cat smile tugging at the corners of his mouth. He watched in amazement as Koernig's demeanor quickly changed as he leaned forward to speak; his smile became a serious frown born of feigned pain.

The Vice President cleared his throat loud enough to gather the attention of all present. "Due to the extreme gravity of the situation, we wanted the leaders of both parties in Congress to know that while we are not seeking your approval for what we are about to tell you, in the name of national unity, we are asking for your support and understanding. We, in this administration, unanimously concur that the situation is intolerable and jeopardizes our national security. Mr. President?"

"Thank you. In the folder in front of you is a copy of the ultimatum that will be delivered by me personally to the Russian Ambassador at 1:00 p.m. today. Below that is a copy of the announcement to our NATO allies of the unilateral action we are being forced to take. Our military forces are about to be placed on DefCon One status and a press conference is scheduled for 1:30 p.m. today. Also included for your perusal is a complete copy of CIA, NSA and DOD intelligence. We think you'll find our decision is of sound mind and our action appropriate. If there are any questions, please feel free to ask them at this time."

***

Jim Marston had finally dragged himself out of his bed and thought, I don't think I can take another sleepless night from hell. I've already had two of those nights in a row; first that red-eye from Warsaw, now this. Shit! Why hasn't that bastard called me? His fingers pushed back the hair from his forehead as he opened a cupboard door in his fashionable Brownstone kitchen searching for a coffee mug. Looking up at the plastered ceiling, he could tell by the squeaks in the floor that Sally had risen and was slowly making her way to the bathroom. What do I tell her…how? Where do I start? I'm so damn tired I can't even think straight. *Why doesn't he call me?*

It seemed as if his mind would explode if this information didn't get out. Jim's conscience was tearing him apart and he needed to right the wrong he had participated in, before it was too late. And he needed to do it *now*! His hand shook as he poured the steaming brew into his mug.

"Damn it!" he bellowed as the scalding coffee burned the fatty crotch of his thumb and index finger. As the mug dropped and shattered on the tiled floor, he felt more burning pain as the coffee splashed up his ankles.

"*Damn it*! I can't take anymore!" he screamed, dancing away from the burning mess at his feet.

Sally rushed into the kitchen in her oversized robe. "What's the matter? Are you all right?"

Spinning around and seeing her loving concern, Jim hung his head in despair, his hands reaching upward, covering his eyes. All the years of burying his conscience poured out in one release of uncontrolled weeping. "Oh Sally, what have I done?"

***

OVAL OFFICE
WHITE HOUSE

The President stood with his hands clasped behind his back, staring out the window. It was a crisp, sunny day and the singing of a robin seemed like a harbinger of a long-awaited spring. He wished his soul could be renewed as easily as Mother Nature was every year as the frost left her womb. President Cook felt frozen by circumstances that had made this the winter of his entrapment. Most of those circumstances were completely of his making, some were not. He longed for freedom—redemption, really. The difficulty was in knowing where to find it, or where to even begin the search.

"Any responses back yet, John?" he asked, never turning to face his Chief of Staff.

"Prime Minister Weaver has sent a typical British response—they would prefer to take up the issue either at a NATO conference or an immediate session of the EU. Although they don't support our unilateral action, they will however, refrain from any statements that could be construed as open opposition, blah, blah, blah..."

"And the French?"

"Well, you knew what their response would be. Couteau will go on record with total condemnation. The Germans, of course, will be in full support, but Mueller wants to play the role of reluctant suitor. As always, the Canadians will help to the best of their ability. Sorry, Mr. President, that's the best of what I've got."

As Waring gave him the disappointing news, Bob Cook raised his arm, grabbed a muntin bar on the window and rested his forehead on the back of his hand. Pondering the enormity of his decision, he continued to stare blankly for several minutes.

"I just don't feel right about all of this. I feel like the weight of the world is on me. I don't know, it's just—"

"Mr. President, if it helps, your entire cabinet concurs with your decision on—"

He spun around and said, "Damn it, John, it's not my son-of-a-bitch decision! Don't you see? It's not my decision! I'm doing it because I have no other option. And I'm still giving an ultimatum to a lunatic who has his finger on enough nuclear weapons to annihilate the earth. I may be setting into motion something over which I have absolutely no control. None!"

"But, Mr. President, how much more support could you ask for?"

"I'd like support from just one European ally. You know, maybe just one. It's their continent for God's sake!"

"Mr. President..."

"Never mind, I'll see it through. My head is splitting…give me about fifteen minutes." As he motioned for Waring to leave, he slowly sank into his desk chair.

"No problem, sir. You actually have about thirty minutes till the next briefing at 10:30 a.m. It's our last review before we meet Ambassador Selivanov at 1:00 p.m."

"Don't worry, I'll get myself ready," sighed Cook.

CHAPTER 61

LISA AWOKE FROM THE FIRST SOUND SLEEP SHE HAD enjoyed in weeks. As she pulled the hair back from her forehead, she saw Bryan still snuggled under the thick, down comforter. Her heart instantly warmed. Noticing the large, carved armoire, she concluded that the design was of Polish influence and the piece must have been in Karol's family for generations. She thought of the countless ancestors of Karol Tciuszko, then the children that she and Bryan would have someday. She could even picture their future home—a small, chalet-styled bungalow tucked away in a mountain setting with children playing in the lush summer grass. A slight shiver brought her out of her trance. Must be hunger pangs, she thought, as she walked down the narrow hall to the toilet.

As the early morning light drifted over Bryan's closed eyes, he stretched his arm out to feel for Lisa. When only the empty bed was felt, Bryan's eyes snapped open. Disoriented by the unfamiliar surroundings, he tossed off the comforter and hopped down from the tall bed, the cobwebs in his head clearing quickly. His heart raced as he pulled his pants on. Hearing a distant flush, he relaxed as he saw the bedroom door open and fill with her shapely presence.

"How long have you been up?" he asked, as she entered the tiny room.

"A couple of minutes."

"Did you sleep well?"

She squeezed his cheeks with both hands, kissed his forehead and said, "Yes, my love."

Bryan responded in typical male fashion by squeezing her buttocks and snuggling his face into the soft valley between her breasts.

"Nasty man," she whispered, feigning a slap on his head.

"Hmm, I think we'd better clean up and go downstairs. The smell of coffee and bacon is trumping my libido."

As Lisa's foot touched the last step of the steep wooden staircase, it yielded a groaning squeak, announcing their arrival.

"Ah, see Katerzina? I told you, all young people today get up late in mornings." Karol winked at Lisa, "Half the good day is gone before they get out of bed."

"But it's only 7:00 a.m., how long have you been up?" asked Bryan.

"Long enough to go out and visit good friend, Tadeusz, come back and eat fine Polish breakfast."

"And how is your good friend, Tadeusz, today?" Lisa asked.

"Fine, he is pleased to send you his very best and hopes you to enjoy small token of his affection. Now, that is for later, so please to have seat. Katerzina?" Karol nodded for her to bring food.

"Karol," asked Lisa, "do you possibly have a typewriter? I have some blank embassy forms to fill out before Bryan and I go sightseeing today."

"Yes, is old and ribbon worn, but works like good Polish typewriter should."

"Did you know that we have beautiful cathedral here in Wroclaw?" asked Katerzina.

"Ah yes," picked up Karol, "and not too far from cathedral is Convent of St. Mary Magdalene. It is four hundred years monastery until big war—"

"But never damaged by filthy Russians," interjected Katerzina, as she quickly crossed herself and turned her eyes upward. "Always a sainted place, except when The Curse fell upon our village."

Karol explained, "When my family was forced to come to Wroclaw, much suffering, no money, no food and no work. Papa was good stone-cutter in old Poland. Convent was given old monastery before big war. Then angel comes to give them gift of more land and to build more stone walls at edge of property. Papa work ten years on new walls with twelve other masons. Karol big enough to help…then no more hungry. Every night, Papa send Karol home to eat with others and he stay alone and work until very dark. He builds Stations of Cross in walls and always reminds us, 'I give gift back to God.'" Karol beamed with pride, for the walls gave his family a special place of honor in the tight-knit Catholic community.

"Then Curse of St. Mary Magdalene comes into Karol's life," added Katerzina. "His Momma, Papa and sister all killed by maniac. Some say

Russian, some say German...no one knows. Then all other masons die, one by one..."

"How did they die?" asked Lisa.

"It was curse of devil," said Katerzina, crossing herself again. "Some die of heart attack, some by accident, some murdered, but all twelve die... every one...curse did it!"

Karol winced as the words of his wife cut him deep. "But it is still beautiful and sacred—very holy. Hard to see, walls block out everything," he added, "but you can see big, beautiful monastery through gates."

Katerzina added excitedly, "Tourists come to have picture taken in front of gates, very famous. Karol, please to draw map so they can find."

A small, devilish smile broke on his face as he turned his head toward Lisa and gave her another wink of his eye, "Only if you say so, little Babushka."

CHAPTER 62

PARLIAMENT BUILDING
RUSSIAN "WHITE HOUSE"
MOSCOW

THE UNIFORMED COLONEL OPENED THE TALL, ORNATE
doors to President Donskoy's offices and stood crisply at attention.
"Comrade President," he said nervously, "please pardon my intrusion,
but I have an urgent message from our embassy in Washington."

"Don't stand there looking like a wooden fool, give it to me!"

Ripping the envelope open, Donskoy's breath stopped as his eyes
scanned the paper:

> U.S. prepared to deliver ultimatum for withdrawal from Poland
> to Ambassador Selivanov today at 1:00 p.m., Washington time.
> U.S. military placed on Defense Condition One. Please advise.

Vladimir Donskoy felt his anger well up inside and a demonic look
appeared on his face as he slowly crumpled the paper, staring blankly
ahead. The colonel felt his lower eyelid twitch as he knew the President
was prone to shooting the messenger. His body temperature rose and he
wished he could open his tunic for relief. Then, as if a thunder clap had
just exploded, he jumped at the sound of his President.

"Get me an immediate security meeting! I want the entire committee
in the Situation Room within thirty minutes—no exceptions!" Donskoy
thundered. "And call General Grinsky; I want our military placed on
highest alert...immediately!"

The colonel saluted, quickly turned and made his grateful exit.

"Bastards!" The colonel heard as he turned the corner of the hall.

***

OVAL OFFICE
WHITE HOUSE

"Ambassador Selivanov," the President said, acknowledging the diplomat with a curt nod as he rose from his chair. Tension filled the air as the two men shook hands. Cook gestured for the Ambassador to take the seat across from his desk. "Please be seated, Mr. Ambassador."

"Good morning to you, Mr. President, and to you, Mr. Secretary," Selivanov said. "And I also wish a good morning to you, Mr. Waring."

"Mr. Ambassador," said Cook, as soon as the Russian had seated himself, "I'm going to get right to the point. We presently have a situation which the United States considers to be of such extreme gravity, that we are left with no other possible alternative but to follow the course of action which we have embarked upon." Cook paused to fix his glare on the shifting diplomat who appeared unable to find a comfortable position. "Your government has invaded a country whose border has been in place since 1945 and is now a standing member of NATO. Poland is no longer to be considered a Russian footstool. We consider this action to be not only a return to the Cold War, but possibly the beginning of a war between the United States and Russia—"

"Mr. President," the diplomat interrupted, "surely in light of the German situation in Poland—"

"I'm not through, Mr. Ambassador!" Cook interjected. "And I will thank you not to interrupt me again until I am finished. This action is contrary to the Helsinki Accord which allows for peaceful resolution of old borders! It threatens the security of Europe, and in turn, that of the United States." The President paused again, this time weighing his words. "We have, therefore, prepared this document for you to present to your government. It is an ultimatum that Russian troops immediately halt their advance across Poland and begin to withdraw within forty-eight hours. We have nothing further to discuss. Thank you."

Rising, Ambassador Selivanov straightened his tie and adjusted the jacket of his suit. The debonair, career politician appeared almost awkward as he reached down and picked up the envelope containing the ultimatum.

"Certainly, as you wish, Mr. President. I will send this immediately to President Donskoy, the consequences of which I dare not predict. In any case, I will be available, as always, should Secretary Holden need my services." He paused, looked down at the envelope in his hands, then back up at Cook. "I might also add, Mr. President, that I have been a diplomatic warrior all my life and have served many of my country's presidents and chairmen. As you very well know, our current president is...shall we say..." The tired old diplomat paused and, pursing his lips, clutched the envelope and thought better of what he was about to say. He then simply nodded to each of the men in the room. "Good day, gentlemen." Having given away more than he should have, Selivanov turned and unceremoniously walked out the door.

As the gravity of the situation sank in, no words were spoken. Finally, Cook broke the silence. "Well, Bert, what's the read?"

"You mean Selivanov? He's easy and completely predictable. It's Donskoy I don't know about, and that scares the hell out of me. He's capable of going any which way...a loose cannon. I can't seem to get a grip on this, Mr. President, and I haven't felt good about this from the beginning. I guess we can only wait and see."

"When is the next security meeting?"

"3:30 p.m., Situation Room," answered Waring.

"All right...I need some time alone, gentlemen. Thank you both."

***

GENEVA, SWITZERLAND

"Hello."

"It's done," declared Koernig. "The U.S. ultimatum has been delivered to the Russian Ambassador." There was a pause while the large man drew heavily on his cigarette. Koernig waited for the exhale.

"Good," was the response, as the expulsion of smoke gave a hissing sound to the words. "How long did they give them?"

"Forty-eight hours," Koernig said.

"Did you stay well distanced from it?"

"It was written by State and delivered by Cook personally. My thumbprint is nowhere to be found. The question is: Will they retreat?"

"As long as they stop their advance, nobody cares. They are only at our old borders now. If they stop, we win...Russia is then Poland's problem."

"What about the virus?"

"It's under control," said Dillon.

"What about Harmon's kid and the broad?"

"Still alive, but they'll be taken out today."

"How will we know for sure?" Koernig persisted.

"Why do you question me? It's not your concern!" he snarled, while taking another deep drag and exhaling loudly into the phone. "They left Warsaw for Breslau. They will go to the convent because they have no other option, and we'll take them out there."

CHAPTER 63

"EXCUSE ME, MR. VICE PRESIDENT," INTERRUPTED THE Senate Page. He handed Koernig a small envelope and said, "I have a message for you, sir. It's from Ambassador Barnes. He told me to deliver this to you in the Senate cafeteria."

Without even acknowledging the page, Koernig took the note, turned his back and walked toward the rear hall door. A look of concern appeared on his face as he read the small white note with the coded phrase:

Washington Symphony, Chopin Concerto

He knew immediately what he had to do. Motioning to his lead Secret Service agent, he moved in the direction of his parked limo. As the agent opened the side door of the parked vehicle, Koernig barked his order with a flick of his hand, "Go to the White House—make it quick!"

***

OFFICE OF THE VICE PRESIDENT

With a hurried gate, Koernig passed through his secretary's office. A quick flick of his hand in a sipping fashion gave the attentive assistant her immediate task. "Ambassador Barnes will be here to see me momentarily. Usher him in straight away," he snapped, slamming the door behind him.

It was a code that he and his father-in-law had worked out together in the event they needed to talk immediately, and in private. The time would always be fifteen minutes hence, the place—his office, the subject—always the same—the German and Polish border.

Within minutes, the secretary gently knocked and opened the door. Ambassador Barnes thanked her as he passed by, took the two mugs of coffee from her tray and waited as she closed the door behind him. He paused long enough to be sure she wasn't eavesdropping.

Handing over one of the mugs, Barnes said, "Morning, Bill," then eased himself onto the sofa.

"Peter, what's the news?"

"Not good. I talked to Dillon about an hour ago—the Russian troops are still on the move. They're closing in on the east side of Wroclaw as we speak. They could take control of the city within forty-eight hours."

"Do we know for certain that the Russians know about the virus?" asked Koernig.

"We have to assume that they do, which is why we needed to talk. Listen, Bill, it's no secret how extremely imperative it is that the Russians do not regain control of Wroclaw. Their advance must be stopped—and stopped *now*!"

Koernig, looking confused over the conversation's direction, said, "But the Russians have received our ultimatum. Surely—"

"Surely is not enough!" hammered the Ambassador. "The pressure must be increased—whatever it takes! You have a National Security meeting beginning at 1:00 p.m. You must take control and pressure the President to send in the Rapid Deployment Forces immediately. It is imperative that they be dropped at the forward front of the Russian line—and that means Wroclaw."

"But they couldn't possibly stop the Russian advance!"

"Of course they couldn't!" Barnes replied, his patience wearing thin. As he glared at Koernig, he raised one eyebrow. Then with a devious smile, he said, "However, a small loss of life would prompt the showdown we desire, would it not? Perhaps even a preemptive strike. *You must* force Cook's hand, Bill. I want to be sure that you fully understand the urgency of this."

"I do, but..."

"We own you, Bill. We created you and your position and placed all our trust in your mission. You hold the key to the fruition of sixty years of hopes, dreams and a massive amount of intricate planning. I don't even want to think of the consequences of you disappointing us."

An icy chill ran up Koernig's back.

CHAPTER 64

WROCLAW, POLAND

FOLLOWING KAROL'S CRUDE MAP WAS THE EASIEST PART OF the trip to the Convent of St. Mary Magdalene. Heavily lined with century-old, low-hanging oak trees, the narrow gravel road that they negotiated appeared to Lisa as something out of some black and white World War II documentary. The sun filtered its streaking rays through a canopy of deep green only sporadically, and the shadow-covered potholes had become a nightmare.

"Bryan!" she said as her knuckles turned white gripping the edge of the dash, "if you can't see the ruts, for God's sake slow down."

"Sorry, can't help it. I don't know how the hell Karol thinks we're going to bring explosives down this washboard road."

"Do you think this road has ever been repaired?"

"I don't think they've done anything since they built the original walls four hundred years ago." He winked at her and said, "Some things never seem to change."

"Look Bryan! Over on the left—there's the start of the wall...and that must be the convent. Wow, now that is incredible; it looks as if it continues on forever."

Bryan pointed and asked, "There's the gate. You want to review our cover story one more time?"

"I don't think so. There's really nothing to review. We're either ready or we're not. It might make us more nervous than we already are."

"How's your Polish?"

"Lousy, as always," she said, shrugging her shoulders, "but I'll get by. Just stop at the gate and I'll see if we can even get in."

Lisa opened the car door, stepped out on to the cobblestone approach and looked up. A strange, spiritual sense of awe infused her, giving her the courage she needed to continue. Rising up in front of her was the most imposing iron gates she had ever seen in her life. Intricate, sculpted scenes woven of bronze and iron depicted the story of the creation of Adam and Eve, taking one visually through the Garden of Eden and ultimately to their fall from grace. Lisa actually felt transported to another place in time, as if the breath of God gently blew His spirit on her face. She closed her eyes and warmth entered her body as she felt it touch the depths of her soul.

Lisa jumped, her trance broken by the raspy squawking of a small speaker mounted on one of the stone column. "Who is it? May I help you?" asked the garbled voice in polite Polish.

"My name is Brandt, Lisa Brandt. I'm with the Assistant United States Ambassador to Poland. We have been sent by the American Embassy in Warsaw to gather information on the Russian invasion. Could you please let us in and help us?"

The speaker did not reply.

Lisa fumbled to get the papers out of her purse, said, "I have papers and official documents that I can show you,"

More time elapsed. Nothing broke the silence.

"Hello? Hello?" Lisa shouted. She looked back at Bryan with a puzzled look.

Thirty seconds more. Lisa wondered if the intercom had gone dead. Finally the speaker crackled again. "You will have to wait a moment. Someone will be down to examine your papers. Please have them ready."

CHAPTER 65

"MR. PRESIDENT!" KOERNIG SHOUTED IN EXASPERATION, HIS voice reaching an embarrassing crescendo. "It is your sworn constitutional *duty* as Commander-in-Chief to protect and defend this country! You have just heard from your own National Security Advisor and you have just seen the CIA recon data. For God's sake! They are positioning nuclear submarines within striking distance of Washington!"

Realizing he was perilously close to losing control of himself, he took a deep breath before he continued. "You have given the ultimatum and the Russians have absolutely not backed down. Worse still, they are continuing their advance into Poland as we speak. This is a sovereign NATO member, and for whatever reason, NATO is paralyzed to act. Is there no one who will stand against this naked aggression? Mr. President, you must act boldly and you must do it *now*! It is your duty, sir—your sworn duty!"

The room was silent as those present dared not interrupt Koernig's carefully crafted tirade. The President, taken aback by the outburst, fumbled for his thoughts and struggled to regain his leadership void that Koernig had filled.

"The Rapid Deployment Forces are our only hope. This is a calculated decision, it is a sound decision, *and* it is a decision that is encouraged by an overwhelming majority of your advisors. Mr. President," Koernig paused for emphasis, "you are sworn to do your duty."

Embarrassed silence again engulfed the conference table as Koernig resumed his seat and scanned each of the occupants for support.

Cook finally looked at his National Security Advisor Doering and asked, "Norman?"

"Sir, I'm afraid I concur with the Vice President. We all knew this was a possibility when we issued the ultimatum. We've now run out of both time and options. We simply cannot, at this point, know for sure whether Donskoy will order a preemptive strike against us or not, but all indications are that he'll back down. The deployment of our forces in Poland is, to me, a sensible move. The size of the force is immaterial… it's just a presence—an *American* presence. When the Russians come face to face with our troops, Donskoy will have to make the decision: Do I attack or do I stand down? If I attack, do I invite a nuclear exchange with the most powerful country on earth? If I stand down, do I negotiate and hope to keep most of what I have already gained? This move will either cause Donskoy to back down or force him to attack, giving us full justification for our own preemptive strike, if necessary. I see no other sensible option, and I believe our military concur."

The President sat motionless as the gravity of his decision weighed so heavily, his breathing became strained. Finally, his eyes rose, focused and looked leftward across the table. "General Belden, order the start of Operation Oaken Shield—troops to be deployed immediately. Charles, what is our current missile status?"

"…Fully operational, fully checked and fully targeted, sir."

CHAPTER 66

TICK-TOCK, TICK-TOCK…THE LOUD TURNING OF THE GEARS inside the massive grandfather clock reframed Lisa's mood to anxiety. She was fully aware of where the sound was coming from, but the hollowness of its tone began to play tricks on her nervous state. The drone began to sound as if it were coming from within her head, louder and then louder. She had never been comfortable with deceit—her self-confident demeanor had always found it foreign, beneath her. Exasperated by her growing sense of guilt, the ticking of the clock had become a form of self-punishment. Shifting in her seat, she wondered how any person could work with such an overbearing irritant. With its ornate scrollwork glistening in the small shafts of sunlight that penetrated the murky window, the large brass pendulum had an almost hypnotic effect on her, seeming to draw her mind into its dark cabinet. She saw medieval craftsmen carving in a work—

Bong! Bong! Her body jumped in a singular spasm as the majestic clock boomed out the hour. Her hand reached across the chair, finding Bryan's.

"I wish she would come in," Lisa said, her eyes scanning the carved moldings on the ceiling. "I don't like this. This room is beginning to give me the creeps."

"Calm down, we'll get through this together. Actually, this convent is rather awesome, isn't it? I wish we could explore it sometime, without a care in the world, just you and me—"

The creaking of the door signaled them to rise from their chairs. Apprehension turned to surprise as a frail, diminutive Mother Superior entered the room. The sudden redness in their faces spoke the embarrassing truth.

"Good morning," the Abbess said with a softness in her voice that delivered a sense of peace to both of them. "I am Mother Anastasia, the Abbess of this convent. Please, sit down," she said with a gesture of her hand. "Let me guess, you were expecting someone taller than four feet, six inches...or was that before I shrunk?" A slight smile broke on her face as she raised her right eyebrow and exposed the twinkle in her eye.

Bryan was the first to recover from his surprise. "Well, uh...yes! We're very pleased to meet you, Mother Anastasia." He released her handshake. "I am Bryan Harmon, with the American Embassy. May I introduce my associate, Lisa Brandt?"

"Mr. Harmon and Miss Brandt, I'm pleased to meet you both. Now, may I see your papers, and perhaps you could share with me what this most unusual visit is all about?" she said with a disarming smile.

"Certainly." Bryan shifted in his seat, betraying uneasiness with his charade. "I'm sure that even here in this cloister, you must be aware of the Russian invasion."

"Yes, even here, Mr. Harmon. It just so happens that I have been closely following these events on the Internet. I am eighty-three years old and have witnessed more Russian troops than I care to remember. Perhaps it would be more accurate to call it a reoccupation. You see, Poland is not America. We have a long history of brutalization by Huns: East, West, South, German, Russian, Mongol or Turk. Which would you care to discuss? I'm afraid we have always been Europe's doormat."

"Please excuse my ignorance of your cloister, Mother Anastasia, but I had no idea that you would have such immediate access to the outside world. Let me explain. My government has asked Miss Brandt and myself to come down from Warsaw and do an in-depth analysis of strategic points of defense that might be used, if necessary, to defend Poland." Bryan again shifted in his seat and looked away from the Abbess as he continued. "Wroclaw is to be our last stop before we present our findings to both our government and to the Vatican. It's the hope of our government to appeal to the Papacy for behind-the-scenes mediation."

Lisa noticed he was looking down at his shoes and thought, More eye contact, Bryan.

"So you are a military strategist as well, Mr. Harmon? To think, we have a budding Henry Kissinger and General Petraeus right here in Warsaw. To have both men wrapped in one person, your government must be very lucky, indeed." Anastasia had fought this battle her whole life. Her petite size had convinced many that she would be a pushover. She learned early on that her tongue could make up for any shortfall in height.

Lisa quickly cut in, "Well, we don't know if there is any strategic value to this property, Mother Anastasia, which is why we would like to just look around...if you would grant us permission, of course."

"You do know that this is sacred ground. This property has been in the loving hands of our Holy Mother, the Church, for over four hundred years. It was a monastery until 1944, when our Order was assigned its use. I am only the second Abbess it has ever had, and I was there to breathe life into its birth. Through God's grace, we've clawed and scratched out an existence in a land of chaos and misery. No, I don't like the feel of this, Mr. Harmon, Miss Brandt, and I am sure that these grounds will survive any invasion by Russia, Germany or anyone else."

"Mother Anastasia, please excuse me," Bryan responded, his boldness now rising with his disappointment, "but this monastery was occupied by German soldiers in 1939 at the order of its own government until it was liberated in 1945. It was a German monastery...in Germany. It could just as easily return to Germany as to Russia. We merely want to help—help it stay Polish, but we can't do that without your help. Please, may we look around?"

The aging Abbess sat with her elbows on her oversized desk, hands folded together, as if in prayer. *What is it about them?* she thought, peering over her hands. *He's a terrible liar, but there's an innocence about him that somehow feels right. I've begged God for this day never to come, but I'm so old, so tired. Are they sent from God? If they are and I send them away, am I fighting against the very will of God? Would I be denying HIM the answer to my prayers?* She stared directly at Bryan, then at Lisa, and nodded her head slowly.

"Alright," she said with resignation, "you may peruse the grounds, but do not go into any of the sleeping quarters, and no questions will be asked of any of our sisters. Is that understood? They are not to be bothered in any way."

"Yes, Mother, thank you. We will respect the privacy of the sisters; you have our promise on that," Lisa answered.

As Bryan opened the door to leave, he heard Mother Anastasia's soft voice over the noise of the creaking hinges. "By the way, Mr. Harmon, perhaps you might find a crowbar in the tool bin in the barn. You'll find it most helpful to open the steel lid to the underground storage area if you have it." That same small smile appeared on her face again as Bryan noticeably froze in his step. "Take some limb cutters also; the lid's quite overgrown with wisteria vines. I trust you'll be able to find it."

Bryan felt his face flush with embarrassment. "Uh...I..."

"Go, Mr. Harmon, Miss Brandt," she said, slowing nodding her head as if giving a reluctant blessing. "Oh here, you might want to save these papers for someone a little less discerning than myself."

Awkwardly, Bryan stepped back to her desk and reached for the packet of forged documents held in her extended hand. His eyes were forced back to the nun's when she didn't immediately let go of the papers.

"And stay working for the embassy. I don't believe you have much of a career in acting."

***

As the carved door creaked its way to closure behind them, the image triggered a long-forgotten memory in Mother Anastasia. She leaned back in her chair and saw the stone masons from town dismantling the odd-looking building with no windows. When the upper portion was gone, it left only a slab and a staircase going down into the earth. She saw a short, stocky man cementing in a heavy steel door used to close off the stairway leading underground. His son was always with him, a beautiful boy of seven who tried to carry stones when his father encouraged him. The rest of the time he played in the dirt and ran through the meadows playing with his imaginary friend. How she had loved that little Karol.

She then remembered earth being hauled in, crudely by horse and wagon, because there was no fuel for the trucks, if one were lucky enough to even have a truck. After the earth was spread, the steel door was slammed shut and locked. The petite, young nun was then the only sentry left to guard the deadly secret.

Then they came no more...never was a stone moved again. All the masons died—murdered, she was certain. First, her friend, Lech Tciuszko, murdered with his wife and daughter, then the other eleven... one by one. All that was left was the child, Karol. Sweet Karol Tciuszko; he was truly the son I never had, my joy. Tears filled her eyes.

For years she had walked past the flowering wisteria vine that was planted by her in remembrance of those that had suffered in the heinous experiments and shared not in her blessed immunity. Always her prayers were fervent and long: Please, God, keep this secret from those who would use it.

CHAPTER 67

WASHINGTON, D.C.

JIM MARSTON SAT AT HIS DESK, ELBOWS BENT, WITH HIS two hands holding his sagging head. Below, a glass of sour mash bourbon was drained to its bottom. His head was light, but his pain would not relent. For him, there was no escape—he could neither run nor hide. His world was spinning out of control.

"Coward!" he whispered to himself. "You said that two hours ago… you're just afraid you'll end up like Blaine Harmon." His head fell to his arm on the desk. He saw the face of his old friend and his pain increased. *I don't know what I would have done if Sally hadn't taken me in her arms and forgiven me.* For the first time, he understood why suicide had appeal to the truly desperate.

The loud buzzing of the intercom caused him to jump as if he had been shocked by a cattle prod. With his head jolting upward, his legs shifted and his hand snatched the telephone.

"Ahem," he grunted, clearing his throat. "Yes?"

"Ambassador Marston, the President is on line one."

"Thank God, Mrs. Blakely, thank God." With forced haste, Jim regained his composure and combed his hair with his fingers. "Mr. President, thank you for calling!"

"Well, Jim, desperation caused me to review your report and I saw the note penciled in the margin. I don't know what you want to talk to me about and I'm hard-pressed for time, but by God, I'd walk through hell if it could help me right now. What is it you want to tell me?"

Jim's voice suddenly lowered as his eyes instinctively looked around the room and at his door. "It's more what I have to *show* you, Mr. President," he said, now cupping his hand around the phone's mouthpiece. "We can stop this, sir," he whispered. "I know we can...we can stop *him*... the Vice President."

"Koernig? What do you know about him?"

"I know enough to show you how to stop him and his sordid plot."

"What plot are you talking about?" the President asked.

"I can't tell you over the phone, sir. This is something I must show you in person. Mr. President, believe me when I say that I'm trusting you with my life by telling you this. I only hope to God that you will trust me the same."

Silence hung as Cook pondered his response. Marston was desperate and he couldn't let the moment fail. "Does the name Jack Dillon help?"

"Come immediately to the Oval Office. I'll have you cleared through. No! On second thought, I'll have the Secret Service pick you up and escort you here. Meet them in front of State—*now!*"

"Yes, sir, Mr. President, thank you." He slowly put the receiver down and poured another drink. Fumbling for his envelopes, his arm brushed the full glass of bourbon, spilling a small amount. He paused, knew he needed more strength, and with two gulps he emptied the glass. He grabbed the envelopes and paused again—the amber liquid beginning to course its way through his body. With his heart beating out of control, he closed his eyes as fear retarded his resolve. Finally, the courage to right his years of wrong returned. He would face the music. He owed it to Blaine, to Sally, and most of all, to his country. He opened his eyes, clipped his clearance badge on his jacket pocket and walked past his secretary without a word.

Looking down the hall, Jim saw the elevator light announce his floor. He quickened his pace and reached the elevator as the doors slid open. Attempting to enter, he stopped in his tracks as SecState Holden was exiting the elevator cab. Both men were caught in an awkward freeze.

"Ah, Jim, I was about to call you. I—"

Holden stood, mouth agape, his head turning in bewilderment as his underling clutched his briefcase to his chest, walked past him and entered the elevator. Jim's slight pause was the only acknowledgment of Holden's presence as he pushed the "close door" button.

"Jim? What the hell is the matter?" As the doors slid to meet each other, the Ambassador disappeared from sight.

CHAPTER 68

"YOU MAY FOLLOW ME, FATHER WETZEL, SISTER ANNA. Mother Anastasia is in her office. I'll take you there."

Ilsa was taken aback by the happiness that seemed to emanate from the jolly, round-faced nun. There was an unmistakable joy that contrasted the solemn surroundings. How could anybody find happiness in this dreary tomb?

Walking down the dimly lit hallway, Ilsa gave a careful look at the line of six nuns that passed them. Their faces, though tightly bound by their habits, had purity and a sense of contentment as they smiled a welcome acknowledgment to their visitors. Looking down, she noticed the smooth stone floor, steeped in tradition, honed over the centuries by thousands of prayerful monks and now devoted nuns. Her eyes then caught sight of her long, black habit with her large wooden rosary bouncing against her thighs with each step. She was intrigued by their devotion, and the fact that it was devotion to God mattered little to her. It was the pure devotion, the sacrifice of one's self to a higher calling that caused her to feel a kinship with these strange women. Yes, I rather like this black habit, she thought, her gait taking on a bounce that only comes from pride in one's self and a true sense of purpose.

Contrasting Ilsa's walk and demeanor was that of Franz. His was the movement of a wolf stalking his prey, his keen eyes taking in and processing every detail of the labyrinth that was now under his control, his body aged but trim, taught and sinewy, his mind sure and focused, knowing the deadly hour of the kill was drawing near. It gave him a satisfying adrenaline rush.

***

With each snap of the sturdy branch cutters, Bryan felt naive and inadequate, unsure of being up to the enormity of the task at hand. Without the help of Jim Marston, Karol and Mother Anastasia, where would we be? he thought. Images of his father and Jose lying dead flashed before him. What about them, their sacrifices, Jose's innocence? Who put me in this picture and why did Lisa enter my life? Or was she put here? The complexity of the questions confused him.

At last, shoveling away decades of pine needles, leaves and moss, he made out the perimeter of the rusted steel door. Scraping away the last of the debris, Bryan felt the recessed latch handle.

"Lisa, hand me the crowbar, the latch is rusted shut and I can't budge it." He wiped his eyelids as the cold mist turned into small droplets of rain.

The heavy crowbar did its job and the steel door creaked open. He felt a terrifying apprehension rise in his heart as a stale, musty odor billowed forth, engulfing his senses. Bryan struggled to move the heavy door, and when it was fully open, dark cobwebs filled the open staircase, exposing it to the only daylight it had witnessed in over sixty years. He looked to Lisa and her to him, their eyes betraying fear of the foreboding abyss. Neither knew fully what to do, nor wanted to make the first move. They seemed momentarily frozen in time.

Lisa was the first to move. She grasped Bryan's arm as if to hold him back and said, "Maybe we should just wait for Karol. I'm not sure I can handle this." She swallowed deeply. "I guess I'm having second thoughts."

"It's all right, you can wait up here, but I have to go in. We have to know for sure."

"Then never mind, I'm certainly not going to let you go in there alone."

Bryan moved forward. He descended each step, tapping it lightly, then heavier, checking if it would bear his weight. As he brushed sticky cobwebs aside with the long handled flashlight, grizzly photographs of the diabolical experiments shot through his mind. His heart pounded harder with each downward step. When his head finally ducked under the top of the slanted door frame, he sensed the presence of those that had suffered cruel deaths long ago. Feeling the touch of Lisa's hand on his shoulder, he was reassured. His strength returned and he swiped at more cobwebs, moving forward. The light shone down the narrow hallway, exposing somber, crypt-like walls and ceilings. Still painted on the musty gray walls was "Krankenhaus," the German word for hospital, with a directional arrow stenciled below. Bryan felt he had descended into the house of Satan himself and fear began sucking the very breath out of him. Lisa tapped him on the shoulder, causing him to jump in fear.

"Shit! Don't do that!" he whispered.

"Sorry. I just wanted you to see that word, Krankenhaus, above the arrow on the wall. Here, give me the flashlight!" She took it out of his hand and directed its beam. "See? That's the same wall shown in the pictures we found in your father's safety deposit box."

They crept down the hall, one small step at a time, till they came to a stop at the first door. Bryan tried to turn the handle, but the door was swollen shut. He leaned back and then slammed his shoulder into the door. It broke free and he lost his balance, plunging forward into a mass of cobwebs that clung to his face. Half crazed, he flailed at the clinging mass that seemed to swarm over his face and stopped only when he finally freed himself of its entanglement. He calmed down, but his reaction left him embarrassed. Then, to his relief, the light exposed an empty room.

"C'mon," he snapped. He walked past Lisa, grabbed the flashlight out of her hand and again led the way.

"Bryan! This room! This is the room with all the infected patients in beds lined up in long rows. I recognize these big concrete columns. This is where all the experiments were going on."

"This gives me the creeps; I'm glad there's nothing in here," he responded, flashing the light around the room.

Two more doors surrendered the same results, until Bryan finally turned a locked handle that would not yield. Slamming into the door twice with his shoulder, he reluctantly accepted that it was locked, not jammed.

"This one's locked; hand me the crowbar," he whispered.

"Look!" She pointed to the emblem on the door with the flashlight. As the beam slid across the door, the only identification stenciled on the flat surface was the small death-head skull of the infamous SS.

***

"Please have a seat," said the Abbess. "Father Wetzel, Sister Anna, we are very honored here at St. Mary's to have two such workhorses of our holy Church choose to visit us. The schedule of your global ministry of healing must be extremely grueling."

"Yes, indeed Mother Anastasia, that is why we requested our Archbishop to grant us a three-day rest and retreat here at your secluded cloister. I'm confident that if you weren't so isolated here, you'd be aware that Sister Anna cannot go anywhere in the real world without throngs of suffering people pleading for her healing gift. As for my involvement, every mission that Sister Anna holds requires Mass and Reconciliation, which can last for hours upon end."

The Abbess measured her words as she struggled to calm her ruffled feelings. "Well, there is no question that our sanctuary is somewhat isolated, Father Wetzel, but I can assure you that we are certainly not out of touch with what you call, the 'real world.'" Then, drawing upon the wisdom of her eighty-three years, she sensed that something was not quite right with the pair in front of her. She decided to dispense with the banalities in order to pinpoint her probe. "I apologize if I might offend you, but I have never personally heard of the mission of Sister Anna," she added dryly.

As she expected, Franz reacted right on cue, feigning hurt at the cutting remark. His voice, resonating loud with indignity, said, "Am I getting the impression that the most holy Sister Anna and I are not welcome here? Perhaps we should return to our Archbishop and see if we can find other more inviting accommodations."

Displaying calm, Mother Anastasia pulled off her small wire-rimmed glasses and rubbed the bridge of her nose. Her years had given her not only wisdom, but the courage not to be intimidated by bombast. Studying the face of her arrogant guest, she wondered what type of priest this man was. She decided to let out the leash on this hound, but just a little.

"I'm quite confident that our humble convent, so remote from the rest of civilization, will give you and Sister Anna all the prayerful rest and solitude that you may require, Father Wetzel."

Rising to his feet, Kreuger attempted to position himself in a commanding posture of superiority. "I trust that our rooms are ready?" He preened like a Cheshire cat with his chin held high.

The abbess remembered the last man to strike a Teutonic pose in her presence. She questioned their connection. "It should only be a few moments, if they're not already prepared. You have to forgive us, Father

Wetzel; it is not often that our cloister should have four visitors in the same morning."

Franz froze at the sound of the words. His eyes flashed immediately back to Mother Anastasia, his mind now racing. "Did you say *four* visitors…this morning?"

"Why yes, this morning we had two visitors from the American Embassy in Warsaw."

"And where are these young people now?" asked Ilsa, trying to take the edge off Franz.

"They went off on their own to tour our beautiful grounds some time ago."

"And what were they looking for?" Kreuger asked, a stare piercing the Abbess.

Mother Anastasia felt the pressure of an interrogation. Something was definitely amiss here…she felt imminent danger. Why should this religious pair be concerned about American diplomatic people? Her brow furrowed. And why did Sister Anna say *young* people? I didn't say they were young. She felt a steady uneasiness rise in her stomach. My God, what have I done? she thought.

"I don't know, nor do I particularly care." She decided to reflect the pressure back to them. She stared at Kreuger, her instincts convincing her that these two were impostors, and possibly sinister ones. There were too many questions and too much arrogance. Why was it she had never heard of Sister Anna's ministry in all of her reading, either in religious publications or on the Internet? After a pause, she continued, "Why do you ask, Father Wetzel?"

"Just curious, Mother. If you will excuse me while you show Sister Anna to her quarters, I think I'd like a prayerful stroll outside. It's been a hectic week and the fresh air would do me well. Guten Tag." Kreuger stood, giving an unconscious click of his heels.

With haste, Kreuger made his way down a winding staircase that led to the sloping hills behind the convent. Simultaneously, his hand slipped under his tailored black coat and unsnapped the shoulder holster at his side. Opening the door at the base of the stairs, he scanned the broad meadow before him. Through the light rain he saw a barn off to the left, and in the distance a thin copse of large trees surrounded by barren fields. From where he stood, he saw that the whole property was enclosed by an old stone wall that rolled with the terrain.

Relying on his instincts, Kreuger knew exactly where he needed to go. As if guided by an internal compass, he set off in that direction, noting every detail of his surroundings. Although the barn was not in the general direction of the grove of trees, Kreuger veered off course to give it a quick walk-through.

Bryan and Lisa reached their fill of the storage facility and had made their way back to the barn. Nothing was said between them. In spite of the fact that nothing had occurred, their minds were in sensory overload from physically being where heinous abominations had taken place and they needed a break.

It was Lisa who first noticed the menacing figure approach the barn as Bryan returned the borrowed items to the tool crib. The barn window was filthy from neglect and looking through it was difficult, but she could never forget the sinister man from the Polanie Restaurant. Her heart stopped.

"Bryan! Quick, get down!" she whispered forcefully. "It's that killer from Karol's place...he's dressed like a priest. Shh...don't move."

While Bryan and Lisa crouched in a corner behind a horse stall, they saw the thin shadow of Kreuger as he stealthily slipped into the barn. Crawling along the floor, the silent shadow crept near, revealing an extended arm holding a weapon. The sound of Kreuger's shoes crackling on the dry earthen floor intensified as each step crunched closer and closer. Their breathing suspended, lungs feeling as if they would explode. Lisa steeled herself, ready to lunge at the gun the second it passed the stall divider. Then, as quickly as they had come, the sounds ebbed and the shadow receded and disappeared.

Bryan raised his head and looked over the edge of the stall, then crept over to the door, praying he was not exposing himself to the would-be assassin. His eyes peeked around the jamb of the open door. Relief came over him as he picked up the figure of the black clad hulk moving down the meadow.

"Come on," Bryan whispered, scrambling toward the opposite door. Hearing no sound behind him, he turned, only to see Lisa still crouched in the corner of the stall, rocking silently back and forth.

"Come on, Lisa!"

"I can't," she said. "I'm too frightened."

Bending over, Bryan drew Lisa to him and helped her to her feet. "We've got to hurry," he said, cupping the side of her face with his hand. Looking into her eyes, he implored, "Please trust me. I love you and I won't let anything hurt you, but we have to get out of here, *now*."

With her eyes never leaving his, she took a deep breath and said, "I do trust you…you are all I have in the world. Let's go."

"Stay low," he whispered. They ran stooped over toward the safety of the convent.

As they bounded through the door at the bottom of the stairs, Mother Anastasia's small body frame was thrust against the wall by the incoming door.

"Mother!" Lisa cried out, her words barely audible from her exhaustive run. "I'm so sorry. We've got to go—"

"Did you find what you were looking for?" the Abbess asked, raising her arm for help.

"Yes, but we'll have to explain later," said Bryan, pulling the abbess up off the floor.

"Quickly! Top of the stairs—turn right, then straight out. It will take you to your car. Go!" the nun said.

Lisa bolted up the stairs and cried out, "Bless you, Mother!"

Half running, half stalking, Franz quickly reached the grove of trees. The strewn mulch and cut limbs came into view and were processed in his mind with the speed of a computer. Coming in close, he slowed down, his head turning left then right, taking in every sight and sound. He crouched down. His hand slipped into his jacket, pulling out his instrument of death. He touched the closed steel door and felt the loose chips of mortar. He slowly lifted the latch of the lock—what's that? In the distance, the sound of a car's ignition starting up broke his concentration. His head snapped around and his eyes spotted the gate. On pure instinct, he was in full gallop, his gun returning to its holster. With his strides long and his vision intense, he sprinted across the field, his mind honed in and his eyes never leaving the moving car. He pushed his tiring body further, believing he could cut off the car if he ran diagonally to the rapidly approaching gate.

Three hundred yards, now two hundred yards, the distance shortened. He saw Bryan leap from the car, run and pull open the iron gate. Kreuger knew he could get them. One hundred yards—Bryan jumped back into the car. Fifty yards—the car began speeding away. "I've got you, you bastard," Kreuger whispered to himself. Twenty-five yards—Kreuger dropped to one knee, pulled out his Glock pistol, both hands clasping the semiautomatic. He drew a bead on the driver of the car.

Spit! Spit! Spit!

Stone chips exploded every which way as the bullets hit a stone column that came out of nowhere between him and the fast moving target. Spraying gravel, the car disappeared behind the high stone wall shrouded in a cloud of dust. Franz dropped his head. They had beaten him…again. Disappointment trumped his shortness of breath and he slipped his gun back into its holster and slowly rose, feeling a burning pain in his knees. His only solace was the surety that they would return and he would not fail a third time.

Standing in her office window, out of Kreuger's keen sight, Mother Anastasia witnessed the unfolding drama in its entirety. She slowly turned, laid her shoulders against the wall and let her head fall back. Closing her eyes, she said a prayer and thanked her loving God.

CHAPTER 69

AS JIM MARSTON EXITED THE MAIN DOOR OF STATE, waiting Secret Service agents quickly grabbed him by the upper arms and whisked him into an awaiting black Suburban without losing a step.

Standing ramrod straight at the White House checkpoint, a Marine sentry passed them through with barely a foot touching the brake. Within what seemed a matter of only seconds, the vehicle's side doors flew open under the covered entrance to the lower level of the White House. Agents moved quickly ahead, clearing the way and practically dragging Jim along in the vacuum left behind. People, cars and checkpoints seemed like eddies of turbulent water camouflaging partially submerged boulders waiting to smash his fragile craft. By command, he quickly emptied his pockets of all metal objects onto a tray and was pushed through a metal detector unscathed. When his hand gripped his briefcase off the inspection table, Jim was again hustled off by a flowing cadre of Secret Service, this time leftward into a hidden staircase. As Jim Marston passed the Chief of Staff's office, John Waring rushed out, extended his hand while still moving and gave him a welcoming handshake.

"Good to see you again, Jim," the Chief of Staff said, shaking his hand while directing him into the Oval Office with his other arm, "the President is most anxious to see you. Please go right in."

The effects of the sour mash bourbon and the whirlwind of the past few minutes had the old diplomat's head swimming. Added to this was the fact that he was from the old school, and no matter who the president was, he was always in awe of the office itself. When he finally cleared his head, he was staring into the face of an anxious President Cook rounding his desk, hand extended.

"Jim, I thank you for coming so quickly. I hope what you have to show me is worth the extraordinary measures we've taken to get you here."

"Mr. President, I believe it is," Marston said, taking a seat and pulling his briefcase up on his lap. He fumbled with the latches and noticed that a bead of sweat had dropped from his forehead onto his eyelash. Awkwardly, he reached into his back pocket, pulling his handkerchief out to wipe his forehead.

"Are you okay?" asked Cook. I've never seen this man so flustered, he thought. What the hell's going on? I didn't think that old prig could even sweat.

"Yes, sir...I mean, no, sir. I don't know..." Marston flipped opened his briefcase and his eyes rose to meet Cook's. As he passed the dental records of Hilda Maier and Eva Braun to the President, he said, "Sir, let me start with these."

Cook examined the records, turning them over in his hands with only a cursory look. "What do these mean to me? I mean—" He paused with a confused look that begged for help and finally said, "Who the hell is this Hilda woman?"

"Her body was the one found by the Russians lying next to Adolph Hitler outside the Bunker. She was Eva Braun's double and stood in for her at most of the public functions. Their dental records were switched."

"Switched...what the hell for?" The President, never quick on the uptake, seemed out of place, as if a joke was being played on him. Finally, the cloud lifted in his head and he asked, "Then what happened to Eva Braun? Are you trying to tell me she escaped and is alive and hiding somewhere?" Concerned that his ambassador was losing his wits, Cook asked somewhat sarcastically, "We're not doing some Amelia Earhart thing, are we, Jim?"

"No, sir, I can only ask you to please take me seriously. Yes, Eva Braun did escape and no, she is not alive. She died in Buenos Aires a month ago."

Cook showed his impatience as he placed the dental records down on his desk and slid the cuff of his shirt past his watch to catch a glimpse of the time.

"Jim, I'm, uh, really fascinated by this and I'm sure it would make for a great movie, but time is critical right now and I think that—"

"Sir, please bear with me," he interrupted. "These birth certificates should clarify everything." He leaned forward and handed them to Cook.

Studying the papers, the President paused and turned them over twice in disbelief. Finally, with an incredulous look, he addressed the diplomat, "Are you seriously trying to tell me that the Vice President of the United States is Eva Braun's…son? This sounds like crap out of a ten-cent Nazi novel. Jim, if this is some kind of a joke…"

"It's not a joke, Mr. President! People have died trying to keep this secret hidden, including Blaine Harmon!"

"Did you say Blaine Harmon? No, he was killed by terrorists in Switzerland."

"They were not terrorists, sir."

Cook was astounded, rolling from confusion to disbelief. "But then who? I mean, who the hell would do this, and why?"

"It's an international cartel, Mr. President…a group of banking and industrial magnates—people whose loyalties and interests transcend countries, wars, governments. Don't you see? It's all about power. Not the kind of power that necessarily eliminates governments or militarily conquers them. I'm talking *economic* power; the kind of economic power that can set up controlled governments and invisibly meld them together to form economic super unions. These unions will regulate peace, war, population and above all, the flow of money! All the total power to shape the world will be in the hands of no more than a dozen *chosen* people! And there is more, so much more that I don't even know where or how to begin…"

Shaking his head in utter disbelief, Cook rose from his desk, walked over to the window and stared out at the thawing White House grounds. He was deflated. He had hoped that the diplomat had something that actually would help him out of his deepening quagmire. His mind turned back again to the problems at hand, realizing he needed to quickly end this pointless conversation with the obviously burned-out man. Pursing his lips, he turned to face Jim Marston once more. Looking down at the seated man, Cook saw not a broken old fool, but a man begging for help. What is it about his face, his eyes? Why is he so believable?

"This isn't one of those New World Order conspiracy theories, is it, Jim?" Cook asked, trying to extricate himself from the situation, yet sparing the feelings of the pathetic person sitting in front of him.

"In a way, yes," replied Marston, totally unfazed by the sarcastic question. "That trial balloon was floated by Bush senior, but it didn't work.

The world wasn't ready for frontal honesty...that's why you were *chosen*."

The word grated on Cook's senses. "Chosen? Damn it, I was elected!"

Pausing to choose his words with care, Marston decided to shed the demeanor of the quintessential diplomat and said with sincerity, "No, Mr. President, you were handpicked and the economy was manipulated to guarantee your success, but you were chosen only to be a caretaker until Vice President Koernig, Eva Braun's *son*, would assume the presidency upon your engineered impeachment."

He paused to let his words sink in and to carefully phrase his next words. "Sir, I'm sorry, but you were just an obscure governor of an unimportant state with a sleazy and exploitable past. Don't you see? You were chosen to be governor because of your sexual weakness. The women... they weren't there because you were some irresistible stud. They were either manipulated or paid. For God's sake, it was all a setup! You are a prisoner of your past and a product of your own weaknesses—just as I am."

As the unvarnished words sank in, Cook choked on the reality of the unpalatable truth. He knew it was true. How could he pretend it wasn't? In the deepest part of his soul, he knew it had been true, and it had been obvious from day one. At the time he never really thought of it as a pact with the devil, but now there was no denying it.

"But how do *you* know all this?" he demanded.

The diplomat dropped his eyes in shame and whispered, "Because I have been a part of it...a willing part of it."

"Oh my God! Who else?" Cook gasped.

"Blaine Harmon was, until his recent death, Peter Barnes, your Ambassador to Germany is, as well as all of the new members of your cabinet...and of course, you."

"Me? What the hell are you talking about?" demanded Cook.

"My contact was Dillon. He is the one that picked you personally, and that you can't deny," said Marston.

The pain of the truth shook the President to his foundation. For the first time in his life, the glib politician could muster nothing to say. He felt like a horse had kicked him in his gut. Ashen, he turned his chair around, slowly putting his hand on the seat and slumping into it. The name of Dillon pained him, and the reality of his pending impeachment flashed in his mind, draining his last ounce of arrogant indignation.

Turning the birth certificates over in his hands, Cook stared blankly at the floor. Finally, his mind turned back to Marston and asked in a low voice, "How could this so called economic super union be controlled—or Russia for that matter?" His voice, conveying both confusion and resignation muttered, "You can't control the world without controlling two countries: Russia and China."

Marston knew the sordid answer to that question lay in his lap. He paused and said, "You need to take a moment to look at these." He passed the photographic record to the President, one disturbing piece at a time. "I think these will give you an idea of what you are up against."

Cook's face wore a complex frown of questions as he looked at the first photograph. Soon his face and eyes winced in disgust as the grisly pictures were presented to him in rapidly ascending order. His head slowly turned back and forth in disbelief. When the last of the photos had been viewed, Jim immediately presented the President with the written reports. Impatience with reading the lengthy results caused Cook to sporadically shift in his chair, while his hands held the material as if it were toxic to the touch. Marston waited patiently for him to finish, hoping the information would be self-explanatory. When Cook finished, he straightened the papers in his hand and handed them back to the somber diplomat.

It was obvious to Jim Marston that the light had not gone on and the President was struggling to see the big picture, so he shifted positions in his chair and opened his mouth to speak, but before his first word came out, the President queried, "Jim, where are you going with all this? We all know there were atrocities…concentration camps, etcetera, but hell, that was fifty some odd years ago."

"Sir, excuse me!" Marston's frustration was now almost belligerent. He knew the time had run out on his meeting and he had only one chance left. "These are not photographs from one of a hundred concentration camps. This was an experimental hospital with biological germ warfare experiments—experiments designed to infect entire populations! Don't you see? They developed a virus, and this virus was genetically engineered to target the races *east* of Germany. And only the ones that *they* deem the undesirable races…Mongols, Alans, Siberians. Only the clean Northern Russians and Poles would be unaffected. Three quarters of the old Soviet Union and China has *some* Mongol DNA. God knows how much Alan DNA is in Turkey, Iran and Afghanistan—even India."

"Still, what's the connection to the present?" Cook asked, understanding the details, but not connecting the dots.

"These pictures are proof that they actually *produced* the virus! It's been stored all these years at this facility."

"How can that be? All the camps were dismantled after the war," Cook asked.

"Not this one. Not entirely anyway. The land was deeded over to the Catholic Church which had converted an old abandoned monastery into a convent on the adjacent property," Jim answered, handing the transfer deed over to Cook. "But there's a stipulation in the deed. The land was to be given to that particular order of nuns from Krakow and they had to encompass the new property within the old monastery facilities; the stipulation being that their old wall was to be extended to include the entire combined property. Now," Marston said, reaching over and pointing to the last sentence for emphasis, "the property reverts to the benefactor should the nuns ever vacate the property for any reason whatsoever. And who is the benefactor?…None other than Hueber Chemical, A.G."

Marston let the words hang until he saw the President's eyes finally focus. Cook's forehead and brow furrowed, betraying his politician's face.

"Now you know why they need Germany to return to its former borders. Wroclaw becomes Breslau again, Germans move in and Poles move out. When the Poles go out, the nuns go with them and the property reverts to its original owners. Bingo! Germany gets the virus. It's so simple—we protect Germany under our nuclear umbrella, they get the virus and silently infect three quarters of the old Soviet Union. They send in massive medical teams to save the day and quietly set up a puppet government. Economically and politically they will have de facto control over the country, including all their natural resources *and* their nuclear arsenal. With Koernig in power in the United States, a super union will form to dominate the world. Right now, Mr. President, you are the only one who can stop them."

Cook rose, put both hands in his pockets and walked over to the window. Again deep in thought, he just stared. Too much had been thrown at him in too short a time. Clear thinking, that's what I need now, he thought. Can this be true? It's all so damned unbelievable.

Koernig…that prick! I should have put the pieces together on my own. If this is true, I can handle him—even the Germans. It's that damned nutcase Donskoy I'm not sure about.

Rubbing his face with his hands, Cook turned back to face Marston. "What about Holden…is he in on it, too?"

"I don't know one hundred percent, sir, but I don't believe so. He's always told me privately he hated Koernig."

Cook pursed his lips and reached for the intercom button. He beeped through to his Chief of Staff. "John, you'd better get in here immediately and call Bert Holden. I want his ass over here in five minutes… but quietly!"

CHAPTER 70

AS THE SECRETARY OF STATE READ THROUGH THE PACKET of documents, the President fixed his eyes on every nuance in the man's reaction. It was a gamble to have this meeting, but he had to trust someone and Bert Holden was his only choice. Cook prayed his instincts were right.

"Well, what do you think?" Cook asked.

Placing the papers slowly onto the coffee table and taking off his reading glasses, Bert Holden paused, shaking his head in disbelief. "Mr. President, I don't know what to say...Jim, I've known you for twenty-five years. Your involvement both saddens and sickens me. I don't know how you became involved in this, but if you weren't sitting here in person, I'd say this was dog shit and throw this packet of crap back in your face. On the other hand, it's so enormous in its implications that it defies reason. This situation is either true or untrue. If it's untrue, then everything we do in reaction won't matter—it simply goes away and we have egg on our faces.

If it's true, then we have two options: we react or we dismiss it. I'm afraid that if it's true and we dismiss it, then we will be party to one of the largest crimes perpetuated against mankind."

"John?" The President turned to his trusted Chief.

"Sir, I'm flat out scared. I agree with Bert in that I don't see how we can walk away from this, but also I don't know what the hell to do *with* it!"

"Well, we had better come up with something, and damn quick," Cook said.

"Excuse me, Mr. President," Marston said, his eyes telegraphing his shame, "I think that I've had a little more time than anyone to think this through, and God knows, I need to help...even if it's only for my own redemption. First of all, the Vice President doesn't necessarily have to be neutralized at this point—only your political enemies in Congress. You'll need to work out a deal with them. Secondly, stop the Russian advance and Germany will have no choice but to fall in line."

"Brilliant, Jim," Bert Holden said sarcastically, "and just how do we stop the Russians short of nuking them?"

Marston was confident and focused. "Do you remember several years ago when Yeltsin left Moscow for a vacation in the countryside? His political enemies tried to have him overthrown. The military then surrounded the Russian Parliament Building with tanks and troops, they fired a few rounds into the building, and just like that it was over."

The Secretary's face winced in disbelief. "Are you suggesting the President surround Capitol Hill with tanks, Jim? Are you completely out of your mind?"

"No. I'm talking about Russia! It has always been rumored that Gorbachev had his hand in putting down that coup. He's been out of power for years, but he still has highly placed moles in both the military and the government. I believe that if he were given the right situation, the right timing, he would risk making a move on Donskoy."

Jim scanned the granite faces of the men sitting opposite him—their blank stares yielding to a slow squinting of their eyes as the picture became clear. He resumed his scheme. "He's in New York, as we speak. He's attending the World Disarmament Committee's annual meeting."

The president stood and slid his hands into his pants pockets. This is it...one chance. He boldly placed his hand firmly on the Secretary's shoulder. "Bert, I think he would listen to you," he said solemnly. "There's always been a bond of trust between you both."

The more Bert Holden thought the idea through, the less he embraced it. "The Ruskies wouldn't take Gorbachev back!" he protested. "The military hates him—too many of them blame him for the breakup of the Soviet Union."

"No, not Gorby—I'm talking of bringing Vasilov to power!" Marston said. He turned his head to the President, hoping he would jump in and somehow support his plan. "Donskoy would be arrested and overthrown."

"Under what pretext?" Cook finally asked.

"Crimes against the federated countries!" Marston replied, nodding his head as if it were a given. "He *has* invaded the Baltic States, Belarus, Ukraine—now Poland. Vasilov would come to power, and with the hidden hand of Gorbachev, the country would lay out the red carpet."

The President rose, walked around his desk and half sat on its corner, his arms crossed. Deep in thought, he looked at the floor—all the while biting his lower lip.

Shit! He's not buying into it, Marston thought. His breathing suspended as he thought all was for naught. His deflated eyes dropped to the floor as he clenched his hands.

Seconds crept by like hours. After what seemed an eternity, Cook finally spoke. "Bert, it sounds improbable, but it could work...Hell, what other option do we have?"

The Secretary shrugged his shoulders in doubt. He directed his next question straight to Marston. "Tell me again why the Russian military would go along with this?"

"To begin with—"

"Wait a minute, Mr. President," Bert interrupted. His mind was focused on the correctness of the plan. "I'm not totally convinced that they'll go along with it, but then again, they just might, but if, and only if, you follow up on the ultimatum already given by openly threatening a nuclear exchange. After all, this is *the* central core of the Mutually Assured Destruction policy, M.A.D....nobody wants mutually assured destruction, but it might be the impetus needed to push them over the edge against Donskoy."

"And, it might be the impetus to push Donskoy into a preemptive strike against us," warned Cook.

A somber hush settled over the room as the enormity of the moment hung over the three men, each avoiding eye contact with the others. Cook broke the self-imposed silence. "Bert, who can we trust outside the four of us?"

"Sir, right now I don't know of one person, not one that I think I could honestly trust."

"Then how do we get Gorbachev into Washington without the blood-hounds in the press corps finding out?" Cook asked.

"Washington? Impossible to do," answered John Waring, "but you might be able to secret him into Camp David."

Cook paused and thought of all the women he had slipped into the retreat. He knew he could pull it off again. "Bert, you reach Gorbachev and coordinate with John to get him and yourself there tonight. I'll need your help to make this work, John. Get the Camp readied and get me a private meeting with Senator Naisbitt—this afternoon!"

"Naisbitt? He's the son of a bitch that's trying to fry your ass!"

"I have a plan, John. I think it's high time he and I talk privately."

CHAPTER 71

RETURNING TO WROCLAW, BRYAN AND LISA WERE STRUCK by the emptiness of its streets. When they had left in the morning, the roads were crammed and the city was bustling. Rusted-out cars had choked the streets with smoke, people had crowded the narrow sidewalks, some walking to work or shopping, while others washed down the soot-covered facades of their buildings. It now appeared as if a curfew was in place. Only the risk takers were out on the streets or sidewalks, and those that were scurried about in a cautious manner.

Bryan and Lisa arrived without incident at Karol's restaurant, but saw the closed sign in the window with the lights off. Dusk was upon them and the position of the setting sun gave the ancient city a strange golden glow.

Reaching Karol's house, they faintly saw dimmed lights glowing behind tightly drawn curtains. With caution, they walked up to the front door, their heads looking left and right. They were relieved when they heard voices inside, even if it sounded like a heated argument. Bryan gave a soft rap on the entry door. The voices faded to silence. Thirty seconds passed and Bryan gave Lisa a questioning look. To their left, a curtain was carefully peered through, and seconds later the door was unlatched. Karol's hand quickly grabbed their coats, pulling them in, while he looked over their shoulders beyond.

"You not hear news?" he asked. His face darted from one to the other.

"Heard what?" Lisa asked. "There isn't a radio in your car. Karol, what's going on?"

"Russians is what's going on. They come to outskirts of city—tanks, guns, many troops. Did you not see them on way back from convent?"

"No. We were forced to take a detour and got lost in the countryside. We thought we were being followed, so we hid out several times. Are they in the city yet?"

"Not yet. Word on radio and television say much moving around city, but they stop and not come in. Katerzina, would you please to get coffee? Have seat. Oh yes! Your American government gave ultimatum for Russian pigs to leave Poland…two days or else." He emphasized by dragging his index finger across his throat.

"Or else what?" asked Lisa.

"Or else...or else...I don't know 'or else.'"

As Katerzina left the room, Karol turned and looked back over his shoulder to be sure she had not stopped to listen. Satisfied, he turned his attention to the tired pair and whispered, "Explosives, they are in back storage, behind house. If we go to do blowup, we must go soon. Tomorrow, Russians will control whole city."

"What about your wife?" Lisa asked.

"She go to her Momma's house, no problem. I tell her I must go to check restaurant, then come later. She will worry and yell and scream at my poor head, but she is good Polish wife and will do what I ask."

"Do we know if the Russians are anywhere near the convent?" whispered Bryan.

"No, but I know back way to convent—old work road through forest will take us right near blowup spot."

"When do we leave?" asked Lisa.

"Right after coffee. I take Katerzina to Momma's house and come back. What you see at convent…you find hidden place?"

"Yes," said Bryan. "We got in and went underground. The storage boxes are there, all right."

"You open boxes?" Karol asked. "You see canisters inside?"

"No," Lisa said, her eyes showing fear. "We were too afraid to disturb them."

Hearing the clinking of coffee cups, Karol quickly changed the subject. "Please to come help me close up restaurant after I take Katerzina to Momma's." Taking his first sip, Karol said, "Ah, good Polish coffee! Thank you, Babushka."

CHAPTER 72

"MR. PRESIDENT, GOOD EVENING," THE FORMER COMMU-
nist Party Chairman said stiffly in formal Russian. Why is it that these
Americans always wait until there is some world crisis before they will
consider working with us? Mikhail Gorbachev thought, examining the
U.S. Chief Executive. First they let our economy sink into an abysmal
swamp, and then they bring Poland into NATO. I'm sorry, but that was
the final insult.

"Good evening, Mr. Chairman," Cook replied. "I can't tell you
enough what an honor it is to have you here tonight. Thank you for
coming on such short notice."

The simultaneous chiming of an old grandfather clock gave Gorbachev the opportunity he was looking for. As his eyes darted to the
source of the rhythmic bongs, he decided to allow them to stay there,
letting Cook know that his predictable sucking up would score no points.

"Uh, Bert," the President finally said as the snub by Gorbachev
sank in, "I think we should get right down to business, so I'm going
to let you start this meeting with some background information for
the Chairman."

When Holden finished showing the ex-chairman the CIA data and
reconnaissance photos, Cook felt reasonably assured that Gorbachev was
not aware of the existence of the deadly virus. Displaying no emotion
or surprise during the long presentation by the Secretary of State, Gorbachev played his cards like a riverboat gambler and simply allowed
Holden to finish without adding any comments.

When it became apparent his Russian guest would not be the first to
speak, Cook broke the ice of the embarrassing moment. "Mr. Gorbachev,
as you can see, due to the extreme gravity of the current crisis, we are
attempting to diffuse the situation by exploring all possible avenues that

would be in the best interest of both of our countries."

"I understand all that you are saying, President Cook, and I also fully understand that any actions you take are, and will always be, done solely for the interest of the United States, not Russia," Gorbachev replied. He raised one eyebrow while tilting his head in a gesture of incredulity. "I simply do not understand what it is that you wish of me. Certainly you do not expect that there would be anything I could do to assist you. As you well know, President Donskoy is in power now, and he and I are not exactly on speaking terms."

"Mr. Chairman, I must tell you in the most direct and forthright manner that this crisis over Poland *could* result in a nuclear exchange, which could escalate to an Armageddon. The entire defensive and offensive capabilities of the United States have been placed on the highest alert. I'm telling you as straight forward as I can—we simply cannot rule out a preemptive strike against your Mother Russia, nor can we rule out one directed against us. The situation is intolerable, and I *will* do what I must to protect the United States and our allies...even if it means a nuclear exchange." Gorbachev saw Cook almost shaking with intensity, his stare piercing the cool front of the Russian.

Gorbachev shifted in his seat and said, "Mr. President, surely you do not believe that you or anyone else can possibly win a nuclear war."

"Mr. Chairman, let me be blunt as hell. If ever there was a time that was favorable to the United States, that time is right now. The old Soviet Union as we both knew it is dead and in total disarray. The new Russian army couldn't even handle a country as pathetic as Chechnya. Your missiles have been sitting in silos for well over twenty years, and the required maintenance was never done. Your military doesn't know the viability of them launching, let alone whether they can reach their intended targets. Yes, I believe the time favors the United States—now!" The President stood and brushed the hair on the side of his head back with his hands, then bent over the chair that Gorbachev sat in. He positioned his face within a foot of the Russian's and said, "We can live with a madman like Donskoy as head of *Russia*, but not of an old Soviet *Union*. I *will*, I repeat, I *will* do whatever is necessary."

"Still," said Gorbachev, leaning back and away from the President's hot glare, "I do not see what you think I can—"

Cook's hand slammed down on the armrest of the chair. "Damn it,

Mikhail! You know exactly what I am asking! We both know that it was you who restored Yeltsin after that coup attempt. I ask you, no, I implore you, in the name of world peace, for the sake of millions of Russian and American lives, to intervene one more time. Please!"

Gorbachev sat perfectly still in his chair. He knew what was being asked, and the thought of what he must do nearly paralyzed him. Dealing with Kostinov and his patriotic band was one thing, but going up against a rabid dog like Donskoy sent a chill to his core. Will the generals even listen to me one more time? Do I have any political clout left? Maybe, if they knew the dire consequences, I might be able to count on Perchenko, possibly Victorlav...I don't know. What about my children and grandchildren? If I fail, that crazed animal will kill them all, but if I do nothing, they could all die in a nuclear exchange. His face grew somber and ashen; he seemed dazed.

"Mr. Chairman...Mikhail?"

It was the calm voice of Bert Holden that broke his trance. Looking up to the Secretary, then to the President, with a look that belied his inward panic, Mikhail Gorbachev softly stumbled through his words. "Mr. President, Mr. Secretary, you ask far too much of me. I don't know if I can accomplish what you desire. I might be able to contact some people...to let them know what is really happening." He paused and wiped his moist forehead. "I don't know if they would be willing, or even able, to do this again. Maybe, who knows?"

Holden reached over and placed his hand firmly on the Russian's forearm. "Mikhail, we've known each other for over thirty years now, and we've had many differences in the past, but you also know that I wouldn't lie or deceive you, nor would I do that to anyone else. You *must* help us with this—for Russia's sake, as well as our own. After your missiles were retargeted, our missiles followed suit. The sands of the hourglass are running down and we desperately want peace. Please, say that you'll try."

He looked down at the floor and slowly ran his fingers over his birthmark. The ex-Chairman was pensive and silent. He drew a deep breath, raised his head and asked, "Under what pretext? I mean, we'd have to be able to charge Donskoy with something—something that would stick."

"May we suggest crimes against the federated nations? After all, Russia has concluded solemn treaties with these nations," the Secretary responded.

The Russian sat in thought for a moment. He nodded his head, and with a frown he said, "That *might* work. What about the Germans? For this to work, they must force their citizens to retreat. Who will handle that?"

Cook stared directly into Gorbachev's eyes and affirmed, "I will. And you can take it to the bank that they *will* leave."

"Bank?" Gorbachev asked with a puzzled look.

Before Cook could explain his remark, Bert Holden explained the slang.

Gorbachev returned the glare into Cook's eyes. "Do I have your solemn assurance that the Germans will affect an immediate withdrawal? I can't see any success on my part without that guarantee."

"You have that assurance, Mr. Chairman. You have my word on it, and the solemn guarantee of the United States of America."

"Pardon me, Mr. President. You will have to forgive my candor, but in the last year your word has been tarnished not only in the U.S., but internationally as well. I'm more than just a student of international affairs, and in particular, I have special interest in the workings of NATO," Gorbachev said with the arrogance of a schoolmaster.

Cook stood dumbfounded, yet quickly recovered and said, "Mr. Chairman, I'll live with that slap—perfectly justified, but by God, my word still stands. Just give us your assurance to help." He then extended his hand for a shake of agreement.

"Then you have my word on it, Mr. President, or at least that I will try." He stood, clutched Cook's hand and, pulling him inward, gave him the customary Russian hug. Cook, caught by surprise, awkwardly returned the embrace and patted the Russian on the back.

"Now," Gorbachev said, as the two separated and stood face to face, "if you would excuse me, I had better make some immediate calls. Time is passing...I assume transportation is waiting?"

"Would you honor us by staying here at Camp David?"

"Thank you, Mr. President, but I do not think it appropriate to be rescuing my country from the confines of an American Presidential Retreat. Do you have a safe house nearby?"

"We understand, Mikhail," said Bert Holden, "and, in anticipation of your cooperation, I've already taken the liberty to make all the necessary arrangements."

"Americans are always so confident," Gorbachev sighed with resignation. "It must be nice to command a robust country."

"Mr. Chairman, thank you again and we wish you every success. No. We *pray* for your success," said Cook.

"Thank me tomorrow, or the next day...that is if we are still alive."

As Holden led Gorbachev out the door, the President buzzed his Chief of Staff.

"Yes, Mr. President?"

"John, get Chancellor Mueller on the hotline and come in."

***

"How did it go with Gorbachev? Will he help?" asked Waring.

Cook raised his eyebrows and gave a helpless look. "It's not a question of will he, only if he can. Pray to God he'll be successful."

"What's his opinion?"

"He honestly doesn't know, John. What about Naisbitt, did he call back?"

"Yes, sir, while you were in with Gorbachev. He said to tell you the deal is on."

"Good."

Both men turned their heads as Bert Holden knocked two short raps and reentered the room.

"The chopper just left and he's all set and on his way," the Secretary announced.

"Thanks, Bert. I must admit, I don't think it would've worked without you. John, check and see what's holding up Mueller."

As the three men sat drinking their coffee, the intercom buzzed, interrupting the tension of their grueling wait. Waring rose and reached for the intercom, all in one motion.

"Mr. President, Chancellor Mueller is on the hotline now."

CHAPTER 73

THE POLISH NIGHT AIR WAS UNUSUALLY CRISP AND THE moon shone a bright path through the gloomy forest leading to the convent walls. Karol Tciuszko's rust-pocked auto struggled to negotiate the narrow winding road. With the road having been virtually reclaimed by nature, Lisa's anxiety rose with every jolt from every pothole, and every branch that dragged against the metal of the car seemed like fingernails on a chalkboard.

"Karol! Are you sure this is a road?" she whispered.

"Oh yes, is fine Polish road…many years fine Polish road. Road built after big war by good Polish people. Papa discovered natural path in forest when he build walls. It took little work to make fine Polish road. We coming to wall soon then turn left and old gate will be quarter kilometer down. And best of all, looks like no Ruskie pigs."

Bryan grabbed Karol's arm and blurted out, "Stop the car, quick! I saw lights through the trees—*over there*! See them? They're moving!"

The old Russian Lada came to an abrupt halt as its tires slid on damp, moss-covered gravel. Karol killed the lights, then the ignition and looked intensely in the direction Bryan pointed.

"I see them!" whispered Lisa, her heart pounding in her chest. "Over there—swirling light patterns."

"Please to forgive, there *are* Ruskie pigs. Looks like patrol beginning to search back of wall. See how lights go right and run long, now go left and stop short. Left side is wall side. Lights move this way—not good."

"Do you think they've seen us, Karol?" asked Lisa, her mouth dry from fear.

"No. If they see, they come fast." After a lifetime of shameful groveling, Karol's newly found freedom refused to cut and run. He weighed the consequences, but in his heart he knew his time had finally arrived. This would be his redemption. "We still have time if hurry—grab backpacks, run for gate. Come—quick!"

Karol loaded the backpack onto his shoulders. "What about the gate?" Lisa asked. "Will it be locked?"

"Yes, but not to worry, is fine Polish lock, so I will open with pocket knife," he said with a sly grin. "Bryan, you to wear this pack and carry that one, I take these. Now, please to follow, and remember, stay low."

With only the slight crunching sound of dried leaves on the old gravel road beneath his bowed legs, Karol moved forward with the intermittent brightness of the moon to guide his path. Hearing the sounds of the soldiers on patrol, he wondered what the hell he was doing there. Then the images of his parents flashed through his mind, and his determination again steeled.

Without notice, Karol's bent-over body stopped as they reached the end of the road, and an enormous, ten-foot-high wall jumped out of the dark shadows. Startled, Lisa abruptly stopped, lost her balance and fell to the ground. Hitting the gravel with a deafening thud, Lisa inadvertently let out a small yelp of surprise. Their terrified eyes riveted on the advancing Russian patrol, five hundred feet away.

"Shhh," Karol growled. He reached over and pulled Lisa to her feet. "Go! Go—that way. Hurry!" He shoved Bryan and Lisa leftward. Within seconds, Karol had them at the heavy timbered gate. His backpack slid off and in one motion, his hands frantically groped the outside of his pockets, searching for his trusted pocketknife. First the pants in front, then his hands rapidly moved upward, helter-skelter to his jacket, his hands crumbling the canvas material. Where is it? I know I brought it—there! Feeling the small object in his back left pocket, his hand slipped to the inside. The knife came out and fell through his fingers to the ground. His body froze. The voices grew louder, closer. Panic set in. He dropped to his knees. Sweet Jesus, please to help me. In a swirling motion, his fingers clawed through the damp leaves and loose gravel...nothing. No, that's it! His fingers clutched the small pocketknife in a death grip. He nervously fumbled to open it and began picking the lock. Thirty seconds went by. Karol wiped the sweat from his eyes and nose, looked at Bryan and Lisa and then franticly began picking again.

"Karol, they're getting too close, I can hear their footsteps now..." whispered Lisa. Fear gripped her throat, denying her effort to swallow. The lock would not relinquish its rusted hold on the door.

"Karol, forget the damn lock, they're too close!" Bryan whispered. "Let's make a run while we can."

"Karol, please!" begged Lisa, watching a beam of light strike the branches of the trees above her head.

Suddenly, the sweet sound of the tumblers' click allayed the panic that had gripped them. "See? Fine Polish lock," whispered Karol. "Now pray gate not to squeak."

Inch by ever-so-slow inch, he pushed the massive door open enough to let them squeeze through as the beam of a Russian searchlight dropped to the road where they had been standing. He pushed the door closed and prayed the lock would reset without noise. He hesitated, then let go of the latch. Sounds of footsteps came to a halt on the opposite side. His breathing stopped. Beams of light shot through the gate's joints as a searchlight washed across the door.

Without knowing what was said, Bryan knew the order had been given to enter the gate. The lock rattled under the soldier's investigation, then, the sound of a shoulder trying to budge its timbers. The gate and soldier groaned, but the gate did not yield. Lisa covered her chest with her hands to muffle the explosive beat of her heart. Karol raised his knife high, ready to attack as he hid behind the column. Finally, the rattling stopped. The footsteps started up again and the Russian voices faded away. Lisa bit her lip, fighting back tears.

Karol resumed control and said, "Please to follow—now!"

CHAPTER 74

THE BOOK BY THOMAS MERTON FELT ODD IN ILSA'S HARD-
ened hands. Why had Mother Anastasia given me this book to read?
What is it about her that disarms me? I feel like putty in her hands. She
should know that I wouldn't be in need of so simple a book as this drivel.
Yet like iron drawn to a magnet, Ilsa kept returning to the underlined
paragraph that stirred her senses:

> "But as long as you pretend to live in pure autonomy, as your
> own master, without even a god to rule you, you will inevitably
> live as the servant of another man or as the alienated member of
> an organization. Paradoxically, it is the acceptance of God that
> makes you free and delivers you from human tyranny, for when
> you serve Him, you are no longer permitted to alienate your
> spirit in human servitude."

Is this what I've been searching for my entire life? Am I merely the
sum total of human tyranny? Even the quick knocking on the door to
her room did not register with Ilsa as she read the paragraph again.
Finally, as the rapping grew louder, Ilsa closed the book about her index
finger, walked to the door and opened it slowly. Her face was expressionless, her gaze going right through the interloper.

"What the hell is the matter with you, Frau Bachmann? Why didn't
you answer the door sooner?" Franz demanded.

"I didn't hear the door," she said. Her eyes only now reacted to Franz,
yet she felt hollow and lost.

Looking at the book in her hand, Franz became agitated. As he
raised his hand to strike the contemptible bitch before him, he held
back, regained his senses and yanked the book from her hand. He turned
it till he saw the title, *The Seven Story Mountain*. His face snarled as he
threw the book into the corner in disgust. For the first time in her life,
Ilsa felt serene—peace in her humiliation. Her hand didn't reach for her

needles in self-defense, anger or even instinct. What is this feeling of liberation, of power? she thought. I see him, but I don't loathe or fear him. I just pity him...and me. After all these years, could there possibly be a new life for me?

CHAPTER 75

CAMP DAVID
MARYLAND

"MS. CHANCELLOR, THANK YOU FOR TAKING MY CALL SO late," President Cook said, trying to disarm Mueller before she went on the offense. "I'll omit the pleasantries and get directly to the point. I want your citizens removed from Poland and I want their withdrawal to commence *immediately*!" Cook had turned the corner and his sense of purpose was clear. "Ms. Chancellor, I understand that it used to be German territory. Yes, I understand the Helsinki Accords only too well... Yes, for peaceful changes in the borders...Yes...Ms. Chancellor! I don't care what the Vice President has promised! *I am still in charge here*! Understand that I'm not conferring with you on this...No, I won't put this off until NATO meets next—Chancellor! *Listen to me*! The Russian army is knocking on your border with Poland as we speak. I will not allow a nuclear war to start over this border dispute. Now, I want those citizens of yours removed, and I want them removed *now*!" Cook was fuming. His eyes stared coldly at his desktop, his knuckles white as they gripped the phone tightly to his ear.

"I don't care what it takes, Ms. Chancellor. Your threat to pull out of Afghanistan is no threat at all. As a matter of fact, I am informing you now that I will announce tomorrow that it is the intent of the United States to begin withdrawing our troops from that region...Again, I don't care what the Vice President has told you. *I'm* telling you to get your people out, and get them out *today*! Just deal with it!...Yes, that's all. Oh, one more thing. If you attempt to contact the Vice President behind my back, you need to know that all his calls and moves are being monitored as we speak. Good night, Ms. Chancellor."

Exhausted, the President slumped back into his chair, exhaled a deep breath and turned to Bert Holden. "Well, there's another mess for you to smooth over. They'll begin pulling out in the morning...so far, so good. Now it's up to Gorbachev...John, wait till morning before you call Koernig. Tell him to meet me—no, tell him I'll meet him at *his* office at nine sharp. Just make damn sure that Mueller doesn't get a call through to him—or anyone else. I want his phone disabled to incoming calls."

"Wouldn't it be better if I called him now?"

"No, I don't want to give him time to do much thinking. Now, let's call it a night...I'm even too tired to screw."

"Sir?"

"Never mind."

CHAPTER 76

WITH NO TIME TO SPARE, BRYAN AND LISA SLIPPED ON their backpacks, watching Karol off and running several meters ahead toward a small grove. Reaching the underground storage bunker, Karol dropped his satchel, crouched on one knee and motioned for the two to hurry. They responded by pushing themselves harder than ever to reach him. Out of breath with his thighs on fire, Bryan dropped to his knees and bent over till his head touched the ground. Struggling to get air to his burning lungs, he said, "Shit, Karol, how can you run like this? I'm half your age and it's killing me." He looked over at Lisa and saw she was winded, but fairing well.

Karol winked at Lisa and said, "Simple, I get you to carry heaviest packs."

Lisa returned a quick smile before her face returned to business. "Do you think the Russians are inside the convent?"

"No. Russian soldier mean and nasty soldier, but Russian army very bureaucratic—too political to invade most holy place—is why they camp in field across road to entrance—will wait orders. Come, let us open door, do blowup and get hell out."

***

Mother Anastasia had finished her vespers and retired to her room for the evening. Walking to the window, she shook her head; the uneasy feeling would not leave her. *What is it with those two? Somehow, I—*her hand froze while drawing the curtains. In the bright moonlight, she saw Father Wetzel half walking, half running down the path leading to the old storage facility with Sister Anna closely behind. *Was this the moment she had dreaded for fifty years?* She was certain that evil dwelt in the heart of the priest, or whatever he was. The Abbess had been a keen judge of character all her life, and it was the pain she felt in Sister Anna's heart that saddened her now. She had hoped that the woman, who pretended to be a nun, would be one lost lamb that an old shepherdess could bring back to the flock.

Unsure of why she was hurrying out the back door toward the barn, Mother Anastasia knew she had some role in the unfolding drama that she believed was being directed by God himself.

The steel door, stenciled with the small death-head skull, was held open by Lisa as she watched the two men set the explosives. Keeping watch, she stared down the long hallway, chills running down her back every time she saw cobwebs eerily sway like ghosts roaming through the incoming air.

Bryan was having difficulty setting two satchels into the corner behind the strewn crates. "Lisa, shine your light over here," he whispered, "I can't quite fit this in." She flashed the light his way, but directly into his face. He raised his hand to cover his squinting eyes. "Not in my face! Down here!" he said in frustration.

"Sorry."

A cold breeze blew on her neck, magnifying the chill she already felt. Out of nowhere, a steeled hand snapped across her mouth and locked her head backward. The flashlight fell to the floor, pain shooting up her arm as her elbow was twisted upward behind her back.

"Damn it, Lisa, give me some light!" Bryan snapped in frustration.

"Bryan, look again," Karol said, stopping dead in his tracks.

Bryan froze. His eyes beheld a nun holding Lisa with the dreaded monster from the Polanie standing at her side, his Glock aimed straight at Bryan's head. Only the slight wave of his black gun broke the tension that seemed frozen in time. Ilsa released Lisa, shoving her downward and in the direction of Bryan. Kreuger took one step forward and motioned with his free hand for his opponents to rise. Bryan's heart sagged as he pulled Lisa into his arms. He realized their long, arduous journey had come to a disastrous end.

"So, Herr Harmon, we meet again, yes? It was so nice of you to leave the door open for us. And you, Herr Poleski, it is time I pay you for the pot of scalding coffee. Move over next to Herr Harmon, bitte."

Karol moved to the left and spit into Kreuger's face. The assassin's gun sprung in one fierce motion and slammed into the cheek of Karol. His body lurched backward, sprawling into the corner. A tight smile formed on Kreuger's face. "It seems our friend has no taste for cold steel," he said, dripping with sarcasm. He then reached into his jacket pocket, pulled out a silencer and methodically screwed it onto the barrel of his weapon. His cold, dark eyes stared at Bryan, projecting the image of Lucifer himself. He then fixed on the slumped body of Karol, now beginning to stir. The dark outline of the gun made its descent, sights honed in on Karol's forehead.

Out of nowhere, a light flashed behind Kreuger. His body turned, smooth and instinctive. Mother Anastasia had entered the doorway. The beam momentarily blinded his vision, but he drew a bead on its source.

"Sister Anna? What is going on?" her soft voice asked.

The sight of the gun swerving in the direction of her newfound mentor pierced the heart of Ilsa. Panic turned into action. Her hand sprung from her habit, the long needle flashing in the light. Instinct turned to fury. She heard the gun spit two bullets. The saintly Abbess was hurled backward into the hall.

"Aaagh!" Ilsa shrieked in total rage. Her arm shot into the air, plunging the syringe into the base of Kreuger's neck. His eyes bulged in burning agony, his body froze. Then, he slowly turned and let one more bullet fly into Ilsa's forehead. Her head snapped back, her body twisting, as she saw the fallen body of Mother Anastasia lying in the hall. She staggered, took two steps and fell next to the nun's crumpled body.

Kreuger struggled to extract the stinging syringe from his neck. He frantically stretched and clawed, his fingers finally grasping the deadly cylinder. It broke in his clutches, the needle remaining. With his muscles tightening, he felt a searing pain race down his spine and impede his movement. Staggering forward, he swept his gun, slow and purposeful, toward Bryan. The red-hot poison shot up his spinal cord, contorted his body like a hunchback and seized his brain. He stumbled once more, then fell face down on the concrete floor. The horror of the shocking scene numbed the amateur saboteurs, leaving them helpless.

It was Karol who first regained his wits. He leapt over Kreuger's body and reached the dying Abbess. Tears poured from his eyes as he carefully slid his hand under her head, eased it slightly upward and gently kissed her forehead. Her fragile body tenaciously clung to life. Her eyes quivered to open and she strained to focus on the blurred image in front of her. Karol's face came slowly into view. Shaking, her hand rose, and with love, cupped his blood-soaked cheek, then pulled on his neck to draw his ear close to her trembling lips.

"Sweet Karol Tciuszko...you look so much like your father. I can see him still; laying the stones in our new wall...Your father and me...we had a special mission." Her hand gripped his neck tighter as she coughed up blood, gasping for precious air.

"I know, Mother—"

"No! You don't know..." She coughed again. "Every day...you would be sent home with the stone cutters, but your father would stay for an hour or two more..." Her nails dug into his skin as her coughing got worse. "Then...then we would build the Stations of the Cross into the wall—"

"Yes, Mother, I know—"

"Listen to me, Karol," she scolded as she raised her head so her lips touched his ear. "I told your father what was stored underground...we knew they would come someday...he promised to help me..." A spasm of coughing began again while blood ran down her cheek from the side of her mouth. "We took the canisters out of the crates...we...buried them into the wall..." Coughing up more blood, she could barely be heard. "... behind the stations of the cross." Her hand slid from his neck and rested once again on his cheek. Her gentle touch became a death grip. Karol winced in pain from the wound inflicted by Franz, but covered her hand with his and pressed it even tighter.

With her gasping whisper now barely audible, she said, "The Russians...they will come tomorrow for the virus...they know, Karol, they know! You *must* make them all think it is destroyed...you must protect this secret at all costs." Her coughing interrupted her dying plea. "Promise me...as your father did..." Her eyes opened wide and he felt his spirit merge with hers. With tears streaming down his face, he answered, "Yes, Mother, yes! This I promise you."

Upon hearing the words, Mother Anastasia surrendered her life. Her head fell limp in Karol's hand. With a heavy heart, he slowly laid his head on her bloodied chest and a low guttural wailing droned from his lips. His fingers grasped her habit, pulling her even closer, desperately taking in the last ounce of her maternal warmth.

Bryan started to move toward Karol, but Lisa pulled him back. Her eyes told him to give Karol the time he needed. Kneeling in a semifetal position over the fallen Abbess, Karol's mind drifted with the rocking motion of his body to a sunny day forty-five years earlier. He remembered a small boy looking up at the nun with the tender loving face. She was planting beautiful lilies around a steel door laying flat on the ground. Oh, please God, give her back to me...please. His rhythmic rocking turned to convulsion as his sobbing face buried further into her bosom.

Feeling a soft, tender hand touch his shoulder, Karol opened his eyes, raised his blood-streaked face upward and was startled to see the face of Lisa, sorrowfully looking at him. Regaining his senses, he gently laid his lifelong friend back on the ground and kissed her cheek.

With new resolve, he jumped to his feet, wiped his eyes with his sleeve and scanned the room. "Listen," he snapped, "convent too remote... Russian troops here for one reason—they come tomorrow and search for virus canisters. Must make large explosion...*now*! And destroy this agent of death...forever. You understand?"

His demeanor had changed to a man on a sacred mission. His promise would be kept. Bryan and Lisa, still shocked by the multiple deaths, meekly shook their heads in affirmation.

"Quick, put satchel in corner." He pointed with one hand as he grabbed the other two satchels himself. "Lisa, please to hold light, we must work fast."

"What is the delay time on the fuse?" she asked.

"Not long—maybe two minutes."

"Two minutes...can't we make it longer? We won't even get halfway back to the gate before this place will be crawling with soldiers," said Bryan.

"Not time to worry—load satchels—*now!*"

Drawing on the energy of Karol, Bryan and Lisa responded with renewed purpose. The three became a team requiring no direction, as if the task at hand had been performed many times before.

"That should do it," said Bryan, drawing a deep breath.

"Looks like good Polish blowup. Lisa, please to go bottom of stairs with light, Bryan, go center of long hall. I light fuse...run like hell. Go!" he said, pointing down the hall and pushing their backs.

Karol turned and looked once more at Mother Anastasia. Her eyes were still open. Gently he closed them and slid his fingers across her cheek. He made a sign of the cross and said a short prayer. His heart broke to leave her there. "Please to forgive," he whispered. He turned to go and took a step, turned one more time to the fallen Abbess. "Karol keeps his promise."

When Lisa reached the end of the long hallway, she saw the base of the stairs with its cobweb-draped handrail. She waved a beam of light in the direction of Bryan signaling her station and a warm sense of justice engulfed her. As soon as Bryan saw the light crisscrossing the hall, he turned and looked backward to Karol. There was a short, bright flash and immediately he heard Karol's footsteps running toward him.

"Go! Go!" he heard, then made out Karol running with his arms motioning for him to move out fast. He ran toward Lisa's light, holding his beam behind him and motioning her to start upward as he drew near. They crawled out of the door and momentarily knelt, waiting helplessly for their Polish friend. Like an eruption, Karol appeared out of the earth and pointed in the direction they should run, motioning to stay low.

Within fifty meters of the wooded grove, they were pummeled off their feet as the satchels discharged their explosive contents. The air surrounding them was shocked by wave after wave of deafening percussion. The sky lit up from a gigantic fireball, as if Satan himself was clawing at them from the underground inferno. Lisa spit dirt from her mouth and felt a massive heat wave singe her hair as it passed over. Her heart raced and her breathing choked by the intense heat entering her lungs. She buried her face in the cool, wet leaves on the ground. In her mind flashed the scene of her mother engulfed in flames.

Then, strong hands under her arms pulled her up and the sound of Bryan's voice, the anchor, brought her back to the present. "Lisa, what's the matter…are you okay?" It was all she needed. They ran again, stumbling over the rutted terrain, with sounds of army vehicles starting en masse. Lisa's head turned. She saw headlights breaking the fog as they circled the distant convent walls.

"They're coming!" she screamed. She tried to keep up with Bryan's tug. The pain in her elbow felt as if her arm was being ripped from its socket.

"Come on Lisa, hurry—hurry!" Bryan knew they had but seconds.

Her foot caught a hole vacated by some field animal. A twisting, burning pain shot up her thigh. Her hand clutched hard on Bryan's, causing them both to fall again. He recovered quickly and was on his feet, pulling at Lisa's tortured arm once more.

"Aagh!" she cried out in agony. "I can't walk on my foot—I think it's sprained."

Karol heard the cry and rushed back to help. He nodded to Bryan and put his arm around Lisa's other side. Bryan reacted in tandem and they gathered her up and proceeded to half run.

Two hundred meters from the gate, large searching beams from the patrols bounced through the dewy air signaling their pincer-like entrapment as they converged toward the gate. One hundred meters and the shouting of the soldiers could be heard above the din of distant motorized vehicles. Fifty meters, a flare shot into the smoke-filled night sky, creating a bright whitish glow.

The muscles in Bryan's legs burned with a fire that increased with every step. Karol said nothing, his eyes remaining fixed on the gate itself. He knew the trap was closing. What to do?

Lisa cried out in agony, "Stop, Karol, please—I can't make it!"

Karol dug deeper. "Shut up, damn it! Keep moving!"

As they reached the gate, Karol released Lisa, her limp body falling to the ground like a sack of potatoes. He reached into the pocket of his field jacket and pulled out two sticks of dynamite. Their fuses had been shortened. He lit them both. He counted to ten and hurled one in each direction over the wall. He threw his back against the gate. With fire in his eyes, he looked at Bryan, nodded and threw open the gate. Nothing had to be said. They grabbed Lisa like a rag doll and ran through. The dynamite exploded within seconds of each other, raining dirt and debris down on their heads.

CHAPTER 77

ASSOCIATED PRESS

WARSAW, POLAND - U.S. RAPID DEPLOYMENT FORCES landed in Poland today in the early hours of the morning and have taken up position in a line from the capital of Warsaw and extending southwest through the city of Wroclaw to the southern border with Slovakia. Although greatly outnumbered, the forces have been deployed immediately opposite their Russian counterparts. Administration officials insist the mission of Operation Oaken Shield is purely defensive and are cautiously optimistic that a direct conflict resulting in casualties can be avoided. The U.S. State Department has announced Secretary of State Holden will meet with members of NATO for an immediate update.

OFFICE OF THE VICE PRESIDENT

WASHINGTON, D.C.

In the three years that she had been Executive Secretary to William Koernig, Margaret Wheeling had never been graced by the President visiting the Vice President's office.

"Good morning to you, Mr. President, may I pour you a cup of coffee?"

"No thank you, Mrs. Wheeling, the Vice President and I will be having a closed meeting...so please hold all calls," he said, opening the door to Koernig's office, then shutting it with force behind him.

Standing rigid at his desk, the Vice President assumed an aura of guarded superiority. Without extending his arm for a handshake, he motioned for Cook to have a seat opposite his desk and coldly said, "Mr. President..."

Feeling the hair on the back of his neck stiffen, Cook took pleasure in what he was about to say. "No, thank you. What I have to say is best said looking at you face to face."

"Suit yourself, but I would encourage you to get on with it as time is spare," Koernig responded, looking down his nose at his guest.

Cook glared back with piercing, fiery eyes. The Vice President felt the acid in his stomach rise, but did not divert his eyes from the President's fervent glare. He knew something must be unraveling—he had to recover.

"Certainly the President did not need to travel to my office if he wished to confer with me," he said with arrogance.

"That is correct, but for the sake of our country and the office that you currently occupy, I felt this was a most appropriate method."

"Where are you going with this? If you have something to say, Cook, maybe you should just get on with it."

Cook threw the envelope on the desk in front of Koernig. "Perhaps you would care to review *these* documents...Herr Braun!"

"What did you call me?" he asked, as his hands fumbled to open the envelope.

"You heard me correctly, Herr Braun..." the President repeated. "Do I need to read the birth certificate for you? Or how about the dental records or the money transfers?"

"These...these are fakes!" stammered Koernig as he quickly perused the papers. "You're trying to destroy me."

Ripping the second envelope open, Cook slammed the facility photos and experimental data down on the desk. "Maybe you'd like me to review this shit with you?" Cook snarled. "It's over, you stinking Nazi bastard! Do you understand? It's finished!"

Koernig's arrogance suddenly melted away and his hands sweat as he nervously sifted through the photos. He knew it was over. He saw the experiments report with its official cover emblem. Slowly he sank into his seat, said nothing and stared blankly ahead at the photos still held in his trembling hands.

"I have scheduled a press conference at ten o'clock this morning," said Cook. "I've already worked out a deal with Senator Naisbitt...they'll drop all impeachment proceedings against me and I'll announce plans *not* to seek reelection. This way we'll present a united front to the Russians. And what about you? *You* will be allowed to resign immediately in a policy dispute over my announced plans to withdraw our troops from Afghanistan. You will go into political obscurity, never to hold public office or leave this country again. You will be given Secret Service 'protection' and will be allowed to golf to your heart's content. Do I make myself perfectly clear?"

The President then turned and walked to the door. As he placed his hand on the knob, he paused and looked at Koernig with eyes filled with both vengeance and disgust. "It's strange, isn't it, how things turn out? All my life I've chased after a piece of ass and the almighty buck...I suppose to some that seems pretty corrupt, but what you did, to jeopardize your country, that's treason! You're just god-damned lucky you don't have to face a trial because I'd ask for the death penalty! You are beneath contempt!"

Koernig's eyes never rose from the devastation contained within his hands—the only sound was that of the door slamming behind the newly liberated President.

***

NEW YORK CITY

"Yes!" said Mikhail Gorbachev. "I do believe he is sincere. CNN and all the major networks will carry his press conference *live*. Yes comrade, he will announce the pullout in Afghanistan...No, I don't think he will be able to change his mind about reelection. Comrade...it's best you listen to me and listen carefully. The time is *right*, the time is *now*. You *must* move the tanks around the Parliament Building...Yes!...I understand...I know what you are saying because I also have a family, but if you do not do this quickly and succeed, there *will* be a nuclear exchange. I know this to be true! Given the state of our unreadiness and the unreliability of our ICBMs, we must do this *now*—quickly...Yes, I have personally talked to General Gurenko and he will move upon your command... No comrade, it must be now...Yes, he is in the building as we speak. You must order his immediate arrest—make it 'crimes against the federated countries.' Yes. It will stick—you have my assurance."

***

WHITE HOUSE PRESS ROOM

The air in the room was electrified with the buzzing anticipation of the usual suspects that comprised the Washington press corps. They were all true to their collective reputation—they were blackbirds on a wire. When one flew off in any direction, the rest would eagerly follow. Although word had leaked that the press conference would be a blockbuster, speculation was rife as to exactly what was going to be announced. When one of the major network reporters preened and gave his prediction, the others dutifully followed suit.

Reaching the level of a discordant din, the feigned "insider" prattle among the seasoned correspondents quickly vanished as the door opened and President Cook entered. Without hesitation or fanfare, he proceeded directly to the microphone. Gone was the usual glad handing and mutual sucking up that had characterized his four-year love fest with the national press corps. His presentation was short and focused, and the television cameras caught every nuance.

"Good morning," the President said. "As of eight a.m. Eastern Standard Time, I have informed party chairman Conner that under *no* circumstances, and I repeat, under *no* circumstances, will I seek or accept my party's nomination for reelection to the presidency."

The press corps went ashen as the murmuring grew out of control. "Please!" Cook said while he raised his hands for silence. "This painful decision has been made in order to free me from the political hindrances that would have inevitably restrained me from making my next announcement. I have instructed Secretary of State Holden to inform our NATO allies that the United States will begin immediate withdrawal of our troops from the conflict in Afghanistan. This withdrawal will be completed within one hundred and twenty days.

"The Rapid Deployment Forces that have been positioned in Poland will remain there, pending further developments in that country. I will again affirm that Operation Oaken Shield is purely a defensive measure and will cease as soon as Russian forces have been withdrawn from Poland. This is all I have to say at this time. Questions will be handled separately by party chairman Conner and JCS Belden. Thank you very much for your understanding."

"Mr. President...Mr. President...Mr. President!"

CHAPTER 78

"WHAT? ON WHOSE ORDERS?" DONSKOY BELLOWED, AS HIS body jerked itself upward from his desk and toward the window overlooking the broad plaza below. Seeing the long line of tanks begin to circle the Russian "White House," his eyes became demonic as the rage inside him boiled over and took possession of him. "I want those goddamned tanks out *now*!" He took the phone receiver and slammed it twice on his desk. "You get me General Gurenko on the phone. That stinking, rotten, bastard, son of a bitch! I know he is behind this shit. I'm going to fry his nuts! I'm going to cut him up into little pieces—*bastard*!" Donskoy slammed his fist on the wall next to the window with such force the plaster cracked under its blow. With spittle now hanging from the corners of his mouth, his face took on the look of a crazed, rabid dog.

"Wait…Gorbachev! Yes! That fat-ass Gorbachev and that pig Kerensky are in on it too…they both want me gone. Where are they—are they in Moscow? They must be—yes, the sniveling vermin are hiding, hiding like women. I'll kill them—I'll kill them all! Get that bastard general on the phone! Do you hear me?"

"Yes, comrade President…" his aide responded. "I tried, but his office does not respond."

"Then get me General Porchenkavich!" He turned and looked out the window again—his shock was now complete. "They're pointing those god-damned tanks at this building! How dare that filthy scum point those guns at *me*! I will have every one of them sent to Siberia—no! I will kill them with my own hands—kill them for treason. Get that bastard—"

The large double doors suddenly burst open and a startled Donskoy spun around from the window. To his shock, four soldiers with carbines in hand stood in his doorway with a stern-faced General Gurenko standing amidst them.

"Comrade Donskoy, by the power invested in me by the Dumas of the Russian people, I place you under arrest for high crimes committed against the sovereign federated countries of Lithuania, Estonia, Belarus, Ukraine and Poland. Your government has been suspended and control is now in the hands of comrade Vasilov, pending formation of a new government." General Gurenko paused and sized up the man who had humiliated him time and again since coming to power. "If you will follow me, please..." he said taking two steps forward.

Without warning, Donskoy bolted toward his desk drawer, yanking it open and exposing his semiautomatic pistol. As his hand reached in, the drawer came crashing in on his wrist as Gurenko's aide lunged forward. He heard the cracking of bones when he was immediately thrown over his desk by two of the soldiers. Donskoy's face slammed hard on its wooden top and his arms jerked in pain as the soldiers pulled them behind his back and handcuffed him.

"I'll kill you, Gurenko! I'll have you shot before a firing squad! Then I'll have your family shipped off to Siberia—no, I'll keep your daughters and rape them. Do you hear me? You bastard! It was Gorbachev, wasn't it? Yes, of course Gorbachev, that bastard coward! I'll kill him too. Are you listening to me?"

CHAPTER 79

ASSOCIATED PRESS

WARSAW, POLAND - RUSSIAN TROOPS HAVE BEGUN A BROAD pullback out of all federated countries. A spokesperson for interim President Boris Vasilov has announced the formal pullback, based on a U.S.-brokered agreement with Germany to complete the forced evacuation of its own citizens who had illegally entered Poland from the west. Former President Yeltsin emphasized that Russia stands by the Helsinki Accords and recognizes no changes in the boundaries established by these accords. A spokesperson for the German Republic insists the Helsinki Accords do allow for peaceful change to those borders. The U.S. has announced that its Rapid Deployment Forces will begin pulling out of Poland immediately in step with its withdrawal from Afghanistan, which is already under way.

MCLEAN, VIRGINIA

"Peter! Your private phone in the den is ringing!"

"Thanks, honey," said Peter Barnes. He hesitated, debating whether to answer it. The events of the last several days weighed heavily. I'm too old for this, he thought. How can I get out…death? I've already died. I died the day I sold my soul…It will never be over…They will *never* stop trying.

"Peter?"

"Yes, I'm getting it."

Looking out his window, he watched his great-grandchildren playing on the jungle gym in his backyard. I've got to protect them. Why can't it just stop? His hand tentatively grabbed the receiver. He knew what he must do and it sickened him. I can't let them hurt Alicia and the kids.

"Hello?"

"Have you seen the CIA report that went to the President?"

"Yes, their operatives went in the next morning after the explosion.

They were thorough."

"Well, what about the facility?"

"The explosion was enormous, apparently there is nothing left of it—or its contents."

"We only need one canister..."

"There was nothing, not even one—a total meltdown."

The silence of the line was deafening. He wondered if he still had a connection.

"What about Harmon...the girl?"

"There is nothing in the report on any positive identification. The Abbess of the convent is missing and is presumed to have died in the explosion. They speculate on a male and two females, that is all."

"Our people?"

"We don't know yet, there were no traces of them either. It is possible the Russians got them. There's no word," Barnes replied.

"Are you sure the report is reliable?"

"Yes, you know our source is impeccable."

"Get me a copy anyway...the usual means."

Silence. Barnes prayed the conversation was over. Then, his worst fears were realized.

"What about your son-in-law?"

"He...he is leaving Friday with his family, a skiing trip." He closed his eyes and bit his lip. Please, please don't ask. The dreaded question came anyway. "What is their destination?"

Peter hesitated. He couldn't open his eyes, almost as if it gave him somewhere to hide. He knew he had to answer. "...Vail," he whispered.

"Send me the itinerary with the CIA report."

"What about Alicia—and the children?" His fear almost caused him to pass out and a burning pain wrenched his stomach. "I *must* know that they will be safe...I—"

"They'll be safe. We have no interest in them. Trust me, they are not our target."

Peter Barnes' body went limp with relief and he could scarcely think. "What now?"

"Go back to your embassy in Germany. We have waited all this time already, and believe me when I say, time is on our side."

EPILOGUE

RELAXING IN THE CALM THAT FOLLOWED THE STORM, SEC-retary of State Holden loosened his tie and unbuttoned the starched collar of his custom-made, white shirt. The couch he was sitting on in front of the President's desk had never felt softer, nor had he felt more relaxed. He also noted that the effects of his Jack Daniels were never quicker. Looking over to the next couch at Chief of Staff Waring, Bert felt a satisfaction of accomplishment that few people ever feel in their entire lives. The President was the first to speak.

"Bert, John...I want to thank you both personally from the bottom of my heart. It couldn't have been pulled off without you—a job well done."

"I guess now that you've officially closed the door to reelection, we can kick back and tell the press corps to go fuck themselves," said John Waring.

"I wish it were that easy," replied Holden. "We still haven't figured out what to do with Koernig and his gang."

"They're not the problem, Bert. They've all been told to submit their resignations in an orderly and spaced manner. The last six months of our administration will have a brand new face on the Cabinet. It's all the moles we *don't* know about that frighten me. All those that have worked themselves into the loop undetected and have become all those small pieces that make up the power jigsaw puzzle of Washington," said Cook.

"What do we do with the information we have on Koernig?" asked Waring.

"We put a lid on it, seal it up and store it in a vault in my Presidential Library when I'm free of this hellhole."

Loosening his tie and top button, Holden drew a pensive look and asked, "What about the rest of the moles? What are we going to do about them?"

Kicking his feet up on his desk and leaning back in his chair, the President took a long sip of the sour mash. "*We* don't; that's a problem our successors will have to deal with, thank you."

***

IN FLIGHT - 747 BOUND FOR WASHINGTON, D.C.

Bryan sat next to the window, looking out into the pillowed nothingness of the white and grey clouds below him. His mind could not erase the events of the last thirty days as they played over and over in the theater of his mind. When he recalled his first glimpse of Lisa, warmth flowed over him that was as unmistakable as it was overwhelming.

For the first time in his life he felt free of the reigns of his father…free to follow his own path, as if the road ahead of him led to some sort of a destination. He basked in this warm feeling of redemption and said to himself, a guy could get used to this. Looking down to his right, he saw the soft curls of her pale brown hair as her head lay on his arm. With his hand, he reached under her chin and softly pulled her face upward till her eyes opened and met his.

"How does life in some quiet little town in Colorado sound to you?" he asked.

"Like heaven," she said, squeezing his arm tighter.

"And how does you living there as my wife sound to you?"

"It sounds wonderful, if you're truly asking me."

"I am."

"Then I'll say yes—but only if it's the boring life of an attorney in private practice."

"Trust me, I am so ready."

Lisa put her head back down on his arm and let her tears slowly run down her cheek.

***

CONVENT OF ST. MARY MAGDALENE
WROCLAW, POLAND

Mother Therese, the newly appointed Abbess, stood at the window of her office looking down on the silent, kneeling figure of Karol Tciuszko.

He was now in front of the seventh station of the cross embedded in the stone walls surrounding the convent.

What a truly devout man he must be, she thought, as she recounted her first visit from Karol one month ago. She remembered the stout Polish man standing at her desk with his hat clutched tightly in his strong, oversized hands. As the request he made of her came out in words choked with emotion, she knew he had more than just pain in his heart over the loss of their beloved Mother Anastasia. He had made a vow to the dying Abbess to pray the Stations of the Cross on their wall every morning till the day he died. How could she refuse him?